"THIS WILL GET OUT OF CONTROL QUICKLY," VAUGHN SAID.

"The minute either Zarin or Worf decides that things aren't going right, that one will call in the cavalry, and five minutes later, the other one will call in his, and this whole thing will blow up in our faces."

"We need to call in reinforcements," Garrett told Captain Haden. "We'll be a sitting duck if those fleets decide to go at it."

"Too risky," Haden said. "I don't disagree with you, Number One, but Monor and Qaolin already have their bowels in an uproar because I let the *Hoplite* out in the first place. They're keeping a close eye on us."

Curzon Dax shook his head. "What we need to do is put our cards on the table and call their bluff."

"That's a quaint metaphor," Vaughn said. "But I doubt they're bluffing."

"I'm sure they think that, too—and will continue to do so, right up until they have to actually play their cards. But one reason why I think they've assembled these fleets in the first place"—Dax looked at Haden—"assuming they *have* assembled the fleets, is because they're far from home. Reinforcements beyond whatever they're hiding behind cloaks or in nebulae are days away, and probably not easily diverted. I'm not sure either Zarin or Worf will be willing to start something they can't finish."

"I've read the transcripts of the me___ ___ said. "I haven't seen anyth___ ___ going to budge. Where doe___

"I have no idea where ___ leaves me with the winning ___

STAR TREK®

THE LOST ERA

THE ART OF THE IMPOSSIBLE

2328-2346

KEITH R.A. DeCANDIDO

Based upon STAR TREK
created by Gene Roddenberry

POCKET BOOKS

New York   London   Toronto   Sydney   Singapore   Raknal V

This book is a work of fiction. Names, characters, places and incidents are products of the author's imagination or are used fictitiously. Any resemblance to actual events or locales or persons living or dead is entirely coincidental.

An *Original* Publication of POCKET BOOKS

POCKET BOOKS, a division of Simon & Schuster, Inc.
1230 Avenue of the Americas, New York, NY 10020

STAR TREK is a Registered Trademark of Paramount Pictures.

This book is published by Pocket Books, a division of Simon & Schuster, Inc., under exclusive license from Paramount Pictures.

ISBN: 0-7434-6405-2

First Pocket Books printing October 2003

10 9 8 7 6 5 4 3 2 1

POCKET and colophon are registered trademarks of Simon & Schuster, Inc.

Cover design by John Vairo, Jr.

Manufactured in the United States of America

For information regarding special discounts for bulk purchases, please contact Simon & Schuster Special Sales at 1-800-456-6798 or business@simonandschuster.com.

When I started this book, a child was born in New York City. When I finished it, seven brave men and women died in the sky over Texas. Both served as sharp reminders of the cycle of life and death that is, in many ways, the theme of the novel you are about to read.

With that in mind, this book is dedicated to the child, Benjamin Palmieri, the Space Shuttle Columbia, and the men and women who crewed it.

"Politics is the art of the possible."
> —Otto von Bismarck, 1867

"What God is he writes laws of peace, and clothes him in a tempest?"
> —William Blake, *America: A Prophecy*, 1793

HISTORIAN'S NOTE

This story commences in 2328, thirty-five years after the presumed death of Captain James T. Kirk aboard the *U.S.S. Enterprise*-B in *Star Trek Generations*. It concludes in 2346, eighteen years before the launch of the *Enterprise*-D in "Encounter at Farpoint."

ON HIGH MY SPIRIT SOARS

A WORLD IN THE KLINGON EMPIRE

The boy could taste the scent of the *lIngta'* on the wind.

"You smell it, don't you?" Mother whispered, a proud smile on her face as they knelt in the underbrush. All three moons were out, casting the plant life and the ground in an eerie white glow. Mother held a *gIntaq* spear in her left hand. The boy was unarmed—Mother was teaching him to track prey in the hope that one day he would be able to hunt on his own. It was their fifth trip into this preserve, and their second at night.

"Lead me to it," Mother said.

Nodding once—an economy of movement was necessary to keep from being detected by the prey—the boy moved quietly through the underbrush. He could not hear Mother moving behind him; indeed, he only knew that she was there because of her scent.

When Grandfather purchased the land on this world, he had declared this area to be hunting ground, and had imported several types of game animal from all across the Empire and beyond, including a dozen *lIngta'* from the Homeworld. The boy had improved his tracking skills with each trip, and he eagerly awaited the day he would be allowed to wield the *gIntaq* and take the beast down.

Within minutes, he sighted the *lIngta'*, bent over a stream, lapping up water.

He stole a glance back at Mother, who did the last thing he expected—though it was something he'd been dreaming about for weeks. She pressed the haft of the spear into his left hand.

Eyes wide, he looked down at the *gIntaq*, then back up at Mother. She simply nodded.

Grinning so widely he thought his cheeks would fold over his ears, the boy turned and got into the proper crouch for throwing. He aimed the spear along the line of his right arm, just the way Mother had taught him. Then he cleared his mind the way his older sister had told him he needed to in order to focus entirely on the prey. Nothing else mattered, not the ground, not the darkened sky, not the three moons, not Mother, not the bush—nothing but the spear and the *lIngta'*.

With all the strength he had, he threw the spear.

At the age of five, said strength was not much. However, he made up for it in precision. The metal tip of the spear penetrated the *lIngta'* directly in its crown. The beast fell to the ground.

The need for stealth now past, both the boy and his mother ran toward the stream. The animal was still alive, but bleeding profusely from the wound in its head. It lay next to the stream, legs twitching. Mother snapped its neck.

Placing a hand on the boy's shoulder, Mother said, "Your first kill, my son. Be proud—today, at last, you are a hunter. You have taken another step on the path to becoming a true warrior."

The boy proudly replayed those words in his mind over and over again as he carried the *lIngta'* corpse across his shoulders back to the tent where Father awaited them both.

"You have brought dinner, I see," Father said in his usual booming voice—one of many reasons why it had been Mother, rather than Father, who taught him how to hunt. Father would stomp through the underbrush and scare away every game animal for three *qelIqams* around within minutes of his hunt commencing.

However, few compared to Father when it came to preparation of the food. Over the next hour, he showed the boy how to skin the *lIngta'*, the best way to strip the meat from the bone, the proper removal of the head, and so much more.

As they feasted on the *lIngta'* while sitting around a fire that was more for warmth than illumination—it barely provided more light than the three moons and the stars—the boy turned to his parents and asked them for a story.

"A new one," he said. "One you've never told before." It was a bold request, but he felt he had earned the right to be bold after his first hunt.

Father threw his head back and laughed, his voice echoing off the trees and hills. "Very well, my boy, you shall have your wish." He gnawed on a piece of *lIngta'*. "Shall we tell him of Kahless and Lukara at Qam-Chee?"

"I know that one," the boy said impatiently.

"Perhaps the tale of the victory over the Romulans at Klach D'Kel Bracht?"

"I know that one, too."

"Or maybe Captain Kang's victory over the creature that fed on warfare?"

The boy knew now that his father was stringing him along. "I know that one, *too*. A *new* story, Father!"

Again, Father laughed. Mother said, "Tell him of Ch'gran, husband."

Blinking, the boy said, "I do not know that one. What is Ch'gran?"

Father swallowed a gulp of stream water from his mug before commencing.

"Over a thousand turns past, after the time of Kahless, the Homeworld was attacked by the Hur'q. Fierce marauders from beyond the stars themselves, they plundered what they could take and destroyed what they could not plunder."

"They took the Sword of Kahless," the boy said impatiently. "You've told this story before, Father. I *know* this."

Smiling, Father said, "And do you know what happened next?"

"I—" The boy hesitated. Whenever Father or anyone else had told the story of the Hur'q, it ended with their disappearance, having devastated the First City and taken dozens of artifacts, including Kahless's *bat'leth*.

"Well?"

Lowering his head, the boy said quietly, "No, I do not."

"Then listen, child, and learn of our people. After the Hur'q left, a great warrior named Ch'gran urged our people to move to the stars—for only by conquering space could we truly become strong, only by taming the stars could we be all that Kahless promised, and only by expanding beyond our Homeworld could we hope to avenge ourselves upon the Hur'q. Besides, we had lost so much to the Hur'q that our best course of action was to find new worlds to provide the resources that the Hur'q's pillage had taken from us.

"And so Ch'gran spearheaded the construction of seven great ships. On the anniversary of the Hur'q's arrival on Qo'noS, Ch'gran ventured forth to the black sky to conquer the stars on behalf of the Klingon peoples."

"What happened?" the boy asked, enraptured.

In a surprisingly low whisper, Father said, "No one knows. Their last words were that they found a world on which to plant our flag. But that was all they said, and then Ch'gran and his seven mighty vessels disappeared, never to be heard from again."

"Not *quite* never," Mother said with an indulgent smile. "One ship was found drifting in the Betreka Nebula, and some say that the other ships were somewhere in that sector."

"Perhaps. But the location of the other six ships, and of

the colony itself, remains one of the great mysteries of the Empire."

Wide-eyed, the boy said, "They never found it?"

"No, my son—at least not yet. Now finish your *lIngta'*. It is time to sleep."

The boy wolfed down the rest of his meat, then prepared his bedroll. After doing so, he turned to his parents. "Mother? Father?"

"Yes, son?" they said in unison.

"Some day, I will grow up to be the greatest warrior in the Empire and I will find the Ch'gran colony!"

Again, Father laughed, this time so hard that the boy was sure that no game animal would come within half a *qelIqam* of the tent for the next several turns. "Of that, my son, I have no doubt at all. But for now, sleep. Tomorrow, we shall return home and tell your sister and brother of your first hunt."

Content with the day's accomplishments, the boy drifted off to sleep. He dreamt of finding the Ch'gran colony and bringing it home to Qo'noS in much the same way he brought the *lIngta'* back to the tent. Today he proved himself a hunter, and some day he would be the finest hunter of all, and bring glory to the Empire . . .

PART 1

SOUND! SOUND! MY LOUD WAR-TRUMPETS

2328

Chapter 1

CENTRAL COMMAND
VESSEL SONTOK

"Entering standard orbit around the fifth planet."

Standing in the center of the bridge of the Cardassian survey vessel *Sontok*, Gul Monor clasped his hands behind his back. "Excellent. Full sensor scan, Ekron. I want confirmation of those zenite readings."

"Yes, sir." Glinn Ekron manipulated a few commands on his console, situated just below and perpendicular to Monor's command chair, which was on a raised platform at the bridge's rear. The console's lighting illuminated Ekron's face, casting shadows that were accentuated by his unusually thick facial ridges. Monor thought the ridges made his second-in-command look like the statue on the grave of Monor's father—*which of course looks nothing like Father, but what do you expect from those idiots who call themselves sculptors these days?* The shadows on Ekron's face actually were an improvement, as it cut down on the resemblance to the statue. Monor's father, of course, looked much more noble in life—he had a good, strong Cardassian face. Ekron, on the other hand, just had an ordinary face, one that didn't stand out in the least. Nobody would ever notice that face, except maybe to comment on how thick the ridges were. Occasionally,

Monor cared enough to wonder whether or not Ekron cultivated that.

The glinn announced, "Preliminary sensor data does verify long-range readings. This world is rich in zenite." That mineral was used to combat botanical plagues, and was vital to the continued efficacy of several Cardassian farming colonies.

Hope in his voice, Monor asked, "Any life signs?"

"None so far, sir."

Monor sighed. "Ah, well. I suppose that'll make annexing it easier. Still, it'd be nice to not have to import a labor force to mine the stuff."

"I'm sure that's true, sir," Ekron said.

"Assuming this isn't another one of those damned sensor ghosts. Damned equipment's never totally reliable, is it, Ekron?"

"No, sir, it isn't."

The gul started pacing the length of the *Sontok*'s bridge, moving away from the command chair, past Ekron's operations console, as well as the navigation and tactical stations. The cramped confines did not allow him much room to have a proper pace. It was a failing in the design of the *Akril* class of ships, to Monor's mind. "Ekron, make a note for me to send a memo to Central Command complaining about the amount of floor space on the bridge."

"Yes, sir."

"But not the lighting. I like the lighting." Again, he sighed. "In any case, what we need is more reliable equipment. We could probably learn a thing or two from the Federation about sensors. They always seem to be one step ahead of us on that. Amazing, for such a backward people. No conception of how to run a government, for one thing." Monor grew tired of pacing, and finally decided to sit in the command chair. "Though at least they have manners, for the most part. The humans, anyhow, and the Vulcans, of course, and those Betazoids. Tellarites, now they're another story. How soon until the scan's complete?" He stepped up the two stairs of the platform and sat in his chair.

Ekron glanced down at his console. "The full scan of the northern continent will be complete in one hour, sir."

"Good. That's what I like to hear." Monor shifted position in his chair; it let out a squeaking sound. Now he remembered why he had gotten up from the chair in the first place. ̣r ͝ n, make a note to have that chair fixed."

"͟I ve already informed engineering of your problems with the chair, sir, but that is the standard command chair for an *Akril*-class vessel."

"Damned excuses. Hiding behind standards like that. In my day, engineers knew how to *fix* things—how to make them better, not just make them adequate. They just don't make 'em like they used to, Ekron."

"No, sir, they don't."

Monor clambered out of his chair, and it made another squeak. "Tell them at least to get rid of that wretched squeaking noise. I assume *that* isn't standard?"

"I'm sure it isn't, sir."

Nodding, Monor once again clasped his hands behind his back. "I should damn well hope not. If we're going to add this world to the Union, we need a vessel in top condition, not one with squeaking chairs. It's unseemly, dammit. Cardassia isn't going to be able to survive in this galaxy without resources, and that means we need zenite. And people to mine it. You sure there aren't any life signs?"

"Only plant life and lower-order animals, sir. No indications of sentient life at all."

Shaking his head, Monor once again started pacing. "Damn shame. That's the nice thing about Bajor—lots of uridium *and* a population we can put to good use. Nice spiritual people, too, Bajorans. Much easier to take control of. Well, in theory, anyhow. I mean, the Klingons are pretty spiritual, too, but I wouldn't want to try to conquer them. At least, not yet. Have we gotten any new reports from Bajor, Ekron?"

Ekron looked up from his console. "Nothing since last week, sir. As far as I know, the new government has been set up and Bajor has officially been annexed, but I'm not completely sure. I can put in a message if you want—"

Waving his arms, Monor said, "No, no, that won't be necessary. We'll get a dispatch soon enough. Central Command's usually good about that sort of thing. Mostly, anyhow, when it serves their purpose. Long as the Obsidian Order isn't involved, anyhow. Damn bunch of voles, the Order."

"Uh, yes, sir."

Frowning, Monor looked over at Ekron. Something sounded wrong with the glinn, like he wasn't paying full attention. That was unusual, in and of itself, so Monor assumed something else distracted him. "What is it, Ekron?"

"We're picking up something odd."

Since neither sitting nor pacing was doing him much good, Monor decided to walk over to Ekron's console. He stared at the readouts, which were utterly meaningless to him—not aided by the intensity of the light from the console. Monor had to blink the spots out of his eyes as he looked over at Ekron. "What do you mean by odd?"

"We've picked up refined metal, and some of what might be DNA traces, in a small area on the northern continent. No life signs as such, though—and there are no other indications anywhere else on the continent." Ekron looked up and almost changed his facial expression, a rare thing. "Sir, the readings we're getting are consistent with a crashed ship."

"A what?"

"A crashed ship, sir. I recommend we send a squadron down to investigate."

Monor frowned. "You've confirmed that the atmosphere is breathable?"

"Yes, sir, quite fit for Cardassian life," Ekron said with

more enthusiasm than he'd ever shown in Monor's presence before. "I'd like to lead the squadron, sir."

That made the gul suspicious. "You've never been this eager to go planetside, Ekron."

"It's a new world, sir."

Shaking his head, Monor said, "It's just a pile of dirt, Ekron. Some day you'll realize that. You children today, you think the galaxy's full of wonder and new experiences, but the damn truth of it is that it's all the same. Just more and more piles of dirt." He waved his arms in disgust. "Well, fine, go check this pile, and see who it is who crashed."

"Thank you, sir." Ekron moved off to the aft doors.

Again, Monor shook his head. "You'd think he was anxious to get off the bridge for some reason."

Chapter 2

RAKNAL V

It had been far too long since Ekron felt the wind blowing through his hair.

Once, Ekron preferred the regulated atmosphere of a ship, but that was before he spent six months on one. Now, he welcomed weather: the smell of salt water on the wind, the uneven feel of the rock and dirt under his feet, the unique song of animal life in the background, the pull of real gravity on his body.

He had no doubt that he'd be well and truly sick of it within the first hour, and go fleeing back to the *Sontok* begging for its artificial stale simplicity, but for now, he was going to enjoy it.

The area into which they had transported was a rocky terrain, not far from one of Raknal V's oceans. Ekron could hear waves crashing against rock to his left, but he and his team were out of sight of the water—it was at least fifty meters away, and several dozen meters straight down, according to his hand-scanner.

"Feels good, doesn't it, Glinn?" one of the troops asked. He stood just behind Ekron—Darnay was his name. "A good stiff sea breeze—nothing like it. Of course, I should think you'd be used to having hot air blasting about your ears, being on the bridge all the time."

Darnay laughed at his own joke, as did several of the other troops.

The laughter ceased when Ekron turned to look at Darnay. "Gul Monor is one of the greatest commanders in the Cardassian military. You should be grateful to be serving under one with his accomplishments."

Holding up a hand, Darnay said, "Oh, of course it is a privilege to serve under Monor's command—as long as I don't have to listen to him." Another laugh. "I think that if I should have to spend my time on duty listening to the old gul ramble, I'd go mad."

"Perhaps you've forgotten," Ekron said sharply, "that Gul Monor led the campaign against the Lissepians. Perhaps you've forgotten about Gul Monor's breaking of the Ferengi privateer ring in the Septimus system, or his destruction of those Orion pirates at Quinor. And perhaps you've forgotten about the penalty for insubordination."

The look on Darnay's face indicated that he had not forgotten the last thing, at least.

Ekron activated the communicator on his left wrist with his right hand. "This is Ekron. Beam Darnay back to the ship and place him under arrest. I will deal with him upon our return from the mission."

"Yes, sir."

Moments later, Darnay disappeared in a burst of yellow light, transported back to the ship.

Looking out at the remaining six troops, Ekron asked, "Is there anyone else who would like to criticize his superior? No? Then let us move on." He looked down at his hand-scanner. "The fragments are this way. Quick time."

In near-perfect formation—there was a Darnay-sized hole in it—the squadron jogged to where sensors had indicated the wreckage was to be found.

In truth, Ekron agreed with many of Darnay's sentiments. Monor was long-winded and tiresome, and sometimes a chore to serve under. But to think it was one thing, to voice it in front of the ship's second-in-command quite another. Ekron supposed that sort of lapse in discipline was inevitable after six long months in space, but that didn't mean he was going to tolerate it. *Obviously,* he thought, *we need to schedule more drills. And maybe we need to start airing those patriotic speeches on the monitors again.* Ekron had stopped showing them after a few months, as Central Command had only provided five of them, and their effect lessened with repetition. Besides, the crew, at the time, hardly needed reminders of the great state they lived under and how privileged they were to be part of the Cardassian Union and its grand military governing body. By serving the military, they served the people, and by serving the people, they served the Union. Until today, Ekron had no reason to think the rank-and-file had forgotten that. *But if discipline has gotten this lax . . .*

Ekron doubted he'd have any trouble convincing Gul Monor to accede to his request. The hard part had been getting him to allow the cessation of the broadcasts in the first place.

When the squadron came within a few meters of the apparent wreckage, Ekron put thoughts of crew morale to the back of his mind. That was for when he was back aboard the *Sontok.* Now, on Raknal V, he had a mission to perform.

The path of their scans led them up an outcropping, which ended in a very steep cliff. The once-gentle sea breeze became gusty when Ekron approached the edge of the cliff, a sheer drop of about thirty-five meters or so. Below them was a circular sandy inlet about a kilometer in diameter. Scattered about the sand—mostly under it—were the metal fragments they'd detected from orbit. Some pieces protruded upward, others were only a decimeter or so below the surface sand. *The changing tide probably affects how high the pieces are.* Ekron's scanner also picked up DNA traces, though it could not distinguish the type.

One of the troops approached Ekron and pointed eastward. "Sir, if we go around the outcropping here, there is a natural path down to the inlet."

Nodding, Ekron said, "Good. Let's go."

Within a few minutes, they had worked their way down a natural rocky pathway that looked to Ekron like it had once been a stream that fed into the ocean. Ekron also saw that the metal fragments were indeed spread across the entire inlet, and also that some of the pieces were corroded.

Another troop said, "Sir, the readings we took on the ship confirm several of the metals present in the alloys of these fragments are not native to this planet."

Ekron nodded as his boots sank slightly into the sand, which was leavened with a variety of small shells and rocks. He turned to the five remaining troops. "Spread out. Standard hexagonal formation. Visually survey and record everything in your sector. Move."

They moved. With Darnay beamed back up to the ship, Ekron took his sector and started examining the wreckage. His own readings confirmed what the trooper had said: this wreckage was from something constructed off world. There was no indication that there had ever been any kind of civilization here, so that meant that this was almost certainly alien.

Then he saw the skull.

Niral Ekron was a soldier, not a scientist, but one of the reasons why he had joined the military was because he loved to look at relics. Sadly, most of the museums on Cardassia had been gutted to pay for the Union's expansion. In order for him to see the treasures of old, he knew he'd have to go off world. But Ekron had been born far too poor ever to be able to afford travel off Cardassia Prime, so he joined the military—which had the added benefit of pleasing his parents, who desperately wanted a better life for their son. Luckily, the Cardassian Union was a nation that rewarded service. By giving his life to Cardassia, Ekron was able to improve the quality of that life, not just for him, but for his family. Thanks to his salary as an officer serving Central Command, Ekron's parents owned their own house in the capital city and no longer had to worry about struggling for their next meal or paying the rent on the hovel in Arinak. Father was able to grow the garden he'd always wanted to have, Mother not only had been able to purchase the best sculpting tools but also at last had the space in which to practice her art, and Ekron himself was finally able to travel to other worlds, and occasionally indulge in a favorite hobby.

So it was with no thought to the dignity of his position as second-in-command of the *Sontok* that he got down on his knees, heedless of the ever-growing pile of sand that was collecting in his boots and would no doubt infest his uniform for the next week, and started digging the skull out.

He found a collarbone next to the skull. Both bones were long since bleached, encrusted with some sand and sea life from the beach, but no evidence of meat or muscle remained. The skull also had an unusually high and pronounced forehead. To Ekron's mind, that indicated Nausicaans, Chalnoth, Klingons, or some other related species.

"Glinn Ekron!"

Ekron looked up to see one of the troops holding up a fragment of metal. "I'm sorry to report prematurely, sir, but I think you should see this."

Peering at the fragment, Ekron saw a trefoil emblem. Ekron recognized it instantly, though the design was cruder than the ones seen on modern ships.

The symbol of the Klingon Empire.

Chapter 3

I.K.S. WO'BORTAS

"Enter," Captain Qaolin of the *I.K.S. Wo'bortas* said after the doorchime to his tiny office sounded.

The door rumbled open, and his first officer, Commander Narrk, entered. Qaolin immediately stood up. Narrk was older than Qaolin, and also shorter. And, while he had shown no overt signs in the ten weeks that Qaolin had been in command of the *Wo'bortas*, the captain found it impossible to credit that Narrk didn't resent serving under someone younger than he was, especially given the amount of time Narrk had served at the rank of commander. There was nothing in Narrk's service record, nor anything in his performance of duty to date, to indicate why he hadn't been given a ship of his own.

"What do you want?" Qaolin asked by way of greeting. He walked around to the other side of his workstation, face-to-face with the commander.

Narrk looked up at the captain, his gray eyes darting and tense, his long mane of hair, which was black streaked with gray, almost quivering. "The crew grows restless. We have been following the Cardassian survey ship for over a month!"

"I am aware of the amount of time that has passed since we began following the *Sontok*, Commander."

"Then why do we just *sit* here, hiding behind our cloaking device?" Narrk's fists were clenched with fury.

"I understand your anger, Commander, but we shall continue to follow our orders."

Narrk now held his fists close to his chest, as if trying to hold himself in check. "If those orders had come from Command, I would not argue with you, but since when do Defense Force vessels bow to the whims of I.I. *petaQ?*"

Qaolin now began to understand why Narrk was still a commander. They had been detached to Imperial Intelligence for this mission, with their specific instructions coming from an I.I. agent, Yovang, who had been placed on board. More for the benefit of the listening device that Qaolin knew was somewhere in this office, he said, "Imperial Intelligence has always had the authority to commandeer Defense Force vessels for missions they deem important. And our orders did not come from I.I., Commander, they came from General Korit. Or do you consider him a *petaQ*, as well?"

If anything, this seemed to incense Narrk more. "Are you questioning my loyalty?"

Moving close enough to smell the *raktajino* on his first officer's breath, Qaolin said, "I question your sanity, Commander. Our orders are to follow Yovang's instructions, which are to observe the *Sontok* while cloaked. Until those instructions change, I will follow them—and so will you."

For a moment, the two warriors locked eyes. Qaolin refused to back down—indeed, he dared not, for it would be a sign of weakness, and Narrk would then attempt to gain a captaincy by rightfully challenging Qaolin for the position.

Instead, Narrk looked away, snarling, and walked over to the bulkhead. "Why do we not simply attack? We can capture those Cardassian *toDSaH* and take the information we need about their attempts at expansion."

"Have you ever tried to interrogate a Cardassian, Commander?"

The silence that greeted Qaolin's question provided sufficient answer.

"Their high-ranking officers have all been conditioned against the usual interrogation techniques, and their rank-and-file have no useful intelligence. No, Commander, we must—"

"*Captain Qaolin.*"

The captain looked up sharply at the sound of the voice that came suddenly over the speakers. *That is Yovang.* "Qaolin."

"*Report to the bridge.*"

The communication cut off. Narrk turned to look at his captain. "He does not even treat you with the respect of your rank. I.I. are honorless cowards who hide in shadows instead of facing their enemies head-on."

Qaolin considered the fact that, in over two months, Narrk himself had also never referred to Qaolin as "sir" or "Captain," avoiding any kind of respectful nomenclature. "I.I. is the scout that precedes the attack party—the swordsmith who sharpens the *bat'leth.* Only a fool goes into battle blindly. The Cardassians have begun an aggressive phase of exploration—but they are not like the Federation. They are not natural explorers who wish to 'seek out new life'—they are predators. For now, they seem to be limiting themselves to lifeless planets in unclaimed space, or easily conquerable worlds like Bajor. But they have been coming ever closer to territory that interests us. It is best to know what they intend before we attack in force."

Narrk said nothing, but instead headed to the exit—not allowing Qaolin to leave first, as was proper.

Up until now, he has not been insubordinate. I will have to deal with this soon.

Qaolin entered the *Wo'bortas*'s cramped bridge to see officers at all the duty stations, and one man standing in front of the raised command chair, between it and the pilot's console: Yovang of Imperial Intelligence. Unlike the others on the bridge, he did not wear a uniform, preferring an all-black one-piece outfit that made him almost blend into the darkness of the bridge—which was, no doubt, the intended effect. He kept his black hair unusually short, and his dark green eyes never seemed to blink. His crest was fairly non-descript—Qaolin had found that, no matter how many times he looked at Yovang, he could not recall the exact pattern of the crest on the man's forehead. The captain suspected that the crest had been surgically altered to achieve precisely that effect, since, thinking back on it, he couldn't remember details of any of the crests of the few known I.I. agents he'd met over the years. Since the crest was a tie to family, and since I.I. claimed no allegiances to any of the Houses—in order to do their jobs, they had to be removed from mainstream Klingon aristocracy—such alterations were probably standard.

As he entered the bridge, he made it a point to look at the crest, and found that it was a fairly straightforward three-ridge pattern, with no marks that Qaolin found distinguishing. *Naturally.*

Without preamble, Yovang started speaking in the near-monotone he favored. "A priority-coded communication has been intercepted from the Cardassian ship. The transmission is being directed to their Central Command. It is being decoded now. Its transmission follows a party beaming to the surface of Raknal V. The obvious conclusion is that they have found something useful."

From the operations console behind the command chair, a *bekk* whose name Qaolin had never bothered to learn said, "The transmission has been decoded, Captain. Shall I transfer the message to your office?"

The *bekk* pointedly did not look at Yovang.

For the briefest of moments, Qaolin hesitated. Strictly speaking, of course, the decision was Yovang's. Leaving aside any other considerations, the only reason why the ship's computer *could* decode the transmission was because of a program Yovang had installed. And Yovang was in charge of this mission.

But Qaolin was in charge of the ship, and had only been so for a few short weeks. His first officer obviously wanted his job. He had to be careful not to seem weak, but also not to incur the wrath of I.I.

"Yes, *Bekk*." He turned to Narrk. "You have the bridge, Commander."

Then he turned his back on Yovang and went into his office. If Yovang wished to follow the captain, that was, of course, his right. He made it clear that he did not consider Yovang to be a threat. Yet he had not actually challenged Yovang's authority on the bridge.

As an added bonus, he had not permitted Narrk to hear the communication, leaving him on the bridge. The commander needed to be taught a lesson.

Unsurprisingly, Yovang did follow him into the office. Qaolin sat at his desk and called up the communication that the bekk had transferred to his workstation.

The message was text only, with sensor data attached to it. "They have found the remains of a Klingon ship!" Qaolin said in surprise. "The wreckage appears to be at least one thousand years old." The captain fell backward in his chair. "A thousand years . . ." He looked up at Yovang, who remained as still as a statue. *Worse*, he thought after a moment. *At least a statue is generally posed heroically*. "You do realize what this probably is? We are not far from the Betreka Nebula . . ."

"Our mission is not to draw conclusions, Captain Qaolin. Our mission is to gather information. You can rest assured that when—"

Angrily, Qaolin stood up. "The Cardassians may have found the remains of Ch'gran! We cannot simply let them—"

"I will decide what we can and cannot do, Captain."

Qaolin hesitated. Then he leaned forward. "We are talking about our history, Yovang. Ch'gran has been one of the great unfinished stories of our people. We *cannot* allow it to fall into the hands of outsiders!"

"Do you challenge my authority, Captain?" Yovang asked.

Again, Qaolin hesitated. I.I. agents were, in theory, exempt from challenges—such matters were handled internally. In reality, of course, they were challenged all the time. However, they were also well enough trained that one only took on an agent if one was supremely confident in one's ability to win. Qaolin considered himself second to no warrior, but if he won, he'd be in a difficult position with I.I., and if he lost, his ship would be entrusted to Narrk—neither a particularly pleasant outcome.

But that exemption cut both ways. Just as Qaolin was not permitted by tradition or law to challenge an I.I. agent, no I.I. agent could issue such a challenge. (Then again, they hardly needed to. They had other methods of achieving their goals.) So Qaolin was able to speak words he could not normally utter to a superior. "I suggest that you reconsider, Yovang. The mission is yours, and if you order me to keep this information from Command, I will obey that order. But you would be unwise to give it."

"Would I?"

For the first time since the agent came on board, Yovang's tone altered from the monotone. Qaolin, however, refused to let it affect him, not when he knew he was right.

"I would not wish to be the one, Yovang, who informed the High Council that we stood by and let one of the greatest discoveries in Klingon history be taken from us."

The monotone returned. "And I would not wish to be the one, Captain, who embroiled us in a war with an enemy we know far too little about. The Cardassians are a military dictatorship, but we still have little information as to the strength of that military. Even if we did know, there is no common territory between our two nations, so any conflict would be a difficult and costly one, as it would require diverting forces away from the Empire at a time when we cannot afford it. The Empire is still replacing the resources lost in the destruction of Praxis. This mission's purpose is to obtain information about the Cardassians because we believe that they may pose a threat—in the future."

Qaolin shook his head. "I had an instructor once who referred to I.I. as bloodless, and now I know what he meant. Look past the analysis, Yovang, and think like a Klingon for a moment. What happens when word of this discovery becomes public knowledge? Do you truly think the Cardassians will keep it quiet? I have seen many artifacts of Cardassia's history in museums on non-Cardassian worlds because they have proven themselves more than happy to sell their past to the highest bidder. Do you think they will treat *our* past any better?" Qaolin stood up. "And when that happens, Yovang, how do you think the Klingon people will react? Do you think they will take kindly to our bartering with outsiders over financial compensation for one of our sacred treasures?" He walked around to the other side of his desk, throwing all fear of reprisal to the wind. "When you were a child, Yovang—and I assume that even *you* were a child once—did you not dream of being one of the Empire's great heroes? I know I did." He looked up, as if seeing a vision in the ceiling. "I wanted to be the one who would bring glory to our people by finding the Sword of Kahless. Or the Hand of Kull." Then he pointedly looked at Yovang's unreadable face. "Or the Lost Colony of Ch'gran. And all those children who grew up to be soldiers of the Empire will *not* stand for Ch'gran being in any hands but Klingons'. And then, Yovang, you will have the very war you seem to think we should not have."

Yovang then did something Qaolin never expected: He smiled.

"Your argument is well taken, Captain. And also anticipated. I have already sent a tight-beam transmission to the Homeworld requesting more ships to take Raknal from the Cardassians."

Oh, it is a good thing I.I. is exempt from challenges, Yovang, or you would be dead by now. Qaolin was wise enough not to say that out loud, but reining in his temper was almost a physical effort; as it was, his hand moved almost unconsciously to the *d'k tahg* on his belt. "You could not possibly—"

"I knew the contents of the Cardassian transmission the moment it came in and acted accordingly. I only ordered your crew to decipher it to provide you with the illusion of control—and to see how *you* would respond to the discovery of Ch'gran, and to my authority."

"Your deception offends me, Yovang."

Yovang nodded in a conciliatory manner. "That was an unfortunate consequence. But I.I. is only effective as an aid to the Defense Force, not a hindrance. Our purpose is to gather information—not just on our Empire's enemies, but on the Empire itself. Our methods are not always honorable, but they serve the cause of honor."

The agent was interrupted by a beeping sound on a padd he carried in a pocket of his all-black outfit. He removed it and activated its display. "Commander Narrk is about to report that Command is sending two ships to rendezvous with the *Wo'bortas* here with orders to fire on the *Sontok*. They will arrive in ten hours. A fleet will be assembled in the Betreka Nebula within two days. If we have not driven off the Cardassians within those two days, the fleet will take Raknal by force."

"Good." Qaolin went back to sit at his desk. "This is now a military engagement, Yovang, and therefore no longer an I.I. mission. If I see you on my bridge, I will have you forcibly removed. Now get out of my sight until I summon you."

It was a risky position to take, but every word Qaolin spoke was true. While Yovang no doubt could make Qaolin's life miserable, the captain had no desire to further weaken his position on the ship—nor did he have any desire to make life easy for Yovang after his deception. *My control over this vessel is more than an illusion, Yovang,* he thought, fervently hoping that it was true.

The agent simply nodded. "As the captain wishes. I will be in my quarters if you require any assistance from Imperial Intelligence."

Yovang left Captain Qaolin wondering if he had won a victory or simply played his role as a piece on Yovang's game board.

He stood up. For the moment, it didn't matter. In ten hours, there would be battle. Narrk would at last get his wish to engage the Cardassians, and Qaolin—

The captain smiled. *I will be the one who at last brings Ch'gran home.*

Chapter 4

CENTRAL COMMAND
VESSEL SONTOK

In the ten hours since Ekron had reported the existence of the Klingon wreck, the young glinn had become more excited than Monor had ever seen his second-in-command. When he finally returned to the *Sontok* and reported to Monor on the bridge, the gul found it difficult to get a word in edgewise, Ekron had so much to say. For the first time, Monor looked upon Ekron and did not see a statue. Ekron gestured frantically as he spoke, the words almost pouring out of his mouth, in stark contrast to the measured tones he usually employed.

"We don't know much about Klingon history, but what we have learned indicates that their expansion into space only happened a few hundred years ago—long after this ship was built. My guess is that they were built by a lone group of scientists—they don't value them much, remember—and sent out into space to try to expand. Obviously, it didn't work, so they didn't try again. It's actually very similar to human history, when—"

Monor finally cut Ekron off. "Glinn, I don't mean to interrupt your enthusiasm—in fact, it's good to see; in general, you young people don't take nearly enough interest in history, if you ask me, so I'm glad to see that *someone* gives a damn—but right now I need to know more about this planet. Central Command isn't going to give a vole's ass about those damned Foreheads and when they first went out into space—even though they probably should. But they're idiots. You know that, I know that, but they don't know that, and even if they did, they wouldn't admit it. What I need to know from you is whether or not I should send a follow-up message to them asking for a colonization fleet."

"Oh, most definitely, sir." Suddenly, Ekron-the-statue was back. A part of Monor missed it, but he also was heartened to see that Ekron recognized that there was a time and place for that sort of thing. "The zenite readings are confirmed, and there's also a good deal of arable land on the other continent." The planet, Monor remembered, had two major landmasses, as well as several smaller ones, and two massive oceans. "Besides, this star system puts us in a good jumping-off position for the Klingon Empire and the Federation. I think it will make a fine addition to Cardassia, sir."

Monor smiled as he turned to sit in his chair. Then, remembering the squeak, he stopped and settled for standing on the step in front of it. "That's what I want to hear, Glinn, that's most definitely what I want to hear. Good work. Get a message to Central Command, tell them to send some ships over here."

"Yes, sir." Ekron turned to give the order to the officer at the communications console, then looked back at Monor. "One other thing, sir."

"What is it, Glinn?"

"It's possible that the ocean might be a suitable place to transplant the *hevrit*."

Monor frowned. He hadn't known this about Ekron. "Glinn, I'm as much an animal lover as the next man, but I'll not have this ship being used for the propaganda—"

"Sir, with all due respect, the *hevrit* are dying out. None of the waters on Cardassia are fit for most marine life now, least of all the *hevrit*. We'll be able to preserve one of the greatest treasures of Cardassia—and one of the finest delicacies."

Shaking his head, Monor said, "If you wish to investigate the possibility while surveying the planet more thoroughly, Ekron, go ahead, I won't stop you, but it better not interfere with the full survey. Our primary concern is the greater good of Cardassia, not the greater good of Cardassian fish, do I make myself clear?"

"Yes, sir."

"Good. I don't want people to think of this world as the place where we saved a few fish, I want people to think of this world as the place where we found a new source of zenite that will make life better for Cardassians all across the Union. That's why we're here, dammit!"

"Of course, sir."

Hoping it wouldn't start another lengthy diatribe, Monor asked, "Anything else about that Forehead wreck?"

"Only that most of the wreckage is well buried, sir. It would take a great deal of specialized equipment to get most of it out. Based on the scans we took, what we found only recently resurfaced due to changing tidal patterns on that beach. If we'd arrived here a year ago, I doubt we would have found it."

"Mmm." Monor found he couldn't work up more than a grunt in response to that. If nothing else, this wreck might prove useful as something to line Central Command's coffers—*maybe even enough to provide ships with command chairs that don't squeak*, he thought angrily as he sat down in his and heard it do exactly that.

"In any event, sir, we placed transporter inhibitors and force fields around the entire site."

"Good." The security was necessary. For now, the only message that had gone out regarding the wreckage was a coded one to Central Command, but the stars had ears bigger than those of the Ferengi, and it wouldn't be long before privateers of all sorts showed up to see about the Klingon treasure. The *Sontok* could provide security against obvious threats; the force fields and inhibitors would work for those who worked more subtly.

Ten hours later, Central Command had confirmed that a fleet of survey vessels, escorted by the Third Order, was en route. Ekron and a team had done a more detailed survey of the planet's surface, which confirmed everything the preliminary readings stated—or improved upon them. The amount of zenite was impressive, and the world was rich in other minerals that were more common, but no less useful and/or valuable for all that. *Maybe I can work something out with Legate Zarin,* Monor thought, *get a piece of prime land on this world cheap now and reap the profits for my retirement. Not getting any younger, after all, and it'd be nice to have somewhere to take the grandchildren.* Monor had seven children and three times as many grandchildren, and he suspected that an exotic location like this would appeal to most of them as a vacation spot. *Well, maybe not Aris and her irritating little brood, but if she doesn't come with that idiot she married, all the better for the rest of us.*

Ekron then suddenly cried out, "Sir, three Klingon Birds-of-Prey decloaking!"

If he had been asked to compose a list of sentences he expected his second-in-command to utter, Monor doubted that those words would have even been put on it. "What the hell are the Foreheads doing here?" This was unclaimed space, after all, not really that close to the Empire—though it was hardly the heart of the Union, either—and, their new discovery notwithstanding, the Klingons had never shown any interest in the sector before. "Defensive posture," he added. "How soon until the Third Order arrives?"

"Another day at present speed," Ekron said.

"Get a message to them, tell them to get here as fast as possible."

"Sir, the survey vessels—"

"Will be useless in a fight," Monor said tightly, sitting in his chair and ignoring the damn squeak. "Think with your brain instead of your neck ridges, Ekron. Survey vessels don't matter a damn right now if the Foreheads want to take us on."

"Yes, sir." Ekron looked down at his console. "Sir, the Klingons are generating a jamming field. I can't guarantee the message got out. And they're arming disruptors."

"Take aim at the lead ship and fire."

"Sir, they haven't—"

"The Foreheads don't decloak like that unless they mean to kill us," Monor snapped. "Fire on them!"

Ekron followed his orders, and phaser fire slammed into one of the Birds-of-Prey's shields.

"Evasive maneuvers. Give us some distance, and get us the hell out of orbit."

"Birds-of-Prey are trying to hem us in, sir. And they're firing."

The *Sontok* felt the impact of the Klingon disruptor fire. Monor checked his display. The Klingons were surrounding them on three sides, blocking all the best avenues for escape.

Fine, we'll take one of the worst ones. He quickly calculated the course necessary to achieve the proper angle. *Haven't done this in years, and it was with a ship a lot smaller than this one.*

"Set course 113 mark 9—and *yes*, Ekron, I know that'll take us further into the atmosphere. Specifically, it'll take us in at an angle to bounce off the atmosphere."

"Laying in course now, sir," Ekron said, stock still as ever.

"When I give the word," Monor said, "adjust attitude and pitch by forty-five degrees." He waited, watching the readings on the screen in front of him.

Another impact. "Shields are down to forty percent, sir."

"Are they pursuing us into the atmosphere?"

Ekron nodded. "Yes, sir, but Birds-of-Prey are atmospheric craft."

"Can't be helped, Glinn." Ideally, the pursuing ships would either avoid the atmosphere or risk being damaged by it—but these smaller Klingon ships were designed to withstand such friction. "Adjust angle!"

The ship lurched, as the *Sontok* made a course change not mandated by the instruments, and therefore slowing the reaction time of the inertial dampeners and artificial gravity. The ship then shot out of orbit at nearly full impulse.

"Set ship's course to match," Monor said. No sense fighting where the ricochet was taking them.

"Now at 94 mark 2, seven-eighths impulse speed." Ekron looked up at Monor. "The Klingons are pursuing."

"Arm aft phasers and torpedoes and fire on the first ship that comes into range. Increase our speed to full impulse."

"Yes, sir." Ekron looked down at his console, the light again casting odd shadows on his deep ridges. "Sir, the Klingons are taking up a wide formation—only one ship will come into weapons range, and that won't be for five minutes."

Monor got up from his chair, ignoring the squeak. This wasn't good. The Klingon captain was driving him from the planet. He needed to even the odds—individually, the Birds-of-Prey were no match for an *Akril*-class ship, but the three of them could pick away at him until he was dead. *And no way to know when reinforcements will arrive.*

"Reverse course, bring us about and hit them with everything we have. Then set an intercept course with the Third Order, warp eight."

"Sir, if they pursue us—"

"They won't," Monor said confidently. "They must have intercepted our message about the remains and want to claim it for themselves. We'll let them have it for now—and return with the Third Order and take it right back from them."

"Very good, sir. Firing on lead ship."

Monor looked at his display. The *Sontok*'s phasers plowed through the shields of one of the Klingon vessels, then came about and—taking several dozen disruptor hits—went into warp.

"Shields down to ten percent. Warp drive intact, and holding course at warp eight. No sign of pursuit."

Nodding, Monor said, "As expected. Fine, let them think they've won. Knowing them, they'll be drinking to their victory within the hour. What's that stuff they like, blood vinegar?"

"Bloodwine, sir."

"I've tasted it, Glinn, trust me, blood vinegar is what it is. Well, we'll come back and take Raknal V from their drunken hands. You *did* protect the crash site, Ekron?"

"Of course, sir. I doubt that the Klingons will be able to penetrate the force fields or the transporter inhibitors."

"Good." Monor sat back down in his chair, wincing at the squeak. *Dammit, I've already picked out my retirement spot. No Forehead's taking* that *from me.*

Chapter 5

I.K.S. WO'BORTAS

"What do you mean we can't *get* at it?"

Qaolin was furious. They had victory within their grasp—they had Ch'gran within their grasp! And now Narrk was telling him that they could not actually close their fists around the prize.

The captain rose from his desk and stood over Narrk, wanting once again to remind the first officer of his lesser height.

"The site is surrounded by force fields of various kinds," Narrk said quietly. "We cannot penetrate them with scanners, transporters, weapons—*nothing* is working. We know only that it is the Ch'gran wreckage by looking at it." He held out a padd, which included the visual record that the landing party had taken of their attempt to inspect the relic. The trefoil symbol of the Empire on the hull fragments was in a style that had not been favored since before the Empire's second, more successful, foray into space. It *had* to be Ch'gran.

And yet, even as Qaolin was fulfilling his dream, the dream of every warrior who served the Empire, he felt it slipping through his fingers. *Damn those Cardassian animals for soiling our sacred past!*

"We've done everything we can," Narrk said almost petulantly. "The force field cannot be penetrated by any means at our disposal."

"Try harder." Qaolin handed the padd back to Narrk. "Return to the surface. I am holding you personally responsible for allowing us access to the Ch'gran remains, Commander. The next time I see you will be either your informing me that you have succeeded or my informing you of your imminent death."

Narrk smoldered, but said nothing. He simply grabbed the padd from Qaolin's hands and departed.

For two days, Narrk supervised the work of engineers from all three Birds-of-Prey, a number that increased once repairs to the vessels damaged by the *Sontok* were complete. However, nothing could get through. The only solution that presented itself was to destroy the inhibitors and force field generators, but that could not be accomplished without damaging the Ch'gran remains, and that Qaolin would not authorize. Were it not for those remains, Qaolin would be more than happy to leave this rock to the Cardassians. This world had no mineral resources that the Empire could not obtain from worlds actually within their borders. This area of space was wholly undesirable, so much so that Qaolin found himself wondering how Ch'gran's fleet wound up here.

By the end of the second day, Qaolin assumed that the fleet had gathered in the Betreka Nebula. According to the orders he had received from Command shortly after the *Sontok*'s departure, they would assemble there and wait to see what actions the Cardassians would take. The *Wo'bortas* would remain on station with its two brother ships for the time being. If the Cardassians returned with superior forces, Qaolin's orders were to lead them to the nebula, and then the battle would be joined.

Then we shall truly learn how strong the Cardassian military is, Qaolin thought.

Still, he was concerned. The fleet being sent consisted of

only six *Birok*-class cruisers—not exactly the cream of the fleet. Again, this system's location proved problematic. Command was not willing to commit a massive deployment to such a remote region.

As he was about to go off-shift and get some dinner—the quartermaster had taken a crate of *gagh* out of stasis—Qaolin's doorchime sounded. "Enter."

Narrk entered wearing a hideous smile on his face. "Success! We have penetrated the force field!"

All thoughts of fresh *gagh* wriggling into his mouth fled, pleasant as they were. *At last!* Qaolin felt his heart singing with joy and glory. "How?"

"Yovang was able to provide—"

Qaolin's heart stopped singing. "Yovang? I gave the entire crew strict orders on the subject of Yovang, Commander. Did you think they did not apply to you?"

Narrk scowled. "He had a method of overloading the force field. You wanted us to get the field down by any means necessary. In order to comply, I felt that it was worth listening to what Yovang had to say on the subject. And it worked."

"Yet you did not report to me that you were approaching Yovang. You did not request my permission."

"*He* approached *me* with—"

Refusing to let Narrk attempt to talk his way out of his insubordination, Qaolin instead slapped him with the back of his hand, then unsheathed his *d'k tahg* from his belt. "You have flaunted my authority for the final time, Narrk, son of Mariq."

Then Narrk threw his head back and laughed. "You cannot challenge me, you ignorant *petaQ*."

"Oh really?"

"Really." Narrk's sneer grew more pronounced. "I had every right to approach Yovang without your approval—after all, he is a fellow member of Imperial Intelligence."

The deck seemed to tilt under Qaolin's feet. *Another I.I. agent aboard? And it is* him? The captain refused to believe it.

"You lie. And there is only one fate for liars."

With that, he thrust his *d'k tahg* into Narrk's chest. The look of surprise that would be forever etched on Narrk's face as his soul departed his body—for *Gre'thor*, if this were a just universe—gave Qaolin some small satisfaction.

After Narrk fell to the deck, Qaolin did not bother to perform the death ritual. That was for worthy warriors who fell in battle, not lying *yIntagh*.

Even as Qaolin summoned the quartermaster and his second officer to his office—the former to dispose of Narrk's body, the latter to congratulate on his promotion—a voice in the back of his head asked, *What if he wasn't lying?*

When he was finished speaking to the quartermaster and his new first officer, Qaolin went to the cabin that had been assigned to Yovang on deck four. All the officers' quarters were on that deck, including Qaolin's own, as well as the one guest cabin. The captain wasn't sure if he would get the truth out of the I.I. agent if he asked, but he certainly wouldn't get it if he didn't.

The soldier assigned to guard the agent's cabin nodded respectfully at the captain as the door rumbled open. Yovang lay on his bunk, wide awake, staring at the ceiling. At Qaolin's entrance, the agent sat upright. Yovang did not, the captain noted, use his hands in any way to aid in making himself upright—he simply rose to the proper position. "Captain," he said in his standard monotone.

As soon as the door closed behind him, Qaolin asked, "Was Narrk an I.I. agent?"

"You speak of your first officer in the past tense."

"Answer my question, Yovang."

Yovang stood up. "Why do you ask the question?"

Qaolin was not about to play Yovang's game. "That is not your concern."

"Oh, but it is. You see, I must deduce from your phrasing

that Narrk is dead, and before he died he gave you reason to think he might be an I.I. agent."

It seems I must play the game whether I want to or not. "The former first officer of this ship has been replaced. Quartermaster has just disposed of his body. He attempted to deny my challenge on the grounds that he was I.I. and therefore exempt. He also used that lie—if lie it truly was—to justify his insubordination, which was in going to you for a solution to penetrating the force field around the Ch'gran wreckage."

"In that case, Captain, Commander Narrk deserved his death."

Qaolin snarled and slammed his fist into the bulkhead of the small cabin. "I'm fully aware of the fact that Narrk deserved to die! If I were not, he would still draw breath! That is not my concern now, Yovang—my concern is, was he telling the truth?"

"What does it matter?" Yovang asked with that small smile he'd used in the captain's office two days ago. "If he was lying, he dishonored himself and died the death he deserved. If he was not, then he was using his position—and, I might add, violating his infiltration—in a craven act of self-preservation. Whatever one may think of I.I. and our methods, we are not cowards, nor are we *totally* without honor. No agent worthy of the name would ever stoop to what you claim Narrk has done."

The captain closed his eyes for a moment, restraining his temper. It would do no good to lose himself to anger with this one. *The fact is, I will get no answers from him, and any answers he might provide are not ones I can trust.* Though, thinking about it, he doubted that Yovang had ever actually lied; he simply was parsimonious with any useful information.

When this was an I.I. mission of reconnaisance, Qaolin accepted that Yovang's authority on this ship was highest, and he would obey the agent's orders. Now, however, it was a military engagement, and purely the purview of the Defense Force. That meant that Qaolin's authority was the highest.

So the captain killed Yovang with his *d'k tahg*.

The look of surprise on the I.I. agent's face as Qaolin thrust the knife point into his heart was even more of a treat than the one on Narrk's, mainly because Qaolin doubted that Yovang had ever *been* surprised before.

However, Yovang did not go down without a fight. Even as the life's blood drained from his chest, the I.I. agent wrapped his fingers around Qaolin's neck in an attempt to take the captain to the afterlife with him. Qaolin found breaths suddenly difficult to come by. His vision clouded as Yovang's fingers clenched his throat.

Then the agent's iron grip loosened. Qaolin was able to breathe freely again even as Yovang fell to the deck.

Down the line, Qaolin had no doubt that he would be made to pay for this action. But that was for later. Right now, Yovang's presence on his ship was a liability he could not afford. Whether or not Yovang approached Narrk with the solution to the Cardassian security, whether or not Narrk was truly an I.I. agent, didn't matter. With them both dead, the *Wo'bortas* was under Captain Qaolin's control. If there were consequences, he would face them, but he would not be put in a position where he had to fight the Cardassians with one eye on his back to make sure that someone wasn't about to stab him in it.

Coughing in an attempt to clear his throat of its recent constriction, Qaolin cleaned the blade of his *d'k tahg* carefully, making sure there was no overt sign of Yovang's blood remaining on it.

When he departed the agent's quarters, he said to the guard, "See to it that Yovang is not disturbed by *anyone* without face-to-face confirmation from me."

"Yes, sir."

"*Bridge to Qaolin.*"

The captain looked up. "Qaolin."

"Sir, *long-range scan is picking up a fleet of Cardassian vessels on direct approach for the Raknal system.*"

Qaolin smiled. *And so the battle begins anew.* "How many ships?"

"*Nine, sir.*"

At that, Qaolin reared his head back and laughed. It was perfect: they had sent as many ships as the Klingons had. *Truly we shall test our enemy's mettle.*

Chapter 6

CENTRAL COMMAND
VESSEL SONTOK

"The *Eldrak* and the *Golnor* have both lost their shields."

Monor pounded the arm of his command chair at Ekron's report. The *Sontok* had combined with the Third Order to do considerable damage to the enemy ships, but despite being outnumbered three to one, the damned Foreheads still had put up a fine fight, critically damaging two of the Cardassian ships.

"Set course—"

"Sir, the Klingons are breaking formation!"

That threw Monor off guard. "What?"

Ekron looked up from his console. "They are setting course outside the system."

"Follow them!" The Klingons may not have had the neckbones to chase after a fleeing foe, but Monor did. "Pursuit course, top speed."

"They're going to warp."

"Overtake them, dammit! We'll show those damn Foreheads how to win a fight."

Ekron nodded. "Yes, sir. Course is 111 mark 47. Klingon ships are at warp seven."

"Increase to warp eight."

Shaking his head, Ekron said, "We can only achieve warp

seven-point-three, sir—and the other ships can't even break warp seven."

Monor stood up; the damn chair squeaking again. "Fine, then, warp seven-point-three. Inform the fleet to keep up as best they can." He paced down the length of the bridge. "Project course ahead. Where are they leading us? Assuming they're leading us anywhere and not just flying off like the cowards they are. They can brag about honor all they want, but give them a real foe and they show their true colors, that's for damn sure."

"Heading for the Betreka Nebula."

Monor laughed. "Those idiot Foreheads think they can lose us in the nebula, do they?" He shook his head. "That trick is so old, my grandfather would be embarrassed to use it. Have I ever told you about my grandfather, Ekron?"

"Many times, sir. We'll reach the nebula in fifteen minutes—that's before we'll be able to intercept."

"Watch their course carefully, Ekron. Sensors'll go out once we get inside that soup, so we'll need to extrapolate their course."

"Yes, sir."

Monor moved to sit in his chair again. "Damned Foreheads aren't going to make a mockery of me. Can't believe they'd pull this sort of trick, like we're some kind of rank amateurs. That's the sort of thing that'll work against Kreel or Kinshaya or those other weaklings that the Foreheads pick on to make themselves look strong, but we Cardassians are made of sterner stuff. Ready a full spread of torpedoes, fire them the instant we're in range."

"Sir," Ekron said, "we won't be in range until we reach the nebula."

Sighing, Monor said, "Then we'll fire the damn things into the nebula! Their shields are low enough that we should be able to penetrate their hull—that'll make going into the nebula all that much more dangerous for those idiots. Then we'll show them what the difference is between a warrior and a soldier. Because that's the important thing, you know. They go on and on about honor and being warriors and all that other muck, but what matters is obedience—following the chain of command to make a better life for your homeland. *That's* what war's all about, Ekron, not this nonsense about glory and honor—that's just an excuse to kill people."

"Yes, sir." Ekron looked up. "Sir, the Klingon ships are slowing to impulse."

"Reduce speed." After standing in front of it for several minutes, Monor finally sat in his chair. Amazingly enough, it *didn't* squeak. Monor decided to take that as a good sign. "Let's show these Foreheads that we mean business."

"Coming out of warp."

"Fire torpedoes!"

Ekron passed on the order to weapons control, then added, "Sir, the Third Order will be coming out of warp in six minutes."

"Damn." Monor shook his head. *If only they'd been able to keep up.* "Well, we ought to be able to hold them off for six minutes. Let's try to get them before they enter the nebula."

However, Ekron seemed vexed by something on his console. "Sir, the Klingon ships *aren't* heading for the nebula."

It took a moment for Monor to realize what his second-in-command had just said. "What?"

"They're holding position approximately two hundred thousand kilometers from the nebula's perimeter."

Shrugging, Monor said, "Fine, if they want to make it easy on us. Target the lead ship and fire with full phasers and torpedoes. Then—"

"Sir, now picking up multiple energy signatures from the nebula. Charged particles are increasing by fifty percent at the perimeter." Then Ekron looked up in shock at Monor. "Sir, six Klingon ships are emerging from the nebula!"

"A trap." Monor shook his head. "Damn me, here I thought they were pulling the oldest trick in the book, and I fell for an older one. Should've given the Foreheads more credit." He sighed. Suddenly the six minutes that it would take the Third Order to catch up were an eternity. "Evasive maneuvers."

Chapter 7

I.K.S. WO'BORTAS

The bridge was coming to pieces around Captain Qaolin. His new first officer was dead, their stock of torpedoes were almost gone, and their shields were down to fourteen percent.

"Those Cardassians fight better than I thought."

His gunner, an old *grishnar* cat named Tolkor, said, "They still die like dogs when facing true warriors."

Qaolin wished that that were more true than it was. He and the fleet managed to destroy three of their ships, but they in turn crippled six of the Defense Force vessels—including the *Wo'bortas*. The shields had taken the brunt of the impact, but they were now down to almost nothing. *One more shot, and we will be defenseless—and they still have superior firepower.*

"Sir," Tolkor reported, "the *Kazin* is coming around and firing on three of the Cardassian ships—it's heading straight for them at ramming speed!"

Qaolin stood and said, "Is G'Zar insane? On screen!"

Sure enough, Captain G'Zar was taking the *I.K.S. Kazin*, one of the *Birok*-class strike ships, right at three of the ships. According to the tactical data on the screen, their shields and communications systems were down and their weapons were spent. Their warp power was also nonexistent.

Tolkor then laughed. "Oh, he's insane, all right, sir—insane like a Romulan. The *Kazin*'s warp core is about to breach. He's maneuvering into position to take as many of those *petaQ* as he can when it goes."

The captain grinned. No doubt G'Zar thought that, if he was going to die anyhow, he would take the enemy with him. "Set course for the nebula, full impulse—warn the rest of the fleet of what G'Zar is planning."

As what remained of the bridge crew carried out his orders, Qaolin saw that the *Sontok*—the ship they'd been spying on—was following them into the nebula. *Good,* Qaolin thought.

The *Sontok* then fired on the *Wo'bortas*. "Damage to the secondary hull and port wing," Tolkor said. "We're venting plasma. Sir, if we enter the nebula—"

But Qaolin had already thought of what plasma interacting with the particulate matter of the nebula would do. "Set course 111 mark 22, full impulse. Is the *Sontok* pursuing?"

"Yes, sir," the pilot said.

"Excellent. When I give the word, reverse course and eject the containment unit in the port wing."

Tolkor spoke up again. "Sir, we have a hull breach on deck four—all the cabins on the port side have been exposed to space, sir."

Qaolin could not help it. He laughed, long and hard.

The guest cabin where Yovang's body still lay was on the port side. It, along with all its contents, had just been blown into the vacuum of space.

A more fitting fate, I could not imagine. He suspected that he would not be rid of I.I. so easily. Qaolin was quite sure that a recording had been made of his assassination of Yovang, and he was equally sure that such a recording would survive a firefight, and even explosive decompression. Still, any destruction of evidence suited Qaolin just fine.

"Approaching nebula," the pilot said.

"Reverse course." A pause. "Eject the unit."

One second later, the viewscreen became filled with static, as the charged particles of the nebula did their work in interfering with the image translator. Three seconds later, several consoles blew apart from the impact of a nearby explosion.

"Report!"

"The *Sontok* is dead in space." Tolkor laughed. "Your timing was perfect, sir. The *Kazin*'s warp core breach happened at the same time as our containment unit ignited the nebula. However, we were caught in the backwash of both. Our engines are offline."

"What of the other ships?"

"Attempting to locate them, now. We're drifting away from the nebula, so that should improve sensor resolution— Aha!" Again, Tolkor laughed. "It would seem, Captain, that we have achieved a stalemate. Only two Cardassian ships are left intact—the *Sontok* and the *Golnor*, and both are showing no power output worth mentioning."

"What of our forces?"

"In *Sto-Vo-Kor* with the Black Fleet—except for us." Tolkor manipulated his console. "Now getting debris readings—it would seem that the *Dogal* followed the *Kazin*'s lead and took our foes with them when their ships proved too unstable to remain intact."

"They died well," Qaolin said. "Time to repair warp drive?"

"I do not know, sir. Internal communications are down. However," and Tolkor laughed a third time at this, "external communications are functioning normally. We can contact Command."

"Do so." Qaolin turned to the viewscreen, the image on which was starting to clear up. "I will not let Ch'gran be taken from my hands now, not when we've come this far . . ."

He stared at the *Sontok* as it drifted through space, powerless, its momentum carrying it slowly closer to the Betreka Nebula. *You fought well, my enemy*, he thought at whoever it was who commanded the *Sontok*. *But I still draw breath, and I swear that I will never allow you to take Ch'gran from me.*

Chapter 8

CARDASSIA PRIME

Enabran Tain had never been to the headquarters of the Detapa Council before. But then, before he hadn't been the head of the Obsidian Order.

Indeed, going to this emergency meeting—which was to be attended only by Tain, his counterpart at Central Command, and the First Speaker of the Council—was Tain's first official act as head of the Order. It was a position he had long anticipated. He had expected to be appointed several months ago, in fact, and he no doubt would have been, had his information that his predecessor was fatally allergic to Locan powder been accurate.

Tain straightened his dull green tunic as the doors parted to let him into the meeting room. The tunic did an adequate job of hiding the fact that Tain was putting on weight. Since his Order duties had been more administrative of late, he had let his weakness for rich food get the better of him, and without the concomitant exercise inherent in field work, he found his middle getting rounder.

Then again, Tain had never been a particularly impressive physical specimen. Though large, he was not intimidating, and even at his slimmest, he presented a bland figure, more circular than stocky. He cultivated that, as it gave the impression that he was weak—useful for someone in his profession to convey.

The room's purpose was to hold meetings such as this where only one member of each body was required. Decorated in bold browns and greens, with tasteful-yet-harmless spacescape paintings on two of the walls, the room's most prominent feature was the window on the back wall opposite the door: an etched-glass window in the shape of the Cardassian Union's emblem. From the outside, the window looked glorious when the sun hit it, and Tain supposed that the brilliance was even more astounding in here. Sadly, this meeting was taking place in the dead of night, so all that illuminated the facets of the glass were the city lights—a woefully inadequate substitute. Tain himself would have preferred stained glass, of course, an art form that the humans of Earth had apparently perfected over the course of their history. Tain had learned of it from one of his operations. *Perhaps I'll copy this design for my own house, only using the human technique.*

Legate Kell was already seated in one of the chairs around the crescent-shaped table. The table had three large chairs, one in the center, one on each of the ends. Kell had taken the seat to the right of center, as was traditional for Central Command. Tain was expected to take the one on the left.

The First Speaker had not yet arrived.

Kell looked up at Tain's arrival and grunted. He wore the gray uniform of the military, in his case decorated on the left breast with a golden version of the Cardassian emblem. Tain had always thought that the decoration that indicated a legate to be overly ostentatious—but then, the military by its nature was ostentatious. That was why the Order was necessary, to counteract that belligerent tendency.

"Good to meet you, Tain," Kell said, not sounding in the least bit sincere in that sentiment. "Your record is fairly impressive."

Tain nodded as he took his seat. Kell would, of course, be

familiar with Tain's record, since Central Command had final approval over any appointment to the Order. Usually that approval was a formality—Central Command hadn't exercised its right to deny an appointment in centuries—but that wouldn't stop them from reviewing any such appointment. *Not,* he thought, *that the opinion of a legate, even this one, is of any great interest to me.*

Kell gazed for several seconds at Tain. For his part, Tain sat in his chair, his hands folded on the table, and waited for Speaker Alnak. *No doubt Kell is waiting for me to return the compliment. Well, let him wait.*

"Hmph," Kell said, then went back to studying his padd.

Tain had not brought such an item with him—in his position, he could hardly put his work in an unsecure portable device and view it in public. So he watched Kell, observing the older man's body language, the way he stabbed at the display of his padd impatiently, the fact that he paid no attention to the mug he was drinking from. That, in particular, piqued Tain's interest. Kell was, by all accounts, a patriot and a credit to his position. Unfortunately, it was a position often occupied by fools. *The day may come where his foolishness will damage Cardassia. When that day comes, I must be ready to deal with it.* The ease with which Kell could be poisoned was something Tain might be able to use some time in the future.

The door opened again, and an older woman in civilian clothes entered. White-haired, wearing no makeup, it took Tain a moment to realize that this was Speaker Alnak. She looked nothing like the image of her in her file—but then, she probably had gone through a certain amount of grooming before that picture was taken. Now she looked like someone woken out of a sound sleep. Her arms were laden with half a dozen padds. "I'm sorry I'm late," she said in breathless rush of words, "but I'm afraid this business has caught me rather off guard."

Kell grumbled something. Tain, however, said, "That's quite all right. I only just arrived myself."

Dropping the padds rather unceremoniously on the table, Alnak took her seat at the center. "I assume you both know what this is about. There was an incident at the Betreka Nebula. We're facing the possibility of war with the Klingons. Now—"

"I say we live up to that possiblity," Kell said without hesitation. "If they refuse to acknowledge our prior claim to Raknal V, let them pay for it in blood."

"The Klingons feel that their claim is more prior than ours, Legate," Alnak said dryly, "and not without reason."

Kell made a noise that sounded like a *chiral* breaking wind. "A thousand-year-old wreck? Please. The Klingons themselves didn't even know it was there until *we* found it."

"And yet they thought it worth sending nine ships."

"The Klingons do not need a reason to fight, they simply fight when the opportunity presents itself."

Tain chose this moment to speak up. "Perhaps, Legate, but this time they *do* fight for a reason. According to our records—" hastily looked up and memorized by Tain on his way here "—the Klingons believe this to be the remains of the Ch'gran colony. One of their sacred legends."

"What, some kind of spiritualistic nonsense?" Kell said disdainfully. "We get enough of that from the damned Bajorans."

"The Klingons are a spiritual people, Legate, but not in the same way as the Bajorans." Tain then turned to look at Alnak. "The Bajorans look to gods who guide their path; Klingons are a bit more self-determinative. According to our information, Klingon myth has it that they killed their gods. The only personage they hold in any kind of reverence is a historical figure called Kahless, who set down most of the code of honor that they claim to follow."

Kell leaned back in his chair. "I see, Tain, that you have the tendency of most of your kind to show off your precious intelligence gathering for no good reason. What, pray tell, does any of this have to do with what happened at the Betreka Nebula?"

"That they will fight to regain something they deem sacred," Tain said plainly, since subtlety seemed lost on the legate.

"Let them offer to obtain it from us, then. But they cannot refute our legitimate claim on Raknal V!"

Tain had nothing to say to such tiresome posturing. Alnak, however, did: "I wonder, Legate, how you would feel if a Klingon ship lay claim to a planet on which they found ruins of the First Hebitians."

This is it, Tain thought. Kell's answer to this question would resolve for Tain once and for all whether or not the legate had two brain cells to rub together, or was just another typical Central Command drone.

But Kell did not answer the question. He did not say, "I would react the same way as I am now," which would serve to strengthen his position. He did not even say, "That would be a different matter—Cardassian ruins are a matter of national import," which would be ethnocentric, but at least in character and reasonable.

Instead, he simply sat there, fuming. It was the worst possible way to respond to the speaker's question, and it firmly lodged Kell in the "fool" column of Tain's mental ledger.

Part of him was relieved. Such a fool would be child's play to manipulate. Another part was disappointed that he would be denied the challenge of a worthy adversary in Central Command. *Ah, well—perhaps there are some lesser legates or guls who can at least keep things interesting.*

Alnak riffled through her padds, finally coming up with one. "We received a message from the Klingon High Council, saying that they wish to stake a claim to Raknal V. They are willing to negotiate, but will fight to regain the wreckage if they have to."

"Pfah," Kell said with a dismissive gesture. "Those imbeciles don't negotiate. It's a ploy to gather their forces."

Tain tried to keep the disdain out of his voice as he responded to Kell. *He had his mind made up before he came in here.* However, Tain preferred to glean information before making any kind of decision—not that he ever made a decision that he couldn't go back on if the need arose. But the news that the Klingons were willing to negotiate was telling, and fit the available data. "The Klingons are only three-and-a-half decades removed from the catastrophic destruction of their moon. Even with Federation aid and the passage of time, their resources are limited. I would surmise that they do not wish to go to war unless they have to."

"Then let them. If they are as weak as you seem to think, Tain, then they should be easy to destroy."

"If they were that easy to destroy," Tain said with a small smile, "why have we not conquered them? Or the Romulans? The Federation?"

Kell sneered. "I should think that even one such as you would understand the military reasons for that, Tain. They are too distant from our current borders. To invade the Klingon Empire would mean a great commitment of resources to a distant campaign that would leave our internal defenses weakened."

"Congratulations, Legate," Tain said with an amiable smile. "You have just made the best case for why we should not pursue this matter militarily."

"Tain is correct," Alnak said before Kell could reply. "While the Betreka Sector is closer than the Klingon border, it is still too distant for us to wage a proper campaign."

"Your military expertise tells you this?" Kell asked, turning his sneer on the speaker.

Again, Alnak riffled through her padds. "I have here a complete list of the present troop and ship deployments of the ships under the jurisdiction of Central Command.

There are only two ways to divert the necessary resources to wage war in the Betreka Sector—to leave other sectors undefended and abandon our current plan of expansion, or to construct more ships and draft more troops. The former is unacceptable—Cardassia needs to expand its borders if we are to continue our food and jobs programs—and the latter would be costly."

Just as Tain had consigned Kell to the fool column, he found himself forced to move Speaker Alnak from "irrelevant" to "worth keeping an eye on." The Detapa Council was mostly toothless, but they served a purpose, and knowing that its First Speaker had a brain in her head was another useful nugget of information. Tain was already thinking of ways to exploit that nugget.

Even as those thoughts turned over in his mind, he said, "The Obsidian Order's position is the same. The expansion program is far more important than getting into a protracted and distant skirmish with the Klingons—one that we are not guaranteed to win. And even if we do," he added quickly, cutting off the wounded reply that he knew Kell would give at his show of disrespect to the Cardassian military, "the Klingons will make this a bloody and costly conflict. Few of their wars have ever been simple or quick."

"I appreciate the concerns that you both raise," Kell said, "but ultimately, they are irrelevant."

The legate's stupidity knows no bounds. "Really?"

Kell smiled. "Central Command needs no one's permission to wage war, Tain. That is solely our purview. If we wish to fight the Klingons for Raknal V, then we shall fight them. The Cardassian people need zenite, and Raknal V has it. That is all that matters."

Tain smiled right back. "And who will provide intelligence reports for your military?"

Dismissively, Kell said, "We have our own intelligence resources."

It was all Tain could do to keep from laughing in Kell's face at the very idea. One of the reasons why the Obsidian Order existed was because of the military's woeful lack of "intelligence resources." Every attempt they had made to cultivate some had met with dismal failure.

Alnak fixed Kell with a gaze that might have been penetrating had her hair not been in such disarray. "And with what will you pay for this war, Legate?"

That brought Kell up short, and for the second time, the speaker left the legate speechless. *Two times too many*, Tain thought.

"It is true," Alnak continued, "that the Detapa Council cannot actually stop you from waging war if it is war you wish to wage. But it is the Council that must approve of any budgetary amendments you might want to make—and you will need to make several in order to fight the Klingons. It is also the Council that is responsible for overseeing any new taxes or conscriptions that must take place. I can assure you right now, Legate, that the Council will feel no obligation to make life easy on Central Command if they choose this course of action."

Tain was grateful that, in this at least, Alnak was on his side. He'd hate to have to kill her.

Whatever Kell's failings, however, he knew when he was defeated. Without the support of the Order or the Council, his ability to fight the Klingons would be severely curtailed. Leaning forward in his chair, he said, "Very well. If we are to negotiate, who is to mediate?"

"The Federation," Alnak said without hesitation. "It is the wish of the Council that we attempt to rehabilitate our relationship with the Federation after that unfortunate incident on Vulcan last year."

Tain of course made no reaction; Kell did seethe a bit, though. It had been a joint Central Command/Obsidian Order operation to disrupt the summit at Vulcan in order to sever ties between the Federation and the Legarans. Unfortunately, as with most joint operations betwee. the two bodies, it was a disaster. Central Command had, of course, insisted that the saboteurs were renegades, but the Federation was not made up of fools. Legara IV remained under the protection of the Federation's military arm, Starfleet, and the Federation now viewed Cardassia as a potential foe instead of a potential ally. It was, in Tain's experience, much harder to slip a knife into the heart of an enemy than that of an ally.

Not that Tain was too put out by the failure of that operation—it had proven that his predecessor was no longer fit to run the Order, and allowed Tain to gather support for his own candidacy for the job, once his predecessor met with his unfortunate accident.

Still, using the Federation made sense. They had been allied with the Klingons since Praxis, and they were very good at filling the air with pointless words—the perfect diplomats.

"Very well," Kell said reluctantly. "However, we will be preparing for a conflict—in case the Klingons prove to be less than amenable to negotiations," he added with an insincere smile.

"Excellent." Alnak sounded relieved. Tain was disappointed in her being so transparent. But then, she hadn't been called upon to do this sort of thing often. As a general rule, Central Command and the Order looked after their own affairs, with the Detapa Council's oversight being little more than a formality. But the potential magnitude of this crisis required the cooperation of all three organizations.

From Tain's perspective, this entire incident was proving to be incredibly valuable. In the short term, he had obtained useful information about Legate Kell and First Speaker Alnak. In the long term, this negotiation would allow his people to observe both the Klingons and the Federation more closely. The expansion program that had brought them Bajor and attempted to bring them Legara IV was also bringing their borders much closer to the sphere of influence of both powers.

The Klingons were an empire that had been bringing worlds under their heel for centuries. They had a reputation for fierceness and cruelty that Tain was sure was well earned. As for the Federation, though they claimed to be beneficent and egalitarian, they were as imperialistic a state as Tain had ever seen, expanding to an astonishing number of worlds. Tain would have thought that their democratic system would collapse under its own weight, especially at the size the Federation had achieved, but it seemed to function efficiently.

If Cardassia is to take its place as the leader of the galaxy, we must know as much as we can about these nations that will oppose our destiny.

The meeting adjourned soon thereafter. Tain could see that Kell was furious. He could also see that the legate was trying desperately to read Tain's own expression and was frustrated at his inability to do so. *Get used to disappointment*, Tain thought.

He rose from his chair. "Thank you, Madam Speaker," Tain said with a small bow. Turning to Kell, he added, "And best of luck to you, Legate."

His polite response only seemed to anger Kell more. Tain simply smiled the blandest smile he had in his repertory and moved to the exit, all the while trying to decide which agent he would send to infiltrate the negotiating team.

Chapter 9

U.S.S. CARTHAGE

When Lieutenant Ian Troi had been given permission by
Commander Rachel Garrett to attend the reception, he had
forgotten how damned uncomfortable Starfleet dress uniforms were.

*Maybe participating in a Betazoid wedding has changed
my opinions on clothes just a bit,* he thought with a smile as
he shifted the collar on the red dress uniform in the vain
hope of keeping it from rubbing against his Adam's apple.

Resigning himself to spending the evening scratching his
neck, he left his quarters and headed to the *U.S.S. Carthage's*
recreation lounge. The room had been converted into a reception hall for this, the first night of what hoped to be a fruit-
ful negotiation between the Klingons and the Cardassians
over the disposition of Raknal V. In the three weeks since the
Betreka Nebula Incident, the three sides had agreed to hold
negotiations aboard the *Miranda*-class *Carthage*, with the
Sontok and the *Wo'bortas* bringing the representatives of the
Cardassian and Klingon governments, respectively. Troi had
noted during his previous bridge shift that both ships had
taken considerable battle damage, and that their repairs were
adequate, but not one hundred percent—in a firefight, neither ship would be able to make much of a show of things,

whereas the *Carthage* was in tip-top shape. Troi wasn't sure if that boded good or ill.

On his way down the corridor of deck twelve, Troi turned a corner and almost bumped into a man also wearing a Starfleet dress uniform. However, Troi didn't recognize the taller man, which meant he couldn't have been part of the crew. Troi prided himself on knowing every one of the *Carthage*'s complement of two hundred at least by face, and this slightly lined, clean-shaven visage framed by dark brown hair amply flecked with gray didn't belong to any of them. *One of the passengers we took on at the starbase, then,* he thought.

"Excuse me, Lieutenant," he said, taking note of the older man's collar, indicating he was a full lieutenant and therefore one grade rank higher than Troi.

"Quite all right," the man said in an all-business tone, then offered his hand. "Elias Vaughn."

"Ian Troi, science officer," he added, though Vaughn had not indicated his own position. "I take it you're going to the reception, also?"

"Yes."

Troi smiled even as he scratched his neck. Lieutenant Vaughn had packed quite a lot of disdain into that one syllable. *Not the party type, apparently.*

They entered the lounge together, and Troi found his ears assaulted by a cacophony of sound. *I'm willing to bet most of it is from the Klingons,* Troi thought with a wry smile. He'd never actually met any Klingons (or Cardassians, for that matter) until today, but he knew their shared reputation for boisterousness.

The lounge didn't have any external windows, but someone had thought to activate the large viewscreen that took up most of one bulkhead—it showed the Betreka Nebula, the swirling gases and particulate matter making for a lovely backdrop. Ever the scientist, Troi was hoping they'd get the chance to explore the nebula in more depth on this mission. Garrett had already given him a we'll-see on the subject.

Speaking of the *Carthage* first officer, she walked over to greet Troi. The commander held a glass filled with an amber liquid. *Knowing Garrett,* Troi thought, *it's bourbon.* "Lieutenants, pleased to see you both," she said. "I didn't know you knew each other."

"We, ah, don't," Troi said. "We just bumped into each other in the hall."

"Well, help yourselves to refreshments," Garrett said, indicating the entire room. "And please, mingle. The object of this reception is to help everyone relax."

Troi looked around the lounge, and didn't see much by way of relaxed people. Numerically, the room's occupants were more or less evenly split among the Klingon delegation, the Cardassian delegation, and Federation representatives. Though several *Carthage* crew members were distributed around various parts of the room—no doubt following Garrett's urgings to mingle—everyone else was keeping to themselves. Troi also noted that Captain Haden hadn't put in an appearance yet. But then, he had left most of the details of this to Garrett. Vance Haden had never had much patience with this sort of thing.

Three tables had been laid out with food and drink. The near table with the odd-smelling, ostentatious—and in some cases, wriggling—food and the smoking beverages had to have been the Klingon food. The far table with various peculiar-looking egg and fish dishes was probably Cardassian. In the center of the lounge was a table covered in raw vegetables from several different Federation worlds, slivers of sandwich meats from Earth, fruits from Trill, *gristhera* from Andor, and a bowl of *allira* punch from Betazed. Troi especially appreciated the latter, as he'd gotten all but addicted to the stuff during his six-month tour on that planet.

Of course, I had plenty of it the last few weeks, he thought with a happy smile. He had returned to the *Carthage* from his honeymoon less than a week ago, and he missed Lwaxana terribly.

Garrett added, "I wish more people were intermingling."

"The food could perhaps have been arranged differently, Commander," Vaughn said.

"Really?" Garrett said with the pleasant, small smile that the entire complement of the *Carthage* had learned to fear. "I wasn't aware that catering was a skill cultivated by Starfleet special operations."

So that's who he is, Troi thought.

Vaughn shrugged. "No, but observation is. Not that any of these people are inclined to talk to each other socially in any case, but by keeping the different foods so far apart, you guarantee that each nation will stay near the food and drink they're most comfortable with."

"Yes," Troi said, "but if we put the Klingon drinks near any of the Cardassian food, it'd probably cause a chemical explosion."

Garrett let out a small exhalation that might have been a laugh. "Mr. Troi raises a good point. Excuse me." She went off to speak with one of the Federation delegates.

"Have you ever had *allira* punch, Lieutenant?" Troi asked after an uncomfortable pause.

"No."

"Then you're in for a treat. Come with me." He led the older man to the Federation table and scooped some of the punch into a glass for Vaughn.

"I take it you enjoyed your honeymoon?" Vaughn asked.

Troi almost dropped the glass. "Uh, yes. How'd you—?"

Vaughn came very close to smiling. "I could try to impress you by telling you that I saw the wedding ring, and I know that Vance Haden would only allow that kind of bending of the uniform code if you were recently married, and also observe that you have the glow common to a newlywed—but the fact is I read your service record on my way here."

Suddenly, Troi grew nervous, even as he handed Vaughn his punch. *Why is a special ops goon checking my service record?*

This time Vaughn really did smile. "Relax, Lieutenant—I read *everyone's* service record." In fact, Troi *was* relaxed—but, he noted, Vaughn was finally starting to do so. "The note about your recent marriage just happened to stick in my head, is all. I met your wife once a few years ago. She's quite a woman."

Troi's face split into a huge grin as he said, "Yes, she is. I'm a lucky man."

Vaughn held up the glass. "To the happy couple."

"I'll drink to that." Troi then suited action to words. The punch wasn't as good as what they'd had at the reception on Betazed, but that was fresh, not replicated.

"Not bad," Vaughn said. "A bit acidic for my taste, but quite pleasant. Thank you."

"You're welcome."

"Not just for that—for defusing that little contretemps between me and the commander." He took another sip. "I suspect that my presence here is a bit of an annoyance."

He wasn't kidding about being observant, Troi thought as he grabbed a carrot and a stalk of celery. "So why *are* you here anyhow?"

"To be a bit of an annoyance," Vaughn said dryly. "We may be allied with the Klingons, but that doesn't mean we're going to do something so silly as trust them. There's too much bad blood there, going all the way back to Broken Bow."

Troi smiled at that. The first aliens to land on Earth and make contact with humans were the Vulcans in the twenty-first century, who did so after Zefram Cochrane's famed *Phoenix* warp-speed flight. The second was a Klingon, who crash-landed ninety years later in an American cornfield and blew up a silo. Both, in their own way, set the tone for future relations—the former as a valued ally in forming the Federation, the latter as an implacable enemy until very recently.

"And considering that the last time we made peaceful overtures to the Cardassians they used it to sabotage our relationship with Legara IV, Starfleet Command is concerned about them as well."

A new voice said, "And heaven forfend we disregard the concerns of Starfleet Command."

Troi turned to see a white-haired Trill dressed in a brightly colored tunic and pants that made Lwaxana's outfits look almost subdued. "You must be Ambassador Dax," Troi said, offering his hand. "Ian Troi."

Dax tilted his head quizzically. "Troi? You mean *you're* the one who succeeded in roping down the infamous Lwaxana?" He returned the handshake with his right hand, after moving a large Klingon mug to his left.

Troi wondered what it was Dax was choking down, and how, exactly, he did it. Just from here, the smell was enough to put Troi off his *allira*. "I wouldn't call it 'roping down,' sir, more like going along for the ride."

"Aptly put," Dax said with a hearty laugh. "You have my respect, Mr. Troi. From all I've heard, Lwaxana is quite a woman. I'm sorry I missed the ceremony."

"We tried to keep the guest list down to a manageable few thousand," Troi said wryly. "Plus, of course, my side of the family."

Another laugh. "Such a wonderfully open-minded people, the Betazoids. Literally, if it comes to that. Was it a proper ceremony?"

Troi nodded. "Of course. Betazoids don't have a nudity taboo—what would be the point, really? Their concept of privacy is a lot more fluid than ours in any case, being telepaths and all. I was worried that I'd be self-conscious during the wedding, but I barely even noticed—either that I was naked or that everyone around me was as well. There was a—purity to it, I suppose you could say. It was very refreshing."

Vaughn finally spoke. "A rather philosophical attitude for a science officer."

"I find that science works better with philosophy behind it, Lieutenant," Troi said with a smile.

"Indeed it does," Dax said. "You might be able to learn something from this one, Vaughn."

Pointedly ignoring the comment, Vaughn turned to Troi and said, "Actually, Lieutenant, one of the reasons why I remembered your service record in particular was because you were the second human I came across serving on this ship who was married to a Betazoid."

Troi sighed loudly. *Here we go again.* "Yes, it's true, I've done it all just to suck up to Commander Garrett." He said the words with a grin on his face. It led to another of Dax's hearty laughs, and something resembling a smile from Vaughn. "Seriously, it's a complete coincidence that both the commander and I married Betazoids. That hasn't stopped half the crew from giving me a hard time about it, of course. But actually I met Lwaxana while I was stationed on Betazed. I was part of the team that upgraded their orbital defense system. We met, we fell in love, I decided I wanted to spend the rest of my life with her—"

"And so you proposed?" Dax said with a grin.

"No."

That prompted another laugh from Dax. "What stopped you, man?"

Not actually looking at Dax, Vaughn said, "Not all of us act on every impulse that pops into our heads, Ambassador."

Troi noted the frown that Dax gave Vaughn at that comment. Before Dax could reply to it, Troi said, "The problem was that I had no interest in abandoning Starfleet, and she couldn't really leave Betazed. But when the project was over, there wasn't a Starfleet position available for me on-planet. I was transferred here to the *Carthage*, and I waited six months to see if the feelings were just as strong if I was dozens of light-years away." He smiled. "They weren't. They were stronger."

"So *then* you proposed?" Dax asked.

"Didn't have the chance to." Troi shook his head ruefully. "That's the problem with telepaths, they never give you a chance. I had it all planned out. I had arrived on a shuttle that landed on Betazed in midafternoon. We were going to go straight to our favorite restaurant on the coast, and I was going to do the whole bit—getting down on one knee, giving her the ring. So what happens? The moment I stepped off the shuttle, she said, 'Of course I'll marry you, my darling boy,' and she kissed me right there in the spaceport."

Vaughn raised an eyebrow in an almost Vulcanlike manner. "What was it you said before about different senses of privacy?"

Troi chuckled. "We may as well have been alone for all that I noticed. I don't think I've ever been happier."

"We should all be so happy," Dax said, raising his mug in salute, then drinking the remainder of its contents. "Well, if you'll excuse me, I'm going to refill my *warnog* and try to put the Klingon negotiator at ease." He shook his head, and spoke in more serious tones. "They both sent military people—a general and a legate. That's going to keep things complicated."

"That's what Starfleet Command is worried about," Vaughn said, "and why I'm here."

"Yes, of course, Lieutenant," Dax said, his smile returning. "Far better to go into a tense situation and add a person whose very presence will make it all the more tense. As usual, Starfleet shows a command of logic that would make a Vulcan gibber. Peace will not come about from two people rattling sabers at each other." Grabbing a *gristhera*, Dax turned to head across the lounge. "A pleasure meeting you, Lieutenant Troi." With a nod, he added, "Vaughn." And then he headed toward the Klingon delegation, in particular a white-haired general with a most sour expression on his face.

Vaughn shook his head. "I don't see any way for this to end well. Klingons aren't known for their negotiation skills, and Cardassians aren't known for much of anything except self-interest."

"Still, they must want to settle this peacefully if they asked for our help." Troi popped a cherry tomato into his mouth after he was done speaking.

"Please," Vaughn said disdainfully. "Dax can carry on all he wants about saber-rattling, but they're only rattling them because their sabers have been weakened. Neither side can afford the kind of prolonged conflict that would normally result from what happened here last month. Instead, they're biding their time, going through with this charade until they can find an advantage. If Dax thinks he's actually going to accomplish anything here, he's fooling himself." Then he let out a breath. "Sorry, old habits. I've never been too keen on diplomats. They tend to have their heads firmly lodged in their hindquarters, and have absolutely no sense of the reality of their surroundings."

Troi smiled as he gulped down the rest of his *allira.* "Somehow, Lieutenant, I don't think anyone will ever accuse you of having no sense of the reality of your surroundings."

At that, Vaughn actually laughed. In fact, it was only a small chuckle, but given how taciturn the lieutenant had been up until now, it was the functional equivalent of one of Dax's belly laughs. "I certainly hope not. And please, call me Elias."

"If you insist, but only if you call me Ian."

"Very well, Ian—would you mind pouring me some more of that punch?"

Somehow, General Worf managed to choke down the liquid that Commander Garrett had insisted was *warnog.* It took all of his self-control to keep from spitting it out and dumping the remainder in his mug on the hideous carpet of this Federation ship's lounge.

Then again, he thought, *it was not that long ago that I would have done so regardless of the quality of the* warnog. Klingons did not drink with the enemy, and until recently, the *Carthage* would have been nothing but an enemy vessel.

"Much has changed," Worf muttered to himself as he set the mug down on a nearby table.

"What was that, sir?" his civilian aide, a young man named Lorgh, asked.

Worf looked down at the youth, with barely enough hair on his face to be properly called a beard. "I said much has changed. I have seen a great deal in my lifetime, Lorgh, things I would never have imagined possible before they actually occurred. Praxis destroyed. Peace with the Federation. And now—now, Ch'gran has been found. We live in peculiar times."

"I wouldn't know about that, sir," Lorgh said with a deference that was in every way convincing, and utterly false.

"Of course you would." Once the general would have been happy to play these games, but he was far too old to have the patience for them now. "It is, after all, your function to observe your surroundings."

Lorgh scowled. "My job is to aid you, General. I can assure you—"

"I did not say 'job,' Lorgh, I said 'function.' Precision of language is important in my line of work—as it should be in yours."

"Sir, my line of work *is* yours."

"If you insist on referring to your cover story as a line of work, so be it. But do not insult me by pretending to be anything other than the Imperial Intelligence agent you are."

To Lorgh's credit, he showed no surprise, nor did his facial expression change in any way. "Sir, you cannot think that I would try to undermine your work here."

"You are here to ensure that these negotiations do not conflict with whatever the High Council's agenda is regarding Raknal V and the Ch'gran colony." Throwing caution to the wind, Worf picked the *warnog* back up. "I do not doubt that you will *also* serve me as my aide."

"How did you know, sir?" Lorgh continued to speak in the deferential tones of an aide. That was no doubt for the benefit of anybody observing them. Worf was sure that, just as I.I. had sent their own operative, Cardassia and the Federation had done the same. Typically, the Federation's was out in the open—the dark-haired lieutenant standing over by the Federation food table with one of the *Carthage* crew. Cardassia's equivalent of I.I. had probably used more covert means, as I.I. had, and assigned someone to go undercover as an aide to Legate Zarin. Worf took pleasure in his surety that Zarin had no clue which of his staff was serving that function.

Answering Lorgh's question, Worf said, "I have spent my life observing people. The battlefield on which I wage war is that of the courtroom and the negotiation table, and language is both my weapon and that of my opponents. Language of the body speaks as loudly as that of the mouth, often more so, for fewer hear the words they speak in that tongue."

"It is a pity I.I. never drafted you, sir."

Worf snorted. "Your flattery is misdirected, Lorgh. I am no warrior. I.I. requires a level of martial skill that I have never achieved. The Defense Force, at least, has a place for those of my class who do not live up to the exacting standards of front-line warriors."

"You'd be surprised what I.I. requires, sir." Lorgh let that comment hang for a moment, then continued. "In any case, I have no intention of undermining these negotiations—unless your intent is to do other than what you have been ordered."

Another snort. "Unlikely—and that you would even think so—"

Lorgh held up a hand. "I merely raise the possibility, sir. After all, no one would have imagined General Chang to be a traitor once. Indeed, his statue in the Hall of Warriors on Ty'Gokor had been all but built. Yet now, his name is spoken of only as a curse."

Worf smiled at that. "I faced General Chang once, in the courtroom. It was shortly before his disgrace—in fact, it was a part of it. I had been instructed to serve as advocate for the humans Kirk and McCoy when they were accused of assassinating Chancellor Gorkon. Chang himself chose me, and I followed his orders. I knew the humans to be innocent of the charges, but I did not disobey. If I had, he would have killed me where I stood and assigned another to take my place."

"Sir, I'm aware of all of this." Lorgh sounded genuinely confused—perhaps the first genuine emotion he'd displayed in Worf's presence. "Why do you tell this story now?"

"I had thought that I escaped Chang's disgrace after the near-disaster at Khitomer. Instead, I was passed over for promotion repeatedly, given the worst assignments in the office of legalities, cases that one gave to a novice advocate. It was made clear to me that Chancellor Azetbur knew of my role in the cover-up of her father's death, however tangential." He forced down the last of his *warnog*. "As I said, I am no warrior. I could have challenged those who insulted my honor by treating me this way, but all that would do is deprive my son of his father, my mate of her husband. So I obeyed. And I continued to obey until enough time passed, Azetbur fell from power, and I became a general. Now I represent the Empire on the day of one of its most historic moments. I came to this by obeying my superiors, Lorgh." Worf had been looking at the representation of the Betreka Nebula on the viewscreen during his entire diatribe. Now he turned and fixed Lorgh with what he hoped was a penetrating glance. "If I wished to disobey, I would have done so much sooner than this."

Lorgh said nothing in response to that—at first. The general took advantage of the silence to grab a handful of *gagh*.

Finally Lorgh asked, "How did you know, sir?"

Still deferential, eh, Lorgh? Worf smiled at that. "How did I know what?"

"You said you knew that Kirk and McCoy were innocent of killing Chancellor Gorkon."

"Yes."

"How?"

"I could see into the humans' hearts. Kirk was a warrior born, not one to hide behind assassins. If he wished the chancellor dead, he would have faced him like a Klingon. As for McCoy, he had no heart for such things. It was not within him to kill, whether face-to-face or in the shadows. No, only a fool would think them capable of such an act." Now, he scowled. "The galaxy, however, is full of fools. That one, for instance." He pointed at the Trill ambassador, who was now holding forth with Captain Qaolin and Commander Garrett.

"You mean the great Curzon Dax?"

To Worf's disgust, Lorgh spoke with what sounded like genuine reverence. *Then again, disguising his true feelings is part of what he does. I can only pray that it is so here, or I will be forced to think even less of him.* "Great by his own lights, perhaps, but not mine. He is an opportunist who has taken advantage of warriors of lesser intellect and great ego to insinuate himself into Klingon society—all in aid of furthering his cause as a diplomat."

"Should he not use all the tools at his disposal? Besides, he respects our ways as few outsiders do."

"Believe that if you may," Worf said disdainfully as Dax let out one of his belly laughs—ostentatious by Trill standards, though weak by Klingon ones. "For my part, I would rather the Federation had sent Riva." The general grinned.

"He, too, is an arrogant *petaQ*, but with that chorus he carts around, he at least makes a better show of it."

"More theatrical, sir?" Lorgh also grinned. "I was not aware that you were a proponent of such things."

"The courtroom and the negotiating table are as much theater as they are battlefield, Lorgh."

"That is very true, sir, as I have learned in my service."

Lorgh implied that it was his service to Worf, but the general knew he meant otherwise. *But why court eavesdroppers?* "Of course." *Then again, why let him pretend he is what he is not?* "You may reassure your superiors, Lorgh, that I will do all that I can to make sure that Ch'gran is not soiled by Cardassian filth."

"Ch'gran must be preserved, it's true," Lorgh said, "but so must the Empire. A full-scale war right now would be unwise."

"I.I. preaches that we shirk battle?" Worf asked, feigning surprise.

"The High Council preaches that we fight this battle at the negotiating table."

Worf's instinct was to simply fight and be done with it— but he thought that secure in the knowledge that he would not be among those fighting. No, he thought, *I will continue to obey as ever I have done. Let others dictate where the* d'k tahg *is to be thrust. I am content simply to be the blade.*

The Klingon general was deep in conversation with one of his aides, so Dax instead approached Captain Qaolin, who was chatting with Commander Garrett. *That's a good sign,* he thought. *It'd be a better sign if all the Cardassians weren't on the other side of the room, but a high-ranking Klingon having a pleasant conversation with a high-ranking Starfleet officer is never a bad thing.*

For Dax's part, he thought that joining the chat wasn't a bad thing either, especially when that high-ranking officer happened to be a devilishly attractive woman. Rachel Garrett had a most pleasant face—it wasn't what Dax would call conventionally attractive, but her soft skin combined with a pair of penetrating brown eyes to make for a face Dax wouldn't have minded getting to know the person behind a lot better.

"Ah, you are Curzon Dax?" Qaolin said.

"Indeed I am, Captain."

Qaolin gave a small bow. "I am honored. I served with Captain Koloth, and he spoke highly of you."

"Koloth speaks highly of few save Koloth in my experience, Captain, so the fact that he spoke highly of another in your presence is flattery indeed." He held up his *warnog*, which was among the worst replicated beverages he'd ever had. *I knew I should have had some shipped in from Qo'noS.* "To Koloth." After choking down the drink, he asked, "How is the mad old razorbeast?"

Laughing, Qaolin said, "Mad and old as ever. He won't die, though."

After sipping her own drink—bourbon, from the smell of it—Garrett asked, "Has anyone tried to aid him in that process?" She smiled knowingly.

"Oh, many have tried to send his soul to *Sto-Vo-Kor*, Commander, believe me. None have lived to make a second attempt. It is perhaps less accurate to say that he won't die—more that no one has been worthy of performing the deed."

"Most definitely," Dax said with a grin.

The captain regarded Dax. "I am glad that it is you who leads this negotiation, Ambassador. You understand the Klingon mind—and the Klingon heart." He put a hand on Dax's shoulder. "I know that you will return Ch'gran to its rightful place."

"What I will do, my friend, is preserve the peace. But you can be assured that I will not do so at the expense of Klingon honor."

Qaolin smiled. "I can ask no more. *Qapla'*, Dax."

With that, the captain excused himself to talk to one of the other Klingons.

"I thought for sure he was gonna head-butt you," Garrett said with a grin. Dax noted that Garrett had an unusually wide smile for her face, and the grin completely changed the structure of her visage. Among other things, it changed her eyes from intelligent to mischievous.

"It was a risk," Dax said with mock gravity.

Garrett swallowed the rest of her bourbon, then shook her head. "Next time, I use my own sour mash."

Dax let out a laugh at that. "It couldn't be any worse than the *warnog*. I'm wondering if perhaps we'd have been better off not replicating everything."

"Perhaps. Do you really think you can do this?"

Blinking, Dax said, "Do what?"

Garrett gestured at the Cardassian legate and then at the Klingon general. "This. What you told Qaolin you could do. The Cardassians have a legitimate claim, and the only reason the Klingons even know about it is because they were spying."

"True, and if it were just a simple case of finding a wreck, I'd agree with you. What you must understand, my dear, is that Ch'gran is one of the sacred stories of the Emp—"

"I'm fully aware of the spiritual significance the Klingons put on this lost colony, Ambassador." Garrett spoke snappishly, and Dax realized that he perhaps should not have put on his patronizing tone when speaking to a commander whose service record included more than one trip to Qo'noS. "Gul Monor found the functional equivalent of an old burial ground. Even so, there are such things as salvage rights."

"There's also such a thing as prior claim." Dax let out a sigh that was probably unnecessarily theatrical. "It's a bit of a legal hair that needs to be split, not aided by the fact that there are no treaties between Cardassia and the Empire— nor, for that matter, between Cardassia and the Federation.

Whatever gets decided on this ship may well have an impact for generations to come."

"And you get to shape it. How nice for you."

Garrett spoke in the most pleasant of tones, but Dax could hardly miss the snide undercurrent. "It *is* my job, Commander Garrett. Both the Cardassians and the Klingons are approaching this situation with caution, but for all the wrong reasons."

"What do you mean?"

Now Garrett sounded like she was genuinely curious. *Good,* Dax thought, *perhaps now I can get back in her good graces.* He knew, of course, that the commander was a married woman, but that didn't make her any less pleasant company, and Dax didn't like the idea of an attractive woman not finding his own company as pleasant as he found hers. "Because of that very legal hair, cautious heads need to prevail—we tread over ground that is fraught with a veritable minefield of procedural dangers." In a sweeping gesture, he pointed at both the Klingons and the Cardassians, each standing near their own table of food. "But that's not why they're being cautious. They're concerned about the distances involved, and whether or not they can afford to commit to a prolonged conflict."

Garrett shook her head and started walking toward the Federation food table. "Who would have thought forty years ago that the Klingons would be holding back from a war for economic reasons?"

Dax laughed. "My dear, you cannot possibly be old enough to remember anything from forty years ago."

"No," Garrett said as she grabbed some vegetables and placed her empty glass on the table. "In fact, I was born the year *after* Khitomer."

"Then you are fortunate, my dear," Dax said as Garrett took a bite of some *irrel.* "You've never been alive during a time of conflict between the Federation and the Empire. As lamentable as the destruction of Praxis was, I have to say that it was the best thing ever to happen to either of our nations."

He poured himself some *allira* punch. "Can I interest you in a glass?"

"God no," Garrett said emphatically, "I can't stand that stuff. My husband tried to ply me with it on our first date, and it almost prevented the second date."

"Lucky for him, you got over it, then."

"Mmm."

Dax frowned. *Trouble in paradise, perhaps?* Still, he knew better than to query someone about their marriage difficulties. One of only two results was possible: she would go on for hours about those difficulties, which was the last thing Dax wanted to hear, or she would clam up and lose her charm as a conversational companion.

He turned his gaze over toward one of the tables, where Vaughn and young Mr. Troi were now sitting, having as animated a conversation as someone with Elias Vaughn's utter lack of social skills could have. "Tell me, Commander, you wouldn't happen to know whose ridiculous idea it was to send *him* along, do you?"

"You mean Lieutenant Vaughn?" Garrett asked as she poured herself a *skahtchansohde*. "I'm honestly not sure. All I know is that our orders were to pick up the lieutenant along with you and your staff at Starbase 47 and bring you all here. Then we were to host the negotiations."

Dax shook his head. "Probably some admiral insisted on it. Unfortunately, he's as likely to make a mess of things as help. He's an even bigger impediment to the process than the general and the legate."

Garrett smiled. "He's just here to observe, Ambassador. I doubt he'll even be that heavily involved in the process."

"I wish I had your confidence," Dax said gravely. "I've known far too many intelligence types, and there are two universal truths about them. One is that they are constitutionally incapable of not being heavily involved in the process, even when they're not supposed to be."

"And the other?"

Taking a bite of a celery stick, Dax said, "Their heads are so firmly lodged in their hindquarters that they have no sense of reality. It's the sort of thing that can get us all killed if we're not careful."

At the sound of the doors parting, Dax turned to see the imposing figure of Vance Haden finally putting in his appearance. Large, dark-skinned, with a full head of hair that the captain kept cut close to his scalp, and wide, round eyes that appeared to see everything, Haden had earned a reputation as a hardass, but not an unreasonable one.

He headed straight for Garrett and Dax. "Number One. Ambassador. Good to see you both." Haden had a deep, rich voice that Dax frankly envied. "How's the reception going?"

"A little more segregated than what I was hoping, sir," Garrett said ruefully.

"We knew this was going to be a hard row to hoe, Number One. I'm just glad they're all in the same room and not killing each other."

Dax smiled. "An auspicious beginning, I'd say."

Haden didn't return the smile. "I certainly hope so, Mr. Dax. I'm holding you personally responsible for keeping it that way. Because if anything happens to my ship, it's your ass I intend to put in the sling. Do we understand each other?"

Although Dax was completely unintimidated by Haden's attempt to intimidate him, the ambassador did at the very least respect Haden's position. He couldn't blame the captain for being apprehensive. "We do."

"Good. I'm also keeping us on yellow alert until these negotiations are concluded, with the crew at general quarters. I don't know much about the Cardassians, but I do know how Klingons act when they start getting their bowels in an uproar, and I don't want any of my people caught in the crossfire."

Wonderful—another bit of tension to add. This business will get out of control if just the slightest thing goes wrong.

Taking another bite of celery, Dax thought, *I'll just have to make doubly sure that nothing goes wrong.*

"The biggest problem, of course, are these young children they have coming up through the ranks. It's almost as if all standards have gone completely out the airlock. They get into formation like a group of lifeless *gritta*, and no passion, no enthusiasm. If Cardassia's going to be what it should be, we need young people who enjoy their work. Now you take my second, Ekron—*he* understands how things should be. When I was coming up through the ranks, you didn't have to order anybody to do their jobs, they did it without asking. Now, it's like yanking out a molar just to get someone to take a damn sensor reading."

Legate Zarin did not believe in an afterlife. He firmly believed that when you died, assuming your body was still intact at the time of death, the body decayed and that was all there was to it. Unlike these Klingon savages they were supposed to be "negotiating" with, who were fairly obsessed with some mythical other-dimensional afterlife where they would beat each other over the head for all eternity, Zarin knew better. To him, life was the most important thing.

However, he knew that many other cultures believed in an afterlife where those who had lived unworthy lives had to suffer some kind of eternal torment in punishment. And right at this moment, he knew that, if such a place did exist, Zarin would be spending eternity being trapped in a room with Gul Monor. He could imagine no greater agony.

"The worst are these Foreheads. Expecting us to negotiate with them like they were civilized people. They're as bad as the Bajorans, really."

Zarin blinked. Monor actually said something intelligent

and worth replying to. Swallowing the *kanar* he had been sipping, Zarin said, "Well, they have more territory."

"Luck, most likely. I've heard that they didn't even develop warp drive, but stole it from some race called the Hur'q."

"Never heard of them," Zarin said honestly.

"Well, as I said, that's just what I heard. Then again, these Foreheads are all talk and no action, as far as I'm concerned. They were more than happy to claim Raknal V after *we* did all the work finding it and locating their damn ship. Have you noticed that whenever they're faced with the prospect of a real challenge—a *real* war, a *real* crisis—they back off with their tails between their legs? I mean, all right, I suppose I can see why they begged the Federation for help after Praxis, though I can't see why they couldn't just support themselves and fix their own problems, but then there was the way they backed off after Organia."

Zarin frowned. "I seem to recall that that treaty was enforced by the Organians."

"If you believe that sort of thing, I suppose." Monor's disdainful tone indicated he did not. Zarin covered his reaction by sipping more *kanar*. The Federation had made the records on the Organian situation available during the initial negotiations leading to the Vulcan summit that ended so badly last year. Zarin had familiarized himself with them, and knew that neither the Federation nor the Klingons had much choice with regard to not going to war sixty years ago. "Frankly," Monor continued, "I don't believe in any of that sort of nonsense. Beings of energy pretending to be sapient so they can play games with us—utter foolishness, if you ask me. Just another excuse for the Foreheads not to fight. Like I said, all talk and no action. Mark my words, Legate, they'll spend the entire negotiating time posturing and yelling and spitting. Especially spitting. Never seen a race that enjoyed spitting as much as they do. Except maybe Lissepians. Still, all they ever seem to do is spit."

Zarin looked around the lounge, hoping for some excuse to get away from Monor. Unfortunately, the only other Cardassians were members of his staff, and the only high-ranking Federation officers present with whom it might have behooved him to be sociable were Commander Garrett and the just-arrived Captain Haden. However, they were talking with Dax, the Federation mediator, and Zarin wanted as little to do with him as possible away from the negotiating table. The ambassador was a flamboyant, annoying little *tralk*—more like a Ferengi than anything, and Zarin hated Ferengi.

On the other hand, even being in Dax's presence couldn't have been any worse than listening to Monor ramble.

"I don't see why we need to negotiate in any case. The Foreheads aren't going to do anything sensible anyhow. We should just go to war. Can't imagine what Central Command is thinking going through this nonsense."

That, at least, Zarin could speak to. "Central Command didn't have a choice. Both the Detapa Council and the Obsidian Order opposed going to war."

Monor sputtered at that, and Zarin felt a slight dab of spittle on his cheek. *For someone who objects to Klingon spit, he is certainly free with his own expectoration*, he thought angrily as he brushed a napkin over his cheek ridge.

"That's the most asinine thing I've ever heard," Monor said. "Since when do we need anyone's permission?"

In this, at least, Zarin appreciated Monor's annoyance, since it was akin to the outrage he himself had expressed at Legate Kell when the latter gave Zarin this assignment. "Permission, we do not need. However, the Council does have oversight over our budget."

Monor shook his head. "Pathetic. Isn't that just like a civilian to let something as crude as money be used as a weapon against us? We're no better than those damn Ferengi. As for the Order—well, the less said about them, the better."

Zarin shrugged. "They just want an opportunity to study the Klingons and the Federation. You know how they are."

"Vultures, all of them." Monor scowled. "You didn't let one of those voles into your party, did you?"

"Allow, no, but I would be stunned if one of my staff wasn't reporting to the Order." In fact, Zarin had given a great deal of thought to which of the six aides he had brought along served another master. The only one he'd eliminated was the young intern. Fresh out of Bamarren, Talen Kallar barely knew which buttons to push on his padd, and what he lacked in brains he made up for in lack of brains. The boy was an idiot, through and through. *No,* he thought, *I'm betting it's Doval's new assistant, what's her name? Just joined the staff, young, bright, eager-to-please—exactly the sort the Order loves to culti-vate. Olett, that's her name. Yes, I definitely need to keep an eye on her.* At present, she was talking with Doval and Kallar, and the rest of Zarin's staff. Doval was speaking, and the wide-eyed Kallar seemed to be hanging on Doval's every word, and not noticing that his glass of *hevrit* juice was dangerously close to pouring out onto the precious Starfleet carpet.

"Let me tell you, Legate, the day we let those Obsidian Order vermin have free rein over our lives was the day that Cardassia started going into the waste extractor. Why, I re-member a time . . ."

Zarin refilled his *kanar* glass, and wondered if he could drink enough to make Monor's stories palatable.

Ian Troi's neck still itched the next morning when he got up to report for his shift on the bridge. He found himself grate-ful that Starfleet had recently changed its uniform design to eliminate the turtleneck under the red uniform jacket.

Pausing only to grab a mug of tea from the mess hall on the way to the bridge—he had given himself some extra time to sleep off the evening's festivities—he entered the tur-bolift along with three other members of alpha shift.

As he settled in next to Lieutenant Michael Zipser, the alpha communications officer, the latter looked up and down Troi's frame. "Oh, good, I was worried."

Troi closed his eyes. Zipser had made this joke every day for the last five days. Bowing to the inevitable, he said, "Worried about what, Mike?"

"Well, after getting married on Betazed, I wasn't sure you'd remember to put your uniform on."

Groans were heard throughout the turbolift. The bridge engineering officer, Lieutenant Susan Phillips, said, "Y'know, Zip, that joke wasn't funny the first three hundred times, either."

Wincing, Zipser said, "Hey, c'mon, don't call me 'Zip.' "

Phillips grinned. "Lay off Ian with the nudity jokes, and we might take to considerin' it—Zip."

Zipser turned to Troi. "What did I do to deserve this?"

Troi just grinned. "What, you don't think telling the same dumb joke five days in a row qualifies?"

Whatever Zipser was going to say in his defense was lost by the turbolift doors opening to the bridge. Troi veered right to the science station between the bridge's two lifts, while Zipser turned left and sat down at the communications station to the left of the captain's chair. One of the other officers gave Zipser a consoling pat on the shoulder as he stepped down into the command well, which Zipser shrugged off, while Phillips passed behind Troi.

As she did so, Troi said, "Thanks, Sue."

"Don't mention it," Phillips said in her mild drawl. "I'm thinkin' Zip's still smartin' from Velazquez breakin' up with him."

Troi blinked. "When did that happen?"

"While you were off gettin' hitched. She's too good for him, anyhow."

Shaking his head as Phillips moved on to environmental control, Troi did a quick run-through of the current sensor readings, thinking, *I can't believe I still haven't caught up on all the gossip yet. Maybe I'll give Mike some encouragement later.* Grinning, he amended, *After calling him 'Zip' a few times, anyhow.*

The other turbolift opened to the rest of alpha shift entering, including Commander Garrett. She stepped down into the command well and took the center seat. "All stations, report."

Navigation reported first. "Holding position at one hundred million kilometers from the Betreka Nebula."

Even as the helm officer continued with his report, Troi noticed something odd on long-range from the direction of the nebula. He did a more active scan of the region to be sure, and called up yesterday's scan results, as well as the last Federation survey of the nebula six months ago.

After Zipser told Garrett that there was no unauthorized comm traffic to report, Troi said, "All clear for the most part, Commander, but I'm picking up something odd in the nebula."

"Can you be more specific?"

"Not yet, sir, but I'd like your permission to investigate more thoroughly."

Garrett frowned. "Just do a more active sensor sweep first and report back. I don't want to do anything to make our guests frantic."

"Understood."

Tactical then reassured Garrett that both the *Wo'bortas* and the *Sontok* were holding station, and that they remained at yellow alert. Troi, meanwhile, continued his scan.

As alpha shift settled into its routine, Zipser suddenly sat upright. "Oy."

"What is it, Mike?" Troi asked.

"Another call from Betazed. This is, what, the four hundred and third this week?"

Troi was starting to think there was more to Zipser's ribbing than simple jealousy over Troi's greater success with the opposite sex. "Lwaxana is a very—talkative woman."

"Talkative. Right. Half her little 'notes' to you crashed the comm buffer. This one isn't so bad, though. Let me—oh." Zipser's face fell.

"What is it?" Troi asked.

"Oh, Mr. Zipser?" Garrett said before Zipser could answer the question. "I'm expecting a communication from my husband on Betazed today. Please keep an ear out."

"Uh, actually," Zipser said, "it just came in a minute ago, Commander. I would've mentioned it sooner, but I assumed it was for Lieutenant Troi."

Garrett smiled. "I think you'll find, Mr. Troi, that the frequency of the comm traffic will die down as time goes by."

"You've never met my wife, have you, Commander?" Troi asked.

With a chuckle, Garrett rose from the command chair. "Pipe it into the captain's ready room. Commander Li, you have the bridge."

As the tactical officer moved to the command chair, Troi turned back to his sensors. *Yeah, this is definitely odd.*

By the time Garrett emerged from the ready room, Captain Haden had reported to the bridge and relieved Lt. Commander Wai-Lin Li, and Troi was starting to think that something was rotten in the Betreka Nebula. When Garrett came over asking for a report, he said, "I'm picking up an increase in charged particles. Normally, that wouldn't be unusual—that sort of thing will fluctuate in a nebula—but it's not very even, and the higher percentages are concentrated in a ridiculously small area. None of it's outside the normal range of activity, but I'd like to send a probe in just to be sure."

Garrett said nothing, but stared at the readings for a few moments, bent over the back of Troi's chair. He looked up at her face, which was completely unreadable, but he had the feeling that it wasn't the sensor readings she was thinking about. "You're right, that doesn't look good." She stood upright and looked down at the command chair. "Captain, request permission to have Lieutenant Troi send a class-one probe into the nebula."

Haden turned and fixed Garrett with that intimidating gaze of his. "What for?"

"Some odd readings that may be nothing."

"I'm amazed you're getting anything at all. It's not like sensors are any kind of reliable in that soup."

Troi chose that moment to speak up. "The probe's readings will be more reliable, sir, and give us a better idea if we're chasing sensor shadows or not."

"Besides," Garrett added, pointing at the viewscreen, presently showing the Klingon and Cardassian ships, "all things considered . . ."

"All things considered, Number One, I don't want to piss off our friends out there any more than they're already pissed." He let out a long breath. "All right, fine. Li, prepare a probe. Zipser, inform the *Wo'bortas* and the *Sontok* that we're taking advantage of this opportunity to do a scientific survey of the Betreka Nebula. If they bitch and moan, tell them we'll share any scientific data we obtain as a show of good faith."

"Thank you, sir," Garrett said. "We may want to inform Ambassador Dax as well, in case either of the delegations decides to get their nose out of joint."

"I'd say their noses started out in that position the minute the *Sontok* found Raknal V, Number One." Haden shook his head, then looked at Zipser. "Do it."

Li launched the probe. Haden asked how long the scan would take. "At least a few hours," Troi said.

"Fine." Haden got up and headed to his right. "I'll be in my ready room. Zipser, have Lieutenant Vaughn meet me there. You've got the bridge, Number One."

I wonder why he wants to talk to Vaughn, Troi thought as he followed the probe on sensors. The telemetry was coming through clearly for the time being, but that would change once it got to the nebula. *Hope this doesn't scotch our dinner plans.* Vaughn had agreed to share the evening meal with Troi, duties permitting. Troi had enjoyed chatting with the older man quite a bit—even though, looking back on it, Vaughn hadn't revealed anything personal about himself, nor talked much about his career, while Troi had done a great deal of both. *Well, fine,* he thought. *After all that time on Betazed, it'll be nice to talk to someone I have to actually talk to.*

"Ch'gran is *not* just an archaeological curiosity," General Worf said, pounding his fist on the table. Clad in a red Defense Force uniform and a floor-length beige cassock that had fewer medals than Dax would have thought from someone as old as the general, the white-haired Klingon sat at one end of the *Carthage* briefing room table, staring angrily at Legate Zarin. "It is a holy relic of the Klingon Empire. You *cannot* simply trample on our sacred ground and not expect a response."

Zarin, whose hair was equally white but considerably shorter, looked like he'd just eaten a lemon, his face was so sour. "If we had any indication that it was sacred ground, *our* response might be somewhat different, General, but I'm afraid that rules of salvage seemed more applicable than any attempt to placate the arcane sensibilities of alien species."

"The legate has a point, General," Dax said quickly before this escalated yet again. He was starting to get a headache. Usually, this kind of negotiating session invigorated him, but this was simply wearing him down. Worf and Zarin were going around in the same circle, and doing it so often, they were digging a rut into the ground. "The *Sontok*'s response to the remains was completely acceptable under salvage laws."

"And whose laws would those be, Ambassador?" Worf asked. "The Betreka Sector is unclaimed space. It is covered by no treaty that exists between Cardassia and the Empire."

"There *are* no treaties between Cardassia and your ridiculous little empire, fool," Zarin said.

Worf looked at Zarin and smiled. "That is precisely my point, Legate. Only a *petaQ* would hide behind protestations of 'proper' behavior when the parameters for such behavior do not even exist."

First rule of mediation, Dax thought, *when the parties start calling each other names, it's time for a recess.* "We've been at this for hours, gentlemen." *And I use that word loosely.* "Why don't we take a short break and reconvene at fifteen hundred hours?"

Zarin stood up quickly. His aides did likewise half a second later. One of them, the youngest, stumbled as he got out of his chair. "To that, I have no objection, Ambassador Dax." With a look at Worf he added, "The air in here has gotten foul."

As Zarin and his staff exited through the far door, Dax thought, *Please don't let the Klingons do anything stupid.* Hoping to head off any attempts to reclaim honor at the pass, Dax started, "General, I urge you, don't—"

But Worf had already risen from his chair and gone out the near door, his own aides trailing behind him.

Dax closed his eyes and counted to ten. Then he contacted the bridge, and instructed the communications officer to put a private communication through to Ambassador Sarek on Vulcan.

It took about twenty minutes—during which time Dax had ordered a *grakizh* salad from the food dispenser—for the call to go through. When it did, just as Dax popped the last of the yellow leaves from the salad into his mouth, the old-fashioned triangular viewscreen in the center of the briefing room table lit up with the somber image of Sarek of Vulcan, the garden of his house at ShiKahr visible through the picture window behind him. Dax hadn't been to the house since shortly before his mentor's marriage a year ago to a human woman—his third, and second to a human—and he noted that the plants seemed livelier and larger than they had in the past. *Perchance his new wife has a green thumb.* Dax hadn't yet met Perrin, but as long as she made Sarek as happy as the late Amanda Grayson—whose company Dax had always enjoyed in his younger days as Sarek's aide—then he knew he would like her.

"*How go the negotiations, Curzon?*" As usual, Sarek didn't bother with unnecessary pleasantries.

"Not as well as I'd like, I'm afraid. Both sides are being predictably stubborn. I understand the Klingons' position, but the Cardassians are genuinely baffled by it. I'm trying to be fair to them—after all, they think they have every right to Raknal V."

"*Perhaps. But you must be wary of being too accommodating to the Cardassians.*"

Dax smiled. "Actually, I'm more worried about the opposite. My affinity for the Klingons is hardly a secret."

"*If there are any who are unaware of it, it is only because you have not had the opportunity to provide that information to them,*" Sarek said dryly. "*That sort of emotional attachment can be a detriment.*"

"It's served me well with the Klingons," Dax said almost defensively. *Damn you, Sarek, how is it you manage to make me feel like a twenty-year-old naïf even now?* "In fact, I'd venture to say that our continued good relations with the Empire are due in no small part to that public affinity."

"*Which is why I have not discouraged the affinity in the past. However, in this instance, it may do you more harm than good.*"

Smiling ruefully, Dax said, "Actually, I think my problem is the other way around—I'm overcompensating by being *too* nice to the Cardassians."

"*That would be a mistake. I have seen firsthand what Cardassians are capable of if they are given too much—niceness.*"

Dax grinned. "I'll just have to be more like you, then."

"*I have always felt that you could afford to incorporate more discipline into your personality. It is good to see that you are at last taking my advice.*"

The grin widening, Dax said, "First time for everything." He let out a breath. Just talking to the ambassador made him feel better. "Thank you, Sarek—I needed this."

"*I have done nothing.*"

Dax shook his head. *Only a Vulcan could go from arrogant to modest within two sentences—and make them both sound like simple statements of fact.* "Well, thanks for nothing, then. Give my regards to Perrin."

"*I will do so.*"

"When this mess is over, I'll try to drop by and finally meet her. Looks like she's done wonders with the garden."

Sarek came infinitesmally close to a smile. "*My wife has a great affinity for bringing out the best in living things.*"

"That's good to hear, old friend. Take care."

As Sarek's face faded from the screen, Dax thought back to the glow that surrounded Ian Troi at the reception last night. At the mention of Perrin and the garden, the same glow seemed to suffuse Sarek. *Something about finding your life-mate that improves the disposition, obviously,* Dax thought. *Maybe I should try it again.*

Of course, Curzon had never settled down with any single person, but many of the previous hosts of the Dax symbiont had done so, and found it most satisfying. *But then there was Torias . . .*

Dax banished the thought from his head. More than one fellow joined Trill had accused him of letting the memories of his last host have undue influence on the current one. Torias Dax had been married to Nilani Kahn for less than a year when a shuttle accident claimed the former's life. Curzon still felt the pain of Torias's death keenly, and some had said that Dax's present inability to commit to any kind of long-term relationship was a psychological attempt to never again repeat what happened to Torias. Dax himself had always thought such accusations to be ridiculous. Curzon's roving eye predated his joining—indeed, was the cause of more than one near-scandal during his time as an initiate. Bonding with the Dax symbiont simply did nothing to discourage that tendency.

Still, sometimes he thought he would like to have had that glow.

Shaking his head, he left the briefing room, determined to be more even-handed in his mediating. *I will work out an agreement that won't thrust this sector into a bloody war that neither side can win.*

"So you're telling me that the probe *may* have given you readings that *might* be indicative of something in the nebula and you want to test these possibilities by going in with a shuttle?"

Ian Troi tried to keep the look of disappointment off his face at Captain Haden's words. Somehow, it sounded more promising the way he'd phrased it to Commander Garrett. He sat next to her in one of the two guest chairs in the tiny office off the bridge that was referred to as the "ready room," an appellation that Troi had never understood. Well, that wasn't fair—he'd never given it a second thought until he mentioned it to Lwaxana, who asked, "Ready for what?" Troi's lack of an answer for that question prompted his then-fiancée to declare the term ridiculous, and she promised to use all her influence as a Daughter of the Fifth House to get it changed.

Of course, based on the evidence to date, all that being a Daughter of the Fifth House meant, really, was that they had been obligated to invite half of Betazed to their wedding . . .

Forcing his thoughts back to the present, he glanced up at Vaughn, who was standing against one of the walls, and who had asked to tag along to this meeting. "For what it's worth, Captain, I think it warrants further investigation. Yes, it may be nothing, but I'd rather play it safe."

Haden didn't sound convinced. "There's no such thing as playing it safe when we've got trigger-happy Cardassians and Klingons hanging off our bow. Li gave me the report from security on the meetings so far—most of it has involved shouting. Gul Monor and Captain Qaolin already objected to the probe, and now, with all this, you think I should risk pissing them off again for what may be a wild goose chase?"

Troi found his mouth moving before his brain had a chance to stop it. "Sir, have you ever encountered a wild goose?"

"I beg your pardon, Lieutenant?" Haden said, his wide brown eyes now boring a hole in Troi's forehead.

Troi glanced quickly at Vaughn, whose expression was unreadable, and Garrett, who looked vaguely amused, then back at Haden. "A wild goose, sir," Troi repeated. "Have you ever encountered one?"

"I have seen many things in all my years in Starfleet, Mr. Troi, but I must admit to never having come across a goose of any kind, wild or otherwise, that wasn't part of a meal. I take it you have?"

"Yes, sir, once, in England as a boy. Geese can get very ill-tempered—even ones raised in captivity. This one wasn't, and it was brutal. Wild geese are surly, quick to anger, quicker to violence, and can do an amazing amount of damage with their beaks. The one I, uh, dealt with took a good-sized chunk out of my thigh."

"Lieutenant, I hope to hell you're going somewhere with this."

Me, too. "Yes, sir, I am." He stole a glance at Garrett, who looked half a step away from an out-and-out giggle, which wasn't making Troi feel any better. "My point is, it's better that we chase a wild goose than find ourselves attacked by one. It may go after more than our thigh, sir."

Haden continued to stare. Garrett continued to struggle mightily to keep a straight face. Vaughn had no trouble keeping his. Troi fidgeted.

Vaughn then spoke up. "Sir, I've had some suspicions from the beginning of this mission, and Lieutenant Troi's readings are in line with those suspicions."

"All right, fine," Haden said, leaning back in his chair. "I'll figure out what to tell Qaolin and Monor. I'll wait until I have an hour blocked out, so I can let Monor carry on." Looking at Garrett, he said, "Take the *Hoplite*, but maintain radio discretion."

"Sir?" Troi said.

"Radio silence would draw attention, Lieutenant," Garrett said as she got up. "Radio discretion means we're just on a scientific survey of the nebula, and all our comm traffic should reflect that."

"You're going too, Mr. Vaughn," Haden added. "I know better than to think that you're going to actually tell me your suspicions until they become something stronger, but I want you on-site in case they're confirmed."

"Understood, Captain," Vaughn said with a nod.

As Troi got up, Haden said, "And Mr. Troi?"

"Yes, sir?"

"Good catch. Even if it turns out to be nothing—you showed initiative. I appreciate that."

Troi smiled. "Thank you, sir."

"Besides," and here Haden actually smiled, a facial expression Troi had heretofore never seen on his captain's face, "I liked the goose story."

Chapter 10

SHUTTLECRAFT HOPLITE

"Approaching Betreka Nebula," Ian Troi said as he piloted the shuttlecraft *Hoplite* toward the phenomenon in question. With each kilometer closer they came to the nebula's perimeter, the image on the viewscreen started to get fuzzier, as the image translator found itself incapable of processing the data, scrambled as it was by the nebula's particulate matter: gases, dust, metals, silicates, carbon monoxide and carbon dioxide "ice," and so much more. As they grew nearer, Troi muttered, " 'We are star stuff.' "

"I beg your pardon?" Garrett asked from the copilot's seat.

"Uh, sorry, sir. Just quoting a human scientist from a few hundred years back."

" 'We are star stuff,' " Garrett repeated. "I'm familiar with Carl Sagan's work." She grinned. "Hard to do this for a living and not be, what with him being required reading at the Academy and all."

"Yes, sir," Troi said ruefully. "Sorry. Lwaxana doesn't know much about Earth history and culture, so I keep having to explain my likes and hobbies and things." He grinned, remembering his numerous failed attempts to convey his love for Western stories from Earth's nineteenth century. "I guess I've grown accustomed to getting all pedantic."

"Like your colloquy on geese?"

Troi closed his eyes and let out a long breath. "I suppose so, yes."

From one of the passenger seats behind Troi, Vaughn said, "It's an odd thing, Ian. I recall, when I read over your service record, there was a mention of a leg injury in your medical file. But, if I'm remembering the record properly, you listed it as a boating accident when you provided your medical history upon enrolling at the Academy."

"Yes," Garrett said, her grin growing ever wider. "Come to think of it, I recall that as well, Lieutenant. You have a fine memory. I have to question yours, though, Mr. Troi."

Troi sighed. "I was young, and I didn't think it was very— I didn't—oh, hell." He sighed again. "I didn't want to put 'menaced by a goose' in my medical history."

Vaughn smirked. "I can't believe that—Starfleet cadets are, after all, the epitome of tact and good manners. For the upper classes to ridicule a plebe just because he has an amusing anecdote from his past—why, that would be unheard of."

Laughing, Troi said, "Of course, what *was* I thinking?"

"Sarcasm aside," Garrett said, "you probably made the right choice. I know I would've done the same in your place. Same with the lieutenant here, I'll wager."

"I'd rather not say," Vaughn said with mock gravity.

An alarm went off on the console. "We've lost long-range sensors and about ninety percent of visual. Short-range sensors are—dodgy," Troi said, not finding a better word for it.

"Shields inoperative," Garrett added, looking at her own console.

Then the shuttle shook rather violently. Troi instinctively glanced down to make sure he was securely strapped into his seat, a precaution he had suggested when they first disembarked from the *Carthage*, and which Garrett had wholeheartedly endorsed.

"That shouldn't have happened so fast." Troi started scanning the region. "Damn—the concentration of charged particles is through the roof."

"More than expected?"

"Much more." Troi examined the scan results. "Based on all the previous scans of the nebula, the concentration should be about a quarter of—"

He was cut off by the *Hoplite* shaking once again.

"The hull can't take too much of this," Garrett said. "We may have to abort."

"No," Vaughn said sharply. "We need to investigate this further."

Garrett turned to look sharply at the lieutenant. "*If* we do abort this mission, it will be on my order, Lieutenant, is that clear?"

With a conciliatory nod, Vaughn said, "Of course, Commander, but there's only one reason why there'd be a concentration of charged particles of this magnitude. If there—"

"—are ships in the nebula, yes, I'm aware of that, Mr. Vaughn," Garrett finished.

"Well, actually," Troi said, "it only really indicates the presence of large electrically conductive objects—a ship, or several ships, is simply the most likely such object to move into the nebula."

"You're being pedantic again, Mr. Troi." Garrett looked back at Vaughn. "Besides, there was a fleet of nine ships in this very nebula three weeks ago. It's possible that that's what stirred up this hornet's nest of electrons."

The *Hoplite* shook again. "Structural integrity field holding at ninety percent," Troi said, then turned to his first officer. "The concentration wouldn't still be this high after three weeks, Commander. I think we need to investigate further."

Garrett thought for several seconds. *Please trust my judgment,* Troi found himself thinking, wishing he were telepathic like Lwaxana so he could convey with his mind what words were obviously failing to do: that he *knew* there were ships in the nebula, knew it from the moment he saw the odd reading. From the sounds of it, Vaughn felt the same — or, perhaps more accurately, Vaughn was *worried* that it was true. Either way, they needed to verify it.

Finally, Garrett came to a decision, just as more particles slammed into the shuttle. "All right. But I'm going to keep a close eye on the rate at which the SIF is deteriorating, how far we go into the nebula, what our maximum safe speed is, and how they all compare to each other. The minute those numbers add up to something approaching our inability to make it out in one piece, I'm turning this thing around and heading home no matter what we've found, understood?"

"Aye, sir," Troi said.

"Yes, Commander," Vaughn added.

Garrett's proviso made perfect sense to Troi. After all, it didn't do any good to find something and not be able to report it. "Proceeding forward."

The ship shook again, and this time a console exploded.

"Damn," Troi said. "Damage control response systems are offline." That meant that, if there was a hull breach, force fields would not engage to seal the breach until it could be physically repaired. "And we've got a plasma leak back there."

"I've got it," Vaughn said, unstrapping himself from his seat and moving for the emergency toolkit.

"Be careful back there, Lieutenant," Garrett said, still looking down at her console. "I don't want — *braking thrusters, now! All stop!*"

Troi's hands moved to stop the *Hoplite*'s forward motion before his brain registered Garrett's sudden order. Even as he fired the braking thrusters, he discovered the reason for the order: the proximity detector had picked up a huge mass only a few kilometers away. Had Troi not applied the thrusters when he did, there was a very good chance that the *Hoplite* would by now be flattened across the surface of that mass.

"Can you get a decent scan of that, Mr. Troi?"

"Working on it, sir," Troi said as he tried to coax some kind of reading out of the sensors and the proximity detector. He managed to get an image of at least part of the shape—the mass extended beyond the range of either scanning device—and ran it through the computer for analysis. When it gave him an answer, he swallowed. *I was sure I was right, but I don't think I really wanted to be,* he thought. "According to what we can detect, there's a sixty-five percent chance that we almost crashed into a Cardassian *Akril*-class vessel."

From the aft, even as he operated the tools necessary to seal the plasma leak, Vaughn said, "Dammit. Commander, this is exactly what I thought we'd find in here, and fulfills the very fears that led Starfleet to send me along. The Cardassians have no more interest in negotiating in good faith here than they did on Vulcan last year—they're just trying to find ways to improve their own position, in this case probably by gathering additional intelligence on us and the Klingons before they strike."

"Unless, of course, there's only the one ship," Garrett said.

Vaughn continued to focus on the leak. "Unlikely. Cardassians are like wolves, Commander—they often travel in packs."

"Either way, I don't want to be anywhere near them." Garrett gazed down at her console. "SIF is down to forty percent. Bring us about, Mr. Troi, and set course back for the *Carthage*."

"Yes, sir."

Even as Troi entered the course change into the *Hoplite's* navigation computer, the shuttle shook again. "You okay back there, Elias?" he asked as he turned the *Hoplite* around and engaged the new course.

"Just fine, thanks, Ian," came Vaughn's steady voice from the aft compartment. "Leak is sealed and I've bypassed the fried circuitry on the damage control systems. You should be able to reactivate them."

Troi checked his status board, and saw that the power flow was uninterrupted. He moved to activate the system—

—just as the hull-breach alarm rang out. The noise of the alarm was loud enough that Troi could feel it in his rib cage, but that wasn't the worst sensation. His ears popped from the sudden change in pressure even as his chair lurched backward, the explosive decompression trying to pull Troi and his chair toward the hole that had opened in the aft section of the *Hoplite*.

Garrett grabbed his wrist before he could activate the damage-control system. Troi turned around. Vaughn had apparently been standing very close to where the charged particles had torn through the *Hoplite* hull and was now literally hanging on for life. Each of his hands gripped the ragged edges of the breach, and that tenuous hold was all that kept Elias Vaughn from a rather unpleasant death. Unfortunately, most of his body was outside the perimeter of the hull, so if Troi did activate the damage control systems, the force field would slice through Vaughn's arms at the wrists and consign his handless body to a quick grave.

Of course, if Troi didn't seal the breach, they'd all die in about a minute when the air was gone.

The shuttle carried very little excess material, and it was all secure, so there was, at least, little danger of something hitting Vaughn on its way to being blown into space. That still left them with minimal options.

Either him or Garrett unstrapping themselves to try to physically retrieve the lieutenant wasn't possible, since that would most likely result in Vaughn's would-be rescuer suffering the same fate.

Then he remembered the recent upgrades Starfleet had made to their shuttlecraft—including emergency transporters. Unfortunately, the controls were on one of the side consoles, a meter away.

However, the armbands that activated the transporters

were in a cabinet just to the left of Troi's feet. He reached down, the straps from his restraints biting into his ribs, and opened the cabinet. The armbands were programmed to transport whoever wore them to the center of the shuttle upon activation. They had a total of ten armbands, so if Vaughn wasn't able to catch one, they had nine more chances. *I just hope he figures out what I'm doing,* he thought as he tossed one armband toward Vaughn.

"Toss" turned out to be an inaccurate verb, as all Troi had to do was let go of the armband after he took it out of the cabinet and it, like Vaughn and the air in the shuttle, followed the scientific law that molecules will tend toward an area of lesser pressure from an area of greater pressure.

Turning in his chair, his hand hovering over the control that would activate the force field, Troi watched as Vaughn abandoned fifty percent of his lifeline by releasing his right hand's grip on the edge of the breach. *He figured it out,* Troi thought with relief. Vaughn's bloody fingers managed to catch the strap of the armband. Using his fingers in manner impressively nimble given the copious amount of blood covering them, not to mention the intense rush of air plowing into his body, Vaughn managed to shift his grip to the metal circle in the center of the armband that contained the activation control.

He then dematerialized. As soon as the transporter effect took him away, Troi activated the damage control systems.

Four things happened in rapid succession. Troi's chair rocked forward as the pull of the decompression ceased with the activation of the force field. The hull breach alarm also ceased, though the vibrating in Troi's teeth did not. He heard the sound of a transporter in the shuttle, which placed Vaughn's form upright in the center of the *Hoplite,* the armband still in the grip of his blood-covered fingers. And he heard the sounds of the environmental system laboring to restore the cabin's lost atmosphere.

"Very well done, Mr. Troi," Garrett said, unstrapping herself, then reaching down and grabbing the shuttle's medikit. "Get us out of here before we have to do it again." To Vaughn, she said, "Let me take a look at those hands, Lieutenant."

They managed to get the rest of the way out of the nebula without incident, though the SIF was down to fifteen percent by the time they made it past the nebula's edge. Vaughn's hands were deemed adequately cared for until he could go to the *Carthage* sickbay, but that trip wasn't immediately called for, at least.

"Set course back to the *Carthage?*" Troi asked, preparing to do that very thing.

"No."

Troi shot his commanding officer—now back in the copilot's seat—a look. "Sir?"

"I want to test a theory first."

Vaughn, who now had Starfleet-issue bandages around his hands, and whose brown-and-gray hair was now flying in several directions, lending a comic air belied by the serious tone of voice he always had, leaned forward. "Commander, with all due respect, we need to return to the *Carthage* immediately. Captain Haden—and Ambassador Dax—need to be informed. So does Starfleet. We're going to need reinforcements, and also—"

"Lieutenant, kindly sit back and shut up. You're right, the Cardassians have decided to put a backup plan in place, hiding a fleet in the nebula. But think about it for a second. The Klingons may have a backup plan of their own, and they don't *need* a nebula to hide in, they have cloaking technology."

"So why'd they hide in the nebula before?" Troi asked.

Garrett shrugged. "Power consumption, maybe. Or they wanted to take advantage of their superior sensors in the vicinity of the nebula. Ultimately, it doesn't matter. Mr. Troi, is there any way to scan for cloaked ships?"

Troi blew out a breath. "Not easily. Every time we come up with a way to penetrate a cloak, the Klingons or the Romulans come up with a better cloak."

"Yes or no, Mr. Troi."

"I'm sorry, Commander," Troi said after a moment, hating himself for doing it, "but I can't be that definitive."

Garrett actually smiled at that. "Good man. I prefer an honest answer. Do an intensive scan of the vicinity, long- and short-range, tell me if anything screams 'cloak' at you."

"I'll do my best, sir."

Troi spent the better part of an hour scanning the area. Garrett and Vaughn left him to it, for the most part, both going aft to get some ration packs. Garrett also did a check of all the shuttle's systems, making sure that the *Hoplite* would survive to make it back to the *Carthage* in one piece—with, Troi heard her mention, specific emphasis on the environmental systems to make sure that the air they lost in the breach would be replenished.

The only interruption came when Vaughn walked over with a mug of tea. "Thanks," Troi said as he took the steaming mug from Vaughn's hands. He took a quick whiff, and identified it as the generic tea included in the packs. *Pity, I could go for some raspberry herb tea right now.* Still, Troi appreciated the gesture.

"I should be thanking you. You saved my life, Ian. It's greatly appreciated."

Troi smiled. "You'd have done the same for me."

"Possibly, but I didn't have to. You thought very quickly on your feet, and acted without hesitation. Pretty impressive. I just hope that Haden and Garrett appreciate what they've got."

Troi grinned. "Me, too." He took a sip of the tea, which was bitter, but still warm and comforting.

Then the sensor alarm sounded—a much milder sound

than the hull breach alarm from earlier, indicating that the scan was complete.

Garrett apparently heard it from the aft section, as she came forward seconds later. "Report."

Looking over the results of the scan, Troi shook his head. The final results told the same story that the preliminary findings had been telling him for the past hour. "Best I can give you is a definite maybe, Commander. We're picking up subspace variances that *could* indicate a fleet of cloaked ships. But it could also be simple background radiation."

"I'm willing to bet it's the former," Vaughn said. He looked at Garrett. "Neither the Empire nor the Cardassians have shown themselves to be adept at negotiation where force or guile will do the job nicely."

"I tend to agree." Garrett bit her lip. "All right, enough sightseeing. Mr. Troi, set a course for the *Carthage*. Tell them that we had to cut short our exploration of the nebula, and point to the hole in our rear if they ask why. We'll give the captain and ambassador a full report on board."

Troi nodded. "Yes, sir."

Damn, but I wish I wasn't right. This can't possibly bode well.

Chapter 11

U.S.S. CARTHAGE

In the quarters on the *Carthage* assigned to Talen Kallar, an alarm went off. The alarm emanated from a small device implanted in the ear of the cabin's occupant, so only he heard it. He barely hesitated in his assigned task of organizing files from the notes that had been taken during the most recent negotiating session. Kallar had a reputation as a physical bumbler, and was more likely to trip over his own feet than walk a straight line, but he was good at the dreary paperwork tasks that always fell upon interns. As a youth, and the lowest-ranking person in Legate Zarin's delegation, Talen Kallar was assigned those duties.

However, the alarm was not intended for "Talen Kallar," for the alarm heralded a signal from a device crafted by the organization that had created Talen Kallar. The name and background credited to Kallar in fact had been a fiction written by the Obsidian Order as a cover for one of their newest agents, a recent graduate of Bamarren named Corbin Entek.

While "Kallar" finished coding the latest file for Olett to look over, Entek made mental note of the fact that the alarm indicated that people had entered Captain Vance Haden's ready room.

According to the ship's chronometer, the next communications sweep would be in one minute. After that, Entek had a ten-minute window to activate the transmitter in the same device that had sent the alarm. The *Carthage*'s communications system did an automatic sweep for unauthorized transmissions every ten minutes.

To Entek, that was one of many reasons why he knew that Cardassia would eventually dominate the galaxy. If the Federation—arguably the greatest power in the quadrant—had such lax security on one of their military vessels, they would be ripe for the taking. There was no reason why those scans couldn't be perpetual, leaving no window for such espionage as Entek was performing. Entek's original theory, when he was told of this odd security measure, was that it was to conserve power. However, the very room in which he sat proved that to be a false assumption—the *Carthage* was a momument to wasted energy, from the overly large rooms to the availability of separate quarters for each member of two full negotiating teams.

The other proof of lax security was the very manner in which Entek had planted the device. The captain had ordered the first officer to give Legate Zarin and his staff a tour of the *Carthage*—as if they were vacationers visiting a museum! Entek had actually laughed in the human commander's face when she said she was taking him on that tour, and only a quick conversion of that laugh to a hysterical giggle had enabled him to maintain his cover as a callow youth.

Of course, Entek's supervisor, whose name Entek did not know, would have said that he *was* a callow youth, and he had only gotten this assignment because Zarin would be on the lookout for an Order agent in his midst, so they needed to put in someone the legate would never suspect under any circumstances. Since Zarin generally believed that nobody under the age of forty had any sense or business doing anything responsible, the ideal infiltration candidate was the most youthful member of his delegation.

That cover also provided his means of planting the listening device, which was the size of Entek's thumbnail, under which he had stored it. When the tour took them to the captain's ready room, "Kallar" tripped over the carpet, taking advantage of his clumsy maneuver to place the device in a corner. Its surface was sensor-blind—the only way it could be detected was when it transmitted an audiovisual record of the room to the receiver in Entek's ear.

The chronometer indicated that the time for the communications scan was complete, so Entek removed the device from his ear and plugged it into his handheld computer.

His computer screen lit up with the image of a *tharul*'s-eye view of the ready room, the feet of the room's occupants large, their heads comparatively small. Entek could barely see the perspectively tiny head of Vance Haden from his position sitting at his desk. Also present were Commander Rachel Garrett, the first officer who had provided the "tour," Lieutenant Ian Troi, the ship's science officer, Lieutenant Elias Vaughn, a consultant from Starfleet Command, and Ambassador Curzon Dax.

Entek went through his mental list of facts pertinent to the four humans and one Trill in the room. Troi had recently married an aristocrat on Betazed, a planet full of pacifist telepaths that Entek had always thought would be among the first worlds to fall when the Federation either collapsed on itself like the bloated mess it was or was finally overtaken by a superior force—ideally, Cardassia.

As for the others, Haden was a war veteran, having fought against the Romulans prior to the Tomed Incident, with a reputation for being somewhat blunt. Garrett was an expert fencer, and had had several dealings with the Klingon Empire over the years. Her experience was as nothing compared to that of Dax, who was one of the negotiators at the Khitomer Accords, and had forged personal bonds with several prominent Klingon military figures.

The only person about whom Entek knew nothing of consequence was Elias Vaughn. His official role was as a consultant, a functionally meaningless term that usually signified intelligence work. The Order's knowledge of Federation intelligence was scattershot at best, but Vaughn wasn't part of any of it that he was aware of. *We'll need to change that.*

"*Are you sure about this?*" Dax was saying. The Trill sounded agitated.

Speaking with a certain confidence, Troi replied. "*About the Cardassian ships, yes. About the Klingon ships, not so much.*"

Entek frowned. His first thought was, *What Cardassian ships?* The only Central Command ship in the area was the *Sontok.*

"*But it fits the profile,*" Garrett was saying.

"*That's ridiculous,*" Dax said, making some kind of gesture that Entek couldn't make out from his vantage point. "*The Klingons wouldn't hide out like that.*"

"*What, it wouldn't be honorable?*" Haden's words were laced with sarcasm.

Dax stared at the captain. "*As a matter of fact, it wouldn't. They've been completely up-front with us.*"

"*C'mon, Ambassador,*" Garrett said. "*You know as well as I do how fanatical Klingons get when it comes to anything sacred. Honor's all well and good, but they're not going to give up Ch'gran without a fight, and they're not going to count on winning that fight over a negotiating table. Look what happened thirty-five years ago.*"

Archly, Dax said, "*Unlike you, Commander, I was there thirty-five years ago. I wrote parts of the Khitomer Accords, so kindly don't try to lecture me on the events leading up to them.*"

To her credit, the commander was wholly unintimidated by the ambassador's posturing. "*Then you should remember that even coming to the table was too arduous a concept for some Klingons to wrap their minds around. So much so that they assassinated a perfectly good chancellor. If they can do that, I don't think hiding a fleet nearby in case things don't go their way can be considered out of character.*"

"*This will get out of control quickly,*" Vaughn said. Entek noted that the human spoke in an even tone, and also that the lieutenant's hands were bandaged. *"The minute either Zarin or Worf decides that things aren't going right, that one will call in the cavalry, and five minutes later, the other one will call in his, and this whole thing will blow up in our faces."*

Calmly, Haden said, *"You're projecting a bit, Lieutenant."*

"I don't think so, sir."

"Oh you don't, do you?" Haden spoke as if he were lecturing a child. In fact, his tone reminded Entek a great deal of that of his Order supervisor. *"We know there's something that's at least sixty-five percent likely to be an Akril-class ship in the Betreka Nebula. We know there's a reading that might indicate a fleet of cloaked Klingon ships. Or, conversely, the* Hoplite *stumbled across some debris from the battle here three weeks ago and those subspace variances are just background radiation, and your over-active imagination is transforming them into a pair of fleets."*

It took all of Entek's willpower not to curse out loud.

Dax smiled. *"I wouldn't worry on that score, Captain. I doubt anyone's accused the lieutenant of having an overactive imagination."* His face grew serious. *"But you're both right. We don't know enough, and it is precisely because of that lack of knowledge that the situation is* already out of control.*"*

"We need to call in reinforcements," Garrett said. *"We'll be a sitting duck if those fleets decide to go at it."*

"Too risky," Haden said. *"I don't disagree with you, Number One, but Monor and Qaolin already have their bowels in an uproar because I let the* Hoplite *out in the first place. They're keeping a close eye on us."*

Entek noted the phrases "sitting duck" and "bowels in an uproar" for addition to their growing linguistic database on the Federation. Both had definitions that seemed obvious from context, though Entek tagged them both for verification and a tracing of etymology.

Dax shook his head. *"What we need to do is put our cards on the table and call their bluff."*

"That's a quaint metaphor," Vaughn said with a level of snideness that Entek couldn't help but admire. He also made a note for the Order to determine what that metaphor was—it was obviously some kind of contest involving cards, but that hardly narrowed the field. *"But I doubt they're bluffing."*

"I'm sure they think that, too—and will continue to do so, right up until they have to actually play their cards. But one reason why I think they've assembled these fleets in the first place—" he looked at Haden *"—assuming they have assembled the fleets—is because they're far from home. Reinforcements beyond whatever they're hiding behind cloaks or in nebulae are days away, and probably not easily diverted. I'm not sure either Zarin or Worf will be willing to start something they can't finish."*

"I've read the transcripts of the meetings so far," Vaughn said. *"I haven't seen anything to indicate that either side is going to budge. Where does that leave us?"*

"I have no idea where it leaves you, Lieutenant, but it leaves me with the winning hand. I just have to play it."

Again, the alarm beeped. The ten-minute window was about to close. Cursing, Entek turned off the listening device. He had been hoping to hear more, but he dared not risk a second transmission. Another one so soon might be detected by the *Carthage*'s communications officer even without the automatic scan.

Besides, he'd heard enough. Haden may have had his doubts, but Entek didn't. Central Command had objected to negotiations from the beginning. It was completely in character for them to assemble a fleet in secret and hide it in the Betreka Nebula, not bothering to inform the Order or the Detapa Council about it.

To Entek's frustration, there was nothing he could do. His job was purely to gather intelligence—and this meeting had gleaned a great deal, beyond the significance of this particular mission. He had neither the means nor the ability to act on any of it, though. Indeed, he would not even be reporting back to his supervisor until he was back on Cardassia.

Assuming we survive this negotiation, he added dolefully, a state of affairs which hadn't been in doubt until Entek overheard the meeting in Haden's ready room.

Entek removed the device from the handheld computer and placed it back in his ear. Then he called up his ongoing report for the Order. He had a great deal to add to it now.

"Enter!" General Worf spoke the single word in the Klingon language when the doorchime to his quarters sounded. As expected, Lorgh walked in.

"You sent for me?" his aide who was not his aide asked.

Seated at the too-comfortable chair Starfleet had provided, Worf reached onto the table that held his workstation and grabbed a mug. He handed it to Lorgh. "Drink with me, Lorgh."

Taking the mug, Lorgh asked, "For what reason, General?"

"I have just been informed that my son has taken a mate."

Lorgh smiled. "For that, I will even drink Starfleet's *warnog.*"

"I appreciate the sentiment, but so great a sacrifice will not be required." The general indicated the bottle of bloodwine on the table. "I have been saving this for a special occasion."

Peering at the table, Lorgh saw that the bloodwine was from the Ozhpri vintner—one of the finest in the Empire. "A worthy vintage." He held up the mug. "To your son."

"To Mogh, son of Worf, and soon to be mate of Kaasin, daughter of Prella."

They both drank. Worf reveled in the oily slickness of the bloodwine that seemed to coat his throat as it went down.

"May they both bring you many strong children to perpetuate your House."

Worf laughed. "Well said, though I will settle for at least one heir." He took another gulp of wine, then regarded his aide. "At the reception, you said that the Council preferred to fight this battle across a negotiating table. I am beginning to think that such is a battle we cannot win. The Cardassians refuse to even acknowledge the importance of Ch'gran. They denigrate it, call it a mere pile of wreckage. It has been exceedingly difficult to keep from killing Legate Zarin. I believe that we will never reach an understanding. We may need to call in the fleet."

Lorgh shook his head and walked over to the cabin's window, which had a spectacular view of the Betreka Nebula. "That may satisfy our honor in the short term, General, but it will not gain us Ch'gran—or much else. The Cardassians are strong, and getting stronger."

"As are we," Worf said.

"Yes, but they grow stronger from a position of strength—they are expanding, improving their resources, and their economy can support a military buildup. Cardassia has gone from an unknown and irrelevant nation to an important participant in quadrant politics in a very short time, General. They build on a solid foundation."

The general snarled. "Whereas we rebuild from weakness."

"Sad, but true, sir. The Defense Force's shipyards have lain dormant for several turns. Vessels that should have been decommissioned years ago still fly the stars, some being held together with little more than *targ* guts and wishful thinking. A war with Cardassia is not one we can win."

Worf shook his head. "I fear you are correct." He drank down the rest of his wine and poured more. "We have become too reliant on others—the Federation, the Romulans . . ."

"What have the Romulans to do with this?"

The general gulped his bloodwine. His thoughts took a dark turn, and he wondered how much of Ozhpri's finest he would need to imbibe before he was sufficiently drunk to deal with those thoughts. "Many of our finest Houses have fallen into debt since the destruction of Praxis. Are you familiar with the House of Duras?"

"Yes. As I recall, they brokered many technological exchanges with the Romulans when we were their allies."

Worf nodded. "Our Houses have long been in conflict. Their House head is an old man now. His son, Ja'rod, has rekindled those old ties with the Romulans now in the hopes of alleviating debts they have accrued. Further—they have introduced other families to Romulan sources that can aid them."

"I was not aware of this," Lorgh said, and Worf wondered if he was honest.

"Your superiors should be. If not, they are fools, and we are in worse trouble than I thought." He leaned forward. "Do you not see, Lorgh? Our people are becoming weak, desperate. Honor must be served, but honor does not put food on the table. It is no easy thing for a noble-born Klingon to starve like some laborer in the lowlands. Finding Ch'gran is the thing that can save us, remind us of who we are." He leaned back in the irritatingly pleasant chair and gulped down the rest of his bloodwine. Then he threw the mug across the room; it clattered against the wall, but the noise was muted by the room's carpeting. *Damn Federation even spoils a perfectly good gesture of anger.* "If we lose that, too, after losing so much, I fear for the future of the Empire."

"Our future is strength," Lorgh said with the confidence of youth. "It is our present that is of concern. We will be great once again."

"But at what cost? Will we be ruled from Qo'noS, Romulus, or Earth?"

Lorgh had nothing to say to that.

The doorchime then rang again.

Worf hadn't been expecting anyone else, but he said, "Enter," this time in the human language.

This proved wise, as the door opened to Wai-Lin Li, the chief of security for the *Carthage*. A short woman with a compact form, she moved with a lithe grace that bespoke fine martial skills. Worf would have expected no less from someone in charge of security. While most humans were soft, Starfleet rarely put people in positions for which they were unsuited, and the job of security chief necessitated a certain physical prowess. "General Worf, I need you to come with me, sir. Ambassador Dax has called an emergency negotiating session."

"What for?"

"I don't have that information, sir. I was simply ordered to escort you to the briefing room."

"Very well." Worf rose and exited his quarters, Lorgh falling into step behind him.

When they arrived at the briefing room, Worf noticed a much larger security contingent present. Usually two guards were posted inside the room during conferences, which Worf had thought a reasonable precaution. Now, however, four guards stood inside the room, with two more posted outside.

I do not like this, he thought, and shot Lorgh a look. *Something has changed.* Worf knew that the *Carthage* had sent a shuttle into the nebula, which had then been damaged and had returned to the ship only two hours ago. Initially, the general had believed the captain's claim that they were engaged in scientific research—the Federation never passed up an opportunity to stare at natural phenomena for long periods of time—but now he wondered if something else was going on.

He also wondered if the shuttle had detected the fleet that lay in waiting. *No, the Federation has no way to penetrate our cloaking shields.*

Worf noted that Li took up position in the room as well. Dax was in his usual seat at the center of the table. "What is the meaning of this?" the general asked the ambassador.

"We'll discuss it when Legate Zarin arrives." Dax's tone was much harder than usual.

Escorted by another member of the *Carthage*'s security force—who also took up position, bringing the number of guards in the room up to six—Zarin and his female aide came in. "What is the meaning of this?" he asked, a parroting of Worf's own words that made the general a bit uncomfortable. But then, it was a reasonable question for either of them to ask. "I was in the midst of very important work—"

"This is the only work that should concern you right now, Legate," Dax said, "and it's taken on a new wrinkle."

"A 'wrinkle'?" Zarin asked.

"Obviously something important has changed, Ambassador," Worf said. "Kindly tell us what it is."

Then Dax smiled that insincere smile that Federation diplomats were particularly adept at. "I'll be happy to, General, Legate. These negotiations are over. The Federation has unilaterally decided to take over Raknal V. We refuse to accept any claim made on the world by either Cardassia or Qo'noS, and any attempt to refute our claim will be met with force."

Zarin quivered with rage, and Worf felt similar anger coursing through his own veins. *I knew that trusting these negotiations to this charlatan was unwise. "Great" Curzon Dax indeed.*

"How *dare* you! You have no more claim to Ch'gran than this *petaQ!*"

"I can assure you, Ambassador, that this act will not go unchallenged."

"I'm sure it won't, Legate," Dax said. "In fact, I'm sure you'll start by leaving this room and having Gul Monor fire on the *Carthage*—just as the general here," he pointed at Worf, "will instruct Captain Qaolin to do likewise. But the *Sontok* and the *Wo'bortas* are still under repair, and the *Carthage* is ready for a fight. Captain Haden's record in battle is not inconsiderable, either. No, your best bet would be to call in reinforcements. Luckily, there's a Klingon fleet a few million kilometers away under cloak that can destroy the *Carthage* and move on to claim Raknal V."

Zarin turned angrily on Worf. "What!? You agreed to bring only *one* ship! Typical of Klingons—you claim to be creatures of honor, yet you cannot keep to a simple agreement. We should have known better than to think you capable of negotiating in good faith."

Worf, however, regarded Dax. *It seems I have underestimated the Federation. I am a foolish old man to have let them outmaneuver me like this.* He could feel Ch'gran slipping away from him—and with it, all the work he had done to climb out of General Chang's shadow being undone.

Dax walked around to stand between the two negotiators. "Of course, Legate, you won't be able to take such an action sitting down, as it were. So you'll have to summon the reinforcements you have in the Betreka Nebula."

Blinking, Worf looked at the legate. Based on the expression on Zarin's face, Dax spoke the truth. "You dare to accuse *us* of not negotiating in good faith?" Worf asked.

"We simply wish to protect our claim," Zarin said weakly.

"And we want to restore a sacred relic to our people! Perhaps we have violated the letter of our negotiating terms, but we did so out of a desire to see *justice* done! Ch'gran is Klingon, even *you* cannot deny that! We fight for our heritage. I wonder what feeble excuse *you* have for breaking your word."

Dax said, "Obviously, you cannot resolve your agreements without fighting each other, so fight each other you must. Tear yourselves to pieces. Sacrifice all the gains you have made over the past few decades. Deplete your economies in a costly war that will drive you into debt and devote your forces to a distant region. Plunge your nations into ruin."

"You underestimate Cardassia," Zarin said smugly.

"And you, sir, underestimate the Klingons," Dax said. "They will fight you until their dying breath to reclaim Ch'gran. This is not a conflict either of you can win."

Dax said nothing Worf had not already thought—or discussed with Lorgh. "Do you have an alternative, Ambassador, or do you simply enjoy stating the obvious?"

Again, Dax smiled. "Actually, I do—have a solution, that is, though I will confess that sometimes stating the obvious has its joys. Have a seat, gentlemen." Dax himself sat in one of the chairs, activating the triangle viewscreen at the table's center.

Worf gave Lorgh a nod, and took a seat on one end, Lorgh doing likewise in the chair perpendicular to his. He noticed that the screen gave a topographical view of Raknal V.

Zarin and his aide remained standing. "I refuse to continue these negotiations. The Klingons—"

"Have a *seat*, Legate," Dax snapped. "Right now, the *Carthage* has its phasers trained on the *Sontok*—with photon torpedoes," he added, "targeting the *Wo'bortas*. The only thing keeping Captain Haden from giving the order to fire is my word. All I have to do is nod to Commander Li there, and the *Carthage* will fire."

"You have no right—"

Dax rose and stood face to face with Zarin. "We have *every* right, sir. You have both violated the terms of the negotiations. The Federation is wholly justified in viewing this military buildup as a hostile act." The Trill's nose was now almost touching that of the legate. "Now kindly—sit—*down*."

Zarin sat down. Worf revised his estimate of Curzon Dax upward slightly.

Then the insincere smile came back, and the Trill retook his seat. "What I propose is simple. Both the Klingon Empire and the Cardassian Union have a claim on Raknal V. I think it's patently clear from the joyous times we've spent in this room that neither side is willing to alter its negotiating position, and neither of you would even *be* at the negotiating table if you were willing to go to war over this. So you need to find a third option—one that allows you each the opportunity to legitimize your claims."

Worf's estimate starting sliding back downward again. "If you have such an option, kindly state it."

"For once, I agree with the general," Zarin said. "You may like the sound of your own voice, Ambassador, but I find it grating."

"Sticks and stones, Legate," Dax said, a phrase that Worf found meaningless. "Sixty years ago, the Federation and the

Klingons signed the Organian Peace Treaty. The conflict that predated the treaty involved the dispute of several border worlds. One of the terms of that treaty was that each nation would be given the opportunity to develop those worlds and prove their claim to be the strongest."

Worf frowned. "You suggest that we do the same for Raknal?"

"Yes." Dax pointed to the rendering of the planet on the viewscreen. "The world has two continents. What I propose is the following: The northern continent will be under the direction of Cardassia. You will treat that continent as if it were one of your colony worlds—set up some kind of governmental body and proceed accordingly. The southern continent will be under the jurisdiction of the Klingon Empire under the same terms. Both the Klingon governor and the Cardassian ruling body will make regular reports to me. When I am satisfied that one nation or the other has proven itself best able to exploit the world's resources, I will make a decision as to whom it will be ceded."

Zarin stood up. "Preposterous!"

"On the contrary, Legate. Whoever gains the planet will have *earned* it. Rather than simply gaining it by stumbling across it—or," he added with a glance at Worf, "by the happenstance of one's ancestors having stumbled across it centuries ago—you will have proven that it deserves to belong to you. Or, as the case may be, not."

Even as Zarin fumed, his lips quivering in anger, Worf found himself grudgingly admiring Dax's solution. It was not ideal, but this, at least, was a battle the Empire *could* win. *Bringing worlds under our heel is something at which we have always excelled.*

Worf noted that the Cardassians were being given control of the continent on which the Ch'gran remains had been found. That was wise—it meant the Klingons would have to gain the world in order to gain the remains. However, it did raise a point. "How do we know that the Cardassians will not simply take Ch'gran?"

"The Ch'gran site is to remain untouched until the final determination is made. Any violation of that will result in the unconditional ceding of the world to the Klingons."

Zarin's lips were still quivering. "What possible reason do we have to agree to these obscene terms?"

Dax looked up at the legate. "The only reason you need, Legate—lack of desire to pursue any of the alternatives." He leaned back in his chair. "I don't expect either of you to be able to answer right away. You will need to consult your governments. We will reconvene here in two weeks to finalize the agreement."

"Assuming," Worf said as he stood, "that there *is* an agreement."

Again, Dax smiled. "Assuming, yes, General. Oh, one other thing." He looked at both of them. "Call off your fleets. Captain Haden has already called for more ships—they'll arrive by tomorrow. I expect that both the cloaked fleet and the ships in the nebula will be gone by the time they arrive."

Zarin exhaled loudly, his lips practically on overdrive, as he turned and left, the aide right behind him, two guards behind them.

Worf watched them depart, then looked back at Dax. "You are playing a dangerous game, Ambassador." Then he smiled. "I admire dangerous games."

"Thank you, General. We will speak again soon."

With that, the Trill turned and left.

Lorgh looked at the general. "Would you still rather Riva was assigned?"

"Yes," Worf said without hesitation. "Dax is still an arrogant *petaQ*. A more clever one than I thought—but the designation stands."

Laughing, Lorgh said, "Perhaps. But he does understand the Klingon heart. We will fight for Ch'gran, and we will be victorious. And the Empire will be great once more."

Youth, Worf thought with disdain. "You may be right, Lorgh. Time will be the judge."

"It always is, General."

"Do you honestly believe this is going to work?"

Dax looked up from his *raktajino* and his padd. He sat in the *Carthage* lounge, reading over the draft of a resolution that had been awaiting his perusal for the last week. Minister T'Latrek had sent several communiqués to him asking for his approval of the text, without which the Calabrese Treaty could not go through. Finally, with a lull in this Betreka Nebula nonsense, he could do so.

Now, the slim form of Elias Vaughn stood over him, a querying look in his penetrating blue eyes. Vaughn had, at least, not actively ruined the negotiations, thus not fulfilling the fear Dax had expressed to Garrett, but neither had he contributed anything of use. As with most of his ilk, he was a waste of time and space, and Dax saw no reason to let such a waste get in the way of his work.

"Lieutenant! What a complete lack of pleasure it is to see you. Please, don't have a seat and go away."

"You haven't answered my question."

With a snort, Dax said, "I'm under no obligation to answer questions posed by Starfleet lieutenants, Mr. Vaughn."

"Consider it practice—because you can be assured that I'm not the last person who'll ask it."

Dax closed his eyes and sighed. In that, at least, Vaughn was correct. But Curzon Dax was used to his judgment being questioned. He had hoped that as he got older, as his reputation for success improved, he would no longer be second-guessed so much, but if anything the tendency of others to do so had increased over the years. "Yes, Lieutenant, I honestly believe this is going to work. There's even precedent. Sherman's Planet, Capella IV, Neu—"

"And you truly believe that this is the same thing?"

"Of course it isn't, don't be ridiculous," Dax snapped. "But the basics are still sound. Neither side is willing to commit to a war. Besides, this provides the competition of such a conflict without the concomitant loss of life. I can't see how anyone would view that as a bad thing, myself."

Vaughn shook his head. "How old are you, Ambassador?"

"Older than you think," Dax said cryptically, since one answer to that question would be a three-digit number. That point-one percent of the Trill population lived in symbiosis was not public knowledge off-world, nor that Dax was one of that rare number. Though various Daxes over the years had revealed that secret, Curzon saw no reason to bring Vaughn into that circle.

The lieutenant didn't look happy with that reply, but did not pursue it. "Then you should know better than to believe it will be as simple as you think. Your solution is too neat, and is more than likely going to blow up in all our faces."

I've had enough of this. "Your years of experience in diplomacy have taught you this, eh, Lieutenant?"

"No, but *your* years should have taught you the difference between two sides that aren't *willing* to commit to war and two sides that aren't *able*. This is a case of the latter, *not* the former, and time isn't on our side. What you've proposed is a compromise, and compromises tend to please no one. Neither the Klingons nor the Cardassians have given any indication that they respond well to not being pleased, and the longer this idiocy goes on, the stronger they'll be, and the more likely they are to vent their displeasure in bloody ways."

Dax sighed. *Let me rephrase—I had enough of this when he came on board. We're now up to more than enough.* "Lieutenant, I've been doing this for longer than you've been alive. I also know how Klingons think. They will fight with honor for the right to take this planet, and I'm sure the Cardassians will do likewise. Whoever does gain claim to this world will have earned it. There will be no bloodshed, and there will be no displeasure. Now if you'll excuse me, I have actual work to do."

With that, Dax turned his attention back to the resolution.

"Why not simply cede the planet to the Cardassians?"

That got Dax's attention just from the sheer ludicrousness of it. "I beg your pardon?"

"Let's look at this objectively for a moment. The Cardassians are the ones who charted and discovered the planet, they're the ones who found the Ch'gran remains. The Klingons only found out about it because they were spying on the Cardassians. What possible reason do you have to even give the Klingons a chance at this?"

Dax set the text of the resolution down. Garrett had suggested the same thing, of course, but what sounded reasonable coming from the commander's mouth sounded totally idiotic from the lieutenant's. "Because if we don't, there will be a war. Just because two parties are *unable* to fight a war, as you put it, doesn't mean they won't make an attempt at it. It's all well and good to say, 'let's look at this objectively,' but the Klingons can't do that. This relic is *sacred* to them. Believe me, Vaughn, this is the only alternative to a war that will, in all likelihood, tear this quadrant to pieces." Having nothing more to say, he picked up the padd and started reading again.

"Perhaps you're right, Mr. Ambassador," Vaughn said in a tight voice. "But I've been in Starfleet long enough to know that I have a good instinct for this sort of thing, and that instinct is telling me that this cannot come to a good end."

Seeing nothing to be gained by replying to Vaughn's arrogance, Dax simply continued reading until the lieutenant finally took the hint and walked away.

After the door to the lounge closed behind the younger man, Dax looked up. *I need to find out who sent that imbecile on this mission. Perhaps Sarek will be able to find out.*

Chapter 12

CARDASSIA PRIME

When Zarin's party returned to Cardassia Prime, "Talen Kallar" was dismissed and allowed to go home. Home was a sparsely furnished apartment barely two hundred square meters in area that was nevertheless able to hold all of Corbin Entek's worldly possessions. Entek had never been one for sentiment—one of many personality traits that made him ideal for the Order—and so he had nothing that could be considered a personal item that wasn't directly related to personal hygiene and/or sustenance.

Now he simply had to wait until the Order summoned him. He passed the time by giving a final proofread to his report—which would be hand-delivered once the summons came. Such sensitive intelligence could not be transmitted.

Shortly after he finished reading the report over a third time, his comm unit beeped and a voice read out a coded message. Entek's keen mind decoded it instantly—and then he blinked his wide brown eyes in surprise. He had expected to be sent to the business office that served as an Order front, where he always met with his supervisor. Instead, he had been told to report directly to Order headquarters.

Briefly, Entek worried that someone might see "Kallar" entering that edifice, thus blowing his cover, but the Order would not have summoned him there if they thought that would be a problem. That meant either that the cover was no longer a concern, or his being seen wasn't one. *Besides,* he thought, *Kallar is a lowly intern, not worthy of being noticed. I suspect I could walk right by Zarin or Olett on the street and they would not even know who I was.*

It only took thirty minutes to traverse the distance from his apartment complex to Order headquarters via mass transit—his orders included no mention of permission to use transporters, which were generally reserved for high-level operatives, or agents actually in the field. Entek took advantage of the opportunity to study his fellow Cardassians, all moving about their lives blissfully unaware that they were under scrutiny. Well, truthfully, they probably knew they were under some kind of scrutiny at all times. Monitors in the train car provided a steady stream of governmental decrees—propaganda, truly—to remind the masses of the great nation they lived under. Entek had always been of two minds about the practice. On the one hand, it was good to reinforce doctrine to the citizenry. On the other hand, familiarity could breed contempt. The very omnipresence of the propaganda lessened its effect, as it became part of the background, something that was seen and heard, but not really observed or listened to.

Still, that was Central Command's decision. Like most of Central Command's decisions, it was questionable. *Such as, for example, breaking our agreement with the Federation and hiding ships in the Betreka Nebula.*

When the train arrived at the downtown stop proximate to Order headquarters, Entek disembarked and walked up the stairs. The streets were crowded with pedestrians of all ages at this late afternoon hour—parents with their children, who were just let out of school, workers leaving their offices to return home to their families, merchants selling their wares.

One woman stood at a cart, selling biscuits and assorted libations. Entek noted that she palmed something into the bag of one customer before handing it to him, and she and the customer exchanged what Entek viewed as a significant look. He committed their physical descriptions to memory and made a mental note to report them to the Order. If they were engaged in seditious acts, the Order needed to deal with it. If, on the other hand, they were engaged in legitimate covert business, they needed to be more discreet. True, Entek was trained to notice such things, but the merchant was still too obvious, as far as Entek was concerned.

Entek turned a corner into a dead-end street. Almost the minute he made the turn, the ambient noise level decreased and the number of people on the street dwindled. The fifty-story gray edifice at the end of the cul-de-sac was not one that many Cardassians went to willingly. Entek knew that this was not truly the Order's stronghold, simply where they kept several administrative offices; it was the Order's sole public face, necessary to give the citizenry a point of reference. Still, Entek had never actually set foot in this building before.

He approached the reception desk, the padd containing his full account of the Betreka Nebula incident in a duffel bag he carried over his shoulder.

"I was instructed to report," he said simply.

The woman at the reception desk barely looked up from her computer. She pointed to the retinal scanner. Entek dutifully leaned into it, allowing the amber light to scan his eyes. Moments later, it verified his identity and ran that through the computer, searching for a match in the day's appointments.

"You're to report to Room 2552," the receptionist said a moment later.

"Thank you," Entek said. "I also wish to report a possible act of sedition."

The receptionist activated a recording device, and Entek gave every detail he could about the biscuit vendor and her customer.

Then, content that he had done his duty to Cardassia, he

proceeded to a turbolift and instructed it to take him to the twenty-fifth floor.

The office in question was in the center of the building, on the middle floor. Entek realized that this put it in probably the most secure above-ground part of the structure: its epicenter.

A woman with black-and-white hair sat at a workstation right outside the door marked with the numeral 2552. The moment Entek entered, she looked up, then activated an intercom. "He's arrived," was all she said.

"Send him in."

She looked up at Entek with a bland expression. "You may go in."

Nodding his assent, Entek walked up to the door, which opened at his approach.

Inside was a simple, undecorated office, with a small wooden desk—real wood, as far as Entek could tell, or as good a fake as made no visual difference; expensive either way—and a viewscreen on the eastern wall that showed a view of a swirling nebula. Entek realized after a moment that it was, in fact, the Betreka Nebula. He wondered if that was a deliberate choice.

The desk's occupant was turned facing the bookcase that lined the southern wall behind the desk. As the door closed behind Entek, the chair whirled around—

—and Entek was barely able to control his reaction when he realized that he was in the office of Enabran Tain.

Entek fully expected to spend many years serving Cardassia in the Obsidian Order without ever being in the same room as the Order's head. To have his first field assignment debriefing be conducted by the Order's leader meant—

In truth, Entek had no idea what it meant.

"Have a seat," Tain said in a surprisingly pleasant voice. Entek had expected someone more—well, frightening to be occupying this office. But Tain was a pudgy, unassuming

Cardassian wearing a simple green outfit. Entek doubted he'd even notice Tain walking down the street.

Belatedly, Entek realized that it was probably a deliberate choice on Tain's part.

He followed Tain's instruction and sat in one of the two guest chairs. "Would you like to read my report?" he asked.

"Very much so, yes," Tain said. "Though based on what I've heard from Central Command, I suspect I'm not going to like what I read." Entek must have shown apprehension on his face at that, because Tain quickly added, "This doesn't reflect on you, Entek. In fact, Central Command may well have blundered into a prime intelligence-gathering opportunity. This may well be a blessing in disguise."

If it is, it's a very good disguise, Entek thought, but was wise enough not to say aloud. Instead, he simply reached into his duffel and retrieved the padd. Tain took it from his hands, and keyed the display to show him the report.

While Tain perused Entek's words, the young agent watched the swirl of the nebula. He hadn't had much chance to observe the stellar phenomenon while on the *Carthage*—between his duties as Zarin's toady and his undercover work, there simply was no time—so he took advantage of this opportunity to watch the stellar nursery at work. Entek had never been much of a stargazer, but he had to admit that the swirl of gases and electrons and protostars made for almost hypnotic viewing.

"An excellent report," Tain finally said, setting the padd aside. "You've done well. Your observations on the Federation staff are especially useful."

"I am only sorry I was unable to inform the Order of the fleet in the nebula."

Tain shrugged. "There was little we could have done."

"Central Command made us look like fools before the Federation."

"Don't underestimate the Federation, my young friend.

They may appear soft and unworthy, but they have thrived. They are the true power in this part of the galaxy, and they have resources we can only begin to guess at. The very fact that they saw through Central Command's deception shows that they are a force to be reckoned with."

Entek could not help but blush with pride at the head of the Order calling him "friend." He also had a question, but he did not feel that he should speak out of turn again.

Again, his emotions must have shown, for Tain prompted him. "You wish to pose a question."

"Yes." Entek waited for formal permission to speak, but Tain simply continued to stare at him. Deciding to take that as assent, he asked, "Do you think the Federation will truly be fair judges? They are allies with the Klingons, after all, and have no such ties with us."

Tain laughed. "With any other government, I would share your concern, but the Federation is painfully honest and up-front in their dealings. That is both their greatest strength and their greatest weakness. And, like any strength or weakness, it is something that we can exploit." He smiled. "Besides, as I said, this competition of theirs provides us with a prime opportunity. We will be able to observe the Klingons firsthand. They may seem like buffoons, but they have built one of the strongest empires in the quadrant. If we are to eventually conquer them, we need to know more about how they work, how they think. Sharing a planet with them will be ideal for that."

Knowing it was presumptuous, Entek nevertheless had to ask, "Do you wish me to return to Raknal?"

"No. As well as you've done here, you're still too new for this sort of thing. I'd rather send a more experienced agent. Never fear," he added quickly, "you've proven yourself a valuable resource to the Obsidian Order. I make use of my valuable resources."

Entek beamed with pride.

"Return to your home. Your new supervisor will contact you with your next assignment within the week."

New supervisor? That could only mean a promotion. The specifics would not be forthcoming, of course, but still.

Entek rose from the guest chair. "Thank you, sir."

Tain smiled. "I'm simply putting you in a position to serve Cardassia better."

"This is madness. Utter madness."

Zarin silently agreed with Kell as he sipped his *kanar.* The two legates sat in Kell's plush office along with Gul Monor. The office was over twenty meters squared, containing a huge desk, a full bar, and several couches and chairs. The east wall was taken up entirely with shelving containing padds, data chips, various odds and ends, and even a few codex books. The west wall was decorated with Lissepian paintings, which Zarin knew to be a passion of Kell's. On either side of the door on the south wall were numerous medals, citations, commendations, and a holopicture that rotated images of Kell with assorted Cardassian celebrities and notables.

Most impressive of all, though, was the north wall, which was one giant picture window with a breathtaking view of the capital city. *This,* Zarin thought, *will be my office someday.* The first thing he planned to do was take down and burn those hideous Lissepian monstrosities. Kell had the aesthetic sense of a Ferengi . . .

Zarin and Monor were next to each other on an extremely comfortable *urall*-skin couch while Kell had parked himself in a huge, flared conformer chair that adjusted itself to the contours of the person occupying it. Zarin thought, perhaps unkindly, that it had to do a great deal of adjusting to conform to Kell's rotund form.

"Absolutely," Monor said. "We should be taking what we want, not jumping through hoops for inferiors. What's next, the Federation telling us how to govern Bajor? We shouldn't be letting them dictate terms to us."

"Unfortunately," Zarin said quickly before Monor went on, "we did violate the agreement. If we don't agree to Dax's proposal, we'll risk antagonizing both the Federation and the Klingons."

"We've already antagonized them," Monor said, slamming his *kanar* glass onto the metal table that sat between the couch and Kell's chair. "We're not Ferengi, we shouldn't be bargaining our way out of fighting. They want to take Raknal V, let 'em try, I say."

"All things being equal, I'd agree with you, Monor," Kell said. "But we don't have much choice. The Council won't authorize more funds for a conflict, and we can't commit the resources."

"Especially if it's both the Federation *and* the Empire we have to deal with." Zarin took another sip of his *kanar*.

"Bah," Monor said. "The Federation is soft."

"So is a *gree* worm, but if you poke it with a stick, it'll squirt acid on your face." Zarin leaned forward on the couch. "The Federation hasn't lost a single war since its founding. I somehow doubt that we're in a position to be the first to defeat them."

"A cowardly attitude," Kell said with disdain.

"No, a realistic one." Zarin didn't like what he was saying any more than Kell did, but he also knew that he was right. He just hoped Kell wasn't stupid enough to let pride get in the way of common sense.

Kell let out a long sigh, and refilled his glass with more *kanar* from the large carafe in the center of the table. "Sadly, you're right. For the moment at least, we'll have to play along with this idiotic charade."

"What about the Obsidian Order?" Zarin asked. He hadn't been able to trace the Order agent in his delegation, but he just knew there was one there.

Shrugging, Kell asked, "What about them? They'll probably send someone—or several someones—to the planet to spy on the Klingons. Let them. It's probably better for all of us if we don't know the specifics of what they're doing. If they gather useful intelligence, it'll be shared with us if we need it. If they get caught, we'll be able to deny everything."

"Not to mention the entertainment value," Zarin said with a smile. "If they *do* get caught, I mean. I've heard stories about what Klingons do to spies. There are several people in the Order I'd like to see get that treatment."

All three of them laughed at that. Zarin had no love for the Obsidian Order, and it came as no surprise to the legate that Kell and Monor felt the same. *One of these days*, he thought, *we need to do away with those shadowy imbeciles once and for all. Cardassia is ill-served by their backstabbing ways. Perhaps when this office is mine, I'll be able to implement that plan.*

Kell stood up. "Monor, I hereby appoint you the prefect of the northern continent of Raknal V. The *Sontok* is to be your flagship. Whatever you need, requisition it from Zarin."

Monor nodded. "If that's what we have to do, then dammit all, that's what we'll do. That's the problem with these young officers, they don't know when to shut up and follow orders. In fact—"

"The important thing," Kell said, cutting off yet another of Monor's rants, for which Zarin was grateful, "is to make sure that we are victorious."

"That won't be as easy as it looks," Zarin said. "Most of the zenite we need is on the southern continent."

"Yes." Kell smiled. "I have to give credit to that Trill ambassador—he put us in charge of what the Klingons want and the Klingons in charge of what we want. But we are Cardassians—Raknal V is *ours*, and we will not give it up. I am hereby instructing you both to do whatever it takes to ensure that we secure our claim to it. Am I understood?"

Zarin smiled. "Perfectly."

Chapter 13

QO'NOS

It had been a long time since General Worf had set foot in the Council Chambers. The huge green edifice that stood at the center of the First City on Qo'noS towered above all the other buildings, looking down on the rest of the city—and, symbolically, the rest of the Empire. Originally constructed on top of the First City's highest point as a stronghold of some emperor or other in the dark times before Kahless, when Klingon warred against Klingon in fierce, bloody conflicts, it had been refurbished and rebuilt many times. The most recent of those was after the explosion of Praxis, the fallout from which had come close to destroying it.

Worf admired the design of the main chamber, in which the High Council met. A wide, high-ceilinged space with directed lighting casting harsh shadows, the room's focal points were the raised metal chair and the trefoil Klingon emblem behind it. As Worf entered the darkened room, that chair was occupied by Chancellor Ditagh.

Of course, "occupied" may have been too meager a verb. Ditagh's broad-shouldered form had to practically squeeze itself into the metal throne that had served as the Empire's seat of power for over three decades.

The rest of the High Council stood in a semicircle on either side of Ditagh, with Worf standing in front of them in the room's center, a spotlight shining on his face. That, along with the backlighting behind Ditagh's chair, made the forms of the Council indistinct and shadowy.

"What are your thoughts, General Worf?" Ditagh asked.

Worf considered his words carefully. "My thoughts are not relevant to these proceedings. I have presented my report. I now await further orders."

One of the councillors—a fierce-looking, angular-faced man named Kravokh—said, "Ch'gran *must* be ours, no matter what. It is our most sacred relic!"

"It's hardly that," said another councillor whose face Worf could not make out in the dark room and whose voice he did not recognize. "It certainly is not worth going to war over."

Ditagh turned angrily on the councillor. "Not *worth* going to war over?" He seemed shocked at the near sacrilege of the statement, and Worf had to admit to a bit of surprise at such words coming from the mouth of a warrior.

"I have no great love for the Cardassians, Chancellor, nor do I have any cowardice in my heart. But I also will not take food from the mouths of my children in order to fight a distant war against spoon-headed inferiors in order to retrieve a thousand-year-old ship hulk."

Another councillor stepped forward. After a moment, Worf recognized him as K'Tal, one of the younger councillors. "The Great Curzon understands the Klingon heart. He has given us a way to battle the Cardassians without engaging in a war that will cost us so much, and still retain our honor."

"We cannot afford to lose Ch'gran," Kravokh repeated.

"I'm with Kravokh. We must take Ch'gran."

"And how will we fight the Cardassians? Shall we divert from the Romulan border?"

"The Romulans have not been a concern since Tomed."

"They're just waiting for us to turn our backs on them.

And if we divert our forces from elsewhere, we become vulnerable to the Tholians, the Kinshaya . . ."

"Are we to tell our children that we abandoned our heritage so easily?"

"Are we to bury our children for useless relics?"

"Ch'gran is *not* useless!"

Worf closed his eyes. This was getting out of hand. The last time he had been in Council Chambers was during the reign of Azetbur. Worf had no great love for the daughter of Gorkon, but at least she ran an orderly chamber. After her death, a man named Kaarg had risen to power—with Ditagh as one of his supporters. Indeed, there were rumors that Ditagh had killed Azetbur on Kaarg's behalf. Kaarg had wasted little time in doing what he could to dismantle what Azetbur had built, starting by formally banning any women from serving on the High Council. No such law had existed, but no woman had ever risen to power as Azetbur had, either. Although Worf's active involvement in political doings on Qo'noS was minimal at the time, he knew enough to see that Kaarg's attempts to return to the glory days prior to Praxis were premature, as the Empire was still far too reliant on the Federation for support. Instead of moving forward, the Empire had been in a sort of holding pattern—with some, like the House of Duras, turning to the Romulans for support.

Now the Council had fallen into squabbling and arguing within minutes of the commencement of discussion of a critical political decision, and Ditagh showed no sign of even an interest in calming it down. *Have we fallen so far?* Worf wondered, and was distressed to see that the answer was yes.

"Chancellor!" Worf shouted, trying to make Ditagh hear him over the din. When that failed, he shouted again, even louder.

"Enough!" Ditagh finally cried in a booming voice, which silenced the chamber. "You wish to speak, General?"

"I do." Now Worf was in his element. He had remained

silent out of respect for the Council and the tenuousness of his own position in the Empire. But this Council was worthy of no one's respect, and that made his own position his to determine. Whatever he had done wrong in his life, he was always skilled in the verbal combat of the courtroom, and now he found himself again entering that oratorical arena.

"You asked me my thoughts earlier, and now I believe them to be more relevant than I imagined." He started to pace across the dark room. "For many turns, the Federation has aided us. Despite a history of mistrust and warfare, despite over a century and a half of conflict, they came to our assistance when we were in need, and have asked nothing in return. They have shown us only honor and respect.

"And what have we given them? We have gone back on our word. We swore to send only one ship to the Betreka Nebula, yet we sent an entire fleet. And when they learned of our deception, did they challenge us, as was their right? No. They offered us more aid—a solution that would permit us to at last bring Ch'gran home in a way that allows us our honor."

He looked upon each member of the Council, even the ones he could not see clearly, in succession as he continued. "There should be no debate, and that there is one shows everyone in this room—including myself—to be a coward. We have been given only one choice, and we must take it, or risk losing even more of our honor than we already have by betraying our allies."

Now he fixed his gaze upon Ditagh. "If Ch'gran is to be returned to us, then we must *earn* it. Ambassador Dax—" Worf refused to refer to him as "the Great Curzon," even if the chancellor did "—has given us a battlefield on which we can win, if we are worthy. If we are, then Ch'gran will be restored to us. If we are not, then we do not deserve it."

A silence fell over the Council Chambers. All eyes turned either to Worf or to Ditagh—for the general's part, he locked gazes with the chancellor. The large Klingon was the first to break the gaze, which disappointed Worf. Ditagh was simply a shadow of Kaarg, himself a shadow of the days of yore before Praxis. The Empire needed new blood, not this clinging to the old ways.

"The general is correct," Kravokh said. "We *must* have Ch'gran back, and we *will*. For we are *Klingons!* Let us take the southern continent of this Raknal V!"

Several voices cried their assent in the dark. Worf did not bother to look to see who they were; instead he kept his gaze upon Ditagh.

"Very well," Ditagh finally said. "We will agree to the terms of the Great Curzon's proposal."

"Chancellor," Worf said, "I request the honor of appointment as planetary governor of Raknal V."

"No."

In truth, Worf was not entirely disappointed. He had no interest in such duties, but being in a position to be the one who restored Ch'gran to the Empire was an opportunity he could not pass up.

"Imperial Intelligence has specifically requested that Captain Qaolin be given the position and the responsibility. He was the one who led the mission that learned of Ch'gran's discovery, so the honor should be his."

"Of course," Worf said, understanding, though he could not imagine that a ship captain would find such administrative duties to be fulfilling. But then, perhaps Qaolin was ambitious.

My ambitions are solely to restore myself to a semblance of normalcy. To make our House strong again for Mogh and Kaasin and their children.

"You may return to the Betreka Sector aboard the *Wo'bortas*, General," Ditagh said, "and we shall commence the process of returning Ch'gran to its rightful place. *Qapla'!*"

"*Qapla'!*"

Worf turned and departed the Council Chambers.

Chapter 14

ROMULUS

Praetor Dralath had never liked the look of his chief aide, Timol. Of course, as the leader of the Romulan Senate, it was well within his purview to have the woman killed, but she had proven quite useful to him over the years. She was very young, and very attractive, but not aggressively so. Her features were arranged in a particularly aesthetic manner, her form lithe and athletic, but no one would ever list her as one of the Empire's great beauties—a distinction that would not go to a politician in any event. Still, her innate good looks made it easy to be distracted by her. She knew this, of course; in fact, she cultivated it. It was one of the primary reasons why she had been so useful—men told her things they would never tell someone less attractive, and she was sufficiently charming and self-effacing about her looks that women trusted her.

The very qualities that made her invaluable made her dangerous. Dralath both admired and feared that.

Now Timol came to him for their morning meeting to go over the dispatches and see to the day's itinerary. Running the Romulan Star Empire was a difficult task, and one that required more meetings than Dralath was entirely comfortable with. Power was all well and good, but he had to spend so much time dealing with *people*.

All things considered, he preferred to avoid it as much as possible—hence the meeting with Timol. She was his buffer to the outside world. The Empire already was closed off from the rest of the galaxy—ever since Tomed, Romulus kept its distance from the politics of the quadrant. Dralath had no patience for it—they had enough to deal with at home.

Timol began with reports from the mines on Remus, which was the usual collection of efficiency reports leavened with the occasional bit of Reman rebellions easily put down by the overseers. *The Remans will never be anything but our slaves,* Dralath thought with a smile.

The domestic reports were the usual drivel—acts of sedition put down here, an economic plan involving changes in the tax laws proposed by the Senate there, and other such minutiae that Dralath did not feel the need to concern himself with.

Next were the intelligence reports. "I believe this will be of some interest to you, My Lord Praetor," Timol said in the lilting tones of voice that, Dralath knew, she had perfected over the years. "The Cardassians have discovered an old Klingon wreck on Raknal V near the Betreka Nebula. The Klingons tried to stake a claim on the world as well, and the Federation has brokered an agreement between them."

Dralath frowned. "An agreement? The *Klingons* have allowed an *agreement* to be brokered?" He threw his head back and laughed. "Oh, how the mighty have fallen! Are these the foes we once feared, the allies we once coveted?"

"The Cardassian Union and the Klingon Empire do not share any borders, My Lord Praetor, and the Klingons are still weakened. A war now would not be prudent."

"Prudence has never been a watchword of the Klingon Empire, Timol."

"Times have changed, My Lord Praetor." She then explained the terms of the agreement, and how the planet would be occupied by both nations until one proved worthy of taking it.

Nodding, Dralath said, "I see, they've made it a competition. That is a language the Klingons *do* speak." He rubbed his chin. "Have our agents within the Klingon Empire monitor the situation on Raknal V, but do not inform the Senate. If the Klingons are truly so weakened, we may wish to end our self-imposed exile sooner than planned."

"Sir, we do not have any agents as such, only—"

"I know exactly what we have, Timol. Speak with the appropriate noble houses, they will do the rest."

Timol hesitated. "I know at least one such appropriate house that will feel no great urge to aid you, My Lord Praetor."

"I beg your pardon?"

"The new taxes will have a profound impact on Alidor Ralak and his concerns on Romii."

Dralath again rubbed his chin. Ralak was the head of a house that had close ties to several prominent Klingon families.

"Assure him that he has nothing to be concerned about regarding the new taxes—which I will be vetoing tomorrow."

"My Lord Praetor, that may not be wise. The economic impact on the worker class—"

Pounding the table, Dralath said, "I have no interest in the worker class, Timol! Ralak is not someone I will have as an enemy. It will be done."

"Of course, My Lord Praetor."

Timol then went on to the rest of the agenda, but Dralath barely paid it any mind. *We will be watching you,* he thought at the High Council on Qo'noS. *You will sit in your chambers and rebuild your pathetic empire and beg the Federation for help and forget all about us. But we will be here, waiting for the right moment to strike.*

PART 2

A HEAVY IRON CHAIN DESCENDS

2333–2334

Chapter 15

RAKNAL V

"My fellow Cardassians, I'm sure most of you have heard about the aircar collision on the outskirts of Raknal City."

Noting that Gul Monor—or, rather, Prefect Monor—used the word "collision" rather than "accident" to describe what happened, Ekron stood to the side of Monor's desk while the communications system sent the prefect's image out to all the monitors on the northern continent. This bulletin was interrupting the usual governmental messages, and would be repeated several times until an update was warranted. Normally, such bulletins would be part of the regular news reporting, but the prefect wanted the people to hear about this from his own lips. "Let them know I'm on top of things," he had said. Ekron had agreed with the sentiment in principle, but in reality he feared that Monor's tendency to digress would dilute the message somewhat.

"I'm saddened to say that four loyal Cardassian citizens lost their lives in the crash. I have personally sent the proper authorities to look into this incident, and I can assure you all that they will not rest until the truth about this crash comes to light. And to forestall the questions that I'm sure all of you, as equally loyal Cardassians, might have, let me say this: we have not ruled out Klingon involvement."

Ekron sighed, expecting this. In fact, there wasn't any hint of Klingon involvement, and the investigation team's preliminary report indicated that it was, in fact, an accident. But Raknal V had been plagued with accidents for each of the five years that the Klingons and Cardassians had been sharing the world, and the plague had grown more virulent with time. Where both governments supported the Raknal project in the beginning, as time went on, supply ships came fewer and farther between, and the supplies they carried were less and less state-of-the-art.

Try telling Monor that, Ekron thought with a sigh. At least he wasn't calling the Klingons "Foreheads" on public broadcasts. That would stir things up even more. And he had finally—after five years of steadfast refusal—given Ekron permission to investigate the possibility of transplanting *hevrit* to this world. It might not be enough to save the species, but Ekron felt it was his duty to try. The *hevrit* were as much a part of Cardassia Prime as Cardassians themselves were. If the people of the home planet deserved to have their lot in life improved by colonization, so too did its animal life.

"We will determine who is responsible for this heinous act against our people, and the responsible parties will be brought to justice. I give you my personal assurance as prefect of Raknal V that all of those responsible will be punished."

I wish he'd let me read his speeches before he gives them, Ekron thought, not for the first time. *Too much repetition makes him look like an idiot.* Monor could not afford to look like an idiot in public, especially now.

"We'll find out what happened, and you can be assured that appropriate action will be taken. This planet will be ours, of that you can *all* be assured. No one will take away from Cardassia what rightfully belongs to Cardassia, least of all a bunch of upstart aliens who think they can scare us off with cowardly sabotage. They have endeavored to elude blame for many of the so-called 'accidents' that have befallen loyal Cardassians in the past, all the while refusing any attempt to cooperate on endeavors that would save lives on both sides. They have continually refused to coordinate their orbital control center with ours, resulting in several near collisions in space. It is only a matter of time before a tragedy even more tragic than the tragedy that befell the air-car victims today happens again."

Ekron tried not to gag at the tortured syntax.

The prefect leaned forward in his chair. "Be strong, my fellow Cardassians, and be vigilant. We will overcome these tragedies and emerge a stronger people for it!"

With that, he leaned back. Ekron deactivated the live feed, and the monitors all across the northern continent went back to the prerecorded bulletins and messages.

Knowing full well that the protest would fall on deaf ears, Ekron nonetheless felt compelled to say, "Sir, there's no evidence that the Klingons had anything to do with it."

"One of those damned Foreheads was seen near the site."

Ekron closed his eyes and counted to five. "Sir, that was a merchant named Kall—he's well known in that sector. He's a private citizen. We've checked him thoroughly, as has the Order."

Monor made a snorting noise as he got up from his desk. "As if you can trust anything from those imbeciles. I want that 'merchant' arrested and interrogated."

"Sir, Governor Qaolin will object if you do."

"Let him."

It took all of Ekron's willpower not to say, *That's easy for you to say, you're not the one who has to listen to the objection.* Monor always made Ekron take any communiqués from the Klingons, refusing to speak to the "Foreheads."

Instead, he said, "What if they go to the Federation?"

"Then they'll be exposed as the cowards I've always said they are. Let them fight their own damn battles. Besides, they haven't freed Parrik yet, have they?"

"No." Parrik was a Cardassian accused of sabotaging a Klingon mine and had been imprisoned for six months, interrogated who knew how many times, with no sign of a trial, nor any proof of his involvement in the landslide that—like this aircar collision—was probably a simple accident. *But Monor wants some of his own back, and I suspect this is how he'll get it.*

"Schedule another broadcast for sunset," Monor said. "By then, we'd better damn well have more information, and I'll be ready to announce another curfew."

Ekron winced, but did not argue. "Curfew, sir?" he prompted by way of determining the nature of this latest futile gesture.

"Yes. *All* non-Cardassians must be indoors before sunset."

Once, Ekron would have pointed out that such an action would only serve to antagonize the citizenry, make everyone nervous, create more tension in a situation already laden with it, and, worst of all, stall trade and the economic outlook of the colony. This time of year on this continent, night accounted for seventy percent of a planetary rotation, so much of the business that was conducted on Raknal was done after dark. And a great deal of it involved aliens, particularly Yridian merchants, not to mention the occasional Ferengi.

However, raising such objections only got Ekron yelled at and, after all these years, Ekron had had enough of Monor's rants. He used to consider them part of his job. Of course, he also used to consider a planetside assignment to be a hardship, something to be experienced briefly before retreating back to the constructed environs of a space vessel. After five years on Raknal V, however, he couldn't imagine serving for any length of time in the regulated atmosphere of a ship—nor had he any desire to listen to Monor's rants more than absolutely necessary.

So he simply said, "Very well, sir."

"Damn right it's very well. We're not going to let those Foreheads stop us, or let them take what's ours from us. It's our planet, dammit, *we* found it. Why, in the old days, we wouldn't have put up with all this competition nonsense. We've become soft, Ekron, that's the real problem."

"Yes, sir. If you'll exc—"

But Monor was determined to rant. "I swear to you, I don't know what's happening to us. I hear that some resistance movement has started on Bajor. Can you believe that? Damn fools in Central Command have let the Bajorans' spirituality lull them into a false sense of security. Now they're facing guerrilla attacks. Mark my words, nothing good will come of that. We can't afford to let anything like that happen here."

Ekron refrained from pointing out how impossible that was. "Yes, sir. If you'll excuse me, I have t—"

"And what's more, you just *know* that Qaolin's going to try to find some way to make us look bad here. He'll go screaming at Dax, telling him that this is proof that we can't handle the planet. And that damned Trill will listen to every word he says. You know those Foreheads call him 'the Great Curzon,' like he's a damned circus performer or something. It's enough to make you weep, it really is." The prefect stared at Ekron. "What are you still doing here, Ekron, don't you have work to do?"

"Yes, sir, I do." Relieved, Ekron beat a hasty retreat.

"Be strong, my fellow Cardassians, and be vigilant. We will overcome these tragedies and emerge a stronger people for it!"

Governor Qaolin switched off the recording of Prefect Monor's tiresome speech. "This," he said to the other occupant of his office, "is what I have had to put up with for five years, General."

General Worf nodded. His hair had gone completely white since the last time Qaolin had seen him, which was shortly after the colony on the southern continent was established half a decade ago. He seemed more tired, too—though Qaolin supposed he could have just been superimposing his own fatigue on the general. The governor had not expected to find himself stuck on this rock for a seeming eternity. All the stories he'd heard about sailing on the Barge of the Dead through *Gre'thor* weren't anywhere near as awful as what he endured daily administrating the Klingon colony on Raknal V.

"I take it the prefect's accusations are baseless?" Worf asked.

"Of course they are." Qaolin was surprised at the question. "We do not need to expend any effort to make Cardassians fail, they do so quite well on their own."

"What of Monor's accusations regarding the orbital control centers?"

Qaolin snarled. "More lies. It is true that we have not been cooperative, but it is not for lack of trying. Both sides assign orbital paths to ships that conflict with those assigned by the other side. We have had several near misses because of this. But Cardassian sensors are not sufficiently acute to do the job properly. We have offered to provide a minimal upgrade in exchange for shared duties, only to be rebuffed. They assume that their sensors are adequate to the task and accuse us of trying to sabotage their equipment—and of deliberately causing the difficulties. As if we need to." His hand going to his *d'k tahg* involuntarily, Qaolin stood up and said, "I swear to you, General, I almost wish that something would happen to force a war between our people. Then it would give me the excuse I need to plunge my weapon into Monor's unworthy heart."

"Perhaps. But now would not be the right time."

"There is never a wrong time for war, General."

Worf gave Qaolin a withering gaze. "It is easy for you to say that, Governor. You are not on the Homeworld. You do not see the posturing of the High Council as half of them insist we no longer need Federation aid, and cry out for closer ties to the Romulans."

Qaolin spat on the floor. "Romulans? Those honorless

petaQ are not worthy to blacken our boots! Besides, I thought they closed their borders."

"Their *government* did. But the Romulan aristocracy is like a *pipius*—its tentacles spread everywhere. I do not trust them. And I do not trust *our* government to act sensibly as long as Chancellor Ditagh allows this petty squabbling to go on." The general shook his head. "He does nothing to unite the Council, instead allowing it to grow more fractious, while our shipyards remain barren, our people starve, and once-noble Houses fall into ruin." The general turned to Qaolin. "We *must* win this planet, Governor. We *must* regain Ch'gran. It is all that may save us in the end."

"Perhaps it is, General, but I do not think I am the one to win it." Qaolin stared at the general, and finally decided that he had to ask the question. "Is there any way I may be reassigned? I am a ship commander, not a planetary governor. The colony virtually runs itself, and the duties I do have can be performed by someone more—politically adept than myself."

"I am afraid not. The High Council agrees on little in these dark times, but one thing they are in harmony on is that you are best qualified to run this colony and to win Ch'gran for us." Worf frowned. "Do you not consider it an honor?"

"I consider winning Ch'gran an honor, General," Qaolin said with another snarl, "and you have made it clear that it is an urgency as well. But I do not consider running this colony to be an honorable way of winning it. It is better suited to the shadowy machinations of I.I., not the true battlefield of a warrior."

Worf tilted his head. "Odd that you should say that."

Qaolin frowned. "Why?"

"It was at the specific recommendation of Imperial Intelligence that you were assigned as governor, and at I.I.'s insistence that you remain."

The governor stared at the general in open-mouthed stupefaction for several seconds.

Then he threw his head back and laughed.

Even from beyond the grave, you manipulate me, Yovang. Foolishly, Qaolin had believed that he could easily deal with whatever consequences arose from killing the I.I. agent aboard the *Wo'bortas* five years ago. Now, he knew what those consequences were: exile to this nightmare of a posting.

"This amuses you, Governor?"

"No. But there are times when laughter is the only rational response." He sat back down. "Very well, General. I shall continue to see to the Klingon needs of this continent, and I will win Ch'gran for us, and I shall save the Empire, and we will survive and be strong again."

Laughing bitterly, Worf said, "I will settle for the first two. The others will take care of themselves over time."

"You think so?" Qaolin asked in surprise. "For one who has spoken so cynically, you seem unusually confident."

"We are Klingons. Eventually, we *will* be victorious."

Qaolin reached into the drawer of his desk and pulled out a bottle of bloodwine and two mugs. "In that case, General, drink with me, to our future." He split the bottle between the two mugs and handed one to Worf. "May it be far more glorious than our present."

To that, they both drank heartily.

"Orbital Control, this is the Gratok. *We will be achieving orbit in five minutes. Please verify flight plan."*

Stifling a yawn, Talik, the traffic controller on duty touched a control. "This is Orbital Control, *Gratok.* Sending flight plan now." Talik entered the standard flight plan for the zenite-bearing freighters like the *Gratok.* It would give them one orbit before departing for Cardassia Prime with the precious zenite shipment.

"Flight plan received, Orbital Control. Staying awake up there, Talik?"

At that, Talik smiled. "Barely. I don't suppose you have any holovids to send over, Kater?"

"Don't tell me you watched all the ones I sent last month?"

"All right, I won't tell you." In fact, Talik had traded them for a bottle of real *kanar*—not that swill they provided at the commissary, but the good stuff. But since he got the *kanar* for when he finally worked up the courage to ask Kater Onell for an evening out, he could hardly tell her about it now. "So when're you due back?"

"I'm not, I'm afraid. The zenite yields are too small to justify coming so far out. The company's sending a smaller ship to do the next run."

Panic gripped Talik. He'd spent *months* working up his nerve. Kater, after all, was a freighter captain; he was just a lowly traffic controller. Just the fact that she was willing to talk to him beyond the confines of duty was impressive enough, and was, in fact, the only reason why he even considered the possibility of asking her to dinner. "You—you mean you're never coming back?"

"Well, I wouldn't go so far as to say never, *but probably not for a few months at least."* She laughed. *"Don't worry, Talik, I'm sure you'll find someone else to send you war vids."*

Talik couldn't give a good damn about war vids just at the moment. His love life had been in the waste extractor for years now. No woman had even been interested in talking to him, aside from Kater, and the only comfort women he could afford weren't ones he had any interest in letting near him; he had never been partial to elderly women with strange sores on odd parts of their bodies. "It's—it's not th-that." He tried not to sound like a stammering idiot. "I was kind of hoping—I mean, I was kind of—"

Before he could blunder through the rest of the sentence, he heard an explosion. After a second, he realized that it was coming over the comm line. *"What the hell was that?"* Kater screamed.

Talik checked his sensor display. "Kater, I'm reading an explosion in your engineering section."

"I'm glad you're reading that. Our internal sensors are down."

"You're also off course." Immediately, Talik hit the panic button, which sent out a broad-band message on both subspace and soundwave frequencies, instructing all ships in orbit to get out immediately, either by returning to the planet's surface or leaving orbit altogether.

The voice of Talik's supervisor, Hamnod, sounded from behind him. "What's happening?"

"Freighter *Gratok* has experienced some kind of engine failure. They've lost attitude control."

Hamnod was a large man with a belly that protruded sufficiently far in front of him that most of those in Orbital Control joked that his stomach arrived five minutes before he did. That belly was rubbing up against Talik's console now, as the supervisor peered at the shatterframe display that gave the usual view of about eighty percent of the space around Raknal V. The only thing missing was the area on the far side of the planet—a blind spot at one hundred and eighty degrees from their position, and, not coincidentally, where the Klingons had set up their orbital control center. At present, the only bodies showing on the display were the *Gratok*—which was bouncing around like mad; its guidance systems and gyroscopic mechanisms were obviously completely destroyed—and Orbital Control itself. The supervisor then pointed a pudgy finger at a new item on the display. "What is that?"

Talik frowned. It wasn't a Cardassian ship, which meant either an unregistered ship or a Klingon ship. Talik sincerely hoped it was the former. The last thing he wanted to do was get into a shouting match with a Klingon.

The new arrival just came into view from the blind spot. It was also on a course that would take it directly into the path of the *Gratok,* if both ships held course.

"Get that thing out of there, Talik," Hamnod said.

Good thing you're here, I never *would have thought of that,* Talik thought as he opened a channel to the ship. He had heard a rumor that Hamnod spent most of his off-duty time with the very comfort women that Talik would never go near. Even if it wasn't true, Talik had always taken it as gospel. It was certainly in character for the fat supervisor.

"Unidentified ship, this is Orbital Control. Please leave orbit immediately, we have a ship in distress, and we cannot guarantee your safety."

There was no response from the ship, but Kater cut in. *"Talik, our warp core's going to go any minute, and I can't get the ejection systems to function. I don't think we're gonna make it."*

"Yes, you are," Talik said stupidly. "Just as soon as I get this ship out of the—"

"What ship? I'm blind out here."

Hamnod had been doing a sensor check. "It's a Forehead ship—the *Chut.* Passenger ship heading to Qo'noS." The corpulent supervisor leaned into Talik's comm unit. "Attention *Chut,* this is Orbital Control. If you do not change course immediately, you risk collision. Please, leave orbit *now.*"

"What? Great!" Kater's voice was distant for those two words, then came on more clearly. *"We think we've got the breach under control, Talik, but we still can't change course."*

"Dammit," Talik muttered. Whatever relief he felt at Kater's continued survival was leavened by the continued presence of the *Chut.* The Klingon passenger liner was still on its standard orbital course, which would bring it slamming into the *Gratok* at one-eighth impulse in about seventy-five seconds.

"Chut, this is Cardassian Orbital Control." Hamnod was practically shouting. "Veer off *now,* or you will be destroyed!" He pounded the console. "Why won't they listen? Damned idiotic Foreheads . . ."

Talik tried to run a sensor scan on the *Chut*, but he wasn't able to penetrate their shields. That was typical of the Klingons—trying to protect their secrets, Talik supposed, though what secrets a passenger liner could have was beyond him—but it made it all the more frustrating in circumstances like this. *What if something's wrong with them, too?* Sadly, two vessels breaking down in orbit on the same day wouldn't be out of character on Raknal V these days . . .

The *Chut* was now one minute from colliding with the *Gratok*. "Why won't they veer off? Just a two-degree course change would do it." Talik leaned into his comm unit. "Kater, you've got to abandon ship. Those Klingons aren't moving!" *Then you'll be forced to stay on Raknal V for a while,* he thought. True, she'd be left without a ship, but at least she'd be alive. And maybe she would feel predisposed toward the man who did everything he could to save her . . .

"*My people are getting to the escape pods now,*" she said.

Talik didn't like the sound of that. "Your people? What about you?"

"*Ship-master goes down with the sinking ship, Talik—besides, we don't have enough pods for everyone. I had to cut back to make more cargo room. I'm not about to make one of my people die for a financial choice I made.*"

This was ruining a perfectly good fantasy. "You can't just die, dammit!"

"*Then get those Klingons out of my way.*"

Hamnod let out a breath that whistled through his nose. "We're trying! *Chut*, you are now forty seconds from a catastrophic collision with a Cardassian freighter. Veer off *now!*"

The next forty seconds were the longest of Talik's life. He found himself utterly riveted by the display in front of him, as the yellow light that indicated the drifting *Gratok* grew closer and closer to the red light that indicated the leisurely pace of the *Chut*. Some smaller yellow lights appeared—

those had to be the escape pods Kater mentioned. Talik noted that there were eight of them; freighters of the *Gratok*'s class usually had twelve two-person pods. Hamnod continued to shout implorations to the *Chut*, to no avail. The Klingon ship continued forward, its course unchanging.

The collision itself was almost anticlimactic, rendered as it was by the red light and the yellow light intersecting. A moment later, both lights went out.

If the *Chut* was a typical Klingon passenger ship, it had the capacity to hold a hundred people, staff included. The *Gratok* had a crew complement of twenty, at least sixteen of whom probably got out in the pods, though Talik had no way of telling if the pods survived being that close to the two ships annihilating each other. Plus, of course, the *Gratok* was carrying a valuable zenite shipment.

"Get me Prefect Monor now," Hamnod said.

And Kater Onell was dead.

"Talik!"

The flight controller shook his head and looked up at Hamnod's fat face. "Hm?"

"I said get me Prefect Monor *now!*" The supervisor sighed. "It's going to be a very very long night."

This outrage will not go unanswered, Qaolin!

Governor Qaolin had already gone through the two bottles of bloodwine in his desk drawer, and was fervently wishing for a third as he stared at the outraged face of his Cardassian counterpart. *I suppose I should be grateful that he is at least speaking to me. Usually I only get to talk to that imbecile aide of his.* But the destruction of the *Gratok* and the *Chut* was the worst of the recent disasters, and Qaolin wasn't about to stand for going through an underling. Not with a hundred dead.

"*You* dare call this an outrage, Monor? At least most of your people survived! There were ninety-eight Klingon nationals on the *Chut* who died because of your incompetence!"

"*Our Orbital Control Center did everything they could to get the* Chut *to veer off. They refused to respond to us!*"

"Convenient, is it not, Monor, that these exhortations only occurred after the *Chut* entered the one orbital section we could not scan from *our* Orbital Control Center. Of course, we would have been able to verify your account if you had allowed us to put the boosters in place, or even accepted our offer to cooperate . . ."

"*Oh, no you don't.*" Monor's face was contorted into a rage that was almost Klingon. Qaolin found himself fighting an urge to admire it. "*Don't try to make this into something that's our fault.*"

Qaolin couldn't help but laugh in Monor's face. "Whose fault is it, then? It was not *our* ship that malfunctioned and went catastrophically of course. On the contrary, the *Chut* was following a standard orbital path—which got it destroyed and a hundred innocents killed."

"*Innocent—pfah! I know you Foreheads—you're responsible for this! You're trying to get in good with that damned Trill of yours, and trying to make us look bad by sabotaging our zenite shipment.*"

Restraining himself from reacting directly to the slur, Qaolin instead forced a grin to his face. "We need commit no sabotage to make you look bad, Monor. You are accomplishing that task quite adequately on your own."

"*I will not be insulted by the likes of you! I know you sabotaged the* Gratok, *and I'll prove it!*"

The grin became a snarl. "Are you so deluded as to think that we would murder a hundred of our citizens just to stop your rocks from getting to Cardassia?"

"*Don't try to play the innocent with me, Qaolin.*" Monor leaned forward into his viewer. "*You Foreheads are all alike—fanatics to a man. A hundred dead? That's nothing, as*

long as you can get your precious Ch'gran relic back. I know
your type, and I know that you'd all jump into a black hole if
it meant you could get that stupid wreck back in your hands.
You're all such fools—glorifying the past so much you forget
about the future. Well, let me tell you something, 'Governor'—the future is the Cardassian Union ruling the galaxy,
and you barbarians working as slave labor and wondering
where you went wrong. I'll tell you where—thinking that
being some kind of honorable warrior means something, when
all it's going to do is get you defeated." Monor leaned back.
"Enjoy your victory, Qaolin. It won't last."

Monor's image faded from the viewscreen on the wall of
Qaolin's office, but the governor spoke to it anyhow. "This is
victory?"

He went to take a gulp of his bloodwine, only to find the
mug empty. Furious, he threw the mug across the room.

Stabbing the intercom with a finger, he summoned his
aide, who entered at a dead run. "Yes, my lord!"

"My lord." That is the true joke, Qaolin thought. "Find
out if General Worf has left yet. If he has, call his ship back
here. If he hasn't, I need to see him immediately."

"Uh . . ." The aide shuffled from foot to foot.

"What is it?" Qaolin prompted.

"Sir, we just received the passenger list for the Chut."

Qaolin closed his eyes.

Then he picked up his chair and threw it against the wall
containing the viewscreen. The chair broke in several
places, and the screen shattered with an ear-splitting crack.

The aide stood in the doorway, unmoving.

"General Worf was on the Chut?" Qaolin asked.

"Yes, sir, he was."

"That would mean that General Worf is dead."

"Yes, sir."

Qaolin smashed his fist into his desk. "Establish the insta-
link to the Homeworld. Now!"

"Yes, sir." The aide scurried out of the room.

"And fetch me another bottle of bloodwine!" Qaolin had no idea if I.I. agents went to Gre'thor or Sto-Vo-Kor, but whichever it was, the governor was quite sure that Yovang was laughing at him from there right now.

The insta-link was a tight-beam subspace system that enabled live communication between Raknal V and Qo'noS. It used an appalling amount of energy, and was only to be engaged in emergencies. As far as Qaolin was concerned, this qualified.

Ten minutes and three mugs of bloodwine later, Qaolin faced the image of Chancellor Ditagh on the small viewer on his desk's workstation. Five minutes after that, he had finished briefing the chancellor on what had happened.

"What action do you wish me to take, sir?"

Ditagh blinked. *There is no action to be taken. If the families of those dead wish to claim vengeance, do not stop them. Otherwise, we have won a great victory. The Cardassians' incompetence has led to the destruction of one of their zenite shipments and the unnecessary deaths of our people. The loss of life is regrettable—particularly that of the general—but we can use that to our advantage as well. Ch'gran will be ours— the Cardassians have already given it to us.*

Qaolin frowned at his chancellor. "Of course, sir," he said out of respect for the office, but he did not see that it was nearly as simple as the head of the High Council was making it out to be.

Even as he closed the insta-link connection, he could hear Yovang's laughter.

Chapter 16

I.K.S. PU'BEKH

"Sir, something's wrong."

Captain K'mpec of the *I.K.S. Pu'Bekh* looked up at that report from the operations station behind him, then gave a nod to Commander Mogh, who walked over to that station. "Explain," the first officer said.

"We just sent out routine communications traffic, sir," the operations officer said. "However, when I checked to see if it had been picked up by this system's communications relay, I got no readings."

"None?" Mogh sounded surprised. "Do a full scan of the relay."

"I have already attempted to do so, sir. Sensors aren't picking up any emissions from the relay at all. In order to do a more complete scan, we'll need to get closer."

K'mpec scowled. They had come to the Donatu system on a routine patrol. Incidents with Cardassian ships along the border had increased over the past several months—ever since the destruction of the *Chut* at Raknal V—and Command had sent the *Pu'Bekh* to make sure that all was well in this particular system. It had been the flashpoint of a Federation–Klingon conflict almost a century ago, and Command thought that the Cardassians might try one of their sneak attacks here. They had already made similar assaults on bases and ships in the Archanis and Cursa systems, though the Cardassian government had, of course, denied it—or, at the very least, disavowed the attacks.

Of course, K'mpec thought with bitter amusement, *the High Council has similarly disavowed attacks in the Cuellar and Trelka systems in Cardassian space. Not to mention that skirmish between the* Korvale *and that Cardassian fighter last month.*

"With your permission, Captain?" Mogh said.

K'mpec nodded.

Mogh turned to the helm control station to the captain's left. "Pilot, set course for the communications relay, full impulse. Operations, when we are within range, do an intensive scan. I expect a full report within the hour."

"Sir!" both officers said.

Then K'mpec rose from his chair. "I would speak with you, Commander," he said, his deep voice rumbling throughout the bridge.

"Of course."

The two of them exited the bridge. Entering his office, the captain gathered his floor-length coat of office and sat his slim, athletic form down into the metal chair behind his workstation. There were no guest chairs—K'mpec had never seen any good reason to make other people more comfortable than he—and so Mogh stood.

K'mpec regarded his first officer, who had only been on this assignment for less than a year. He had a simple, yet strong crest, with a raised middle ridge, penetrating black eyes, and wide shoulders. In battle, he had proven a crack shot with a disruptor, but awful with a *bat'leth.* The captain preferred that to the other way around—it was all well and good to be handy with a blade, but ultimately it was disruptors that won battles.

Mogh also waited patiently, standing at attention. He did

not fidget or show any outward sign of displeasure or worry. K'mpec admired that.

"It has been several months since the *Chut* incident on Raknal V, Mogh. Yet you have said nothing."

"There has been nothing to say."

K'mpec chuckled. "I find that difficult to believe. Your father was killed in a cowardly attack. Does that matter to you?"

"Why do you ask me this, sir?"

"Are you questioning me, Commander?" K'mpec asked, his voice lowering.

"Yes, sir, I am."

At that, K'mpec laughed. "Good. I was beginning to wonder if you had any passion at all."

Mogh looked straight at K'mpec. "My father died in an accident caused by carelessness. The only one against whom I could possibly seek vengeance—the captain of the Cardassian cargo ship—is also dead. As far as I am concerned, the matter is closed. My father died in the line of duty. The best way to honor his memory is to continue to serve, as he did."

Silently, K'mpec was impressed. It was quite possibly the longest number of sentences Mogh had strung together in all his time serving aboard the *Pu'Bekh*.

"I have received many reports, Mogh. You have no doubt read them as well. Many of the family members of the *Chut* victims are seeking vengeance against random Cardassians."

With a shrug, Mogh said, "That is their prerogative. But it is a foolish endeavor. It is not true vengeance if it is against someone unrelated who happens to be of the same species."

Before K'mpec could pursue this further, the intercom sounded. *"Bridge to captain."*

K'mpec looked up. "Yes?"

"We have scanned the relay, sir—or, rather, what is left of it."

"Mneh," the captain grumbled, and got up from his chair. Mogh followed him back onto the bridge.

"Report," Mogh said as K'mpec took his seat.

The operations officer stood at attention. "Approximately sixty percent of the relay's surface area has been blasted away. Preliminary scan indicates phaser fire consistent with Cardassian ships."

"Are the relay's security systems intact?" Mogh asked.

"Impossible to be sure."

K'mpec looked at the viewscreen, which the operations officer had provided with a view of the relay. Its oblong shape was pitted, its surface broken, with wiring, circuitry, and chips all exposed to the vacuum of space.

One of the officers sneered. "Only Cardassians would invade our space to attack a mere relay station."

Several other members of the bridge crew snarled and spat in assent. K'mpec had to agree with the sentiment. The relay's sole function was to amplify and redirect communications traffic. Normal ship-to-planet communication, even via subspace, could take days, but relays such as this did much to make interstellar communication as close to instantaneous as possible. However, the machinery was also easily repaired or replaced, and could hardly be counted as a major blow against the Empire.

"Sir," Mogh said, "request permission to beam the relay into the cargo hold. We can examine it more thoroughly that way."

K'mpec nodded his affirmation. "You will supervise the examination personally, Commander. I want to know precisely what happened to that relay, and what it will take to fix it."

"Sir!"

An hour later, Mogh once again stood in K'mpec's office. "We have had success, Captain. The Cardassians showed poor aim. Though I am afraid that the unit will have to be scrapped and replaced, as it is beyond repair, they did not hit any of the security systems." Mogh then smiled. "Lieutenant J'tal was of the opinion that the Cardassians were not smart enough to realize that a communications relay would have a security system."

"Or, perhaps they do not think us smart enough to have constructed one." K'mpec chuckled. "Either way, I assume that the images provided are useful?"

"One might put it that way, yes, sir." Mogh was still smiling as he loaded a dataspike into K'mpec's workstation.

K'mpec watched as the relay showed the emptiness of space. Mogh advanced the recording to the moment when a ship came out of warp. Within moments, the ship came close enough to be visually identified as a Cardassian *Akril*-class ship. *Definitely from their military*, he thought. *Perfect*.

The ship, which the *Pu'Bekh* computer identified as the *Boklar*, then fired on the relay and warped back out of the system.

"I already have the pilot charting their projected course," Mogh said when the recording was done. "Based on the time-stamp of the relay security, this occurred less than seven hours ago."

At that, K'mpec looked up sharply.

"Yes, sir—we just missed them."

"We will not miss them again."

Mogh's smile grew wider. "No, sir, we will not."

"Very well then, Commander, give chase. I will alert Command of what has happened."

"Sir!" Mogh moved to leave K'mpec's office.

"Commander!"

Mogh stopped and turned around.

"For one who swears no vengeance against the Cardassians, you are extremely eager to pursue them."

Dropping the smile, Mogh said, "I merely wish to see that *these* Cardassians pay for their cowardly attack, Captain."

"And that is all?"

"Yes, sir."

After dismissing his first officer, K'mpec ordered a communication be put through to Qo'noS. Then he called up the Defense Force records on the *Boklar*. The only thing they had was its class—which K'mpec knew from looking at it—and that it was most recently known to be commanded by a gul named Onell.

K'mpec frowned, his complex crest furrowing. He knew that name. After a moment he placed it as connected to Raknal V. Calling up the records of that, he saw it: Kater Onell was the ship-master of the freighter that crashed into the *Chut*.

He wondered if Mogh knew this, and if that explained his enthusiasm. *So much for this being over, eh, Commander?*

"*Sir, we have gotten through to Qo'noS. I have Councillor Kravokh for you.*"

K'mpec was impressed. He had expected to get one of Kravokh's functionaries at best. "Put him through."

Kravokh's angular face appeared on the viewscreen on K'mpec's desk. "*Report, Captain.*"

"Our assignment to this system has been justified. A Cardassian ship called the *Boklar* attacked the communications relay in this system. We are in pursuit."

"*Excellent. And you have proof?*"

"Yes."

"*Most excellent. This is a great day, Captain. With this, perhaps we can finally convince the Federation to take Raknal V away from the unworthy Spoon Heads and then, finally, Ch'gran can be ours.*" Kravokh leaned forward. "*I want that ship captured, Captain. I want whoever the gul of that ship is—*"

"Gul Onell."

"*Fine, I want Onell to stand before the Council and speak for all to hear that he destroyed Klingon property at the order of their Central Command. Then he will be executed, and we will have all the justification for taking Ch'gran that we will need.*"

K'mpec thought the councillor was jumping ahead of himself a bit. "And if we do not find the *Boklar?*"

Kravokh shrugged. "*Then we will demand it through channels. We have proof now, after all. I want that proof sealed, Captain—under the best protection your guards can give it. And no matter what it takes, I want that ship intact and its gul alive, even if you are to leave Klingon space, am I understood?*"

"It will be done."

"*Good.*"

After Kravokh cut off the connection, K'mpec leaned back and smiled. His ambitions had always stretched far beyond that of the captain's chair, and currying favor with Kravokh—who was looking more and more to be the favorite to succeed the ailing Ditagh—could only benefit K'mpec now.

At least, the reports were that Ditagh was ailing. He had been less and less visible over the past few months—though some argued that he was already insubstantial, so becoming invisible was not much of a stretch. The current chancellor seemed to be in favor of strengthening the Empire but had never actually implemented any plan to do so. Kravokh, at least, had the welfare of the Empire in mind, though he seemed to think the restoration of Ch'gran would do the most good to restore the Empire to greatness. K'mpec wasn't so sure—but he also knew that losing Ch'gran would be a disaster.

K'mpec also questioned the wisdom of pursuing the *Boklar* out of Klingon jurisdiction. True, most of the space between here and Cardassia was either unclaimed or belonged to the Federation, but engaging the *Boklar* after they left Klingon territory would muddy the issue. They needed to take the *Boklar* in Empire space.

Mogh's voice came over the intercom. "*Sir, we have picked up the* Boklar *on long-range sensors. They are on course for Cardassian space, but still within our borders.*"

"Can we catch them before they cross the border?"

"Yes, sir, if we increase to warp eight."

"Anh!" he grunted, then moved quickly to the bridge. *We will get them,* he thought gleefully.

As K'mpec entered the bridge, the pilot said, "Speed increasing to warp eight."

Standing next to the operations console, Mogh added, "At this rate, we will overtake the *Boklar* in three minutes—long before they reach the border."

"Arm torpedoes, and fire a minimal spread at their engines as soon as they are within range." He turned to face the gunner, a heavy-ridged older lieutenant with gray-and-white hair, and spoke in a quiet tone, enunciating every word even more than usually. "The ship is to be taken *intact.* If it is not, I will hold *you* responsible."

"Sir!" the lieutenant said quickly, understanding that the penalty for the *Boklar* being destroyed would be the gunner's own life.

Mogh then approached the command chair and spoke quietly to K'mpec. "Sir, the *Akril*-class vessels have impressive firepower. I do not doubt the ability of the *Pu'Bekh* to win any battle, but if we hamstring ourselves—"

Matching Mogh's quiet tones, K'mpec interrupted. "Our orders are to take the *Boklar* intact and bring Gul Onell back to the Homeworld for trial."

"Sir, we have the sensor logs from the relay. What need do we have to keep these Cardassian animals alive?"

K'mpec's instinct was to remind the commander of his place and of the foolishness of questioning his orders. But K'mpec also preferred underlings who thought for themselves. *The question being, is Mogh thinking for himself, or thinking only of the vengeance he claims he does not feel the urge to undertake?* This bloodthirstiness was completely understandable—the Cardassians had, after all, invaded—but may have had ulterior motives. Either way, K'mpec felt the need to explicate. "Do not underestimate the power of a living witness and of physical evidence, Commander. We can tamper with our own sensor logs, after all."

Mogh nodded, in seeming understanding. "I withdraw my objection, Captain."

"Weapons range in thirty seconds," called out the gunnery lieutenant.

"Prepare to fire," Mogh said with a smile.

"In range."

Clenching his fist, Mogh cried, "Fire!"

K'mpec watched as the torpedoes traveled through the distortion of warp space, traversing the gap between the *Pu'Bekh* and the *Boklar*, then striking the latter ship's shields, disrupting them.

"Direct hit. They are coming out of warp."

"Stay with them, pilot," Mogh barked. "Arm disruptors and raise shields."

From the operations console, the officer posted there said, "They are hailing us."

A rumble sounded in K'mpec's throat. "I have nothing to say to invaders."

The officer smiled. "Sir!"

"Coming about," the pilot said.

"Fire!"

Disruptor fire now struck the *Boklar*'s shields even as the Cardassians fired their own phasers at the *Pu'Bekh*.

"Shields down to ten percent!" The gunnery lieutenant's voice was tinged with surprise and outrage.

"It would seem the Cardassians have improved their arsenal." K'mpec pounded a fist on the armrest of his chair. "Damage to the *Boklar*?"

"Minimal, sir."

"We must bring down their shields. Continuous fire."

Disruptors and torpedoes burst forth from the *Pu'Bekh*'s weapons arrays, pounding at the *Boklar*'s shields. The disruptors finally brought the shields down, with the final torpedo striking the Cardassian vessel's hull.

A cheer went up from around the bridge, even as more Cardassian phaser fire struck the *Pu'Bekh*.

Consoles then sparked around the bridge. "Shields dow—" the gunner started before the deckplates behind him exploded in what sounded to K'mpec's veteran ears like a plasma fire. K'mpec turned to see that the gunner had been thrown halfway across the bridge and into a bulkhead. Mogh, to his credit, immediately ran to take the gunner's position.

"Programming torpedo pattern," he said.

The gunner managed to clamber back up and return to his post. K'mpec noted that he seemed to have even more white in his hair now. "Thank you, Commander."

Mogh gave the lieutenant a curt nod and made way for him.

"Firing torpedoes and disruptors."

Seconds later, just as the torpedoes were striking the hull of the *Boklar*—and after the disruptors had already started cutting through the vessel's hull—the Cardassian ship exploded in a fiery conflagration that forced K'mpec to avert his eyes from the viewscreen momentarily.

Furious, he unholstered his hand disruptor even as he turned around to face the gunner. Growling in inarticulate rage, he fired.

The gunner's screams seemed to echo long after his body had disintegrated.

K'mpec had no choice. He had already stated to the entire bridge that the destruction of the *Boklar* would mean the gunner's life.

Yet it had been Mogh who programmed the torpedoes' firing pattern.

Then again, the disruptors struck the Boklar *first. It is quite possible—likely even—that it was the disruptors that provided the fatal blow.*

Either way, it no longer mattered. "Damage report."

"Shields and cloak are gone," the operations officer reported. "Multiple hull breaches on the lower decks—we have had to evacuate the entire undersection. Warp drive offline; engineering estimates a day to repair."

"Communications?" Mogh asked.

"Functioning."

"Good," K'mpec said, falling more than sitting back in his command chair after reholstering his disruptor. "Make contact with the Homeworld."

Mogh stepped up to stand beside K'mpec. "It is not what we had hoped," the commander said. "But when I look back on this day, it will be one of celebration. I will not mourn the loss of the cowards who invaded our space to fight a mere communications relay. I will instead see this as a victory against an unworthy foe who deserved nothing less than what they received."

K'mpec regarded his first officer carefully. There was, once again, no glee in his voice, no joy in victory, simply a recitation of duty. *As usual.* But the captain did not know whether or not Mogh had been responsible for the destruction of the *Boklar* or not.

What he did know was that the actions of this day would have long-term consequences. Already, K'mpec was beginning to formulate ways he could work them to his advantage.

Chapter 17

CARDASSIA PRIME

"An excellent meal, Kurrgo."

The Klingon smiled widely at the Hallitz family—a Cardassian man, his wife, their five children, and one grandchild—as they moved toward the exit of his restaurant. In his heavily accented Cardassian, he said, "It is my pleasure to bring food to your plate, my friends."

"I still don't know how you can get such fresh *pipius* claw," the father said, shaking his head.

"I have my sources," was all Kurrgo would say in reply. In fact, his "source" was a Ferengi who made regular trips across the border—though those trips were getting less regular of late.

"Careful," the father said with a chuckle. "I'll have my son-in-law check into your 'sources,' and then we'll be able to get by without you." The eldest daughter's husband—and father to the grandchild—was a respected gul in the Cardassian military. His duties prevented him from joining the rest of the family for meals with any regularity, though he was, at least, posted to Cardassia Prime.

The mother snorted. "As if I could prepare Klingon dishes with anything like Kurrgo's skill."

Kurrgo bowed. "You honor me with your praise."

"I merely speak the truth," the mother said. "Thank you again."

"Mother, my food was *moving*. You said you'd *tell* them!" That was the grandchild, a girl of only three.

Kurrgo squatted down so he was face-to-face with the young girl, whose name, Kurrgo recalled, was Alyn. Her ridges were barely starting to form—her skin was almost as smooth as a Romulan's. "You ordered *racht,* little one. *Racht* is best served live."

Alyn pouted. "I don't like it when my food moves. It's icky."

"Perhaps. But then, if it does not move, it's too easy to catch. You see, we Klingons believe in conquering our food, hunting it. The hunt should not end just because the food has already reached the plate."

The girl brightened. "So it's like a game?"

"Exactly! So next week when you and your parents come here, treat the *racht* as if it were trying to get away from you—and you must hunt it with your fork!"

She smiled. "Okay!"

They all laughed, and soon the family departed, heading for an evening home before the trials of the workday began again the following day. The mother, Traya Hallitz, had been brought here once for a business-related meal. Kurrgo remembered the day well, for she had come in with her nose wrinkled, her lips pursed, and had refused to order anything beyond a glass of water. Her companion—one of Kurrgo's regulars—had laughed and insisted that she at least try the *rokeg* blood pie. She refused at first, but he had managed to get her to take a bite of *bok-rat* liver.

To Traya's own great surprise, she loved it. She wound up ordering a full meal, and a week later, she brought her husband—a self-proclaimed lover of exotic foods—and eventually, the entire family made it a weekly ritual to have their evening meal at Kurrgo's.

It was from exactly such types that Kurrgo made his business. After all, while he was a decent chef, there were better ones in the Empire. To follow in his parents' footsteps and open an eatery on Qo'noS or one of the other Klingon worlds would only allow him to be one of many—and not the best. So Kurrgo instead struck out into the unknown, determined to bring the joys of Klingon cuisine to foreign planets.

Ten years, and several false starts later—it had taken years to pay off the massive debts incurred by his failed attempt to open an establishment on Tellar; apparently too few Tellarites found Klingon food sufficiently appealing to keep a restaurant afloat—he found himself thriving on Cardassia Prime. The expansion of the Cardassian Union had led to a great curiosity among the natives as to the wonders of the galaxy, including the types of foods eaten by all the new species they were encountering every day.

For the first decade or so, business had been good. He finally paid off all his debts, both the ones incurred on Tellar and those he took on in order to get this place going, and the restaurant started to show something resembling a profit—or at least made enough for him to live comfortably.

At last, he had won. He had brought Klingon cuisine to Cardassia.

Sadly, of late, Cardassia seemed less and less interested in the Klingon cuisine he offered. The growing number of incidents between the two governments had resulted in a downturn in business. The regulars like the Hallitz family weren't the problem—it was the walk-in business, the curious thrillseekers, the adventurous tourists, and, of course, the occasional visiting Klingon, desperate for a taste of home. Those were fewer in number with each passing month, and Kurrgo could not survive on his tiny base of regulars alone—especially since the price of importing the necessary ingredients had skyrocketed on account of the strife between the two governments. Most of that, of course, was artificial gouging by that damned Ferengi, but he was also the only one who was willing to cross both borders and acquire the necessary foodstuffs for Kurrgo.

As he said good-bye to a retired doctor who came every night for a bowl of *taknar* gizzards, Kurrgo thought, *Speaking of whom, that little troll should have been here yesterday with that fresh supply of* targs. *Where is he?*

He looked around. *And where is Larkan? He should have been here an hour ago.* It was the height of the dinner hour, and all four of his waiters should have been present. Though the crowd was sufficiently thin that the three who had made it in were more than enough to handle the load. Still, it was the principle of the thing . . .

After seating a couple—Gran Marits with his latest conquest—the young Cardassian errand boy that Kurrgo had hired the previous month came running up to him. "It's Lig on the comm."

"Finally," Kurrgo muttered. He went into the back, and Lig's big-eared, small-eyed face appeared on Kurrgo's battered old viewscreen. The image started to lose focus until Kurrgo slammed the comm unit on the side. Then Lig came into full view, making Kurrgo regret going to the trouble. The Ferengi's face was easier to look at when you couldn't see it.

"*We've got a big problem,*" Lig said without preamble. "*My ship's been impounded.*"

"What? What for?"

"*Apparently, the tariffs on goods coming from Klingon territory have quadrupled in the last week. The customs officer made some comment about how we have to pay a higher price if we want anything that comes from 'those murderers' entering Cardassian space.*"

"Murderers?" Kurrgo slammed his fist into the table. "What are they talking about?"

"*Don't you watch the newsfeeds?*"

Kurrgo snarled. "No, but I have heard people talking. I thought it was just talk, though, not action."

"It is now. The tariff has gone up by a thousand leks."

"So why have they impounded your ship?"

Lig's eyes went wider than Kurrgo had thought them capable of getting. *"Because I don't have a thousand leks in my pocket, you idiot! Plus, they're levying additional fines for violating the tariff law, not to mention storage charges for the impound."* Smiling grimly, Lig added, *"There are so many additional charges, you'd think this was a Ferengi customshouse."*

"I'm glad you admire them."

"Mind you, they didn't say anything until they found the targs. *Until then, everything was business as usual. As soon as they saw that, though, they started double-checking everything, down to the stembolts. And let me tell you, the extra charges all apply* just *to the* targs."

Kurrgo sighed. "What are you going to do?"

"What am I going to do? I'm going to sit here and wait for you to come and pay all these fees so I can have my ship back. Then you can have your blessed targs *and I can get out of this madhouse."*

Kurrgo was outraged. "You expect *me* to pay *your* tariffs? I thought that was covered in our agreement!"

"This is a special case."

"No, Lig, it is not." Kurrgo leaned into the viewer. For emphasis, he grabbed a carving knife. "I have already paid for those *targs*. Our contract obligates you to pay *any* transportation fees or tariffs. You are within your rights to charge me for the goods based on what you'll have to pay, but you cannot change the price of delivery after full payment has been made."

Lig sighed. *"Leave it to me to go into business with the one Klingon who actually reads his contracts."*

"I'm a businessman just like you, Lig. Except, of course,

that I'm better with a knife than you." He started twirling the knife in a manuever that looked like he was about to cut his—or somebody else's—hand off. "And if I don't get my goods, I will declare you in breach and report it to the FCA." He smiled, twirling the knife some more. "Liquidator Gant is one of my more reliable customers." Gant was one of the Ferengi Commerce Authority's agents in charge of external affairs, and he had developed a taste for *bregit* lung. Every time he visited Cardassia Prime—which was usually at least three times a year—he had all his meals at Kurrgo's.

"*Fine, sic Gant on me,*" Lig said, sounding less intimidated than Kurrgo would have liked. "*It doesn't change the fact that I can't get at my ship and you can't get at your* targs *unless these fees are paid, and I can't pay them. Either you come here with the money, or we both lose.*"

Much as Kurrgo hated to admit it to himself, the little *toDSaH* was right. "I'm in the middle of the dinner crowd right now. I'll send Amon." Amon was the head waiter, a wily Cardassian who was smart enough to not let Lig cheat him and Cardassian enough to not be gouged too badly by the customs officers. It meant he'd be two waiters down—unless Larkan had somehow materialized in the last five minutes—but it was better than being out a shipment of *targs*. "He'll bring a chit. Whatever we pay to customs will be an advance against payment of the next shipment."

"*Just send him quickly. I've got perishables in there.*"

Kurrgo felt a momentary panic. "Aren't the *targs* in stasis?"

"*They* are, *yes. What, you think you're my only client on Cardassia? If that were the case, I'd've gone out of business years ago. As it is, if these tariffs keep up, there may not be a next shipment.*"

Only the fact that Lig had been making the same threat for years prevented Kurrgo from worrying overmuch about him making it again.

At least until he added: "*I'm serious this time, Kurrgo. The way things are going, a Ferengi can't make an honest living going back and forth between Qo'noS and Cardassia. I may have to find a less—troubled trade route.*" Before Kurrgo had a chance to reply to that, Lig signed off.

Damn him and his oversized ears. He summoned Amon to his side, handing him a blank credit chit. "Take this to the customshouse. Lig will meet you there. Find out *from the customs officers* what fees need to be paid. Pay everything directly to them. Do not put a single lek into Lig's pocket, is that understood?"

Amon smiled. "Of course."

He left. *It's not like I need all my waiters tonight in any event,* Kurrgo thought sourly, looking at all the empty tables. Usually this was the busiest time of night, yet only a quarter of the restaurant was full. He looked around the restaurant walls, covered as they were with assorted Klingon memorabilia: weapons, Klingon artwork, a fake *SoSnI'* tree, and more weapons. *Perhaps I should make the décor more Cardassian.*

His redecorating thoughts were interrupted by the arrival of three men and one woman wearing military uniforms.

No, there was a fifth with them—a stooped-over figure whose face Kurrgo could not see. At first, Kurrgo thought they were bringing a drunk in off the street, especially since the fifth figure wore civilian clothing.

Kurrgo scowled. He had little use for this world's military. Klingon soldiers were warriors, creatures of honor and duty, worthy of the highest place in Empire society. Cardassian soldiers, though, were just thugs with uniforms. Upon the newcomers' entrance, he immediately moved to the front of the restaurant to greet them before they could come any further inside. "What do you want?" he asked, trying to maintain at least a facade of pleasantness, though he clenched his fists so tightly, his fingernails drew blood.

"This creature says he belongs to you, Klingon," one of them said. He gave a signal to the one dragging the fifth figure, who tossed said figure to the floor between him and Kurrgo.

Only then did Kurrgo get a good look at the figure, and realized that it was a Klingon, his face bleeding from several cuts and covered in bruises, one eye completely sealed shut from the swelling.

It took him a moment to recognize Larkan.

"He is one of my waiters!" Kurrgo knelt down to check on the young man. He was breathing normally, if a bit raggedly.

"I—am—all—right," Larkan managed to say, spitting out blood and a tooth or two as he did so.

Standing upright, Kurrgo faced the lead Cardassian. He kept an old disruptor pistol in the back room, but he'd never get to it in time. Even the *bat'leth* on the west wall was too far to do him any good. *Besides, I will not endanger my customers.* "Who did this to him?" he asked, knowing the answer.

"He was out after curfew."

Kurrgo blinked. "What curfew?"

"The curfew that was announced this afternoon. All Klingons are to be indoors after sundown. No exceptions."

Tightly, Kurrgo said, "I was not informed of this."

The officer looked around. "Yes, I can see that you don't have any monitors in here. Why is that, I wonder?"

"My customers come here to get away from Cardassia, to get a taste of *tlhInghan'a'*." There was no adequate Cardassian way of expressing the word, which basically meant "Klingon-ness." "To have a Cardassian face prominently displayed would spoil the ambience." Clenching his fists once again, he added, "I have all the necessary permits to—"

"I do not *care* what permits you have, Klingon!" The officer spit on the floor. "This restaurant is an abomination. It offends the memory of every Cardassian who has died at Klingon hands, and will be shut down. Your waiter will be arrested for violation of curfew. You will be escorted to your home. We will no longer allow your kind to walk about freely where you can poison our children and murder our people."

At first Kurrgo was aghast. He had now moved on to furious. "This is *my* property! You cannot—"

"This is *Cardassian* property," the officer said, standing face-to-face with Kurrgo. "We simply allow you—or, rather," he added with a supercilious smile, "*allowed* you to use it to poison our people with your vile foodstuffs. But that is over now. I have orders to close this—establishment. If you need a place to work, I'm sure the mines on Bajor could use someone of your bulk." Raising his voice for all to hear, he continued: "Everyone please leave the premises immediately. This restaurant has been shut down. Anyone left within these walls in five minutes will be arrested for trespassing on Central Command property."

"You cannot do this." Kurrgo spoke the words even though he knew them to be a lie—never mind that he had indeed bought the land ten years earlier. Cardassia was a military dictatorship, after all, and that meant that people did what the military said. Now the military had, in the person of this *petaQ* of an officer, declared his deed of ownership to this restaurant null and void.

There were four of them and only one of him. They were trained in combat, where Kurrgo knew a few knife tricks that might allow him to hold his own in a one-on-one brawl. Against these odds, he'd be torn apart.

He decided to wield one last weapon. "Gul Hallitz is one of my regular customers. I do not think he will be pleased by this." In truth, he had no idea one way or the other how important Hallitz was in the grand scheme of Cardassian Central Command, nor what influence he could wield, but at this point Kurrgo had little to lose.

The officer just laughed at that, as did his fellows. "Gul Hallitz is the one who cut the orders to shut this charnel house down."

So, there it is. Kurrgo had hoped it would not come to this. But if they closed his restaurant, he had nothing. He doubted he would be able to make a third attempt to open such an establishment, and he could not live with the shame of returning to the Empire a failure twice over. *If they insist on taking my life's work, they shall do so only by stepping over my corpse to do it.*

Without any warning, he struck the lead officer on his neck under his chin. It was an especially vulnerable spot for Cardassians if one aimed it properly, and Kurrgo did — it was no doubt why they had evolved such tough chins, to protect that weakness. The officer went down like a sack of *HaroS*.

He turned to face the others, but they were too fast. Each of them had unholstered phasers and started firing.

As the phaser fire burned his flesh and muscle, as the pain lanced through his body, as the screams ripped from his throat, Kurrgo thought, *My death may not be worthy of song, but I died defending my land. I could have hoped for no better end.*

As he fell to the floor, he heard the voices of the Cardassians.

"Are you all right?"

"I'm fine." A cough. "Hadn't expected that."

"Who's Gul Hallitz, anyhow?"

"I have no idea. I just thought I'd twist the knife in that alien scum's heart is all."

Laughter.

Oddly, the treachery brought comfort to Kurrgo as he died. *At least my customers are loyal . . .*

Chapter 18

QO'NOS

Of all the mountain-climbing excursions Arn Teldin had taken on dozens of worlds throughout the quadrant, this trip to the Sutor mountains on Qo'noS had been the best yet.

The biggest problem with Cardassia II, where Teldin grew up, was its near total lack of mountains. Teldin had always felt the urge to climb, ever since he was a small boy trying to scale the tree in his backyard. The first time he went off-world was when his father's business took him to Chin'toka III, to a city near the Likra mountain range. His father wouldn't let him climb then—he was only seven—but Teldin studied climbing when he went to school, becoming a champion. He won dozens of competitions and left his mother living in constant fear for her son's life.

With adulthood came responsibility, of course. It was all well and good to indulge in one's fantasies as a youth, but Cardassia gave him a home and a life, and in return for that, he owed the state service. He became an archivist for the Central Command library, soon rising to the position of chief archivist. Eventually, after a long and distinguished career during which he revolutionized Central Command's record-keeping abilities, he retired, determined to spend the rest of his life traveling the galaxy and climbing mountains.

He'd climbed peaks all over Cardassian space and on several Federation worlds. The trip to Qo'noS had been expensive, but worth it. Klingons, for all their peculiarities, had a fondness for preservation of nature, so the wildnerness of Sutor was left mostly untouched by the ravages of industry and technology. It had been the purest climb he'd had since his school days.

Even as he waited for the transport that would take him back to the First City, where he would find lodgings before heading back home to Cardassia in the morning, he missed the sensation of rock under his hands, the searing cold air slicing into his lungs, the feel of the wind through his white hair—more, he missed the *sound* of the wind. When the transport arrived, he planned to compose a letter to his mother—still alive, and well cared for by the state—telling her of the adventure. His mother had long since given up being worried about her son's jaunts across the galaxy. Whether or not it was old age or just resignation to the inevitable, she at least no longer tried to talk him out of it, and pretended to enjoy hearing about his adventures.

It was only after he'd been at the kiosk for fifteen minutes that he noticed the odd looks he was getting from the Klingons around him.

Teldin had never given much thought to Klingons. Until coming to Qo'noS, he'd never even met one. He didn't like the way they all tended to snarl and bare their teeth and shout. But then, they probably didn't like how quiet and unassuming Teldin himself was, so he figured it all balanced out. Besides, they let him climb their mountain, and he couldn't bring himself to be too badly disposed toward them.

"Hey! Cardassian!"

Blinking, Teldin turned to the large Klingon who spoke. "Are you talking to me?"

The Klingon, who was a broad-shouldered young man with a thick beard and a wild mane of red hair framing a heavily ridged crest, laughed heartily. "Do you see any other Cardassians around, old man?"

"Er, no. Can I help you with something?"

Another laugh. "Why, yes! Yes, you can, Cardassian! You can tell me why you're here!" The Klingon walked up to Teldin and stood face-to-face with him. The Klingon's breath was beyond foul—it smelled like something that had lived a very unpleasant life died in the man's mouth. Teldin knew that Klingons had odd taste in food—he was grateful that he'd packed his own rations before leaving Cardassian space—but this was beyond the pale. "You don't belong on a Klingon world, old man!"

"I've—I've been climbing the Sutor p-peak." Teldin started to grow nervous. He was just a retired archivist, after all. In good shape for a man his age, but against one of these brutes—who lived for combat, or so he had heard—he wouldn't stand a chance. *Where is that transport?*

"Oho!" Yet another laugh. It sounded like the braying of a wompat. Several others around him joined in the laugh. Others simply moved away. "Then you haven't heard the news! The High Council has decided, in its great wisdom, to expel all you *toDSaH* from the Empire." He looked around at the crowd. "No longer will we have to allow the thieves of Ch'gran to sully our worlds!"

"Ch'gran? What are you talking about?" The Klingon was ranting. Teldin was prepared to dismiss him as a lunatic, albeit a dangerous one.

But then he saw the rest of the group waiting for the transport. Those who hadn't moved away were nodding their assent. Some were cheering. Others joined the burly red-haired one in his wompat-bray of a laugh. *Could he be speaking the truth?*

Then a noise filled Teldin's ears: the transport. It was coming down to land on a pad some distance before them. An attendant came out to take their tickets and allow them ingress to the transport—but when Teldin reached the front of the line, she would not let him through. "You may not pass."

"I beg your pardon?"

The attendant sneered. "Your kind is not permitted to mix with Klingons, murderer."

This was getting ridiculous. "I'm not a murderer."

"Tell that to the souls of the dead on the *Chut!*"

Teldin was baffled. "I don't even know what a chut is. Please, I just came here to climb the mountain, and—"

"Go back where you came from!" shouted one person from behind him on the queue.

"Thief!"

"Murderer!"

"First you soil our history, then you soil our world!"

"Cardassian filth!"

"Look," Teldin said to the attendant over the din, "I just want to get back to the First City so I can go home."

"Oh, you'll be going home, all right." The attendant signaled to someone. Teldin followed her gaze to see two Klingons in full military uniform approaching. "Just not in comfort."

The two uniformed men violently grabbed his arms. It felt like they were trying to rip them out of their sockets. As they led him off, the cheers of the crowd, particularly the laughing redhead, echoed in Arn Teldin's ears.

The *tik'leth* went flying from Kravokh's opponent's hands, clattering to the wooden floor. Kravokh stood with his *bat'leth*, smiling, ready to strike the killing blow, when Ruuv, his aide, entered the large practice room.

"Oh, good, you're practicing. You'll need it. Ditagh is dying."

Kravokh snorted. "Ditagh's been dying for years. His inability to actually take the final step has grown tiresome."

The councillor touched a control on his belt, and his opponent disappeared in a puff of photons. The holographic technology was every bit as good as the human merchant said it would be.

"What was that?" Ruuv asked.

"A holographic opponent. The Federation has perfected

the technology to the point where one can create a solid object. Makes a fine sparring partner, if programmed right." Kravokh walked over to where the *tik'leth* had landed and picked it up. "We should be trading for such technology, not holding the Federation at arm's length."

"You may have your chance to implement that plan soon."

Kravokh hung the long sword and the *bat'leth* in their respective cradles on the eastern wall of the practice room. Said wall also contained a *mek'leth* and half a dozen other weapons—some of Romulan, Vulcan, Kinshaya, and human design. The opposite wall was a giant window that looked out over the Qora forest. The array of sepia leaves and red bark against the blue-and-white sky provided a fine backdrop for his combat drills.

He regarded his aide. Ruuv was lanky, tall but with skinny shoulders. Still, Kravokh knew he was reliable in battle, and he was also a keen observer—which was why he'd made him his top aide in the first place. "Ditagh is really dying this time?"

"The doctors do not think he will last the night."

Another snort. "These same doctors said he was due to cross into *Sto-Vo-Kor* 'any minute' three months ago."

Ruuv smiled. "In fact, it is a different doctor, and she is quite sure of her diagnosis. She was convincing enough that Ditagh has named an Arbiter of Succession."

Kravokh started pacing across the wooden floor toward the window. When a chancellor died in a manner other than in combat, an Arbiter was chosen, who had the task of determining the two most qualified candidates to become the new head of the High Council. Those two then fought each other for the right to rise to the chancellorship. "Who has he named?"

"K'Tal."

Kravokh whirled away from the spectacular view to give Ruuv a shocked look. "That child?"

"I suspect that is why Ditagh chose him. He is new enough not to have any prejudices."

Laughing, Kravokh said, "Ditagh *must* be dying—it's addled his brains. Since when has he preferred those with no prejudices?"

Ruuv joined in the laugh. "It *is* a wise move. K'Tal may be young, but his House is strong, and he will be the head of that House before long. Making him Arbiter gives him a position of respect, and will indebt the next chancellor to his House even more so."

Kravokh fixed his aide with a look. "I know why it is good for K'Tal, I am merely surprised that Ditagh chose him. I would have thought he'd choose B'alikk to guarantee that the choices were palatable to Ditagh."

"I don't think any choices are palatable to Ditagh." Ruuv walked over to Kravokh's side, his boots clacking against the wooden floor. Kravokh, in the privacy of his home, had been wearing *mok'bara* shirt and pants, and had left his feet bare. "I believe that he has left the Empire in a state of disarray and would prefer the choice go to someone else."

"Of *course* he's left the Empire in a state of disarray. The amazing thing is that *he's* realized what the rest of us have been telling him for the past several years. The only concern now is who K'Tal will pick as the final two candidates."

"There is little doubt of your being one of them."

Kravokh shrugged. "Possibly."

"Definitely. The only successful programs that the High Council has put forth in the last year have come from you."

Ruuv was not one for unnecessary flattery—in fact, his brutal honesty was one of his best qualities. And in this case, he was right. Kravokh had pushed hard for a variety of programs and reforms, and all the ones he'd been able to slam through the Council—which were irritatingly few of them—had gone quite well.

"I would suggest," Ruuv said, "that you program that new hologram of yours with everything you can find about Grivak's fighting style."

Again, Kravokh laughed. "You're sure of this information?"

"Quite sure."

"Good. And you can be sure that my seat on the Council will go to you, Ruuv."

Ruuv smiled. "That has always been my goal, Kravokh. Out of curiosity, who will get the other one?"

"Assuming the other candidate is Grivak, or someone else on the Council, once I kill them, their seat will go to Captain K'mpec."

At that, Ruuv's eyes widened. "I'm not sure that is such a good idea. K'mpec disobeyed your orders at Donatu."

"And it has all worked out for the best. I have seen the record of battle for the engagement with the *Boklar*. K'mpec had no choice but to destroy the invaders. Besides," and here Kravokh smiled viciously, "the promotion of the man responsible for the destruction of the *Boklar* will send a message to Cardassia."

Ruuv didn't sound convinced. "I would think expelling all Cardassian citizens from the Empire would be message enough."

Kravokh waved him off. "That is a tiny gesture, and does nothing to get us Ch'gran back. We were a mighty Empire once. Now we are reduced to a third-rate power, letting the Federation broker competitions while Cardassians hold one of our sacred relics hostage. Meanwhile, our so-called 'leader' lets our shipyards remain closed because he refuses to bring our ties to the Federation closer! Look at this!" He activated the hologram. "We should be trading Raknal's zenite for this technology, but instead we let it sit unused. We—"

"Kravokh."

The councillor blinked.

"I am not the one you need to convince," Ruuv said with a smile. "Save this oratory for after you defeat Grivak."

This time, Kravokh's laugh was a full-throated one that echoed off the high ceiling of the practice room. "Indeed!

And when it is over, you and I—*Councillor* Ruuv—will share a drink to celebrate!"

"I look forward to it."

Ditagh died the next morning.

The *Sonchi* ceremony was held that afternoon in Council Chambers. The corpse of Ditagh sat on the large chair that was the chamber's centerpiece. Five had petitioned to be considered for the chancellorship, and all five, as well as K'Tal—whose job was to reduce that list to two—stood around the chair, along with aides and other companions, as well as the remainder of the High Council. Ruuv stood by Kravokh's side, holding his painstik.

First K'Tal walked up to the chair holding his painstik, and issued the traditional challenge. "Face me if you dare!" Then he jabbed the corpse with the painstik, its red glow spreading across the chancellor's chest.

Ditagh did not move.

The purpose of the ceremony was to verify for all to see that the old leader was truly dead. Like many old traditions, it served little purpose beyond the symbolic in this day and age. Indeed, many of the old rites had fallen away over time like the leaves off a dying tree, but this one remained.

Next was Grivak. Like Ditagh, he was a large, muscular warrior, with enough canniness to make up for an appalling lack of intelligence. His record in battle was excellent; his record in politics unspectacular. In fact, his career was similar to that of Ditagh's when he ascended, which no doubt accounted for the strength of his petition to succeed him.

"Face me if you dare," Grivak said, sounding bored. He barely touched Ditagh with the painstik.

A woman named Altrom then approached. She had no aide, and carried her own painstik. Kravokh knew her as an agitator who mainly wished to reverse Kaarg's decree that women could not serve on the Council.

"Face me," she cried, "if you *dare!*" She practically shoved the painstik through Ditagh's belly.

The other two petitioners took their turn, then, finally, it was down to Kravokh. Ruuv handed him the painstik, and he approached the corpse, now smoking with the remnants of five painstik bursts.

The erstwhile chancellor looked much older in death than he had in life. Yet part of him seemed almost—relieved? *As if the burden of the chancellorship was too much for him,* Kravokh thought. *Certainly I would not argue that point.* Ditagh had succeeded Kaarg, a reactionary chancellor whose entire platform consisted of not being Azetbur, but with no plan beyond that. The Ditagh regime was more of the same. Kravokh vowed that he would be remembered as more than the idiotic footnote that was, he hoped, the only fate that awaited Kaarg and Ditagh in the future.

"Face me if you dare," Kravokh said, and applied the painstik. And of course, Ditagh did not face him, nor anyone else. The *Sonchi* was especially fitting for a chancellor whose regime would be known as an era of doing nothing.

K'Tal then once again approached the chair, this time without the painstik, and spoke the phrase for which the ceremony was named. "He is dead."

Then the young man turned to face the five petitioners. "I will now choose the final candidates to succeed Ditagh, as laid down in the traditions of our people." K'Tal paused, letting the moment stretch. If someone with more of a sense of humor than he credited K'Tal with having were Arbiter, Kravokh would have half expected him to choose Altrom as one of the candidates. But K'Tal was in no position to make so radical a choice without dire consequences to his burgeoning career.

Several seconds passed. The politician in Kravokh admired the delaying tactic, though the warrior in him cried out for blood. Kravokh had worked his whole life for this moment, and he did not want it delayed because some boy wanted the spotlight on him for a few extra seconds.

"Kravokh, Grivak, come forward!"

It took all of Kravokh's willpower to keep from smiling.

The fight did not last very long. Kravokh had been up all the night, spending half of it researching Grivak's fighting style and programming it into his holographic sparring partner and the other half engaging the hologram in combat. Grivak's thrusts and parries were all from above—if Kravokh emphasized strokes that came from below, Grivak would have a harder time defending or moving to the offensive. Although the real Grivak proved more adaptable than the hologram—the latter was limited by the short timeframe and its programming—Kravokh still made relatively short work of his competitor.

His *bat'leth* firmly lodged in Grivak's chest, Kravokh now stood over his fallen foe. *I've done it,* he thought. *I lead the Empire.*

It almost didn't seem real. He still remembered the day he set himself on this course: it was when Kaarg announced that no women would serve on the Council shortly after he ascended. It was then that the simple thought entered his head: *I can run the Empire better than this fool.* He spent the next two decades consolidating his support, making a name for himself, gaining a seat on the High Council. Then, when the Ch'gran colony was at last found, he stepped up his efforts. The remains of Ch'gran *had* to be retrieved at all costs, and he knew that Ditagh would not—indeed could not—be the one to do it.

Now he had succeeded. The battle was won. He was chancellor.

Before him, the entire High Council, the other petitioners and their aides, all stood. Several of them cheered his name, as they had been doing since the tide of victory started to stem his way during the fight with Grivak.

The first order of business was to honor his fallen foe. Though Grivak was an unworthy fool, he died a good death, and deserved all considerations due him for that. Kravokh knelt down, pried open the warrior's eyes, and then screamed to the heavens. Around him, the other Klingons did likewise, warning the Black Fleet that another Klingon warrior was crossing the River of Blood to *Sto-Vo-Kor*. Their screams echoed throughout the high-ceilinged chamber for several seconds after the screams themselves ceased.

Then Kravokh rose and walked over to the chair on which Ditagh's corpse still sat. As he did so, the assembled Klingons rumbled in anticipation of Kravokh's first words as the new Klingon supreme commander.

"Centuries ago, Ch'gran ventured forth into the black sky to bring greatness to our people after the Hur'q left us ravaged. The destruction of Praxis left us ravaged again, and we have let the Empire flounder and grow weak. We have even let the remains of Ch'gran—found after all these turns—lie fallow in the hands of outsiders."

He walked back to Grivak's corpse and yanked his *bat'leth* from his fallen foe's chest. Holding it aloft, the blade dripping Grivak's blood onto the chamber floor, he continued. "Today dawns a new day for the Empire. No longer will we sit while the Federation and the Cardassians grow stronger! No longer shall we allow outsiders to sully our sacred relics! Cardassians will remain pariahs on our worlds! Any Cardassian ship that violates our borders will meet the same fate as the *Boklar*! And Raknal V *will* be ours! The Klingon Empire will once again be a force to be reckoned with! We will be strong! We are Klingons, and we will achieve our destiny!"

All of those present cheered his words, even those who, Kravokh knew, were his enemies, for none could deny the heart of what he said. Even Ditagh's most fervent supporters knew that it was time for a change.

Kravokh would bring about that change. And he would bring Ch'gran home to Qo'noS. That was the most important thing of all . . .

PART 3

FIERCE FLAMES BURNT ROUND THE HEAVENS

2343–2346

Chapter 19

SHUTTLECRAFT WOODLAWN

"Have you found her yet?"

Lieutenant Elias Vaughn—or, rather, Lieutenant Commander Elias Vaughn; he still wasn't used to the new rank—spoke through gritted teeth as he piloted the shuttlepod through the turbulent storm that was ravaging the northern continent of Devniad, the restraining straps cutting into his chest. The *Woodlawn* was a small craft, with only room for four people to sit, and at that it was cramped. All remaining space was given over to the experimental warp engine—*and why they felt the need to field-test the new miniature propulsion system on this mission is a question I will probably never get an adequate answer to,* Vaughn thought as he compensated for yet another updraft. The staccato pounding of the rain against the hull and viewport combined with the difficult maneuvering to give him a sharp pain behind his right eye that he knew would be a full-blown headache in about five minutes.

Next to him, Lieutenant Commander T'Prynn manipulated her console, a receiver protruding from her pointed left ear. "I am still registering neither a human life sign, nor any signal that can be identified as Federation." She looked over at Vaughn. "We have now scanned the entire continent. Logic suggests that we expand our search."

"If nothing else, the weather's probably better." Vaughn set a new course. "Can't imagine how a Federation special emissary would get to another continent while a hostile military takeover's going on around her, but you're right—it *is* the most logical course of action."

One of T'Prynn's eyebrows climbed up her forehead. "Do you not believe that Special Emissary Tartovsky is capable of fending for herself?"

"If she is, she's unique among the diplomats that I've known." Gunning the thrusters, Vaughn took the shuttle southward—the next nearest continent on Devniad was to the south—and keeping an eye on the sensors for Cardassian ships. So far, their tiny shuttle had evaded detection, but that couldn't possibly last. *Damn you, Tartovsky, why couldn't you stay put so we could have found you and gotten you out?*

But that was hardly fair. All Vaughn knew for sure was that the Cardassians had suddenly, and violently, taken over this planet in neutral space while Raisa Tartovsky was in the process of negotiating a trade agreement with the natives. According to the gul in the fancy new ship of a type that Starfleet Intelligence had thought was still on the drawing board, Federation citizens were permitted to remain on-planet but would be subject to Cardassian law.

Relations with the Cardassians and the Klingons deteriorating, while both powers are engaged in a massive military buildup. Relations with the Romulans nonexistent. Relations with the Tholians and the Tzenkethi never all that great to begin with. We do live in interesting times. The Federation was on the brink of four potential wars—five, if you counted the Romulans, which Vaughn generally did. True, they'd been withdrawn since Tomed, but Vaughn was *there* for Tomed, and he knew that the Romulans' isolationism would not be permanent.

"Approaching the southern continent." Vaughn noted with relief that the rainstorm did not extend southward, and the weather was clearer. Unfortunately, that also meant that the shuttle was not masked by cloud and rain cover, which made their being seen by the Cardassians a greater likelihood. He deliberately did not mention this to T'Prynn, as her quoting the odds of same would just add to his headache.

"I am receiving a Federation signal," T'Prynn said. She adjusted her console. "Computer verifies that it is the frequency and code assigned to Special Emissary Tartovsky. However—" She hesitated. "I am receiving no readings from that position."

T'Prynn had transferred the coordinates of the signal to Vaughn's display. "No life signs means she may be dead." *Dammit.*

"I did not say there were no life signs, Commander, but that I am receiving no readings. However, scans indicate a cave system at those coordinates, and the initial planetary geological survey of Devniad indicated a high fistrium content in the crust."

"So Tartovsky could be alive and hiding where she can't be scanned. Luckily, her transmitter can penetrate the fistrium."

Again, T'Prynn's eyebrow raised. "Fistrium only interferes with the signals from sensors and transporters. There is no evidence that it has ever impaired subspace transmissions."

Vaughn smiled through his recently grown salt-and-pepper beard. "Isn't that what I said? I'm going to bring her in for a landing."

"Acknowledged. And, of course, the fistrium has also rendered moot your objection to this vehicle."

I guess I should have expected that, Vaughn thought, holding in a sigh. He found a clearing about ten meters from the source of the signal where he could put down the *Woodlawn.* When he and T'Prynn had been given this assignment, Vaughn had objected to their being issued an experimental shuttle with no transporters. After all, transporters were a most valuable tool in an extraction. However, they needed a warp-capable craft small enough to avoid easy detection by the Cardassian conquerors. The fresh-out-of-the-shipyards *Woodlawn* fit the bill, but it was too small to be equipped with a transporter.

Ever since Ian Troi saved his life with a shuttle transporter in the Betreka Nebula, Vaughn had come to appreciate shuttles that were so equipped.

As he brought the pod down, he thought about Ian. When Rachel Garrett was given the *Enterprise,* Ian had been promoted to second officer of the *Carthage,* and he was likely to become first officer any day now. Vaughn hadn't seen him since Kestra's funeral. The thought of that poor child drowning at such a young age made the sixty-eight-year-old Vaughn grateful that he'd had as much life as he did—and, at the same time, feel deeply sorry for Ian and Lwaxana that their oldest daughter would not have that opportunity.

Good Lord, that was seven years ago. Deanna's the same age now that Kestra was when she died. Time's slipping away too damn fast. He made a mental note to send a letter to Ian on the *Carthage* when he got back to the starbase.

But first, he thought as he touched the *Woodlawn* down on the dirt of Devniad's southern continent, *to business.*

Just as Vaughn unbuckled himself from his seat, T'Prynn said, "Picking up several Cardassian life signs—one-point-three kilometers away and closing." She looked over at him. "It is likely that they also detected Special Emissary Tartovsky's signal and are tracking it. You must move with dispatch."

Smiling grimly, Vaughn grabbed a tricorder from the small supply cabinet under the console. "I wasn't planning to dawdle, believe me."

Opening the hatch, he stepped out into the warm air. A stiff breeze blew through his graying hair, and he had to hold up his hand to shield his eyes from the bright, red sun.

Gazing down at the tricorder, he confirmed that Tartovsky's signal was coming from a position nine-and-a-half meters from where he stood. He was also picking up a human life sign. *How the hell—?* Then he realized—from the ground, he could detect Tartovsky through the mouth of the cave in which she hid. But that also meant that those Cardassians—who were now just one kilometer away and closing awfully fast—could also detect that life sign. Not to mention Vaughn, T'Prynn, and the shuttlepod . . .

Pumping his legs—with, he was proud to say, the same vim and vigor with which he ran as a youth in the Academy—Vaughn dashed toward the cave mouth. Pulling up seconds later, he saw a two-meter-wide opening in a large chunk of rock that looked like it was embedded in a grassy hill. *Not a bad hiding spot*, Vaughn thought, revising his estimate of Tartovsky upward a bit.

Proceeding slowly into the much cooler cave, he activated the light beacon on his tricorder. All it served to do was illuminate sheer rock.

"Don't move!" cried out a female voice from deeper inside the cave. Vaughn shone his light toward the voice, and the beam framed a round face that blinked in the onslaught of light. Said onslaught did not cause her to lower the phaser pistol she held in her right hand.

"Special Emissary Tartovsky, I presume. I'm Lieutenant Elias Vaughn from Starfleet. I'm here to get you out of here. I have a shuttle."

"Nice try. You should tell your Cardassian masters to train your spies better."

What the hell is she talking about?

"That rank insignia on your shoulder patch is for a lieutenant commander, not a lieutenant."

Hell's teeth, he thought. *Of all the times for a slip of the tongue . . .* "I was only recently promoted, ma'am. I need you to put the phaser down so we can get out of here."

"Recently promoted? You look like you're at least fifty. Still only a lieutenant?"

"Lieutenant commander, as you pointed out, ma'am. We really need to leave."

She shook her head and made a *tcha* noise. "You Cardassians are pathetic. You definitely need a better breed of spy. If you're so damn good at rescue missions, why are you still a lieutenant at your age?"

Because the kind of work I do requires a low profile, but telling you that would go against that very principle. "Ma'am, there are actual Cardassians on the way who will most likely shoot both of us if we don't get to my shuttlepod and get out of here. In fact—oh, the hell with it." With one swift motion, he unholstered his own phaser and shot the special emissary.

She crumpled to the ground, stunned.

Vaughn ran over to her unconscious form. He saw that she was bleeding from a badly bandaged wound in her leg. *She'd have fallen unconscious from blood loss if we'd kept up that inane conversation much longer.* Under any other circumstances, he would have been willing to wait her out, but they didn't have the time. Picking her up in a rescue carry and securing her with his right arm, he ran back out the way he came, the hot air blasting him in the face as he exited the cave.

Tapping his combadge with the butt of the phaser he held in his left hand as he ran, he said, "Vaughn to T'Prynn. Get ready to go, Commander."

"Cardassian patrol approaching. They will be within sight of the Woodlawn *in thirty-five seconds, Elias."*

No way he'd be able to close the distance that quickly—not while burdened with Tartovsky. And the *Woodlawn* wasn't armed.

"The hatch is open, and I am armed with a phaser rifle, Commander. I will cover your approach."

Vaughn grinned. "You read my mind, Commander."

"Hardly."

The *Woodlawn* came into Vaughn's sight just as the phaser fire went flying over his head. *Dammit,* he thought as he fired back.

Another shot hit about a meter in front of him, tossing rocks and dirt into the air. Pain sliced across Vaughn's head as one rock collided with his forehead. *And here I was hoping to stave off that headache.*

He ran around to see a Cardassian trading phaser fire with T'Prynn. Said Cardassian was between Vaughn and the *Woodlawn* hatch. Vaughn fired off a quick shot, which missed, and a second, which didn't. Between those two, the Cardassian took a shot into the *Woodlawn* before collapsing to the ground.

Vaughn yelled, "Go!" even as he leapt into the *Woodlawn*'s rear two seats, his own body and that of Tartovsky forming a rather ungainly pile in the shuttlepod.

To his irritation, the shuttle did not move.

Clambering up from under the unconscious special emissary, he saw why: the Cardassian's last shot had apparently hit T'Prynn in the shoulder. Green blood pooled under her red uniform and also poured forth from a wound in her head. *Dammit.*

Slamming his hand on the control that would close the hatch, Vaughn got into the pilot seat and noted that T'Prynn had already run the preflight sequence—all that was left was for the hatch to close and for Vaughn to engage the engines. Pausing only for a half a second to smile at his comrade—a pause he needed to take while waiting for the hatch to seal in any event—he then lifted off, the sound of Cardassian phaser fire hitting the shuttlepod's hull with the same intensity that the rain was hitting it less than half an hour earlier.

Now let's hope we're small enough to stay off the sensor screens of those big ships in orbit—which are now looking for a small Starfleet shuttlepod. Well, nobody said this job would be easy.

Chapter 20

CARDASSIA PRIME

It had been fifteen years since Corbin Entek had set foot in the Obsidian Order's fifty-story public headquarters in the cul-de-sac. Back then, he was being debriefed by Enabran Tain himself on the disastrous Raknal V negotiations. Since then, Entek had thrived, becoming a top operative for the Obsidian Order.

In all that time, he had never again laid eyes on Tain. He had simply received instructions from assorted supervisors and then carried out his assignments. He had the feeling that soon he would be one of the supervisors rather than the supervised, and in fact he'd hoped that this summons would be a prelude to that.

A different receptionist sat at the main desk, of course, and instead of a retinal scanner, he now had to place his hand on a device that would verify his DNA.

Once again, Entek was to report to Room 2552. *Tain again*. Entek was pleasantly surprised.

When he arrived on the twenty-fifth floor, Entek saw that a different woman, this one with longer, blacker hair, now sat at the workstation outside Tain's office. As her predecessor had a decade-and-a-half earlier, this woman activated her comm unit and said simply, "He's arrived."

"Send him in."

Entek entered Tain's office to find that, unlike the identity of his assistant, very little had changed. The office was still sparsely furnished, the east wall still contained a large viewer—this time the image was of the Dakhur Hills on Bajor. Entek chose to take this as a good sign. He knew that there was a supervisory position open administering Order affairs on Bajor, and he had hopes for it. Central Command had, typically, let the situation on Bajor get out of hand. The resistance movement was growing in strength and needed to be crushed. Central Command's more overt methods were not getting the job done, and it was Entek's considered opinion that more subtle means were required.

Of course, it was also possible that Entek was not here to receive good news. One thing he had learned in his time as an agent of the Order: it was best *not* to come to the attention of Enabran Tain if you could avoid it. If he had known fifteen years ago what he knew now, he would have approached his Tain-led debriefing following Raknal with a great deal more trepidation.

One other thing had changed over the years: Tain was a lot bulkier around the middle than he had been. *I suppose that comes of working in an office rather than out in the field.*

"Come in, Entek, come in, have a seat," Tain said.

Entek sat down, noting that the guest chair was of a different type than the one from fifteen years ago, and yet it felt the same: neither particularly comfortable nor uncomfortable. It served its purpose as a chair, no more, no less.

"The last time you were in this office, you asked me if you would be assigned to Raknal V. I told you then that you were too young, too raw to take such an assignment." He chuckled. "I never imagined that the situation would still be an issue fifteen years later. How closely have you followed the situation with the Klingons?"

"As closely as duties have allowed," Entek said honestly. "I do know that no Klingons have been permitted on our worlds and that the Klingons have done the same to our people in their territory. Border skirmishes have been on the upswing."

Another chuckle. "That is an understatement. Any time a Cardassian ship and a Klingon ship are within a parsec of each other, there's a good chance of torpedoes being exchanged sooner rather than later. The *Grannal*, the *Pa'Dan*, and the *Baknab* have all been engaged by Klingon ships in the past month alone. The Klingons still blame us for the *Chut*'s destruction, and they're very good at holding grudges. In addition, relations with the Federation have gotten worse since that incident with the *Enterprise* seven years ago." Tain shook his head. "There was a confrontation just yesterday— the *Alkar* got into a running firefight with a Federation ship, the *Stargazer*. Every attempt at trade talks with the Federation have failed, and Central Command insists on being aggressive with them and letting the situation grow worse. An all-out war is one thing, but these hostile skirmishes with both powers without a formal declaration pick away at us."

With that, Entek had to agree. He also was starting to suspect the true reason for his summons. "It does not bode well. There are also rumblings on Romulus. Praetor Dralath is losing popular support, and their emperor has become little more than a figurehead. It is quite possible that they may come out of the shell they have been hiding in since Tomed and strike at either the Klingons or the Federation—or even us."

That seemed to intrigue Tain. "What leads you to that conclusion?"

Entek shifted nervously in his seat. He had made a report to this effect only the previous week, and his new assumption was that it had come to Tain's attention, hence his summons here. "Dralath is not an imaginative man. The Romulan economy is failing, the people are disaffected. Successful Romulan politicians tend toward long-term planning, but every indication points to Dralath being an unsuccessful one. His profile is one that prefers simple short-term solutions."

"You believe he will start a war."

It was not a question. *Perhaps he* has *read the report.* "It is a common solution to declining popularity among ineffectual leaders. And we would be a ripe target—an upstart power that is already in conflict with the Klingons and the Federation."

"A fine observation." Tain smiled. "To answer your unspoken question, yes I read your report. It is a very canny analysis, and indicates that we need to do further study of the Romulans, especially while Dralath remains in power." Entek tried not to be too obvious in letting his pride show. "In the meantime, however, there is the matter of our continued difficulties with the Federation and the Klingons. If the Romulans are planning an assault on us, we need to be prepared, not engaged in petty squabbles. Federation–Klingon relations are not at their best at the moment, but they might well unite to fight a common enemy in us."

A thought occurred to Entek. "The same might be true if the Romulans attack one of them."

"If they choose to go that way, yes." Tain leaned back. "What we have here, Entek, is a powder keg, one that will explode in the face of Cardassia no matter who lights it. What we need to do is apply some water. The root and cause of all our difficulties with the Klingons is Raknal V. Central Command insists that all is well on the planet. I'm more skeptical. Our last operative on-world was killed in what appears to have been an accident—certainly the planet has had enough of them. However, it was probably an assassination by one of Prefect Monor's lackeys."

Entek tried to avoid a sigh. This was not what he had been hoping for. Fifteen years ago, he had been eager to return to Raknal V; now, the planet held little interest for him. Bajor was, to his mind, more important to Cardassia's future.

Tain, however, thought otherwise, and Entek knew better than to argue with him. "What is my assignment to be?"

Tain leaned forward. Up until now, his tone had been pleasant, conversational—he discussed the political situation in the quadrant with all the ease and comfort of an uncle chatting about the latest sporting events with a favorite nephew. Now, though, his voice hardened, his hands folded on his immaculate desk. "Cardassia needs fewer enemies right now. The longer the situation on Raknal goes on, the more likely it is that we will have to go to war. Klingon military forces have built up impressively since Chancellor Kravokh came to power, and our own forces are divided among the Federation, the Klingons, and internal difficulties on Bajor and Chin'toka VI—and Raknal V, which now has a garrison dedicated to defending it, despite its distance. What I want from you, Entek, is to observe the situation on Raknal V. Central Command may be convinced that it's worth devoting the resources to; I'm not. If it's possible to cede the planet to the Klingons and end this—and give them their precious Ch'gran relic back—I think it's something we should consider."

Where fifteen years ago, Entek considered Tain to be sensible, despite Entek's enthusiasm, for not sending him to Raknal V, now Entek thought Tain unwise for doing so. Entek's expertise was on the Romulans and the Bajorans. Why devote such a resource to a backwater planet that was the flashpoint of a conflict with a species Entek hadn't even thought about since he disembarked from the *Carthage* a decade and a half ago?

But he also knew better than to question an assignment from Tain himself. Just the fact that he was leaving this office in one piece—and with an assignment that the head of the Order considered important—spoke well for Entek's future.

Tain stood up. Entek did likewise. "Your supervisor will have all the details of your cover on Raknal V at your next meeting. Make your reports to her."

Entek nodded and turned to leave.

"Oh, and Entek?"

He stopped and turned to face Tain again.

"I told you once that I make use of my valuable resources." Entek noted that the avuncular tone had returned, as had his bland smile. "I still do."

The words did not fill the older Entek with the same pride as they did the younger one, but he, at the very least, was willing to take it guardedly as a good sign . . .

Chapter 21

STARBASE 47

"Starbase 47, this is the shuttlecraft *Woodlawn* requesting permission to dock."

"This is starbase control. You are cleared to dock at Pad E."

Wiping the blood on his forehead away from his eyes, Elias Vaughn said, "Thank you, starbase control. We'll need a medic to meet us—we've got wounded."

"Acknowledged."

Vaughn looked over at the still-unconscious forms of Special Emissary Tartovsky—who would no doubt be fuming when she awoke—and Commander T'Prynn—who would not be. "Oh," he added, "and tell Chief DeMartis that I banged up his shuttle."

"He'll be devastated, I'm sure," the starbase control officer said dryly. DeMartis was the one in charge of the team that built the *Woodlawn*, and Vaughn had spent the hour before the mission listening to the young man go on at some length about the pod's capabilities, limitations, and, above all, the necessity of bringing it back in one piece.

After he brought the shuttle in for a landing on the designated pad, he opened the hatch to see three people in white medical uniforms, one in the red-and-white engineering uniform—DeMartis, with an expression on his face indicating that someone should draw a dark cloud over his head—and an elegant-looking older woman in a captain's uniform, who was the last person Vaughn expected to see.

"Captain Uhura. This is a surprise." And, given Uhura's position at Starfleet Intelligence, which was arguably as high as it got, rank notwithstanding—Vaughn wasn't the only one who kept a low profile, after all—probably not a good surprise.

"Walk with me, Commander," she said in an almost musical tone of voice that couldn't hide the fact that she was here on serious business.

Pausing only to give the medics a quick précis of what he knew of the damage T'Prynn and Tartovsky had taken, and to ignore the wails of agony coming from DeMartis, Vaughn did so.

They walked through the hallways of Starbase 47 in silence for several seconds. Finally, she asked, "Your mission went well?"

"About as well as expected."

Uhura smiled. "That bad?"

Returning the smile, Vaughn said, "We did what we were supposed to. I had been hoping to extract Special Emissary Tartovsky without drawing any attention from the Cardassians, but I knew that was wishful thinking. I'm content with the fact that we got the emissary and ourselves—and Chief DeMartis's precious shuttlepod—back in one piece."

"More or less. How did Commander T'Prynn and the emissary—and you—get hurt?"

Vaughn told her. When he got to the bit in the cave, it prompted a pleasant laugh from the elderly captain that sounded like wind chimes. *Elderly, listen to me. She may have passed her hundredth birthday, but she's as formidable a presence as she was when I first met her. More, even. I hope I'm half as sharp when I hit her age.*

When he finished his tale, Uhura said, "I've met several diplomats in my time for whom shooting would have been a useful option to have. In any case, this latest bit of Cardassian imperialism has a lot of people worried. They've made similar moves in the Bryma, Umoth, and Cuellar systems in the last year. The Cardassians are building their forces, and getting into more skirmishes with us and the Klingons. Did you hear about what happened with the *Stargazer* two weeks ago?"

Vaughn nodded. He had met Jean-Luc Picard a few months earlier, and knew that the younger man had a reputation for not ducking a fight—this one, though, he ran from. The Cardassians were definitely getting more aggressive.

Uhura continued. "To make matters worse, the Klingons are doing likewise, and starting to remember what it's like to be a major power—and an enemy of the Federation—again."

Vaughn frowned. "You think they're gearing up for war?"

"I think they both wanted to fight a war fifteen years ago over Raknal V. Ambassador Dax managed to put that off by pulling a rabbit out of his hat, but now it's coming to a head again. And if it does happen, we'll *all* feel the effects."

"Why are you telling *me* this, Captain?" Vaughn asked, though he suspected he knew the answer, given that he was *at* Raknal V when Dax came up with his so-called rabbit.

"To the point, as usual, eh, Commander?" Waving off Vaughn's slightly abashed look, she said, "It's all right. To the point, then: I want you to go to Raknal V and check up on things."

Snorting, Vaughn asked, "Shouldn't that be Ambassador Dax's job?"

"Dax isn't Starfleet. And he has a vested interest in telling us what we want to hear. I'd rather be told what I *don't* want to hear—and you've always been very good at that."

Vaughn smirked. "Is that a compliment, Captain?"

"A fact, Commander." They arrived at Uhura's office. The doors parted to reveal a small space, with a desk, workstation, and an entire wall decorated with various exotic sculptures, masks, and a Vulcan lute that looked to Vaughn's eye as if it had to be at least eighty years old. As Uhura took her seat at the desk, she looked at the computer screen on her desk. "Your orders are to observe the situation and report back." She looked up and fixed him with a penetrating gaze. "I want a *full* report, Commander. Not just facts—I can get those anyplace. I want your *opinion* as to the situation on Raknal V, and what it means for Starfleet, and for the Federation. Is that clear?"

"Crystal, sir."

Then Uhura smiled, and the room seemed to brighten. "One bit of good news—you'll be going back the same way you went there last time. The *Carthage* is in the area, and I had her diverted. Captain Haden will be by to pick you up tomorrow. That will give you enough time to make sure that Commander T'Prynn is well and is also soon enough for you to avoid Special Emissary Tartovsky's wrath."

"It's appreciated, Captain," Vaughn said, referring to both the consideration regarding T'Prynn and Tartovsky and the fact that he'd be back on the *Carthage. Now I'll get to see Ian without having to write the letter.*

Chapter 22

I.K.S. PU'BEKH

When the beams deposited Councillor K'mpec in the *Pu'Bekh*'s transporter room, he felt a swell of pride. *It is good to feel these deckplates beneath my boots once again.* Although K'mpec eagerly took his position on the High Council when Kravokh offered it to him nine years ago, he sometimes missed running a space-faring vessel. The *Pu'Bekh* was K'mpec's first (and only) ship command. It was like your first kill—nothing else tastes quite so sweet. That was why, when he decided to take this inspection tour of an assortment of Defense Force vessels, he made sure that this ship was at the top of the list. The other stops on his tour were chosen at random, but he saw no reason to pass up the opportunity to revisit an old battleground.

His successor, Captain Mogh, was standing before him. "It is good to see you again, Councillor K'mpec," the captain said with his usual formality.

K'mpec laughed as he stepped down from the platform, his boots echoing solidly on the stairs. "Why so formal, old friend?" He slapped Mogh on the shoulder. "It is good to see you. How is your son?"

At the mention of his child, Mogh's face broke into a smile the likes of which K'mpec had never seen on his former first officer before the boy's birth. "Young Worf is three now. Kaasin tells me he has already learned how to hold the family *bat'leth*."

"With any luck, he will wield it more skillfully than his father."

At that, both men laughed. "He could hardly do otherwise. Kaasin has employed a nurse—I think you'd like her. Her name is Kahlest, and Worf adores her."

"I look forward to meeting her—and seeing your son wield the weapons of a warrior." He slapped Mogh on the shoulder. "Come. It has been too long since we shared a meal and a mug of *warnog*."

"Indeed it has. And such a meal has been prepared—for three."

"Anh?" K'mpec didn't like the sound of that.

Mogh's old formality quickly returned. "An old family friend is on board, sir. When he heard you would be taking this tour, he arranged to be on board as well. He wishes to speak with both of us."

K'mpec frowned. He did not like surprises. Still and all, he followed the captain out of the transporter room. Trailed by two guards—Mogh's own personal guard and the one that had been assigned to K'mpec—they proceeded to the captain's cabin.

With a grinding rumble, the door opened to reveal the smell of fresh *rokeg* blood pie, *racht*, *bregit* lung, and plenty of *warnog*. K'mpec smiled, and both his stomachs—which had grown distressingly wide in his years on the High Council—rumbled in anticipation.

That smile turned into a frown when he saw the room's occupant.

"Lorgh." The word came out as a low rumble from deep within K'mpec's throat, almost harmonically balanced with his hungry stomachs. "This I.I. *petaQ* is your 'old family friend'?"

"Yes," Mogh said simply. The door closed behind him,

leaving both guards outside. Mogh took a seat, as did Lorgh. K'mpec remained standing, staring angrily at the I.I. agent.

Smiling widely, Lorgh asked, "Aren't you glad to see me, K'mpec?"

"I have no use for you, Lorgh, nor for the rest of your organization." K'mpec practically spat the words.

"We're aware of your designs to have Imperial Intelligence disbanded, K'mpec."

K'mpec snorted. "I have made no secret of it. Nor do I make a secret of this, now: I will not eat with you. I will not drink with you. Leave this ship, or I will have you put to death."

"This is *my* ship, K'mpec." Mogh, as ever, spoke in a respectful, professional tone. "And Lorgh was a friend to my father. That makes him a friend to me."

That was foolish, K'mpec admonished himself. If K'mpec took any action against Lorgh, Mogh would feel the need to avenge it. Mogh was passionate about few things, but family loyalty was one of them. The more time had passed, the more certain K'mpec was that Mogh had made sure that the *Boklar* and Gul Onell were destroyed nine years ago to avenge his father's death at Onell's sister's hands. Three years ago, Mogh and his mate, Kaasin, had their first child, a son, whom they had named Worf after the boy's grandfather. If Lorgh was a friend to the dead general, then he was a friend to Mogh, and therefore a friend to K'mpec as long as he considered Mogh a friend.

K'mpec had been able to use Mogh's actions against the *Boklar* in his favor, as they put him in the good graces of Kravokh when he rose to power. K'mpec had aspirations of his own, after all. And Mogh was now a ship captain, who owed that posting to K'mpec, and who, in turn, commanded great loyalty. It was an alliance K'mpec could not afford to jeopardize just because he despised Imperial Intelligence and all it stood for.

At least not now.

"Very well." K'mpec sat his ample frame down in the third chair, gathering his floor-length cassock around him. "I will hear your words, Lorgh."

Chewing on a couple of serpent worms, Lorgh said, "That is quite generous of you, K'mpec." He swallowed his *racht,* washed it down with some *warnog,* then let his own smile fall. "I can assure you, what I have to say is of great moment."

"So you indicated." Mogh stuffed a piece of *bregit* lung into his mouth.

Lorgh looked at the captain. "Years ago, your father told me of knowledge he had of certain Klingon Houses' dealings with the Romulans. The House of Duras, for example, sold ships to the Romulan military."

"That was decades ago," K'mpec said dismissively as he cut off a slice of blood pie.

"So was Praxis. But its destruction led to economic ruin for many strong Houses—and opportunities for smaller ones to improve their fortunes. There are many Houses—some of whom have ample representation on the Council—who owe a great deal to Romulan assistance given during the last four decades."

K'mpec frowned. He knew that several of his fellow councillors had favored keeping good relations with Romulus. K'mpec hadn't given it much consideration one way or the other, seeing as how the Romulans had remained isolationist for the most part since Tomed.

Mogh asked, "How much of this is due to the influence of the House of Duras?"

"It is safe to say that it is considerable."

"Based on what?" K'mpec asked.

Lorgh regarded K'mpec with a withering expression. "Intelligence we have gathered."

This provoked a deep-throated growl from K'mpec. "Be

wary, Lorgh. I do not appreciate being lectured to by the likes of you."

"I.I. knew of some of this, but since General Worf's death, I have pursued the matter more closely. I have learned two things. One is that many on the High Council are linked to the very Houses that owe the Romulans a considerable debt."

"So you said. Have you any proof?"

Lorgh smiled. "Nothing I could present in a *meqba'*, but I do trust my sources."

Before K'mpec could object further to this foolishness, Mogh said, "What is the second thing you have learned?"

K'mpec had to force himself not to call his former first officer a fool for even listening to this, but he held back. Lorgh, curse him, had chosen his words wisely when he mentioned the involvement of the House of Duras. The rivalry between that House and Mogh's own went back several generations. In fact, K'mpec had contributed to it when he chose Mogh as his first officer over Ja'rod, the current House head. Regardless, if the House of Duras was involved, Mogh would be interested.

"The current Romulan praetor, Dralath, is losing the support of his people and the military. The former are chafing under economic restrictions that threaten to crush them, and the latter grow frustrated with their continued isolationism. Their emperor is an old weakling. Dralath may decide to restore his position by making a strike against us."

K'mpec stood up. "I will listen to no more of this idiocy. I do not know what game I.I. is playing, Lorgh, but you may remove my piece from the board."

Mogh also rose. "K'mpec, at least hear him out."

"I have heard all that I need to. If Romulus has such influence over the High Council, why would they attack us? And why would they break over thirty years of hiding now?" With that, K'mpec turned and moved toward the door. "I assume the guard you assigned me can escort me to my cabin."

As the door opened at K'mpec's approach, Lorgh said, "We are letting ourselves be distracted, K'mpec. This ongoing conflict with the Cardassians, tension with the Federation when they have been naught but our staunch allies—it leaves us vulnerable. Romulans are like *wam* serpents: they can sense weakness, and then they strike."

"Mneh." The grunt was all K'mpec could bring himself to say as he departed. *Let Mogh believe this I.I. fool. I will have no part of it.*

Lorgh's final comments were not entirely wrong, of course. Kravokh had insisted on being aggressive with the Cardassians and with the exploitation of Raknal V to a degree that was well out of proportion to the rewards that would be gained. Yes, Ch'gran needed to be restored to the Klingon people, but after so long, it would hardly have the impact on the populace as it would have fifteen years ago. Unfortunately, that single-mindedness led Kravokh to avoid coming to any kind of decision regarding the Federation. Kaarg and Ditagh's incompetence had let the alliance that Gorkon and Azetbur built begin to crumble, and Kravokh was doing nothing to rebuild the foundation.

But the Romulans? No. I will believe such tales when they come from the mouth of one I can trust. Never will such a mouth belong to an agent of Imperial Intelligence.

Chapter 23

U.S.S. CARTHAGE

"When you gonna be home 'gain, Daddy?"

The plaintive tone in his daughter Deanna's voice made Ian Troi's heart break. It had only been a few months since he'd last gotten home to Betazed—and that only because Captain Haden had found an excuse for the *Carthage* to be in the sector—but to a seven-year-old, a few months was an eternity.

"Soon, Durango, I promise," he said, using the nickname he'd given her during one of their joint readings from Troi's large collection of Westerns. "Daddy has to finish another mission on his ship, and then we'll all be together again, okay?"

Deanna pouted. *"Okay,"* she said, not sounding in the least bit happy about it. *"Why do you have to be far away all the time?"*

"Because Daddy's doing what he loves."

"Don't you love me and Mommy?"

His heart broke all over again. "More than you could ever know, Durango. And when I come home, you'll see just how much." He smiled. "I may even have a surprise for you."

At that, Deanna's black eyes widened. *"A surprise? Really? What'll it be?"*

"If I told you, it wouldn't be a surprise, now would it?"

"I guess." Deanna didn't sound convinced. But this was

one area where Troi would never give in. After years of being unable to surprise his wife, thanks to her telepathy, he took great joy in being able to at the very least surprise his children, at least until they developed telepathic skills of their own as teenagers.

Assuming that at least one of them lives that long. The thought fell into his head unbidden, and he banished it quickly, along with the image of poor Kestra's face that accompanied it.

"I can't stay on too much longer, Durango, so why don't you put Mommy on, okay?"

"Can we read Cowboy Ralph *again when you come home?"*

Troi sighed. The *Cowboy Ralph* adventures by a twenty-second-century hack writer named Ernest Pratt were Deanna's favorites—and also by far the worst in Troi's extensive collection. *Does she like Zane Grey or Larry McMurtry? No, she goes for Ernest Pratt. There's no justice.* However, he gamely said, "Of course we can, Durango. Now put Mommy on, okay?"

A smile brightened the seven-year-old's face. *"Okay, Daddy. I love you!"*

"I love you, too!"

Deanna ran off, her black curls bouncing, and Lwaxana's lovely face filled the screen a second later. *"I'm sorry, dear one, but I couldn't* bear *to read that* Cowboy Fred *any longer. So she's been a bit deprived of her precious Eastern books lately."*

Troi laughed. "It's Ralph, and they're Westerns." Sometimes Troi was convinced that his wife deliberately misremembered things in order to draw attention to herself. Of course, everything about Lwaxana was designed to do that. "And it's not a problem. I'm just glad she still likes them."

"Is it true that you'll be coming home after this assignment?"

"Captain Haden's approved my leave. But they need me for this one—we're going back to Betreka." He smiled. "It's actually like old home week. We're ferrying Elias to Raknal V."

"*Dear Elias. How is he?*"

"We haven't picked him up yet, but I'm sure he's fine. Of course, I haven't seen him since—"

"*That reception on Babel ten years ago, wasn't it? That was such a lovely time. Elias can be quite the gentleman when he isn't being all special-operations stuffy.*"

Troi closed his eyes, counted to ten in Greek, and then said, "Of course." In truth, they had both last seen Elias Vaughn at Kestra's funeral, but Troi had long since given up trying to get Lwaxana to cease her attempts to eliminate all evidence of Kestra's existence. She had erased all her journals from the day she learned she was pregnant with their first daughter until after the funeral, would not speak of her, nor acknowledge any event connected with the girl. Troi found it maddening and frustrating—and an impediment to his own ability to grieve—but after seven years, he had surrendered to the inevitable. To try to address it now would only lead to an argument. Troi had never won an argument with Lwaxana in his life—which put him in company with the rest of the universe—and fifteen years of marriage had taught him that it was better to avoid the issue altogether.

She'll deal with it when she's ready, and not a minute before. In the meantime, both Troi and their valet, Mr. Xelo, had kept a few mementoes of Kestra hidden from Lwaxana for when that day finally came.

And Deanna deserves to know about her sister, he thought, *before her telepathy develops and she yanks that knowledge out of my head.*

Lwaxana said, "*You should ask Elias to come with you when you visit. It would be wonderful to see him again, and he could meet Deanna.*"

Not bothering to point out that he met Deanna at Kestra's funeral, Troi simply said, "That would be nice. I'll ask him." Besides, Deanna was an infant then. "Given his usual work schedule, it's as likely as not that he won't be able to, but it couldn't hurt to ask." Glancing down at the time stamp on the screen, Troi noted that he'd already gone over his allotted personal comm time by three minutes. "I need to go, love." He smiled. "You know how much I miss you?"

"*Of course I do,* imzadi," she said with a mischievious grin. "*I wouldn't be much of a telepath if I didn't.*"

"Oh, right. Explain to me again how your telepathy works over subspace?"

"*You can be such a killjoy, Ian Andrew Troi,*" Lwaxana said with a smirk.

"So how much *do* I miss you?"

"*As much as I miss you.*"

For a moment, they simply locked eyes. Troi took in every line of her face, every facet of her beautiful smile and her lovely dark eyes.

Then, finally, he said, "I have to go. Be well, *imzadi.* I'll see you soon."

"*Not soon enough.*"

Reluctantly, Troi cut the connection. The screen embedded in the wall of his quarters went dark.

"*Bridge to Troi.*"

Troi sighed. *Can't I just bask in the glow of my family for a few more minutes?* But it was not to be. He knew what was involved when he took his oath after graduating the Academy. Despite everything, though, he couldn't bring himself to resign his commission. He was happy in Starfleet—it was where he belonged. One of the advantages to being married to a telepath was that Lwaxana understood that implicitly—in fact, she probably understood it better than he did—and wouldn't hear of him resigning, and settling for a job he wasn't as content with in order to make his family happy. "When the time is right," she had said once, "we'll know it, and then we can be a family together. For now, it's right that we be a family apart."

Of course, explaining that to a seven-year-old girl is a bit harder.

Tapping his combadge in response to the call from the bridge, he said, "Go ahead."

"*Report to Transporter Room 2, sir. Commander Vaughn's ready to beam on board.*"

"Acknowledged." Troi was grateful that Captain Haden had allowed him to perform this duty, which could just as easily have gone to the first officer, Commander Li, or the security chief.

Instead, it was the second officer of the *U.S.S. Carthage* who entered the transporter room to greet Vaughn as he beamed on board.

Vaughn had changed a bit in seven years: more lines to his face, more gray in his hair. Most notably, he'd grown a beard, which matched the brown and gray colors of his hair.

On the other hand, the body language hadn't changed at all. Troi had never known anyone who was quite as in control of himself as Elias Vaughn. Troi envied it in a lot of ways, though Troi had found that a lack of control had its appeal. He often wondered how someone as centered and as private as Vaughn would fare in a relationship with a telepath.

Smiling slightly at the sight of his escort, Vaughn said, "Ian. Good to see you again."

"Same here. I like the beard."

Vaughn smirked at that. "Thanks."

Troi tapped his combadge. "Bridge, Commander Vaughn is on board."

Haden himself replied. "*Acknowledged, Mr. Troi. We'll be getting underway to Raknal V immediately. Escort the commander to my ready room.*"

"Yes, sir." He looked at Vaughn and grinned. "If the commander will come this way."

"Be happy to."

As they proceeded to the turbolift, Vaughn asked, "How are things at home?"

"Quite well. Deanna's an incredibly bright child. After this little trip to Raknal's over, I've got some leave coming, and I'm going to spend some time with them." Remembering Lwaxana's suggestion, he added, "You're welcome to come along, if you want. It'd be nice to have you visit when there isn't a funeral involved."

"It's a possibility," Vaughn said, which was a better answer than the "no" Troi had been expecting. "Let's see how things go on Raknal V first."

They entered the turbolift. "Fair enough," Troi said to Vaughn, then added to the computer, "Bridge," causing the lift to head upward.

Within moments, they arrived, and entered Haden's lair. The captain's wide eyes fell on Vaughn's face, and he scowled. Troi tried to cover a smile. The last fifteen years had not been kind to Haden's hairline, which had receded quite a bit, and he seemed to derive a certain irritation from the fact that Vaughn, who was older than Haden, not only still had a full head of hair, but had poured salt in the wound by growing a full beard.

"Welcome back, Commander."

Vaughn nodded his head as he and Troi took their seats in the captain's two guest chairs. "Thank you, Captain."

"It's almost like a reunion. Pity we can't divert *Enterprise* here, we'd have the whole Betreka gang back again."

Troi smiled. Commander—or, rather, *Captain* Garrett had been given command of the *U.S.S. Enterprise* four years after the Betreka Nebula incident, and had spent the last decade-plus doing everything she could to live up to the reputation that the name of her ship carried. Most of the crew complement from the *Carthage's* last trip to the Betreka Sector had either been promoted—like Troi and Lin—or moved on to other assignments—like Phillips and Garrett. The captain and Mike Zipser at communications were the only ones still in the same position they were fifteen years earlier. *And*

Zip's close enough to retirement that he probably doesn't care all that much about the lack of promotion.

Haden leaned back in his chair, folding his arms over his barrel chest, looking like a particularly cranky Buddha. "What's your take on the Raknal situation, Commander?"

"I don't have a 'take' just yet, Captain. That's part of what I'm taking this trip to find out. From what I do know, I think my feelings fifteen years ago that this was an incredibly bad idea were justified."

Snorting, Haden said, "That's an understatement. The Cardassians and the Klingons have spent more time spitting on each other in space than they have actually exploiting the planet. They've both done lousy jobs of making use of Raknal's resources, and half their equipment doesn't work. You'd think that disaster with the *Chut* would've been a wake-up call, but it hasn't improved a damn thing."

"Personally, sir, I'd rather wait until—"

Whatever Vaughn wanted to wait until remained unsaid, interrupted as it was by the Klaxon of the ship going to red alert. Commander Lin's voice came over the intercom. *"Captain Haden to the bridge."*

Troi looked up in shock, then all three of them immediately went through the door. "Report," Haden barked at Lin, who was standing between the command center and the helm. Troi stepped into the bridge's lower level to take his position at the operations console to the left of the helm even as Haden moved to sit in the command chair. Vaughn remained on the upper level, standing just to the right of the communications console.

"We just received a distress call from Raknal V," Lin said. "We've increased speed to warp eight."

Troi winced. Lin looked over at Zipser, who said, "According to the signal, a building in the Klingons' capital city on the southern continent has been destroyed." He cast a quick glance at Haden. "Governor Qaolin thinks it's because of Cardassian sabotage."

"What kind of building?" Haden asked.

"They didn't say, but there was an indication that people were trapped."

Haden and Lin exchanged a glance, then the captain looked at Vaughn. "Looks like this just mutated into a damn rescue mission."

"So it would seem." Vaughn, Troi noticed, spoke in a neutral tone.

Zipser then said, "Sir, we're being hailed directly by Governor Qaolin."

"This oughtta be good. On screen."

Troi blinked in surprise at the face that appeared on the forward viewer. Fifteen years ago, Qaolin had given the impression of a vibrant man, dark hair framing a fierce face. His voice had a deep, confident timbre to it.

The voice that issued forth from the gray-haired wreck of a Klingon with several missing teeth had none of that confidence left. From the way he slurred his consonants, Troi's best hypothesis was that he had drunk all the confidence away. "I demand the immediate arrest of Prefect Monor and the ceding of Raknal V to the Klingon Empire!"

"Greetings, Governor Qaolin," Haden said dryly. "This is Captain Haden. We're on our way to assist you. Is there anything we can do—"

"I don't have any interest in your Federation politeness," Qaolin said with a snarl. "There are Klingons dying and dead in that building, and Cardassian treachery has killed them, just like it did the good men and women who died on the Chut."

"Do you have any evidence to support this accusation?"

Qaolin slammed his fist on his desk. "I need no evidence! I have lived on this mudball with Monor for fifteen years! I know his heart, Captain, and he will stop at nothing to keep Ch'gran from us!"

Troi could hear Haden's sigh. "So no evidence, then?"

Before Qaolin could say anything in response, Zipser said, "Sir, we're now being hailed by Prefect Monor."

That prompted a laugh from Qaolin. *"The petaQ no doubt wishes to curry favor with you by spinning lies of his innocence."*

"Split screen, Mr. Zipser," Haden said. "Let's all talk together."

Qaolin's image shifted to the righthand side of the viewer, with the left side now taken up by Monor's visage. The Cardassian showed less evidence of the passage of time to Troi. His face, hair, and bearing were much the same as they were. The only difference Troi could see was in the prefect's eyes, which looked tired. Then he checked the library computer and discovered that, in the Cardassian capital city on the northern continent, it was the middle of the night right now.

Both leaders stared straight ahead, though Troi knew that they were each getting the same split-screen view that the *Carthage* had. *"Greetings from Raknal V, Captain Haden. I'm sure Governor Qaolin has already laid the blame for this at my feet. As if the Foreheads need our help to construct buildings that fall down at the drop of a rock."*

"Are the souls of the Chut *not enough for you, Monor? Will you not rest until all the Klingons on this world cry out for vengeance against Cardassian treachery?"*

Monor made a dismissive noise that sounded like a leaky pipe. *"You're drunk."*

"Of course I'm drunk! I drink to the souls of the dead— slain by Cardassian cowardice!"

"The only coward I see is an old wreck who should be embarrassed to let himself be seen like that! Look at you—inebriated, unkempt. You wouldn't last an hour on a Cardassian ship. That's why you Foreheads will always—"

"That's enough!" Haden barked, which came as a great

relief to Troi. "Both of you shut the hell up. Mr. Troi, what's our ETA?"

Troi double-checked the navigational computer. "Thirty-five minutes at this speed."

"When we arrive, the *Carthage* will aid in any rescue endeavors, and our sickbay will be at your disposal as well."

"*That is appreciated, Captain.*" Qaolin spoke in a more subdued tone. "*The Federation, at least, has always been honorable.*"

" '*Honorable.*' " Monor made the leaky pipe noise again. "*That's your catch-all word for everything, isn't it?*"

"*Worry not, Monor,*" Qaolin said with a wide, half-toothless grin, "*it will never be applied to you.*"

Haden continued as if the two men had not spoken. "After that, as per the agreement signed at the Betreka Nebula by both your governments, we will investigate the destruction of the building, and report our findings to both of you—and to your respective governments, and to Ambassador Dax and the Federation Council." He turned toward the communications console to look at Vaughn. "Lieutenant Commander Vaughn, you will lead the investigation." Then he turned back to the screen. "I expect both of you to cooperate fully with Commander Vaughn and his team. If you don't—well, that will go in our report, as well."

Monor scowled. "*I can't imagine what help we can provide, Captain, since the incident had nothing to do with me or anyone from—*"

"*Do you fear that the Federation will learn what I have known for fifteen years, Monor?*"

"*What, that you're a pathetic drunken—*"

"Screen off," Haden muttered, and Zipser quickly cut off the communication, returning the main viewer to the image of the distorted starfield that signified the *Carthage*'s warp-speed travel. Then the captain rose from his chair and moved toward the turbolift. "Commander Li, let me know when we arrive, and have the transporter chief prepare for multiple transports. And put all shuttlecraft on standby, just in case."

As Wai-Lin Li sat in the command chair she said, "Should I alert sickbay also?"

"I'll do that. I'm going there now to do something about this headache I just acquired." As he passed Vaughn, Haden added, "Mr. Vaughn, feel free to use whatever *Carthage* personnel you need, but get to the bottom of this thing quickly, understood?"

Vaughn nodded. "Yes, sir. With your permission, I'd like Lieutenant Commander Troi to assist me."

"Permission granted." As the turbolift doors opened, he said, "You have the bridge, Number One."

Chapter 24

RAKNAL V

By the time the *Carthage* arrived, there was comparatively little rescuing to be done. The building in question held several residences as well as three merchants. Most of the debris had been cleared by Klingon rescue workers. Fifty-three people were in the building when it collapsed, of whom twelve were dead. At Commander Li's insistence, the remaining forty-one were transported to the *Carthage* rather than brought to the local hospital, on the logic that a starship sickbay was better equipped than any Klingon hospital, a point no one could truly argue.

Once that was done, all that was left was the wreckage — and twelve dead bodies. Troi stood before what was left of the building as the last of the rescue workers started to leave. A semipermeable force field was keeping all but the workers and Starfleet personnel away from the site. The field would allow those with a particular transponder to pass through it, one held by all the workers and by Vaughn, Troi, and the other *Carthage* personnel on-planet.

At the sight of the twelve corpses being left on the ground, Troi grabbed one of the departing rescue workers by the arm. The worker looked at Troi's hand like it was diseased. Troi quickly removed it.

"What's to be done with the bodies?"

The worker shrugged. "Disposed of in some manner."

"Don't you have any—well, funerary rites?"

Again, he shrugged. "They are not warriors. If they lived dishonorable lives, then *Fek'lhr* will escort their spirits to the Barge of the Dead, which will take them to *Gre'thor*."

Troi knew that that was the Klingon equivalent of hell. "What if they lived honorable lives?"

At that, the worker scowled. "Then they deserved better deaths than *this*."

Troi found he couldn't argue with that either way.

After the last of the rescue workers departed, Troi was alone with the building. Vaughn was interviewing people who were nearby when the building collapsed, and had asked the *Carthage* security chief to do the same with the survivors in sickbay.

Troi, meanwhile, was tasked with examining the site itself. He looked up at the building. It had been made from plastiform over a metal frame. Parts of the frame—which looked to be an alloy of rodinium, iron, and a metal the tricorder couldn't identify—remained intact. A preliminary scan with the tricorder indicated that the frame had weakened and collapsed in the southwest quadrant of the foundation. When that gave way, a large chunk of the building went down.

Troi proceeded, as Vaughn had instructed him, to go over every millimeter of the building. All the evidence pointed to a simple structural collapse, which would make Monor happy, if not Qaolin. *Wonder what that third metal in the alloy is*, he thought. *That may have been responsible. Iron and rodinium are pretty tough, but that third metal's an x-factor.*

It took two hours to do most of the job. The items he found in various states of repair ranged from the obviously personal—clothes, furniture, pictures, artwork, padds labeled in the angled Klingon script, well-worn weaponry, cooking implements, food—to the assorted items that were for sale in the stores.

When he came across a small figurine that was vaguely in the shape of a *targ*, Troi felt a lump in his throat. Up until this point, he had managed not to think about what it had been like going through Kestra's things seven years ago—a task that had been left to Troi alone, since Lwaxana had already started her campaign to eradicate Kestra's very existence—until he came across this toy *targ* which, despite looking nothing like Kestra's teddy bear, reminded Troi almost painfully of My Bear. Troi had given Kestra the stuffed black bear when his daughter turned four. It had floppy arms and legs, a tiny smile, wide brown eyes, and a sufficiently soft interior to make him eminently huggable—a feature Kestra employed often. Kestra had never come up with a name for the bear, insisting on simply referring to the toy as "my bear!" The name stuck.

After Kestra's death, Troi had given My Bear to Commander Li for her daughter.

He set the toy *targ* back down amid the wreckage. Once he and Vaughn were through, someone was supposed to come and sort through all this. Troi was grateful that his assignment to Vaughn's detail meant he would be spared that duty. Once was more than enough.

The one part of his job he hadn't done was to do a full check of the southwest quadrant. He clambered over pieces of plastiform and shards of blades and precious stones—the store over the collapsed part of the building sold weapons and jewelry; both proprietors and one customer were among the dozen dead—to see if he could better determine the cause.

Unfortunately, the weakened beams in question were under more material than he could move safely, because of both the weight and the number of items with sharp edges. Besides, it was only a matter of time before the building collapsed the rest of the way—the remains of the foundation couldn't bear the added concentration of mass for much longer.

Luckily, Troi didn't have to move it himself. He trained his tricorder's sensors on the broken beams under the wreckage, then tapped his combadge. "Troi to Sulma."

"Sulma here."

"Chief, I need some help here. Can you tie in to my tricorder?"

"*Hang on.*" A pause. "*Yeah, okay, got it.*"

"Can you lock onto the pieces of metal I'm scanning and beam them to a position about three meters to my left?"

"*Don't see why not. Hang on.*" Another pause. "*Got it.*"

"Thanks, Shawn. That's a big help."

The transporter chief laughed. "*No big deal. It's not like I'm doing anything difficult. Not like that time Commander Li needed me to beam that funky alien gourd off her arm. Anyhow, energizing.*"

Seconds later, several bent, broken, and shattered fragments of metal materialized three meters to Ian Troi's left.

"Thanks again, Shawn. I owe you lunch. Troi out."

Now Troi did an in-depth scan of the beams. The tricorder still couldn't identify the third metal in the alloy—but it did identify some resonance traces that matched a similar investigation they'd done in the Barradas system near the Romulan border a few months earlier. "Oh, this isn't good."

"What isn't good?"

Troi turned to see that Vaughn had come back inside the force field.

Before Troi had a chance to answer the question, Vaughn added, "Just so you know, I've cleared the area of all onlookers. There's one Klingon guard outside the force field, but otherwise, it's just you and me for dozens of meters around."

Smiling at his friend, Troi said, "The joys of a sparsely populated colony that has transporter technology. No need for crowding. In any case, I've discovered two things."

"Which is the one that isn't good?"

"Both, unfortunately. One is that the rest of this is going to come crashing down in the next half-hour or so. We'll want to bring the force field in a little, use it to minimize the damage to the surrounding area."

"Good idea. What's the other thing?"

Pointing at the shattered framework, Troi said, "This wasn't because of shoddy construction. That beam was weakened by an explosion."

"What? How the hell did we miss that?"

"It was a very small bomb with a very low yield and a detonator that works well at this size. That's all they needed, as long as they put it in the right spot. This beam, as it happened, was."

"What kind of explosive?"

"Standard triceron. That's not the kicker, though. You ever hear of molecular-decay detonators?"

"I've *heard* of them." Vaughn shrugged. "I know that they're virtually undetectable and that Romulans are the only ones who've been able to get them to work reliably."

Smiling grimly, Troi said, "Only half right. Yes, Romulans are the only ones who use them, but they're not as undetectable as they used to be. A few months ago on the *Carthage*, we figured out how to detect them in the Barradas system." He held up his tricorder display so Vaughn could see it. "I'm picking up residue of one now."

"That doesn't make sense. The Romulans have pretty much kept to themselves since Tomed. Why would they get involved in *this* mess?"

Troi shrugged. "I don't know, Elias, but this is definitely a Romulan operation."

"Or someone trying to set up the Romulans."

"I doubt it." Troi barked a laugh. "I mean, if someone else figured out how to rig an MD detonator, I doubt they'd use it for something like this. They'd go around selling it to the highest bidder—or at least using it for an explosion with a bit more oomph than this."

Vaughn let out a breath through his teeth. "Probably, but I have to consider all the possibilities. You're right, though, Romulan sabotage is the obvious answer. Which leads me to wonder what *they* want with Raknal V."

Troi shrugged. "Maybe they just want to—" Before he could continue, his tricorder beeped an alarm. "Elias, someone's penetrated the force field."

"What?"

Expanding his tricorder range outward, he asked, "You said you posted a Klingon guard?"

"Qaolin's people did, why?"

"The only life signs I'm picking up are you and me—and our intruder, but it's masked with some kind of screening field."

Vaughn started to look around, seeming to take in the entire three hundred and sixty degrees around him at once. Then he sprang into action rather suddenly, leaping to push Troi to the ground. "Get down!"

Even as he did so, Vaughn unholstered his phaser and fired it.

Green beams of coherent light sizzled over Troi's head, which meant the weapon they came from could well have been a Romulan disruptor. *Or, as Elias pointed out,* Troi thought, *someone trying to set the Romulans up.*

Somehow, despite the weight of Elias Vaughn on top of him, Troi managed to get a look at his tricorder. It was still picking up the life reading, and also the masking field. Whoever was firing at them didn't want to be identified by species. Troi had no idea what that meant in the grand scheme of things, but that was Elias's problem.

Troi's problem was getting out of this alive.

Vaughn had gotten into a crouching position, covering Troi's prone form, and fired again. Right after he did so, the life sign reading fluctuated. For a moment, it registered as Vulcanoid. *My God, it really could be a Romulan.*

"We've got to get out from the open," Vaughn said. "We're sitting ducks out he—"

Then a green beam struck Vaughn, and he went down— albeit with no obvious physical trauma. *Since when do Romulan disruptors have a stun setting?*

That question was the last thing Troi thought before a green beam struck him in the shoulder. As blackness started to claim him, he heard a rumbling sound. *The building's about to collapse!* He tried to make his arms and legs move, but they refused to respond to his brain's commands. The ground started to shake under him even as consciousness slipped away, and he felt something heavy smash into his chest . . .

Intellectually, Elias Vaughn knew he had opened his eyes. However, he had no empirical evidence to back this knowledge up, as there was no qualitative difference between what he saw after he opened his eyes and the pitch blackness of unconsciousness.

Immediately, he assessed the situation. His head was pounding, and there was a coppery taste in his mouth that he knew was blood. Although he was aware of the presence of his body below his sternum, he couldn't really *feel* that part of him as such. There was also a very heavy weight that was keeping him in place—probably one of the metal frames of the building. That weight pinned both his arms, and attempts to wiggle free proved futile. He wasn't moving.

He also couldn't get at his combadge to call for help. If his combadge was even still on his uniform, which he couldn't tell from the darkness.

Vaughn also had the vague queasiness that often accompanied awakening from a phaser set on stun. The weapon that fired on him and Ian Troi looked and sounded like a Romulan disruptor, which didn't traditionally have a stun setting, but Vaughn himself knew how to reprogram its lower settings so that it could mimic a stun blast, so it stood to reason that their assailant might know how, also.

All in all, he thought, *I've been in worse spots.* That thought was a rather telling commentary on the kind of life he lived, Vaughn realized.

"Oooooh."

The noise sounded like Troi's voice. "Ian?" Vaughn's voice was a barely legible croak; he cleared his throat, and repeated himself.

"E—Elias?" The voice sounded weak.

"I'm here, Ian. Where are you? Are you all right?"

"Wha—wha' happen'?"

"Best guess is that our assailant rendered us unconscious, then left us in the building for when it collapsed."

"M—makes sense."

Vaughn frowned. "Why?"

"Well, feels like there's a big piece o' plastiform 'n my chest."

Oh, hell. Instinctively, Vaughn once again struggled against the beam that held him in place, but he had neither the strength nor the leverage to budge it. He was trapped. *And given the numbness in my lower body, I doubt I'm in any shape to move even if I could get this thing off me. Dammit.*

"Can you reach your combadge?"

" 'S not there." Troi's voice was weakening. "Musta fallen off."

Or more likely was removed. "Stay with me, Ian." He couldn't afford to let Troi go into shock. "Talk to me."

"Why'd 'e do 't?"

Vaughn blinked. At least he assumed he did. It was still pitch black, after all. "Why did who do what?"

"Th' Romulan. Stunned us. Coulda jus' killed us."

"Assuming it was a Romulan, then—"

"Was."

That confused Vaughn. "Was what?"

"Was Romulan. Or Vulcanoid, anyhow. Gotta readin' after y' shot 'im."

A pity that Ian's tricorder probably went the way of his combadge. "In any case, the lighter setting means less physical evidence on the bodies of being shot. All there'd be is nerve damage. If the saboteur shot to kill, either there'd be evidence of the disruptor blast on our bodies, or we'd just disintegrate, in which case our missing bodies would raise a red flag. Much easier to leave our bodies in the collapsing building, where cause of death would be blindingly obvious, and likely no one would investigate further. It's just his bad luck that we both survived."

"Jus'—one—of—"

"We're both going to make it," Vaughn said sternly. "The *Carthage* will send someone to look for us." He couldn't imagine Vance Haden letting his second officer and a mission specialist stay missing for any length of time.

"Not—if—combadges—gone."

Troi had a point. "They're still going to look for us. And once they find that we're not with our combadges, they'll search. We're virtually the only humans on this planet, it won't be too hard to pick us up."

"Mebbe." Troi made some kind of noise. "Hell'va s'prise."

"Surprise?" Vaughn asked after a moment, when no explanation was forthcoming. *Besides, silence could be deadly.*

"Tol' D'anna I'd have—s'prise f' her. Not—what I—had 'n mind."

Normally, Elias Vaughn did not believe in giving people false hopes, but he was damned if he was going to sit here and listen to Troi bury himself. "You're not going to die, Ian. They'll be by soon to rescue us." A pause, which Vaughn refused to let go on for any length. "What was the surprise going to be?"

"Dunno. Hadn'—decided yet. Was part'a th' fun." Troi's breathing was getting more labored. "Th's really hurts."

Trying like hell to sound encouraging, Vaughn said, "We'll be rescued soon, Ian."

"Sorry I—c'dn't see you one las' time—*imzadi.*"

He knew that last word was a Betazoid term of endearment of some sort. Lwaxana was an especially powerful telepath, even by the high standards of her species, and Vaughn wondered if Troi thought his wife could hear him.

Futilely, Vaughn tried once again to move the beam, but his strength had diminished—probably because of blood loss, based on the increasing coppery taste in his mouth— and his leverage certainly hadn't improved.

Dammit, Haden, find us already! I can't just sit here and listen to him die!

But it seemed that was exactly what was going to happen.

"Elias?" Troi's voice was barely a whisper.

"I'm here, Ian."

"Thanks."

Vaughn couldn't imagine for what this man had to be grateful to *him*. "For what?"

"Didn'—wan'—die—'lone. Gladjer—here."

"You're not going to die, Ian. We're going to make it out of here, they'll patch us up on the *Carthage*, and we're both going to go back to Betazed to visit Lwaxana and Deanna, and you're going to give Deanna her surprise."

Silence.

"Ian?"

Nothing.

"Dammit, Ian, *talk* to me!"

Elias Vaughn still remembered, with crystal clarity, the day a decade and a half ago when charged particles tore a hole in the shuttlecraft *Hoplite*. Vaughn had fully expected to die when the explosive decompression blew him toward the vacuum of space, and the only reason he hadn't was because of the fast thinking of Ian Troi.

Now he sat helplessly, kept by a piece of metal from returning the favor.

Snarling, he tried once again to shift the beam, pushing his entire body upward in an attempt to free himself.

Blue and red spots danced before his eyes, shockingly visible in the total darkness, but still he struggled. *Ian's going to die unless I can get this thing off me.*

Chapter 25

U.S.S. CARTHAGE

The next thing Vaughn knew, he awoke in the *Carthage* sickbay.

"About time you woke up. You've been out for the better part of a day."

He looked around, blinking his eyes repeatedly. The red and blue spots were still there, but started to fade after a few moments. The last thing he remembered was trying to shift the beam. Now Commander Li was sitting next to his biobed. Vaughn could hear sounds around him—no doubt the usual business of sickbay.

An attempt to speak was a complete failure, even after he cleared his throat.

However, Li answered his unspoken question. "Commander Troi didn't make it. He was DOA. Somebody made off with his tricorder, and both your phasers, transponders, and combadges. Your legs were crushed—doc says it's going to take months before they're back to normal, but they can be healed."

Many thoughts went through Vaughn's head. One was that the Romulan connection needed to be investigated. One was that somebody needed to find Curzon Dax and beat him until he admitted that his solution to the Raknal V problem was a total disaster, just as Vaughn had predicted. One was that "months" was a long time for him to be out of commission.

But the thought that remained at the forefront was how a seven-year-old girl was going to react to the news that her father was never coming home.

Chapter 26

RAKNAL V

The specially designed transporter beam deposited Corbin Entek in the apartment that he had rented on Raknal V's northern continent.

The stealth transporter was a handy tool of the Obsidian Order. It masked its signal by hiding amid the authorized transporter patterns that flew back and forth from the surface to orbit and from orbit back to the planet. In this case, Entek had beamed here from the wreckage of the sabotaged building by hiding amid the transporter traffic going from the surface to the *Carthage*, "bouncing" the signal off the Starfleet ship and coming back to the planet behind a beam from the Cardassian Orbital Center to the spaceport on the northern continent.

The technology was years ahead of anything Central Command had, of course. It was the benefit of seeking out, hiring, and paying top money for the best, as opposed to getting one's equipment on the open market.

As soon as he materialized, Entek checked the time. It was still two hours before he was to make his report. He decided to get a meal. The apartment was conveniently located near an especially good restaurant, which Entek had discovered upon his arrival two weeks earlier. They served an especially fine *sem'hal* stew made from some local vegetables, marinated in *kanar*, and the thought of having some now cheered Entek a great deal.

Especially after what he'd just observed.

Though he was not able to get near the wreckage of the collapsed building—as a Cardassian in the Klingon section of the planet, that would be quite impossible without surgical alterations that Entek did not have the means to have performed—he was able to release a small roving imager. It told quite the story.

Romulans. Between the two Starfleet lieutenant commanders' conclusions regarding the molecular decay detonator and the type of weapon used by the person who subsequently attacked those two men and tried to bury them alive, it was patently obvious that the Romulans were trying to stir things up between the Klingons and Cardassians even more. *It would seem that Praetor Dralath truly wishes a war.*

As he entered the restaurant, Entek wondered if Tain suspected this all along. *It would explain why I was sent.*

A monitor screen showed a Cardassian speaking. Entek recognized the man as Prefect Monor's aide-de-camp Ekron. *"The tragedy on the Klingon continent is just another example of the shoddy work we have come to expect from Klingons, who believe that their alleged prowess at hand-to-hand combat somehow entitles them to domination of the galaxy. In truth, they cannot even keep a building from falling down. It is more proof that Cardassia deserves—"*

"What rot," said Entek's server, who chose that moment to come by. "I take it you'll have your usual?"

"Sem'hal stew, yes. And some water. What do you mean, rot?"

"Hey, look, I'm the last person to say something nice about the Foreheads, but I mean, come *on*—they know how to put a building up. That was sabotage, plain and simple. And you *know* Monor was behind it. And did you hear? One of those Starfleeters died, too."

Only one? Entek had assumed that both Elias Vaughn and Ian Troi died when the building collapsed on them. "No, I hadn't heard."

"Yeah, two people from their ship were investigating the mess, and the building fell on them. One of them died, but they got the other one back up to orbit and saved him. Now you *know* that was Monor. I mean, come *on*—the Klingons aren't going to go around dropping buildings on their allies like that, but Monor? He'd do it in a minute."

The server went off to place Entek's order. The Obsidian Order agent brooded, even as he mentally prepared the report he would make to Gul Monor's office of the sedition he had just heard. The server would not be working here for long.

This isn't good. If even the Cardassian people are believing the worst of the government, then the Romulans' work is being done for them. A Federation death won't help matters. Cardassia needs to get out of this conflict. Perhaps we can use the Romulans' hatred of Klingons to give Dralath the very war he seems desperate to fight and also restore some of Cardassia's lost lustre.

As he waited for his stew, Entek finished his mental composition of the sedition report, and began to compose his report to his supervisor—and to Enabran Tain.

Chapter 27

DEEP SPACE STATION K-7

Lorgh wasn't sure why simply walking the hallways of this ancient space station made him tense. Perhaps it was the odd looks that the station's denizens—mostly humans—gave him. Perhaps it was simply the reputation that this place had in Klingon history. After all, it was here that the infamous tribble infestation got its start, a plague that had menaced several Klingon worlds until the foul species was finally eradicated like the vermin they were.

Still, this was the ideal meeting place—close to the Federation–Klingon border, administered by civilians rather than Starfleet, and sparsely populated these days—for his meeting with the human Vaughn.

He entered the drinking establishment where they were to have their meeting. The diamond-shaped door slid open slowly, briefly stopping halfway before finally opening all the way. That, sadly, set the tone for the entire place. The décor was no doubt the height of human fashion eighty years earlier, but it also looked like it hadn't been maintained in almost as long. The tables were cracked and balanced unevenly on legs that had fallen off and been given inadequate replacements, the cushions on the chairs were split open or missing, and the trays on which the bored-looking servers brought the drinks were worn and gray.

One of those servers gave Lorgh a sharp look upon his entrance. "Can I help you?" she asked in a snide tone. She wore a pink outfit that revealed more than it concealed. Lorgh found the sight of so much soft, human flesh to be nauseating.

"I'm meeting someone."

Her face indicated a mind that was torn between not believing Lorgh and not caring much one way or the other. The latter apparently won out, as she shrugged, indicated a table in the corner with her head, and said, "Have a seat. I'll be with you in a minute."

"I'll have a—"

"I *said* I'll be with you in a minute." Then she turned her back on him.

Lorgh knew that wasn't an insult to quite the same degree among humans as it was among Klingons, but he decided to accept it as such in any case.

It was considerably more than a minute before the server finally came to take his order. Knowing that this establishment was unlikely to have any proper drinks, he ordered an Altair water.

Just as she brought it over, the diamond door slid hesitantly open once again, and Elias Vaughn entered. Lorgh noted that the human was walking gingerly, which made sense, given the gravity of his injuries on Raknal V months ago. What impressed Lorgh was that he was walking at all. If a Klingon suffered a like injury, the legs would not have been salvageable, and would have been amputated. A Klingon warrior—or I.I. agent—would probably insist on *Mauk-to'Vor* at that point, since one cannot go into battle without legs, and a warrior would rather die than be forbidden combat.

Vaughn had proven to be a valuable resource. They had first met aboard the *Carthage* during the Betreka Nebula incident, and they had remained in contact on and off in the decade and a half since—each had found the other a useful font of information at times, and the constant exchange had served to allow both of them to do their jobs more efficiently. Neither of them had informed their superiors or colleagues that he used the other as a source. I.I. knew only that Lorgh was visiting one of his confidential informants; he assumed that Vaughn's own people knew exactly as much.

Lorgh wondered if symbolism as much as practicality entered into Vaughn's reasons for choosing this as a meeting place. Deep Space Station K-7 was the nearest Federation outpost to Sherman's Planet, one of several border worlds in dispute during the hostilities that led to the Organian Peace Treaty. Under the terms of that treaty, the Klingons and Federation had to show who could develop Sherman's Planet most efficiently; the Federation won that battle a year later. The Great Curzon had used Sherman's Planet as one of the precedents for his Raknal V solution at the Betreka Nebula. Now Vaughn, coming off an injury sustained at Raknal V, was meeting here with Lorgh, a contact he first made near that world.

Then again, this human has never struck me as one to appreciate that type of symbolism.

It didn't take Vaughn long to spot Lorgh, even in the corner—he was one of only half a dozen customers in the place, and the only Klingon—and so he immediately walked over and took the seat opposite Lorgh.

"You seem to be recovering nicely."

"I suppose," Vaughn said. "It's good to see you again."

Sipping his Altair water and trying not to gag, Lorgh said, "I feel the same. Especially now that you have finally grown a beard. It is unfit for a warrior to be without one."

"I'll take that as a compliment."

The server came over; Vaughn ordered something that sounded like *t'qIla'*, which turned out to be a clear liquid that came in a very small glass.

"I believe you requested this meeting," Lorgh said by way of getting the conversational ball rolling.

Vaughn sipped his drink. "Yes, I did. The incident on Raknal V was the result of sabotage by Romulans."

At that, Lorgh's eyes narrowed. He'd been investigating the Romulans for months, and learning some disheartening things about the direction their government was taking, but this was a new wrinkle.

Lorgh chose his next words carefully. "I take it by the fact that the official report listed the building's collapse as an accident means that either you wish to keep the Romulan involvement a secret, or that you have no proof."

"The latter, believe me." Vaughn sounded especially angry. Lorgh remembered that the Starfleet officer who died in the building was a comrade of Vaughn's. "If we could expose their involvement, we would. Unfortunately, they had an agent on-site who dropped a building on Commander Troi and myself and made off with our evidence. Bringing accusations of Romulan sabotage into Raknal without anything to back it up will only make a disastrous situation worse."

Lorgh tapped the glass that held his Altair water, which he had no intention of finishing. "You brought me this information for a reason, I assume."

"You know as well as I do that Qaolin is furious that we didn't blame the Cardassians for sabotaging that building, even though everyone assumes they did." He snorted. "From what I was hearing on Raknal before the *Carthage* left, half the Cardassians on the planet thought Monor orchestrated it, and they're on *his* side. Meanwhile, the Cardassians know they didn't do it, and are blaming us for spreading the rumors."

Grinning, Lorgh said, "Sounds like a difficult situation."

"What I need to know from you is what the High Council's position is."

Lorgh's grin fell. "Divided. Some wish to strengthen our ties with the Federation, some wish to strengthen our ties with the Romulans, some think we need to find our own path."

"What about the Cardassians?"

The grin came back. "They die well." Skirmishes with the Cardassians had increased in the months since the latest Raknal V disaster, with the Klingons being on the winning side more often than not. Kravokh's recruitment drives for enlisting in the Defense Force and his initiatives to construct newer ships had borne fruit. The Klingon military was stronger than it had been in fifty years. *As long as no more moons explode, we should thrive,* he thought wryly.

None of that, however, was the human's concern—nor would Lorgh's glib response truly satisfy the human's need for information. The question was, how much was Vaughn's intelligence about Romulan involvement in the Betreka Sector worth?

More to the point, how much was it worth to Lorgh's own investigations for the Federation to be more aware of the situation?

"The fervor which gripped our people sixteen years ago over the recovery of Ch'gran has abated with time, as all things do. True, we would prefer to have it in our possession than it be in the hands of murdering outsiders, but the number of dead without any true gains made by their sacrifices makes us weary."

Vaughn frowned. "So what's the problem?"

"Kravokh. He is obsessed with Ch'gran. Everything he does seems geared toward our wresting Ch'gran from Cardassian control. The benefits to the Empire are merely a fortuitous side effect—but one that masks his true intentions, and also prevents those who oppose his obsession from doing anything about it. I fear that his insistence on keeping our eyes on Cardassia will blind him to the dagger that the Romulans will insert in our backs." Lorgh thought a moment, then decided to open up further. "And that dagger will come soon. I have information that Praetor Dralath suffers from an incurable blood disease called T'Shevat's Syndrome. That, combined with his declining popularity and the age of their emperor, points to a man who is desperate enough to attempt something foolish."

"Like start a war?"

Lorgh nodded.

Vaughn sipped the rest of his drink in silence. Then he rose. "Thanks for seeing me. You've been a tremendous help. The next one's on me."

Again, Lorgh nodded. Obviously, Vaughn felt he had gotten the better end of this particular information exchange. *Which means that next time, he will be even more forthcoming. Good.*

I just hope that revealing so much to the Federation benefits us as I pray it will. I.I.'s attempts to convince the High Council that the Romulans were a threat had fallen on deaf ears, mostly because of K'mpec's efforts in blocking I.I.'s every move. Part of Lorgh thought it would be best to simply remove K'mpec, but—his animus for I.I. aside—he was an effective councillor. He was a consensus builder, and a charismatic leader who had avoided the factionalization of the Council. That made him an ideal candidate to succeed Kravokh, and perhaps truly unite the Council for the first time since Azetbur's time.

If only he will come to my way of seeing things . . .

Throwing common sense to the wind, Lorgh finished his Altair water, and also departed the bar. His work on Deep Space Station K-7 was done.

The much more difficult work lay ahead.

Chapter 28

RISA

The sun shone gently on Curzon Dax's face as he relaxed in the reclining chair. *It has been far too long,* he thought. He hadn't had a proper vacation in over a year, and it had been considerably longer than that since he'd been to Risa.

The world was everything Dax could want in a vacation spot, especially after months of dealing with a group of Gallamite delegates who nit-picked every aspect of a trade agreement. His reward for thirteen weeks of staring at delegate brains (and what evolutionary quirk of fate led to a species with transparent skulls?) was to spend a week at his favorite place to relax. Risa had a regulated atmosphere that was heavenly to most humanoid species, an open policy of happiness, and a desire for all its inhabitants to have a good time.

For today, at least, his first day back after so prolonged an absence, Dax just wanted to turn off his brain and relax. He had deliberately left all his work in his office on Earth, and even his staff didn't know where he was, just that he was "indisposed." No one could find him, no one could conscript him to negotiate a treaty or settle a dispute or keep people from killing each other—at least not this week.

And so he lay on the recliner, thinking about nothing. He brought no reading material, had not even gotten a *Horga'hn.*

Frankly, he was too tired for *jamaharon*. *No, for today at least, I am simply pretending that the galaxy outside Risa does not exist.*

He closed his eyes and started to take a nap.

When he no longer felt the sun on his face, he woke up, assuming night had fallen—only to realize that the sun was still up, it was simply being blocked by a man wearing a red Starfleet uniform with a lieutenant commander's symbol on the shoulder patch.

"You know, I was just saying to myself, 'Self,' I said, 'the absolute last person in the entire universe that I want to see right now is Elias Vaughn.' So naturally, you show up to ruin my vacation. Do me a favor and go away, would you please?"

Vaughn didn't move. "I'm afraid that won't be possible, Ambassador Dax. I need you to come with me."

Dax let out a very long sigh. "I'm on a holiday. And what's more, how did you find me?"

Smirking slightly, Vaughn said, "You're getting predictable in your old age, Ambassador. When I realized that nobody on your staff knew where you were, I figured you came either here or to Wrigley's Pleasure Planet. Risa was closer, so I tried here first. Luck of the draw."

"Luck of the irritating, more like. Look, Vaughn, I'm sure that whatever it is that led you to track me down seems very important to you, but it isn't important to me. What's important to me is lying in this recliner for a week."

"The death of innocent people isn't important?"

Dax closed his eyes and exhaled. "Don't get melodramatic with me, Vaughn. People die all the time. It's the one guarantee of living."

"Yes, but those responsible should try to atone, should they not?"

Rubbing the bridge of his nose with his thumb and forefinger, Dax said, "Vaughn, when I came here, I had a splitting headache, the unfortunate result of thirteen weeks spent negotiating with a tiresome collection of Gallamites. The headache was *this close—*" he now held the thumb and forefinger very close together in the air between him and the lieutenant commander "—to going away when you showed up. Now it's back, full bore. I'm about half a step away from having you forcibly removed from the planet—and don't think I'm bluffing, I'm quite well known to the higher-ups hereabouts, and they'll take my side a lot sooner than someone uncouth enough to wear his uniform to a resort. Kindly tell me why you're here so I can ignore you and get back to my nap."

"Do you remember Ian Troi? He's dead."

Dax blinked. "I'm very sorry to hear that." He meant it, too. Troi was a good man.

"He died on Raknal V, investigating a building collapse—that building then fell on both of us. I managed to get out, he didn't. The kicker is that the building was sabotaged by Romulans."

"Romulans?" Dax sat up. His headache grew worse, but the involvement of Romulans on Raknal V changed everything. "What the hell do they have to do with it?"

"A very good question to which greater minds than yours are trying to come up with answers," Vaughn said dryly.

"I sincerely doubt that you know any minds greater than mine, Vaughn, though I don't expect you to admit it, either."

Vaughn stared at Dax with his steely blue eyes for several seconds. Finally, he spoke. "Do you remember what I said to you on the *Carthage* sixteen years ago?"

Dax sighed. "Yes. You said that this wouldn't come to a good end and that it would blow up in our faces."

"I'd say I'm two for two on that score, Ambassador. Hundreds of Klingons and Cardassians have died, and now a Starfleet officer's been killed. This idiocy has gone on so long, the Romulans are using it as an opportunity to foment chaos for their own reasons. It has to stop."

"Agreed. Though I doubt I'll be able to get Prefect Monor and Governor Qaolin into a room together so they can kiss and make up."

"No, but you might use some of that clout with the Klingons that you're so proud of to get them to focus. They're pouring all their resources into developing their military for a fight against Cardassia while ignoring the planet that's the source of the conflict." Vaughn's eyes were fairly smoldering. "I'm not leaving this planet without you, Ambassador. One way or another, you're coming with me to clean up this mess that you've made."

"Relax, Vaughn, you sold me the moment you mentioned the Romulans. Although I am impressed. I didn't think you had this level of fire in you."

"Ian Troi was a good friend. He died because of your carelessness."

"Don't try to put that on me, young man," Dax said, standing up. A breeze blew through his white hair. "You said yourself that Romulans killed him by dropping a building on his head. Troi took an oath that he would die in service of the Federation if called upon to do so. I took no such oath, but I did promise to oversee the development of Raknal V."

"Obviously it has not developed as you hoped."

"Obviously," Dax snapped. "Well, let's be off. We can take whatever ship you and your intelligence friends commandeered for the purpose."

"Fine, we can go back to your room and pack. Where is it?"

Dax grinned. "No need." He indicated the short-sleeved shirt and shorts he wore. "This is all I brought with me. I didn't expect to need any clothes beyond this. I intended to purchase a *Horga'hn* tomorrow, you see."

"Your self-confidence is—"

"Well earned," Dax interrupted, his grin widening, "I assure you."

Vaughn scowled. "If that were the case, we wouldn't still

be tallying the damage from your solution at the Betreka Nebula, would we?"

"Touché," Dax said with a dismissive gesture. "Shall we?"

As they walked toward the resort's exit, Dax couldn't resist one final shot. "By the way, I see you've grown a beard. I don't like it. Looks like a *sehlat* died on your face."

Chapter 29

QO'NOS

For years, K'mpec had heard stories about "the Great Curzon," mostly from Captain Kang, who had gone so far as to name his firstborn after the Trill. So, when the High Council received a request from the ambassador to speak before them, K'mpec had been looking forward to finally seeing the person behind the legend.

What he got was a small, middle-aged, white-haired, smooth-foreheaded humanoid who was indistinguishable from any other small, middle-aged, white-haired, smooth-foreheaded humanoid. Except for the spots. Hardly the subject of song and story.

However, the body was just a shell. The true heart of a warrior cannot be seen with the eyes—and Kang was also not one to name his firstborn after a weakling. So K'mpec gave the Trill the benefit of the doubt as he stood before the assembled Council, one of the high-ceilinged chamber's giant floodlights shining down on him, making the black spots that ringed his face almost glow.

"Councillors—Chancellor Kravokh. I thank you for allowing me to speak before you."

Kravokh nodded. "Your service to the Klingon Empire and its people is well noted by the Council, Ambassador."

"Again, thank you. It is one of those past services that I wish to discuss with you now. Sixteen years ago at the Betreka Nebula, I proposed—and you all accepted—an arrangement whereby the Klingon Empire and the Cardassian Union would each be given a continent on Raknal V to develop. Whoever proved better able to exploit the planet would be granted full control of it—as well as the sacred remains of Ch'gran. I did this because I knew that a true Klingon would not shirk such a challenge, indeed would rise to it, and fight like warriors to the end."

Dax started to pace the hall, looking each councillor in the eye as he spoke. "Yet here I stand before you, sixteen years later, and what have you done? Instead of fighting like warriors, you skulk like vermin!"

Several members of the Council rumbled in outrage. Recognizing the obvious rhetorical technique, K'mpec was not among them. Still, had anyone other than the Great Curzon made this statement, their lives would be forfeit—but had it been anyone other than the Great Curzon, they would not be speaking before the High Council in the first place.

"The Klingon colony on Raknal V is a joke, a model of inefficiency run by a drunken former ship captain. The equipment is substandard, the work uninspired, the population barely interested in sustaining their own lives. Hundreds have died due to incompetence, mismanagement, or the dozens of small battles that have erupted between Klingon and Cardassian. Now a Starfleet officer has been killed, a man with a widow and child who cry out for vengeance. What is it we may tell them?"

K'mpec admired the effectiveness of Dax's oratory. Humans, of course, did not cry for vengeance when their loved ones died—they simply cried. That, and whined about the injustice of it all, as if it were some great revelation that the universe was cruel. But that did not change the fact that an honorable ally died on a Klingon world for no reason other than the apparent incompetence of Klingon builders—or

Cardassian sabotage, but K'mpec believed the Federation report that the Cardassians were not responsible.

"I ask you, Councillors—honorable Chancellor—is this how the heroes of Ch'gran are to be remembered? Are the pioneers who paved the road to space with their sacrifice— with their blood—to be remembered as the instigators of a drawn-out, futile conflict? Are we—"

"Enough!"

K'mpec's attention had been focused on Dax. He turned now to see Kravokh standing in front of his chair of office, his face contorted in fury.

And something else—something K'mpec never imagined he would see in the eyes of a leader of the High Council: fear.

"I have let you speak out of respect for all you have done, Ambassador, but do not try the Council's patience any further! You are not one of us, you *cannot* understand the importance of Ch'gran to our people!"

"I understand completely, Chancellor, that is why I think it is important to—"

"Raknal V will be a Klingon world! We have not attempted to take it by force because we abide by our agreements. Do *not* ask any more of us, Ambassador, or we will be forced to test the limits of our willingness to placate our allies."

"Are we allies?" Dax asked, a wry smile on his face. "I see an empire that has engaged in a massive military buildup without informing its allies of its purpose or number. I see an empire that has rejected every trade overture made by the Federation over the last ten years. I see—"

"Chancellor!"

K'mpec followed this new voice to its source: the large entryway opposite Kravokh, through which ran a young man in a warrior's armor.

"Why do you come before us?" Kravokh asked sharply, though to K'mpec's ears he sounded almost relieved at the interruption.

"We are invaded! The outpost at Narendra III is being at-tacked—by Romulans!"

Council Chambers then burst into a chaotic jumble. Speculations, accusations, denials, all of them ran rampant through the hall.

"Are they mad?"

"The Romulans would never attack!"

"We must destroy them!"

"Narendra III is of no consequence."

"We must have vengeance!"

But all K'mpec could think was, *Lorgh was right. Curse his beady little eyes, I.I.'s information was correct.*

"Enough!" Kravokh's voice silenced the chamber. To Dax, he said, "Ambassador, for obvious reasons, we must sus-pend your—discussion until this crisis is resolved. You are welcome to stay in the First City for as long as you wish. We will summon you when we are ready to proceed."

Dax, to his credit, was completely conciliatory. "Of course, Chancellor. If there is anything I or the Federation can do to be of assistance, please inform me immediately."

With that, the Great Curzon took his leave.

Once he was gone, Kravokh snarled. "Summon General Krin immediately! Why were we not warned of this possibility?"

The councillor to K'mpec's left muttered, "We *were.*"

K'mpec growled, but his fellow councillor was correct. *I was a fool. And thousands will die on Narendra III to pay for my foolishness.*

"We must be cautious," said one councillor whom K'mpec knew to be sympathetic to the Romulans. "These could be the actions of renegades among the Romulans. They have been inactive for over thirty turns—why attack now?"

Another who had no clear position on the Romulans said, "Their leader is weakened. Perhaps he wishes to go out in a blaze of glory."

As the Council continued back and forth while awaiting

the general's arrival, K'mpec found himself tuning it out and thinking ahead to the aftermath of the crisis. He needed to mend fences with Lorgh quickly. Whether this was the action of a few renegades, a new Romulan offensive, or something else entirely, K'mpec needed to know everything that I.I. knew.

A day later, K'mpec found himself calling on Curzon Dax. Although he could have taken rooms at the Federation embassy, Dax instead chose to reserve a room at a Klingon boarding house in the First City—one much closer to the Great Hall than the embassy. K'mpec admired the Trill's fortitude. Few outsiders had the ability to thrive in Klingon accommodations, particularly ones of Dax's age.

K'mpec found Dax in the small room, sitting at the workstation, several padds lying in front of him unread. He was sipping from a mug.

"Greetings—K'mpec, is it not? Join me." Dax held up a bottle of bloodwine from one of the lesser vintners. "We can drink to the honored dead."

That was a toast K'mpec was willing to participate in, especially given the sheer number of honored dead there were to drink to. Exact casualty figures had not yet been tallied, but hundreds of warriors died defending Narendra, not to mention much of the population of that world—and the entire complement of the *U.S.S. Enterprise*, a Starfleet vessel whose captain, Rachel Garrett, sacrificed herself and her ship trying to save Klingon lives. Already Garrett's name was being spoken of in Council Chambers—indeed all over the Empire—with a level of respect that few outsiders had earned.

"To the dead," K'mpec said after Dax had poured him some wine. "May they battle in *Sto-Vo-Kor* for all eternity."

Dax said nothing, but slammed his mug into K'mpec's, some of the wine splashing over the side. Unheedful of it, he drank the remainder, as did K'mpec, who smiled. The wine was weak, but at least Dax knew how to drink like a Klingon.

"I knew her, you know. Garrett. Fine woman. She deserved better."

K'mpec frowned. "She died well."

"I have seen more kinds of death than you would believe possible, K'mpec," Dax said, his voice slurring enough to make one wonder how much bloodwine he had imbibed before K'mpec's arrival. "I have yet to see one that could be classified as dying 'well.'"

Perhaps you do not understand us as well as you think, K'mpec thought, but knew better than to say out loud. Death was life's sole inevitability—how one faced it was the most important thing anyone could do. *How can he understand so much about us and not that?*

Dax gulped some more bloodwine, then continued. "You are the sixth councillor to visit me since yesterday, K'mpec. Are you also here to tell me that you should cede Raknal V to the Cardassians, and would have done if not for Kravokh's insistence?"

Interesting, K'mpec thought. In fact, he had intended to say no such thing. But the fact that five councillors did spoke volumes. Kravokh's support had dwindled even further than K'mpec imagined. Until yesterday, his policies had been good for the Empire, if a bit single-minded. Now, with the embarrassment of the attack on Narendra, Kravokh's Raknal V obsession had cost Klingon—and Federation—lives, and possibly gained them a dangerous enemy. Not that relations between the two Empires were ever all that friendly—the Romulans were tentative allies even at the best of times—but the new Warbird ships that the Romulans had unveiled in the attack on Narendra were as fearsome as anything the Klingon shipyards had produced of late.

And K'mpec could not get the image of Kravokh's fear-laden eyes from his mind.

"No," K'mpec said in answer to Dax's query. "I wish to discuss what may be done to strengthen our ties to the Federation. You were correct in what you said yesterday. Our alliance is weakened to the breaking point."

"Not on our end," Dax said. "I think Captain Garrett showed that quite admirably."

K'mpec rumbled his agreement. "In that spirit, Ambassador, I assure you that the High Council will not forget Captain Garrett's sacrifice. And if they are in danger of doing so—I will remind them."

The ambassador and the councillor spent the next hour discussing possible ways to improve ties between the governments, from trade agreements to increased intelligence sharing between the Defense Force and Starfleet. At the moment, it was simply words, but words led to actions, and the Empire needed to take action.

Especially with regard to the Federation. *If we are not careful, we will make enemies of the entire quadrant. We are far past the point where we can rely solely on our own strength.*

When he returned to his office in the Great Hall near the Council Chambers, K'mpec was met by one of his aides. "There is news, sir," the young woman said. "Praetor Dralath has been overthrown. He has been replaced by an aristocrat named Narviat."

K'mpec smiled. *It seems you overplayed your hand, Praetor.* Then again, the defiant resistance of the Klingons combined with the *Enterprise's* sacrifice made their invasion something less than successful.

The aide added, "And you have received a private message." She handed him a padd.

Dismissing the aide with a wave of his hand, K'mpec sat and thumbed the padd. It scanned his DNA, then decoded the message—which turned out to have the Imperial Intelligence seal.

Lorgh's face then appeared on the padd's display. *"I see you finally wish to hear my words, K'mpec. A pity it comes too late for the inhabitants of Narendra III. I will contact you soon."*

An alarm sounded on K'mpec's workstation: Council was returning to session. K'mpec almost didn't get up. *What is the point?* He knew that the pro-Romulan faction of the Council would see the overthrow of Dralath as a reason not to go to war with them.

But no—he had promised Dax that he would remind the Council of Garrett's sacrifice, and he suspected that such a reminder would be needed now.

A week after his arrival on Qo'noS, Curzon Dax put through a communication to Ambassador Sarek of Vulcan. It was coded with several encryptions that Sarek and his son, Ambassador Spock—who had a facility with computers unmatched in the Federation—had developed. Dax derived a certain amusement from the contortions the Imperial Intelligence eavesdroppers would go through attempting to decode the communiqué, but Dax had every faith in Sarek and his son's abilities to keep the conversation private.

When Sarek's face appeared on the tiny viewscreen, Dax's first words after the pleasantries were of the Vulcan's son. "How was the wedding?"

"It was a most satisfactory affair."

Dax grinned. "I'm sorry I couldn't be there. I've always wanted to meet Spock. But leaving Qo'noS now would be unwise."

"Of course. What way twists the High Council?"

"Every which way, apparently. This situation has gotten intolerable." He leaned back in the uncomfortable Klingon chair. "And it's all my fault. My actions at the Betreka Nebula have led to this disaster."

Sarek raised an eyebrow. *"You can hardly blame yourself. Your solution sixteen years ago was both sound and logical. That events have transpired the way they have is not due to any fault in that logic."*

Smiling grimly, Dax said, "Loath as I am to disagree with

you, old friend, I'm afraid I must. Who else am I *to* blame? The mistake was mine because the solution *wasn't* sound and logical. It was emotional and stupid, and if I'd been thinking, I wouldn't have done it."

"*As you yourself observed at the time, the Klingon mindset is ideally suited for a competition such as what you proposed.*"

"The *Klingon* mindset, yes." Dax leaned forward. "But not the Cardassian mindset. They resented this whole thing from the beginning. I suspect that their disdain for this enterprise is what has led to their continued open hostilities with both the Federation *and* the Empire. How many have died from this conflict? What about the hundred people on the *Chut*, and all the blood feuds that the Klingons started as a result of that? What about Ian Troi?" He leaned back again, suddenly feeling exhausted. "And what about Narendra III?"

"*You can hardly be held responsible for the ambitions of a Romulan praetor.*"

"No, but I can hold myself responsible for giving Chancellor Kravokh something to focus on that distracts him from the possible Romulan threat. I've seen a great deal of death in my time, Sarek. I've lived over half a dozen lifetimes, outlived everyone I've ever cared about, with only recent exceptions— and I fully expect to outlive them, as well, even if I die myself. The joys of joining." Dax pursed his lips. He hoped Sarek's encryptions were as good as they were supposed to be; Sarek was one of the few non-Trill who knew that he was both an old man named Curzon and a centuries-old symbiont named Dax, and he didn't fancy the idea of I.I. finding out—especially this way. But he needed to say this. "So many joined Trill let themselves become inured to it—they allow each lifetime to harden them, make them accustomed to death. But do you know what I've learned from Lela and Torias and Tobin and all the others?"

Sarek came as close to a smile as he was ever likely to. "*I presume that you learned to treasure life precisely because you have seen how fleeting it is.*"

Dax shook his head. "As usual, you know me as well as I know myself."

"*Not a difficult task. You vastly overrate your own self-awareness.*"

"No doubt," Dax said with a bitter chuckle, especially given that he recalled Sarek's father Skon saying something similar to Tobin Dax once. "But that's why this hurts so much. It's not enough that Garrett and Troi and General Worf and so many others are dead—it's that *I'm the one responsible*. More to the point, I have to live with, and go on living with it for a very long time." Dax let out a short laugh. "But enough of my existential ramblings. You know what's truly ridiculous? Klingon Imperial Intelligence *warned* Kravokh about a possible Romulan attack, and he ignored it. His entire being has been focused on the Cardassians and on regaining Ch'gran. It's costing him support. Some of the other councillors are managing to patch up the damage—one in particular, K'mpec, is proving to be a valuable ally—but Kravokh is still focused on Ch'gran to the exclusion of all else."

"*Klingons do have a tendency toward single-mindedness—especially when it relates to something they hold sacred, or something they fear. Since warriors do not admit fear, that makes them all the more fanatical when confronted with it.*"

That got a rise out of Dax. "And what, pray tell, is the logic in telling me something you are damn well aware that I already know?"

Again, Sarek's almost-smile. "*Because, my former pupil, you are not asking the right questions.*"

Rubbing his chin, Dax thought a moment. "Why is Kravokh so focused?"

"*That would be a right question,*" Sarek said with a nod.

Dax thought back to his address to the Council. In particular, he remembered the expression on Kravokh's face when he cut Dax off.

"Fear." He stared at the viewscreen. "Kravokh is afraid of something. Something having to do with Raknal V—or, more likely, Ch'gran."

"If you learn the answer to that question, it may lead you to the path you obviously wish to tread on."

Grinning, Dax asked, "And which path is that?"

"You will learn that when you find the answer."

Again, Dax shook his head. "You've been reading Zen philosophy from Earth again, haven't you?" He held up a hand. "Don't answer that. In any case, you're right. I need to find out more about our esteemed chancellor." He grinned. "And I know just the man to help me." Putting a respectful look on his face, Dax said, "Thank you, Sarek. As usual, you have helped me focus."

"Pray, then, that you do not outlive me, for who shall give you that focus after I am gone?" Before Dax could formulate an adequate retort to that, Sarek held up his hand in the Vulcan salute. *"Peace and long life, my pupil."*

Dax returned the gesture. "Live long and prosper, my teacher."

After Sarek's face faded, Dax contacted Starbase 343 and put in a request with the communications officer there for her to track down Elias Vaughn.

As he walked alongside K'mpec toward the entryway to the seat of the House of Mogh, Lorgh felt a combination of uneasiness and pride. The latter was due to the fact that K'mpec was walking alongside him, and not behind him in an attempt to slide a dagger into his back. If all those Klingons—and Starfleet officers, if it came to that—had to die at Narendra III two turns past, at least their deaths had benefitted the Empire. In general, the *Enterprise*'s sacrifice led to many new trade agreements between the Federation and the Empire, a strengthening of the bonds that Chancellors Gorkon and Azetbur forged fifty-three years ago.

In particular, K'mpec had come to realize the value of Imperial Intelligence. K'mpec had gone from implacable enemy to I.I.'s greatest advocate on the High Council in a mere two years.

A servant opened the door for Lorgh and K'mpec silently, leading them into the sitting room. It was a massive space, with grand double-door entrances (most propped open) to every other room on the ground floor, as well as a staircase leading to the second level. Each piece of furniture sat next to a pedestal on which statuary rested; the walls were hung with weaponry, primarily from the Third Dynasty, and an especially fine tapestry that took up the entire south wall, rendering Kahless and Lukara at Qam-Chee. Lorgh recognized the work of Danqo, an artist renowned for sewing tapestries from the fur of animals he killed with his bare hands—though Lorgh knew that he had become sufficiently renowned that he now had a massive estate where he bred the animals, which were mostly killed by assistants hired for the purpose. Still, only the richest Houses had Danqo's work.

Lorgh noted that one item was missing from its usual place on the wall, but the roar of a small child answered that question in short order, as a six-year-old boy ran through the sitting room, wielding the House *bat'leth* like a champion as he chased some invisible enemy. Lorgh could see traces of the boy's grandfather in the child's face: the old general's eyes and hard-lipped mouth had been passed down.

That, and the deep voice. "You will die, traitor!" he bellowed to no one in particular as he ran into the next room without even acknowledging the two new adults in the house.

"Worf! Get back here!" That was the boy's nurse, Kahlest. Lorgh looked over to see her running down the stairs. "Worf!"

Kahlest was a beautiful woman with lustrous black hair. Her fierce face was lined with the frustrated fury that only a misbehaving child could inspire. Lorgh looked over and saw the lascivious look in his comrade's eyes. K'mpec had made no secret of his desire for Worf's nursemaid.

Upon seeing them, Kahlest stopped short, and stood in a more respectful posture. "Sirs. I was not aware that you had arrived."

"We just did," K'mpec said. "It is *very* good to see you again."

Smiling, Kahlest said, "I'm sure it is. I must chase down Worf before he kills himself or his younger brother."

"Of course," Lorgh said.

The servant who had let them in had already disappeared, and moments later, Mogh and Kaasin came in from yet another entryway. Mogh favored them with a rare smile. "Welcome, my friends, welcome. It is good to see you both. You will, of course, stay for a meal?"

Lorgh could hear both of K'mpec's stomachs rumble at the prospect. "As if we would turn such an offer down."

Soon they were all seated around the dining hall table— Mogh, Kaasin, Kahlest, Worf, and even the newborn, Kurn. It had taken Kahlest several minutes to pry the family *bat'leth* out of Worf's hands. She placed the heirloom— which had been part of the House of Mogh for nine generations—back in its place on the sitting-room wall, then rejoined them in the dining hall.

Almost as big as the sitting room, the hall had two more Danqo pieces on opposite walls. The kitchen staff brought in plate after plate of mouth-watering dishes, from *rokeg* blood pie—which Worf devoured eagerly—to the best heart of *targ* Lorgh had ever tasted.

They spoke of many things, most of them revolving around the infant who spent most of the meal throwing his food around. *He'll be at home in a Defense Force vessel's mess hall*, Lorgh thought with amusement.

"Kurn is a difficult child, but a strong one," Kaasin said as she elegantly placed a handful of *gagh* into her mouth. A *mok'bara* master, Kaasin had already regained her fighting form despite being only a month removed from birthgiving. Some women took years, but one did not become a *mok'bara* master by allowing such trivialities to interfere with being in the best possible fighting condition.

"Which is why he will be coming with us to Khitomer," Mogh said proudly.

At that, Lorgh and K'mpec exchanged a quick look. "That may not be wise," Lorgh finally said.

Mogh frowned. "Why not?" he asked in as dangerous a tone as Lorgh had ever heard him use to a superior.

K'mpec growled slightly, reminding Mogh of his place. Then he explained: "Your assignment to Khitomer is *not* what it appears to be. We *do* require you to supervise the upgrades to the Defense Force installation, as your official orders state."

"However," Lorgh added, "anyone could do that. What we need from you relates to the conversation we had on the *Pu'Bekh* three years ago."

"Romulans." Mogh almost sneered the word.

"What would the Romulans want with Khitomer?" Kaasin asked. "It is merely a research outpost."

"The Romulans place value on symbolism, in particular names and places. Khitomer was the site of the treaty between the Federation and the Empire. The Romulans' attack on Narendra III served to strengthen that treaty. We believe a Romulan agent has been sent there to sabotage the outpost and weaken the alliance."

"How?" Kaasin asked.

K'mpec smiled grimly. "If we knew that, we would not need to send you."

Shaking her head, Kaasin started wolfing down more *gagh*. "Why would the Romulans care? Have they not been our allies also, now that Praetor Narviat is in power?"

Kurn chose that moment to throw his entire plate of

diced *racht* across the room. One of the servants silently moved to clean it up.

"Kurn!" Kaasin yelled. "You are forbidden all food for a day. Kahlest, take him away."

The nurse obeyed immediately, gathering the infant in her arms and taking him out of the dining hall. Kurn rewarded this by spitting on her dress, which Kahlest ignored.

"Quite a woman, your nurse," K'mpec said with a large smile.

"You haven't answered my question," Kaasin said tartly.

Mogh then finally spoke again. "Romulans are not to be trusted. After Praxis, they wormed their way into Klingon Houses like Kreel picking over the remains of our slaughtered enemies."

"Yes," K'mpec said, a serious look returning to his face after his rather weak attempt to distract Kaasin and Mogh with his pursuit of Kahlest. *Unless,* Lorgh thought with amusement, *it wasn't an attempt and he really is that smitten with her.*

K'mpec continued. "While Narviat has remained committed to keeping us as allies, it is unlikely that the entire Senate agrees with this position—nor the entire military. Not to mention those aristocrats who lent support to some of our people after Praxis. The ties between the empires may not be high—but they are deep."

Lorgh swallowed the last of his *targ* heart. "Your job, Mogh, will be to find the tie that is on Khitomer and sever it."

Mogh nodded. "It will be dangerous." He looked at his mate. "Perhaps you and the children should remain here."

"I have already accepted the position on Khitomer, my love," Kaasin said in an iron voice.

"Position?" Lorgh asked. He did not know about this.

"A *mok'bara* instructor," Kaasin said, fixing her gray eyes on Lorgh, her tone losing none of its hardness. "I have given my word to the outpost commander that I will serve this function. I will *not* go back on my word because my mate feels the need to treat me with the same delicacy that he treats his precious tapestries."

"I want to go too, Father!" Worf bellowed suddenly. Lorgh smiled, hearing his grandfather in the child. But young Worf had much more energy than the old general, whom life had so thoroughly beaten down by the time Lorgh met him. "I will help you seek out the Romulan traitor and kill him where he stands!"

"No," Mogh said.

"I am old enough to wield a *bat'leth*! I can fight!"

Kaasin smiled, and now the look in her gray eyes was mischievous. "He already fights better than you, my love, I think he has earned it." Then the iron returned. "Besides, I will not leave him or Kurn behind with Kahlest and the servants for four months."

Mogh laughed, a harsh sound, as if the man's larynx was unaccustomed to it. "I know better than to argue with you, Kaasin. So be it. We shall all go to Khitomer, as planned. And I shall root out the traitor."

Worf let out a cheer. "He will die at our hands!"

Before conversation could continue, a beeping emitted from K'mpec's coat of office. Reaching into one of the voluminous pockets that lined the garment, he pulled out a communications device. "Rnh. The High Council has declared an emergency session. I must go. Tell Kahlest I look forward to seeing her again before you leave." He rose, and activated the device. "This is K'mpec, code *wa'maH Soch*."

A red transporter beam took the councillor away.

"Good," Worf said, reaching over to K'mpec's plate, which still had some half-eaten food. "I can finish his blood pie!"

Mogh and Kaasin both laughed at their older son's enthusiasm for his meal—not to mention K'mpec's—but Lorgh could not join them. He was concerned. Worf could at least defend himself, and both Mogh and Kaasin were the worthiest of warriors. But Lorgh feared the worst might happen on

Khitomer, and he would not endanger both sons of Mogh. He owed General Worf too much to allow all of his male heirs to go to their possible deaths. The one least able to fight was the one who needed to stay behind.

Besides, if the worst happens before Mogh can identify the spy, I will need a long-term backup plan.

"I urge you, Kaasin, to reconsider sending Kurn, at least. He is but an infant who cannot even throw *racht* with any accuracy, much less a blade."

"I will protect him," Kaasin said.

"Of that I have no doubt, but to risk your entire line . . ."

Mogh fixed Lorgh with a stare. "Do you question our strength?"

"No, but I know the Romulans. If they learn of your true mission, or if you uncover theirs, all of your lives may be forfeit."

"So I am to leave my newborn child with servants and inferiors while I teach *mok'bara* to an outpost full of fools?"

If they are such fools, why did you accept the assignment? Lorgh was tempted to ask, but that would have been a mistake. Kaasin was, like any mother, trying to protect her family, and Lorgh could not blame her. So he played his final piece. "One of the warriors assigned to Khitomer is Ja'rod."

That got their attention, as Mogh knew it would.

His mouth full of blood pie, Worf asked, "Who's Ja'rod?"

"My greatest rival," Mogh said. "And his House and ours have been in conflict for generations. You remember Huraga?"

Lorgh recalled that the young warrior was a shipmate of Mogh's on the *Pu'Bekh* and a friend to the House of Mogh.

Worf seemed to know him as well. "He told good stories."

Mogh smiled. "Yes. You remember the one about the time we fought against the House of Duras?"

Nodding eagerly, Worf said, "That was a great story!"

"Ja'rod is the head of that House now." Mogh looked at Lorgh. "If he is on Khitomer—"

Lorgh held up a hand. "We have no proof that he is the Romulan agent. In fact, we have no reason to assume that Ja'rod has any links to the Romulans at all. Yes, his ancestors sold ships to the Romulans decades ago and brought together rich Romulans with destitute Klingons, but that means nothing for the purposes of this mission."

Kaasin bared her teeth. "The House Head is responsible for the actions of his House."

"By law and tradition, yes—but on Khitomer that does not make Ja'rod a spy."

Mogh nodded. "It also makes our entire family a target."

"I will not leave Kurn *here!*" Kaasin said in a tone that would brook no argument.

In Kaasin's emphasis on where Kurn was to be kept, Lorgh saw how to move in for the kill. "*I* will take charge of the boy while you are gone. He will be cared for as if he were one of my own children until you return."

Mogh and Kaasin exchanged a look. Klingons had no telepathy like Vulcans or Betazoids or Letheans, but Lorgh knew from his relationship with his own mate that couples often had unique psionic abilities all their own. Though he could not hear it, an entire conversation took place between the two with that look.

Then Mogh turned back to Lorgh, both challenge and concession in his dark eyes. "If you were any other man, I would kill you for trying to steal my son. But my father named you friend, as have I. For that reason—and because I would not put Ja'rod in a position where he can harm my son before he is of an age to defend himself—I will trust you to care for Kurn while we are gone."

"Thank you," Lorgh said. "Believe me, this way is for the best." He leaned back, resting his hands on his belly. "Now then, what is for dessert?"

Chapter 30

ROMULUS

Only two people still living knew of Koval's mountain retreat. The house was nestled in an outcropping halfway up the peak of Kor Thon, constructed of sensor-proof plastiform. Snow pounded against the outside of the house, drifts cascading on the windows. No roads led to the house; the configuration of the outcropping and the prevailing winds made approach by air all but impossible. It had not been easy to get the house constructed, but Koval had spent his many years in the intelligence field amassing currency of a variety of sorts—monetary in order to acquire material and builders, informational in order to acquire permission and secrecy—that enabled him to have this vacation spot all his own.

Presently, he sat in the sitting room, drinking a hot mug of *tarka* and reading an old-style codex book. It was a philosophical treatise on the efficacy of obedience to the state, written by a Cardassian philosopher from some three hundred years past.

The Tal Shiar agent was relieved to see that the green transporter beam that appeared in the middle of the sitting room coalesced into one of the two left who knew of this place: Timol, his chief aide. (The other was the head of the Tal Shiar, Jekri Kaleh, the only person from whom Koval dared not keep any secrets.) Timol had been a most compe-

tent aide, providing Koval with excellent intelligence on
Praetor Dralath—who had proven especially susceptible to
the pheremone enhancers Timol wore—and the inner
workings of the Senate right up until Dralath was overthrown. Timol had survived Narviat's coup, and gone back
to work directly for Koval.

He did not admonish Timol for disturbing him while he
was on vacation, for she would never have violated his privacy without reason. Instead, he set down the book and regarded her. "What is it?"

"I have managed to intercept the contents of an interrogation conducted by the Obsidian Order."

Irony, Koval thought. *I read Cardassian philosophy and
am now confronted with Cardassian intelligence.* "An interrogation by whom?"

Timol raised an eyebrow. "Not of whom?"

"The conductor of the interrogation will dictate the usefulness of the intelligence provided by its subject."

Smiling, Timol said, "Well then you'll be pleased to
know that the interrogator is Corbin Entek."

This surprised Koval, though he made no outward show
of it. That was one of the Order's top agents. "Entek is not
one to misplace his files."

"He is not, no, but my source is somewhat more susceptible to my charms than others of his species." Timol's smile
became a grin.

Koval nodded. Cardassians were not generally as recep-
tive to Timol as Romulans, but those who were found her as
irresistable as she required them to be. "Very well. Who is
the subject?"

"A Klingon by the name of Dirak, of the House of Kultan."

That was a House that Koval had encountered before.
"They are the ones who have attempted to develop biogenic
weapons—against the wishes of the Klingon High Council."

"Yes," Timol said, though Koval had not phrased it as a

question. "Apparently, the High Council has reversed their sanction. According to the information Dirak provided to Entek, House Kultan has been commissioned to develop a biogenic weapon on their base at Khitomer."

At that, Koval stood up. The Klingons had put together a research outpost of some sort on the site of the hated Federation–Klingon treaty of over fifty years ago. That alliance had shifted the balance of power and indirectly led to the Romulan Empire's retreat from the business of galactic politics—with occasional exceptions, of course. "So, the honorless cowards of the Klingon Empire circumvent the Khitomer Accords on the very soil on which they signed them. How fitting." He scowled. "You are *sure* this is a genuine interrogation?"

She held out the padd she carried. "You may witness it yourself. I also had it checked by every expert we have. There were no changes, no alterations, no trickery."

"At least not on the part of the Cardassians. That does not mean there is no such trickery from the Klingons. It is possible that this Dirak person has led the Order astray—or that the Order has deliberately planted this information with us."

"I doubt that," Timol said. "Believe me, the person I received it from was not expecting me—nor had he any desire to provide the intelligence." Timol spoke with her usual confidence. Koval had no reason to assume it wasn't warranted.

"True. And I find it difficult to credit that any Klingon agent could successfully fool Corbin Entek."

Koval started the display on the padd, which showed a Klingon sitting in a chair in an empty, featureless room. The eyes of the Klingon—presumably Dirak—were equally featureless and empty. He had obviously been drugged. The Order, Koval knew, had an excellent pharmacopeia. A voice in the background asked questions, to which Dirak gave answers in a dull monotone.

Most of the interrogation was full of useless information. That was the problem with drugs, they led to a literal-minded subject. Dirak provided a great deal of "intelligence" regarding his own eating habits and the women he had bedded, none of which was of the slightest interest to Koval. He was sure Entek had even less interest, but the Order agent was patient enough to sift through the chaff in order to find the wheat. Eventually, that wheat was forthcoming, as Dirak told of the secret laboratory at the Khitomer outpost where the biogenic weapon was being developed.

After he had seen and heard enough, Koval turned off the display. This was important enough intelligence that he needed to verify it—and also share it with his superior. "You will set up an appointment with Kaleh immediately. I will also contact our agent on Khitomer to verify whether or not this Klingon spoke true."

"He spoke the truth as he knew it," Timol said.

"Of that I have little doubt. The question becomes whether or not what *he* was told was the truth."

For a brief moment, Koval gazed longingly on the codex book he had set aside on the couch. *Cardassian philosophy will have to wait until a more opportune time.*

"Return us to Tal Shiar Headquarters," he instructed his aide.

She activated a control on her wrist, and a green transporter beam whisked them back to the capital city.

Chapter 31

KHITOMER

After completing her preclass exercises to limber up, Kaasin went to the board to see who had signed up for this morning's *mok'bara* class. She offered two classes, one just prior to the day shift's commencement, the other prior to the night shift's, allowing the warriors the opportunity to begin their work with mind and spirit in harmony and ready for whatever trials would come their way.

When she, Mogh, Worf, and Kahlest first arrived on Khitomer a month earlier, she had over thirty people per class. Unsurprisingly, attrition took its toll on that number, and she was now down to a dozen regulars per class, plus the occasional extra, add-on, once-a-week student, or other straggler.

On this day, sixteen names were on the list—her twelve regulars, one occasional, and three brand-new names. Two were recent transfers to the base—crew rotation and replacement always meant new students.

The other was Ja'rod.

Scowling, Kaasin left the warm-up room, clad only in the white, skin-tight shirt and pants traditionally worn for the *mok'bara*. Unlike her students, the trim on the left half of her shirt's V-neck and cuffs on both shirt and pants were colored maroon, indicating her status as a master.

As she turned a corner, she literally bumped into Ja'rod. The current Head of the House of Duras stood half a head shorter than Kaasin—who was tall for a female—and was presently also dressed for the *mok'bara*.

"What do you want, Ja'rod?" Kaasin asked, restraining herself from instinctively wrapping her hands around the man's throat.

He smiled. "Simply to make your mate's life easier. He seems determined to follow my every move, and I thought if I took your class, it would allow him time to perform his other duties. Or has he been assigned to be my bodyguard without my being informed?"

Still scowling, Kaasin said, "You know the history between our Houses, Ja'rod."

"Yes," Ja'rod said emphatically, "*history*. As in, the past. We should be concerned with the present—and the future. This rivalry between our Houses must end, Kaasin."

"If you are so unconcerned with the past, why did you not change your House name to the House of Ja'rod? If you wish to distance yourself from the past as you say—"

Ja'rod laughed. "It seemed pointless. When my esteemed father ascended to *Sto-Vo-Kor* and I became House Head, I had already named my son Duras. *He* is the future of our House, and it seemed foolish to change our name when he would simply change it back to the name it has had for two centuries." Ja'rod put a hand on Kaasin's shoulder. She glared at it, and he quickly removed it, but he did lock eyes with her. "Kaasin, I ask you please, use whatever influence you have with Mogh to get him to stop. This constant suspicion serves no one. Our Houses are both strong ones—we should be allies, not enemies. For the good of the Empire, if nothing else."

Kaasin stared right back into Ja'rod's brown eyes, and took some measure of satisfaction out of the fact that he finally looked away. "I will convey your message to my husband."

"That is all I ask." He smiled. "I look forward to learning

more of *mok'bara* under your fine tutelage. I've heard many good things about the class."

Ja'rod walked off. Kaasin growled deep in her throat.

An hour later, however, she had to admit that Ja'rod was an excellent student. His movements were expectedly awkward, but he grew accustomed to the forms with as much speed as anyone Kaasin had ever taught, and more than most. By the end of the class, he was already moving as if he'd been doing the forms for weeks.

After dismissing the class, she overheard a conversation between two of the control-room officers, L'Kor and Gi'ral.

"I think we may finally see the Romulans coming out of their shell," L'Kor was saying. "Since Narviat ascended to power, their Senate has actually put through some sensible policies. In fact—"

Whatever else L'Kor planned to say about the Romulan Senate was lost when he departed the building where the classes were held—apparently he intended to change into his uniform elsewhere.

Kaasin proceeded to her private changing room, her crest furrowing in annoyance. Like Mogh, she thought Ja'rod the prime suspect for being Lorgh's Romulan spy. Now, she started to wonder.

That night at supper, she sat with Mogh. Khitomer was a large planet with only four thousand living on it—half Defense Force warriors like Mogh, the other half scientists and other civilian support staff like Kaasin—so there was sufficient space that Mogh was able to obtain use of a ten-room cabin six *qelIqams* from the main base.

The cabin was proximate to a massive forest teeming with wildlife. After much pleading with his parents, Mogh and Kaasin had permitted Worf to take a hunting trip, accompanied by Kahlest. They had left a few hours ago, and would not be back until the following morning. Kaasin noticed that the family *bat'leth* was missing from the wall. "Did Worf take the *bat'leth* with him?"

Mogh smiled. "Of course he did. Can you imagine him using any other weapon? It has been all Kahlest can do to keep him from sleeping with the thing."

"That weapon has been in the family for nine generations. Is it wise to let a child run free with it?"

At that, Mogh laughed. "Were *you* not the one who said he wielded it better than I?"

Kaasin returned the smile. "True." She stuffed some *bregit* lung into her mouth, the smile falling from her face. "I had a new student for the morning class."

Mogh nodded. "Ja'rod."

Of course he knows, she thought. *Mogh has been keeping a close eye on him.* "He claimed that he signed up to make it easier for you to perform surveillance on him. I think, my love, that you are watching him too closely."

"One might argue that I am not watching him closely enough. He is a *wam* serpent, that one, waiting only for the right moment to strike."

"Perhaps, but if he knows you are hovering over him like a predator, do you truly expect him to reveal himself? And what if he is not the spy?"

Mogh snorted, an action that caused him to spit pieces of *bregit* lung onto the table. "Who else could it be?"

"L'Kor, for one." She shared her overheard conversation.

Rubbing his bearded chin, Mogh said, "Perhaps—if nothing else, I should investigate the possibility." He sighed. "You are right, I have let my hatred for Ja'rod blind me to other possibilities. I will observe L'Kor tomorrow, speak with him, see what—impressions I get from him. And, of course, check his service record." Then he smiled. "However, that is for tomorrow. For tonight, Kahlest and Worf are far away. Kurn is even farther away. We have the cabin to ourselves."

Kaasin smiled, tossed her *bregit* lung aside, and ran her

fingernails across Mogh's bearded cheek, drawing blood. Inflamed by the smell of her mate's scent, she leapt into his arms.

The transmission was routed through so many subsystems that even if it was detected—unlikely as that might be—it could never be traced. Unfortunately, that also meant that the image of the Romulan that Ja'rod saw was barely visible, the voice laced with static.

The Romulan—Ja'rod had not been given his name—spoke a few words, but they were lost to that very interference. "Please repeat," Ja'rod whispered. He did not need to speak so softly, of course. He was *qelIqams* away from anyone, and whispering would not confound any decent listening device. Not that there were any, as he had swept for such devices thoroughly before initiating his weekly contact.

"Are you sure of your findings?"

"Not completely, no. But I have investigated thoroughly, and found no evidence of a biogenic weapon. Are *you* sure that your source was trustworthy?"

The Tal Shiar agent hesitated. Romulan faces were difficult to read at the best of times, especially as skilled an operative as this one, and the poor image quality meant that seeing that face was impossible anyhow. It frustrated Ja'rod—he preferred to know what people were thinking. He certainly knew that—while he had not convinced Kaasin of his innocence—he had seeded sufficient doubt in her mind that she and Mogh would, at the very least, ease up on their surveillance of him. Her gray eyes gave all that away in an instant.

Finally, the agent spoke. *"The interrogation record we intercepted from the Obsidian Order passed every authenticity test we could give it. The Klingon they questioned did serve on the team that developed the biogenic weapon prototype."*

"Could he have been lying?"

Even the poor image quality allowed Ja'rod to see the

Romulan's eyebrow rise in a disturbingly Vulcan-like manner. *"I was under the impression that your people preferred not to lie."*

"Is that supposed to be a joke?"

"A small one, admittedly. However, the interrogator in question is known to me, and I truly doubt that he would extract anything but the truth." A pause. *"Still, it does not matter."*

Ja'rod frowned. "Why not?"

"Because my supervisor has already passed on the details of the interrogation to some friends of hers in the military. They are planning an attack on Khitomer in two days."

Now Ja'rod growled deep in his throat. "You cannot be serious. There is no proof that a biogenic weapon is being developed here."

"Proof is no longer an issue. The very existence of an outpost on that world is a constant reminder of your people's alliance with the Federation. That alliance is an affront to us."

"They are 'my people' in name only." Ja'rod spat with contempt. "Our future lies in an alliance with a strong empire, not with a weak collection of fools." He bared his teeth. "The Federation alliance is an affront to me as well, and many other Klingons."

"Just so. Your job is to transmit the access codes to the lead Romulan ship so that they can lower the shields and provide any other means of sabotaging the base." The Romulan then proceeded to outline the exact time and nature of the attack, which ship would be leading it, and several other details. Ja'rod had no doubt that some facts had been left out—like how the Defense Force vessels assigned to this sector were to be dealt with—but Ja'rod knew what he needed to. *"You will die for the greater glory of both our peoples."*

"Yes." Ja'rod smiled. That, more than anything, was why Klingons and Romulans needed to be allies. Romulans understood what it meant to die for one's people. The Federation was far too concerned with the pointless extension and preservation of life, which served only to crowd the galaxy with more weaklings. Without a willingness to give one's life, there was no strength. When the quadrant bowed before the joint Klingon–Romulan Empire, Ja'rod hoped that perhaps all would finally understand that.

He only prayed that his son Duras would live long enough to see that day.

It was with an energized sense of purpose that Mogh entered the outpost control room. Although this room itself was being left mostly untouched, it was from here that most of the upgrades that Mogh was supervising would be implemented. The new shields were already in place, ready to defend the outpost against anything from Romulan disruptors to Cardassian phasers. The new weapons systems would be online within a week, and the old ion cannons were still in place. While ancient, they still had sufficient firepower to disable a ship in orbit.

Today, he was determined to find the Romulan spy. He had already begun a computer search on L'Kor's activities over the past years, and began some inquiries among the contacts Lorgh had given him regarding the man's activities. It might have been nothing, but he had to investigate the possibility. The conversation Kaasin overheard meant he could do little else.

And I will not cease keeping an eye on Ja'rod.

"The upgrades go well," Mogh said to L'Kor.

A big, broad-shouldered man, L'Kor stared at Mogh for several seconds before simply saying, "Yes."

"I wish to run a simulation on the new shields. I assume we have enough information on Romulan weaponry to do so?"

L'Kor stared at Mogh some more. "Do you think such an attack likely?"

"I think such an attack is possible. After all, one praetor

has been overthrown—who is to say another might not be? Politics are unpredictable."

"That is certainly the case. But I cannot imagine why Romulans would attack this base. There is much about them that is honorable."

"True." Mogh pretended to concede the point, though he disagreed fervently. "I have always admired Romulans." He smiled lasciviously. "And their women."

Another of the officers assigned to the control room, a woman named Gi'ral, said, "For shame, Captain Mogh. You are a married man." She smiled. "Though I will admit, I have seen some Romulan men who might be tolerable in bed."

At that, all three of them laughed. Mogh added, "I merely speak of aesthetics. Believe me, I would not do anything to anger my mate."

Gravely, L'Kor said, "Then you are a wise man. Kaasin's *mok'bara* class revealed parts of my body I was unaware could ache in such a manner."

"Kaasin is rather skilled at that. She demonstrated those skills last night very well."

Now it was L'Kor's turn to smile lasciviously. "With a child in the house? Impressive that you would be able to bed your mate without interruption."

"Worf was out hunting with his nurse last night—they returned this morning with an animal that will make a fine feast tonight for the troops. He donated it to the mess hall." Mogh smiled. "And we never actually *made* it to the bed."

Again, the trio laughed.

A voice came from behind Mogh. "If you are to conduct tests, then do so and have done with it."

Mogh turned to see Commander Moraq standing in the doorway to his office, which adjoined the control room. The supervisor of this base, the commander had not been pleased at Mogh's assignment, feeling that he himself was perfectly capable of supervising the upgrades, and that Command did not need to send someone else to do the work of overseeing them. Since his true work on Khitomer could not be revealed to Moraq, Mogh had gone to great lengths to stay out of the man's way and not interfere with his command of the base. Moraq deserved no less, especially after a check of his service record indicated nothing suspicious—quite the opposite, in fact, as his list of kills included a considerable number of Romulans.

Unfortunately, Moraq's attitude did not improve with time. He was never insubordinate, but he kept his desire for Mogh to be elsewhere at the forefront.

"Come," Mogh said, slamming L'Kor on the shoulder, "let us run these simulations, and see what will happen if the Romulans decide to forgo that honor we both admire so."

L'Kor nodded in response. Moraq simply turned on his heel and went back into his office.

Chapter 32

I.K.S. SOMPEK

"Sir, we are receiving a distress call."

At last, a call to battle, Kang thought. For the past week, he had been given the "honor" of conducting several members of the High Council—including Kravokh—on an inspection tour. The *Sompek* was one of the new *Vakk*-class ships that had been constructed as part of Kravokh's ship construction initiatives, and now the Council, in their infinite bureaucracy, wished to see them in action.

Except, of course, Kang knew that there was no action to be had as long as such important personages were on board. The tour was as much to show the people how much interest Kravokh and the Council took in the defense of the Empire, and so not only did everyone know that they were present, but they had a virtual armada for an escort. All the ships assigned to this sector served as protection, as well as *Qo'noS One* and three of the Council's own strike ships. This collection of vessels could no doubt conquer several small interplanetary governments without too much difficulty. No one would be foolish enough to challenge them.

As a result, Kang had spent a week observing. Worse, what he observed were Kravokh and the assorted councillors observing. A scientist, his mate Mara appreciated the value of such tasks, but Kang had no use for them. He was a warrior, one of the most renowned soldiers of the Empire. That made his choice as the captain to lead this nonsensical "tour" as inevitable as it was frustrating.

Now, however, the monotony may be broken. "Specifics," he instructed the operations officer who gave the report.

"It is coming from the Morska system, sir. The *I.K.S. Konmat* is under attack by three *Galor*-class vessels."

"Cardassians." Kang almost sneered the word.

Just as he spoke it, the rear door to the bridge slid open to reveal Kravokh and three of the five councillors who accompanied him—as well as their entourage of bodyguards—came onto the bridge.

"What Cardassians?" Kravokh asked.

Kang turned to the operations officer. "Report to the chancellor."

The officer seemed surprised at first, but recovered quickly and spoke in a far more respectful tone than Kang had ever heard the young officer use to Kang himself. "Sir, according to this signal, the *Konmat* is under attack by three *Galor*-class ships, but—" He hesitated.

"But what?" Kravokh prompted.

The officer looked quickly at Kang, who cried, "Speak!"

"I—I am not sure that the distress signal is genuine, sir."

Kang's lips curled. The officer was too intimidated by the presence of such exalted warriors to be anything other than truthful. If anything, he had probably understated his case. Kang looked at the pilot. "Time to Morska?"

Without hesitation, the pilot spoke, meaning she had wisely already calculated it. "Three hours, ten minutes at warp eight, sir."

Turning to the chancellor, Kang said, "With respect, we should send two ships—I recommend the *Aktuh* and the *Gowlak*—and—"

"No." Kravokh strode to the area between the command

chair and the forward viewer. "I grow weary of these Cardassian invasions of our space. Instruct the convoy to set course for Morska."

Kang seethed. Bad enough that an entire garrison of vessels were being wasted on a glorified publicity exercise, but this . . . "We do not even know that there *is* a Cardassian invasion of our space. And to send a dozen ships on such an errand is akin to using a disruptor cannon to hunt a single *lIngta'*."

To Kang's irritation, that prompted a smile from the chancellor. "In the end, though, the *lIngta'* is dead. Give the order, Captain."

Any other captain might have jumped at that point. To even question the Supreme Commander of the Klingon Empire was courting death. But Kang had lived far too long to be so easily intimidated. He had been leading troops into battle when Kravokh's father was too small to hold a *bat'leth*.

Still, challenging his authority for more than a few seconds would cause more problems than it would solve. For one thing, the other councillors—not to mention their bodyguards—would probably cut Kang to ribbons. Normally he would expect at least some loyalty from his crew, but based on his operations officer's stammering, perhaps this was not a normal situation. Nor did he wish to force his crew to make that decision.

So, finally, he said, "Instruct the convoy to set course for the Morska system, warp eight."

"Course laid in, sir," the pilot said almost immediately. This time, Kang did not welcome the woman's efficiency.

"Execute."

Chapter 33

KHITOMER

Mogh exited the control room with a combination of glee and regret. The former was because the shield tests went better than expected. If they were attacked by Romulan or Breen disruptors, Federation or Cardassian phasers, or even Kinshaya pulse blasts, they'd be ready.

The latter was due to his inability to root out the Romulan spy. L'Kor and Gi'ral both expressed admiration for certain characteristics of Romulans, but neither of them showed any outward indication, and the computer searches had turned up nothing suspicious.

On the other hand, Ja'rod was looking more promising. Mogh was still unable to eavesdrop on the man's residence, and there were several anomalies in his service record. None of it was hard evidence, but it was enough to encourage a deeper digging. *That would be more Lorgh's task than mine.*

As he exited the control room and headed for the exit, he was greeted by Kahlest and Worf. The boy was, of course, holding the family *bat'leth*, as he had been when he triumphantly returned that morning with what would become the evening meal for the Defense Force troops.

Mogh noted with pride that the weapon was clean. Knowing how to maintain the weapon was as important as knowing how to wield it—at least that was what Mogh always believed, especially given how much better at the former he was than the latter—and he was glad to see that Worf had taken that lesson to heart.

"How was your day, my son?" Mogh asked.

"It was all right, Father," Worf said, sounding bored. "I want to go hunting again. Next time, I will catch the beast's father!"

Mogh smiled. "I am sure that you will, Worf."

"Have you found him yet?"

Again, Mogh felt pride at his son's good sense. He knew that Mogh's mission was secret, and so never spoke openly of it outside of their cabin. "Not yet, but I have a suspicion. Now, however, is not the time for—"

"Husband!"

Mogh looked up to see Kaasin entering. She still wore her *mok'bara* shirt and pants, covered with a long maroon coat.

"I was hoping to find you all here," she said. "My class has ended, and I thought we should eat with the troops in the mess hall—partake of the feast our son has provided."

Worf's eyes grew wide. "Can we, Father, please?"

As if I could say no to either of you. "That is an excellent idea, my love."

"Of course it is." Kaasin smiled, her gray eyes almost glowing. Mogh felt his heart sing, as it always did in her presence.

He still recalled the day he brought her to the seat of their House, in the sitting room under the Qam-Chee tapestry and the same *bat'leth* that Worf now carried with him everywhere. There, Mogh's mother gave her blessing to their union. His father, Worf's namesake, had been on a mission, but he gave his own blessing in due course. Mogh would always serve the Empire, always do his duty, but nothing pleased him more than simply being in Kaasin's presence.

As they proceeded toward the mess hall, an alarm sounded.

"Alert status. Alert status."

Mogh immediately ran to a workstation, and called up the current display on the tactical monitor in the control room.

It showed several Romulan warbirds decloaking in orbit.

Such an attack is more possible than either of us dreamed, L'Kor, he thought sourly.

Then the display showed that the outpost shields—the same shields he had just spent the day testing—had gone down.

Slamming his fist onto an intercom channel, he cried, "Mogh to control room! Commander Moraq, come in!"

There was no reply from the outpost commander, nor any of his crew.

"Engineering, this is Captain Mogh, respond!"

Again, nothing. *This is not simply an attack—we are sabotaged.*

But Mogh's first thoughts were for his family. "Kahlest, take Worf to the sub-basement."

Holding up his *bat'leth*, Worf said, "I wish to fight beside you, Father!"

"No!" Mogh closed his eyes for a moment, then opened them. "I need you to protect Kahlest. No harm must come to her, Worf, understood?"

"I understand, Father. I will die before I let anyone harm her."

Let us hope it does not come to that, Mogh thought, now more grateful than ever that he had allowed Lorgh to talk them into leaving Kurn behind. "Good," he said. "Go!"

Before he could say anything to his mate, she spoke. "We have been sabotaged by whoever it was Lorgh sent you to find."

Mogh shook his head. *I knew I loved this woman for a reason.* "Yes. I do not know who to trust—except you. Go to the engineering section, see if you can re-establish the shields. I will go to the control room and see if anyone there still lives."

The entire complex was then rocked with a tremendous impact. Mogh lost his footing and fell to the ground, which seemed to buck and weave beneath him despite being made from the strongest rock available.

Kaasin, of course, had maintained her footing. She moved toward him, concern for her mate overriding a warrior's preference not to be helped in any way. Mogh waved her away. "Go to engineering! Quickly!"

Nodding, she turned and ran toward the access ladder.

Clambering to his feet, Mogh ran in the opposite direction toward the control room.

The base shook twice more during his sojourn, and Mogh fell over one of those times. Plasma fires erupted all around him. The stench of burning plastiform and damaged equipment only served to get his blood boiling. *The Romulans will pay for this—and so will the traitor.*

To Mogh's confusion, the door to the control room was closed. It had never been closed in all the weeks he had been here, and did not understand why it was shut now. Worse, the privacy seal had been engaged.

His own code overrode that, of course, but in the time it took him to enter it, the base was rocked yet again.

When the door rumbled open, a stench like rotting meat assaulted Mogh's nostrils. He recognized it instantly as *SIp*, a gas that rendered one comatose—if left untreated, it could easily lead to death. It was part of the control room's security system, meant to provide the option of incapacitating intruders to leave them alive to be interrogated.

SIp's dense green color also resulted in reduced visibility if used in an enclosed space. Covering his nose and mouth with his hand, Mogh made his way through the jade miasma to the environmental control console in order to clear it. He almost tripped over the prone forms of L'Kor and Gi'ral. Saboteurs were, in Mogh's experience, unlikely to gas themselves, so the two of them were no doubt innocent.

Worry about that later, he thought. As soon as he activated the scrubbers to clean the air of the *SIp,* he sent out a distress signal and ran a diagnostic on all systems.

To his horror, the Romulans themselves lowered the shields. *They had the access codes!*

The base had also stopped shaking, and Mogh was now reading multiple transports to the surface. The Romulans had sent down ground troops to take care of whoever was left.

That number was small. Sensors registered very few life signs, and several were in this room. Mogh turned around and looked over the unconscious forms. He recognized most of the regular staff, but conspicuous by his absence was Commander Moraq—he wasn't in his office or the control room. *Could he be the traitor after all?*

The base shook again, but this was not from disruptor fire. On one of the security viewers, Mogh saw a massive explosion from one of the secondary laboratories in one of the smaller compounds near the base. From the looks of it, the compound's generator overloaded.

Based on the reduction in life-sign readings, two hundred Klingons died in that explosion alone.

Unfortunately, sensors, environmentals, and communications were all Mogh could get to operate. All tactical systems, from the shields to the ion cannons, had gone offline, and nothing Mogh could do would reactivate them. *The saboteur did his work well.*

Mogh was no longer sure if it was Ja'rod or Moraq or someone else entirely who was responsible for this treachery—for this murder—but Mogh swore he would not rest until the deaths of all these good people were avenged. This was *not* a good day—or a good way—to die.

Then he heard a humming sound behind him. Mogh whirled to see half a dozen Romulans materialize in the room. Mogh had his disruptor out before they could coalesce into their natural form, and killed two of them before he felt the heat of one of their disruptor beams slice into his torso.

As he fell to the ground, his final thoughts were of Kaasin and his son Worf, and of Kurn, who would be the only one left to carry on the family name.

Centurion Tokath shook his head as he looked at the three corpses—the two antecenturions the Klingon had killed before Antecenturion Belear cut the Klingon down. "Senseless. The control room was supposed to be gassed."

Belear knelt down over another Klingon body. "This one is not dead."

"Neither are these others," said another antecenturion.

"That one probably entered after the gas. Senseless," Tokath repeated. He had served loyally in the Romulan military for decades, but as he grew older, he found that he had less and less taste for death. *Perhaps it is time I retired.* He had hoped that with the insanity of Praetor Dralath's regime a thing of the past things might improve, but governments were, he had decided, inherently insane. *What is madder, that the Klingons would develop a biogenic weapon or that our response would be to murder four thousand Klingons?*

Either way, Tokath had lost his taste for combat.

Aloud, he said, "No doubt he is responsible for the distress signal we detected."

The young antecenturion snorted. "As if that matters. The Klingon ships in this sector have been led to the Morska system. We have nothing to fear from—"

"Centurion!"

That was Belear, who now stood at one of the control room consoles. "What is it?" Tokath asked.

"Sensors are detecting a ship approaching at high warp!"

Damn those fools in the Tal Shiar, they assured us that Kang's fleet would be distracted!

Tokath walked over to the display—only to see that the

configuration of the ship was all wrong, as was its course. The ship wasn't coming from the Morksa system, it was coming from the Federation. "It's Starfleet," he said after a moment. "They must have been near the border and picked up the distress signal." More foolishness. The commander had not bothered to jam the signal when it began to broadcast, just before Tokath was sent to the planet. The commander had faith in the Tal Shiar's information, forgetting that Starfleet had a tendency to come to the aid of—well, anyone, truth be told. The Federation's desire to help people was as pervasive as it was predictable, and that it wasn't anticipated as a possibility distressed Tokath. *Have I lost the taste for combat, or merely for those who run it?*

"Gather up the prisoners—him, too," he added, pointing at the Klingon they had shot. "The doctor might be able to revive him." He contacted the mother ship. They were going to need to leave sooner rather than later if they didn't want to risk a confrontation with Starfleet. Tokath doubted that the commander wished a repeat of Narendra III, after all . . .

Kaasin arrived in the engine room of the Khitomer Base just in time to see Commander Moraq cut down by a disruptor fired by Ja'rod.

The engine room housed all the control systems and power for the entire base—with the exception of a few of the compounds holding the secondary laboratories, which had their own power sources. She carried only one weapon—a disruptor pistol that Mogh had given her years ago. It had gone unfired, aside from the occasional bit of target practice, for all the time she'd owned it, as Kaasin always came armed with her best weapon: herself. Besides *mok'bara*, she had mastered several martial arts forms, including some from the Federation. She had every faith in her ability to take on even an armed foe with just her hands and feet and teeth.

However, right now she needed more than faith, she needed surety. Hence the disruptor.

"Kaasin! I'm glad you're here!" Ja'rod indicated Moraq with his weapon. "This animal betrayed us to the Romulans! We must raise the shields, quickly, before we are destroyed!"

As Ja'rod moved over to the console, Kaasin looked at the prone form of Moraq. He lay in the midst of the wreckage of a console that had exploded in the attack. In fact, the entire room smelled of burning conduits. The base commander struggled to move, but it was obvious that the disruptor had done its job well. He would be dead in moments, and until then he would be unable to make his limbs function properly, the deadly beam having all but destroyed the function of his nervous system.

But he was able to lock eyes with Kaasin. His body was failing, but Moraq's black eyes burned with the intensity of a warrior.

All her life, Kaasin had heard warriors—mostly old, fat ones—talk about *tova'dok*, the moment of clarity when warriors spoke to each other without words. She had always given those stories the same level of respect and belief that she did all their other exaggerated tales of mighty prowess— to wit, none whatsoever.

Until now. Because when she locked eyes with Moraq, she *knew* that Ja'rod was lying and Moraq died trying to stop the very traitor Mogh had been sent here to find.

Then Moraq's eyes shut.

"Leave him be, Kaasin! You must aid me in bringing the shields back up."

She turned and aimed her disruptor at Ja'rod's back. "Face me, traitor." Even one such as Ja'rod deserved to look his killer in the eye.

Ja'rod did not do so, however, instead ducking behind a console and firing his own disruptor wildly. Kaasin was able to avoid the beam easily, then she too took cover behind one of the damage-control consoles.

"And to think I thought I had you fooled," Ja'rod said. "After all, Mogh was finally starting to leave me alone. A pity that none of us will live to see how futile his efforts were. It's only a matter of time, you know."

Kaasin was still barefoot from her *mok'bara* class. She moved slowly and silently across the room, ignoring the mild pain of the sharpened edges of metal from the damaged consoles as they ripped into the callused soles of her feet. She did not speak, did not breathe, did nothing to give any indication of her position. Only her scent would give her away, but the burning-conduit stink that permeated the room would mask that.

Besides, she somehow doubted that a Romulan-lover like Ja'rod was much of a hunter.

"Soon our people will see the wisdom of a Romulan–Klingon alliance. Together we will conquer the Federation, the Cardassians, the Tholians—all the galaxy will be ours for the taking!"

Keep talking, fool. She only had a little farther to go and she'd be around the other side of the console from where he was crouching.

"You still have a chance, Kaasin—you and your husband, if he's still alive, can lead the vanguard! Think of it! The House of Duras and the House of Mogh united! The wonders we can accomplish would be—"

Kaasin stood behind Ja'rod and blew his head off.

For a moment, Kaasin was concerned that she had dishonored herself and her mate by killing without showing her face—but the moment passed. *He already knows what I look like.*

Stepping over the corpse without giving it another thought, she walked back to Moraq's body, knelt next to it, pried open his eyes, and then screamed to the heavens.

At least I was able to avenge you, Commander—I will see you in Sto-Vo-Kor.

The hum of a transporter grabbed her attention—and that there *was* a hum meant that it couldn't be a Klingon transporter, since they were silent. She raised her disruptor—

—only to have a Romulan soldier knock it out of her hands as he materialized. The Romulan then smiled, thinking her helpless before him.

The smile fell as she grabbed his left arm, yanked it around behind his back hard enough to break it in three places, and then broke his neck. She did not let the body fall to the floor, however, as there were three other Romulans who had come with him, and she needed the corpse of their comrade as a shield.

Backing toward the wall, she grabbed her victim's disruptor and started firing. But the other three fired as well. While two of the shots hit the dead Romulan, one struck Kaasin's leg.

Pain seared through her shin, clad as it was only in *mok'bara* pants, and she found herself sprawled on the floor, her Romulan shield in front of her. She tried to raise the disruptor to fire it, but another Romulan, a female centurion, did as her comrade had, and knocked it from her grip. Kaasin's attempt to grab her in a hold did not succeed, as she simply brushed it off.

Instead she leapt backward in what might have been an excellent flip were she not burdened by an injured leg. Still, even though she landed awkwardly, it got her out of reach of the Romulan and the pain only served to focus her rage.

"You will not take me, Romulan," she hissed.

"A pity," one of the antecenturions, a male, said, his eyes scanning the shape of Kaasin's body. "You might actually be worth taking."

Nausea spread through both of Kaasin's stomachs at the very thought. "I'd rather die."

"That can be arranged," the female centurion said as she shot Kaasin.

Fire spread through her veins as the disruptor did its work. Her penultimate thoughts were glee that she had, at least, killed the traitor, as well as one of those Romulan *petaQ*.

Her final thoughts were of Mogh and her son Worf, and of Kurn, whom she would never see again . . .

As he materialized in what was left of the research outpost on Khitomer, Chief Sergey Rozhenko's entire face scrunched as horrible odors assaulted his nostrils.

Not all the smells bothered him. As a Starfleet engineer of many years' standing, he was well used to the olfactory clues pointing to melted conduits, burnt chips, and fried consoles. That only bothered him insofar as the stench generally led to his having to put together a repair detail.

No, what caused his nostril hairs to scream in protest was the smell of burning flesh.

Rozhenko remembered stories that his aunt Lilya told growing up on Gault, about their ancestors back on Earth in the days before the Federation—indeed, before first contact, before the planet was even united—who had been hunted down and slaughtered, or put in work camps and *then* slaughtered after they had been worked almost to death. Uncle Isaac would usually then interrupt the story and say, "For God's sake, Lilya, that was four hundred years ago on another planet! Things are different. That couldn't happen now."

To which Aunt Lilya would always reply: "That's because we remember what happened *then*. The only way to avoid it is to never forget."

Right now, Rozhenko wasn't particularly heartened by the knowledge that something a twenty-fourth-century human like Uncle Isaac could dismiss so easily was happening literally under his nose in the Klingon Empire. It made him think that his decision not to re-enlist when his term was up in a month's time and return home to Gault—and to his wife Helena and their son Nikolai—was most definitely the right one. *The only massacres we have on Gault are of the vegetables during the harvest.*

"I'm picking up transporter traces. They're not Federation or Klingon," said Lieutenant Tobias, the chief engineer of the *Intrepid*, Rozhenko's commanding officer, and leader of this damage-control team. Captain Deighan had sent down several teams to different parts of the base to assess the damage and look for survivors. Given that the *Intrepid*'s sensor readings indicated no life signs, this second was a vain hope, but the captain was not about to rule out the possibility that *somebody* survived this mess.

Besides, based on the damage, it was quite possible that some life signs were unreadable. *That,* Rozhenko thought grimly, *is, at least, as good a rationalization as any.*

For his part, the chief went over to look at the generators to see if he could coax some life into them. It wasn't quite his specialty, but Tobias, the chief engineer, had made it clear that everyone was to pitch in on this one. The attack on Khitomer was even worse than the one on Narendra III two years earlier—totally unprovoked, and leaving an estimated four thousand dead. *I think I like Romulans better when they are quiet,* Rozhenko thought.

He examined one of the consoles, stepping over the bodies of two Klingons, a man and a woman. The man was missing most of his head; the woman was wearing something that looked to Rozhenko like a martial arts *gi*. A third corpse lay on the ground across the room. All three were obviously the victims of gunfire.

The console was functioning, barely. Rozhenko examined it, and saw that several key components had been destroyed—and several more had been removed altogether. *A saboteur, perhaps? Or the work of whoever killed these three?*

Many of the interfaces were also burned with what the tricorder identified as residue from an energy weapon—specifically a disruptor. That meant Klingon—unlikely, given that it was their base—Breen—unlikely due to Khitomer's rather distant location from the Breen Confederacy—or Romulan—extremely likely, since the *Intrepid*'s sensors picked up ships whose configuration matched those of the ships that attacked Narendra III. To Tobias, he said, "Sir, it would seem that the Romulans beamed down ground troops."

"To finish the job, maybe?" one of the other engineers said with disgust. "Can't believe that even the Romulans would do this."

"Unfortunately," Tobias said with a long sigh, "the evidence is pointing that way. Hell, that's *all* we need." He looked at Rozhenko. "What about the generator?"

"It is functioning at minimal output. There is no way to repair it without replacement parts, and there is little we have on the *Intrepid* that would do the job. I doubt it will function for much longer."

"How long?"

Rozhenko considered. "Two hours."

"Enough time for us to search for survivors, then. With luck, some actual Klingons will show up by then, and *they* can figure out whether to salvage the base or scrap it." He looked at the rest of the team. "Scan for life signs. We're not leaving *anyone* behind to die here."

Adjusting his tricorder to scan solely for Klingon life signs, Rozhenko was surprised to find two indications. "Lieutenant! I am picking up two Klingons, directly below us!"

"You two, stay here," Tobias said to the rest of the team as he ran toward the exit. "You're with me, Chief."

They went into the hallway and searched for some kind of access to anything that might be below them. Setting his tricorder to examine the signs on the doors and translate them, Rozhenko found that one of them said SUB-BASEMENT right over a rectangular seam in the wall that could easily have been a hatch. "Sir, over here."

Despite their years of training, the two engineers found themselves unable to determine which of the assorted buttons, levers, and switches on the door next to the sign actually would open the hatch—if hatch it truly was, as it had no handhold of any sort.

"This is ridiculous." Tobias sighed, running a hand through his blond hair. "Let's see if we can find another way down."

Instead of responding, Rozhenko decided to test a theory. He placed his hand against the hatch.

It started to roll inward and then down, revealing a small vertical tubular shaft, just wide enough to accommodate one person, with a ladder on the back part.

Tobias regarded Rozhenko. "Chief, remind me, why did I bother spending four years at the Academy?"

Rozhenko smiled for the first time since beaming down to this charnel house. "That, Lieutenant, is one of many questions I ask myself every day. As soon as I have an answer, I promise to let you know."

Shaking his head, Tobias climbed into the shaft and started down the ladder. Rozhenko followed the officer a moment later.

The ladder emptied into a relatively small room whose nature Rozhenko found himself unable to properly determine, as most of the floor was covered with parts of the ceiling—the latter had broken and fallen in many pieces, large and small, to the floor.

Panic welling in his gut, Rozhenko did a quick structural scan of the room, which verified what his eyes were telling him.

Before he could voice his concerns, Tobias said, "This room's gonna collapse and take half the building with it in about fifteen minutes."

"Twelve, according to the tricorder, sir."

Tobias smirked. "*That's* why I went to the Academy, Chief—I'm not so dependent on gadgets. Trust me, this room'll hold for three more minutes. Still, I'd rather not risk it. Let's find our life signs and—"

He was interrupted by the sound of something moving. Rozhenko followed the noise to a small pile of rubble.

Then he noticed the tiny hand sticking out.

It must be a child! Rozhenko thought as he and Tobias ran over and started throwing pieces of debris off the hand, which soon revealed an arm, and then an entire body.

It was indeed a child, who clutched one of those Klingon swords for dear life. He was only a little bigger than Nikolai . . .

Tobias practically beat his chest, he hit his combadge so hard. "Tobias to *Intrepid*." He then removed the combadge and placed it on the boy. "Medical emergency. Lock onto my signal, and beam directly to sickbay!"

"No . . ." That was the boy, who had somehow found the strength to speak. "Must . . . protect . . . Kahlest . . ."

Then the transporter beam took him to the *Intrepid*.

"Kahlest is probably the other life sign," Rozhenko said.

"Let's find her, then. We've only got ten minutes . . ."

Chapter 34

B'ALDA'AR BASE

"There I was, on a planet full of *grishnar* cats. The only two of any consequence were a fierce one named Baroner and a Vulcan trader."

Several of the Klingons listening to Captain Kor tell his tale in the midst of the dark, crowded bar made their disdain for Vulcans quite clear. From his seat at a table halfway across the bar, Dax smiled as his old friend silenced their grumbles. "Do not underestimate Vulcans! They can be a fierce and powerful force when provoked. They lull you into a false sense of security by being so insipidly bland," the captain said with a grin, "but they have their moments."

Kor, a mug of *chech'tluth* in one hand, started pacing in front of the bar. It, as well as the stools, railing, tables, and mugs, were all made of the same solid wood that derived from a tree native to this world. The wood had a complex grain and was as solid as many metals. The wood scent, combined with the alcohol, gave the bar a natural feel that most modern bars could not achieve—especially, Dax noted with a smile, in the Federation, where "antiseptic" was all too often the order of the day.

"I soon learned that Baroner and his Vulcan ally were none other than Captain Kirk and Lieutenant Commander

Spock of the *Enterprise*. The honor of killing Kirk would have been great, but it was war, and prisoners had their uses. So I put them in a prison—but the other Organians freed them. I killed two hundred of them for this effrontery, yet they seemed utterly unconcerned. I was prepared to kill more, when Kirk and Spock themselves burst into my office."

Laughing as he poured his *chech'tluth* toward his face—some of it, Dax noted, even actually making it into his mouth—Kor then went on. "Truly they were worthy foes." He cocked his head. "More or less. Humans tend to be sentimental, even in war, and Kirk was no different. But when it came time to fight, he fought—or tried to. That was when the Organians stepped in and forced us to cease hostilities."

The Klingons present had less love for the Organians than they did the Vulcans, but the captain shushed them. "Believe me, no one hates the Organians more than I. They claim to have evolved beyond us, yet they have no joy, no passion, no lusts!" To accentuate this last point, Kor grabbed an attractive Caitian female—who was about a quarter of old razorbeast's age, Dax knew—and gave her a friendly snarl. The woman purred back, and everyone around them laughed. "Besides, if not for what the Organians did that day, I doubt we would have been in a position to gain the Federation's assistance when Praxis was lost to us."

Several grumbled at that—nobody liked being reminded of Praxis—but then Kor laughed. "Of course, that was not my last chance to face Kirk in battle! No, we fought again later, at the legendary Delta Triangle!" He gulped down the rest of his drink. "But that is a tale for another day."

Some were disappointed at this postponement, others were relieved, others simply went back to whatever they were doing before the aged captain enthralled them with his words. Most were Klingons, and therefore had no trouble finding someone to wrestle or head-butt or drink copious amounts with. *I think that's what I like best about these people—they know how to have a party.*

The storyteller himself, though, went straight for the small wooden table where Dax sat, nursing a beer. Dax had no idea how or why a bar located on a base deep in the heart of the Klingon Empire served Earth beer, but he hadn't had any in years, and he found he missed it.

"Now there is a face I didn't expect to see here," the old Klingon said.

"I, on the other hand, fully expected to find your face here as soon as I learned that the *Klothos* was in orbit here at B'Alda'ar. Speaking of your face, you've got *chech'tluth* in your beard."

Kor laughed. "I'm saving it for later." He fell more than sat into the seat opposite Dax. "So—if you were seeking out the *Klothos*, it stands to reason that you were seeking out its captain."

Holding up his beer in tribute, Dax said, "Your powers of observation remain keen as ever, Kor. A colleague and I have been spending the last several weeks doing some—research into the head of the High Council."

Kor frowned. "Why do you wish to investigate Kravokh? He is a good man, from all accounts, and he has made us strong once again."

"Perhaps, but he's also obsessed with Ch'gran. And I've learned why. He—"

"He is the descendant of one of the original colonists, of course."

Dax stared at Kor for several seconds. "My colleague and I—neither of whom are without resources—took weeks to dig that up. The least you could've done, old friend, was let me gloat over our work."

Kor's laughter echoed off the ceiling. "Ah, Dax, I've missed you so. It's not as if you were ignorant of my knowledge, or you would not have sought me out in this lovely establishment." He gestured, taking in the entire dark, high-ceilinged bar. "You know that I served with Kravokh's father, and I suppose now you wish me to provide you with insight into the chancellor's mind."

Dax grinned. "And they say you're getting forgetful with age, Kor."

"Nonsense! No one says that!" He spoke with mock outrage that only lasted about half a second before he, too, grinned. "They say I'm getting forgetful with drink!" And, as if to prove those words prophetic, he gulped down the rest of his *chech'tluth.* "Now, then, where was I?"

"Kravokh."

"No, Kravokh's father. Yes, J'Doq and I served together years ago. I remember once, after we defeated Tholian raiders, we came to a bar—rather like this one, actually—and spoke of glories past. He went on at some length about the great deeds his family had committed—it was quite tiresome, to be honest."

Dax pointedly made no comment.

"Then I remember him saying, 'And of course, there was Ch'gran.'" Kor smiled. "This was something of a surprise, since I had no idea that his House descended from those heroes. I said as much." Kor frowned. "The next part was peculiar, for J'Doq said, 'Bah! Klartak may have been my ancestor, but he was no hero. I know the *truth.* The whole family knows the truth, and if it ever got out it would destroy the Empire.'"

Now Dax leaned forward. *This is even more than I'd hoped for.* "So what was the truth?"

Kor seemed distracted. "Hm?"

"The truth about Ch'gran, what was it?"

"How should I know?" Kor shrugged, took a dry sip of his drink, realized it was empty, then tossed the wooden mug aside. "Right after J'Doq said that, he passed out. We never spoke of it again."

Incredulous, Dax asked, "You didn't question him further?"

"Listen carefully, Dax. I said, *we* never spoke of it again. *I* certainly did, but the *toDSaH* wouldn't say a word after he sobered up—*and* he never got drunk in my presence again." Kor snorted. "He became very dull after that. But enough of this!" He got up, grabbing Dax by the arm as he did so. "Dax and Kor are together again! We must celebrate!"

"Who am I to argue with the hero of Klach D'Kel Bracht?"

Slamming Dax on the back, which caused the Trill to stumble forward toward the bar, Kor laughed and said, "Have I told you the story of how I massacred the Romulans on that day, my old friend?"

"Not for several years, no," Dax said dryly.

"Then you must hear it again, for I tell it much better now. There I was . . ."

The beeping seemed to echo in the Trill's skull.

He tried to remember where he was. Then he tried to remember his name. After several seconds, that came to him: he was Curzon Dax, a Federation ambassador.

And he had the mother of all hangovers.

Then he recalled the first thing: he was on his private transport, a small Trill craft that had an exquisitely comfortable bed—which made the feeling of metal against his cheek rather confusing. He opened his eyes to discover that he had fallen asleep about a meter from that bed on the cold, hard deck.

Ah, well. At least I had the presence of mind to make it back to the ship. "Computer, turn off that damned beeping!"

"Please repeat request."

Dax sighed. Although he had intended to enunciate those words, looking back, it came out more like, "Kapooer, tnoffat dameepng!" So instead, he gathered every ounce of strength he had and sat up.

This was a mistake. The interior of the ship proceeded to

leap about, jump up and down, and generally act quite silly. Dax closed his eyes—which served to give him a burst of color inside his eyelids—then opened them again. The ship had, blessedly, calmed down.

Finally, he focused on the fact that the beeping was the comm system. He managed to crawl over to the workstation and activate the viewer.

Too late, he realized he should have disabled the video feed, but by then the face of Elias Vaughn was already on the screen. *"Rough night?"*

"Vaughn, the last thing I need right now is a high-handed lecture from you about the perils of drinking."

"Good, because you're not getting one—unless, of course, talking to Kor proved a waste of time."

With the mention of that name, the rest of the night came back to Dax. The drinking. The stories of everything ranging from Klach D'Kel Bracht to the Albino to T'nag to the Korma Pass to the Delta Triangle and back to Organia again. The drinking. The flirting with those two rather comely Rigelian women. The drinking. And, oh yes, the drinking.

Vaughn was still droning. *"Believe me, Ambassador, I'm fully aware that the best tool to use in interrogating a Klingon is often a case of bloodwine."*

Dax smiled. Vaughn wasn't as stupid as he looked. *But then, with that beard, he couldn't be.* "Well, you can rest assured it was successful—sort of." Thinking about where he and one of the Rigelian women wound up, perhaps "sort of" was overstating the case, but Vaughn didn't want—or deserve—to hear about that. "Kor *did* serve with J'Doq. And J'Doq—and Kravokh—did have an ancestor on Ch'gran. *And* there's some kind of secret that relates to his ancestor—fellow named Klartak."

At that, Vaughn's eyes narrowed.

"What is it?" Dax prompted.

"It can wait until you're of a better mind to appreciate it."

"Don't coddle me, Commander, this isn't my first hangover. What. Is. It?"

"*I was able to dig up some of the sealed records from the Ch'gran wreck they found in the Betreka Nebula about fifty years back. Klartak was the second-in-command under Ch'gran.*"

"Interesting," Dax said, though it wasn't really. "Still, that doesn't explain Kravokh's obsession."

"*I'm afraid it does. You see, Klartak wasn't just Ch'gran's first officer—he's also the one who led the mutiny.*"

Chapter 35

I.K.S. SOMPEK

K'mpec was livid.

It was not enough that the distress call to the Morska system was a fake. All the *Sompek* found when Morska came on long-range sensors was a buoy of some sort that exploded within seconds of the *Sompek*'s commencement of that very sensor probe. No sign of the *Konmat* or its Cardassian attackers. One of Captain Kang's officers did report, however, that the buoy could well have been a communications relay that faked the signal, though it was impossible to be sure. Kang had the debris beamed on board just in case.

But then, to add insult to injury, they received a disaster call from Khitomer—they were under attack by Romulans. Had the convoy remained on-station, had Kravokh heeded Kang's advice and only sent two ships, then they would have been only two hours from Khitomer. Now they were at least seven hours away.

When they received the distress call from Khitomer, the first thing Kang said was, "Is *this* call genuine?" He stared right at Kravokh as he said it.

"It is a disaster beacon, sir. Those cannot be faked."

K'mpec was touched by the young officer's naïveté, though it was true that disaster beacons were harder to fake than simple distress calls, as they had several added layers of identity markers. That was why the original disaster call when Praxis exploded still got out, despite attempts by the High Council to suppress them.

"Set course for Khitomer, maximum speed." Kang gave the order without consulting Kravokh. The chancellor, for his part, said nothing. *The first sensible thing he has done this day*, K'mpec thought.

"Sir," Kang's pilot said, "do you mean maximum speed of the convoy or of the *Sompek*?"

Kang did not hesitate. "All ships are to execute at their maximum velocity. If some are left behind, so be it!" His voice rising with every word, Kang cried, "We will not leave our comrades to die at the hands of Romulan filth!"

A cheer went up around the bridge, including several of the councillors and their bodyguards.

Only Kravokh remained silent.

However, when the cheers died down, the chancellor did speak. "Captain Kang, while I appreciate the need for dispatch, given the circumstances, I do not appreciate my convoy being taken—"

"It is not *your* convoy, Kravokh." Kang looked directly at the chancellor, not bothering to rise from his chair. Kravokh's office required a modicum of respect, but Kang was not giving him even that. "*I* command this fleet's flagship. And we have seen the result of the last time I ceded my command to you. I will not make that same mistake twice."

A strong chancellor would have killed a ship captain that made such a pronouncement, especially in front of so many other members of the High Council. In fact, a strong chancellor would not have needed to do so, because those other members of the High Council would be falling all over each other to do it themselves.

Instead, they stood their ground.

K'mpec had known that this day would come. The battlements on which Kravokh stood had been crumbling since Narendra III—K'mpec knew this, because he had been standing on the same unsteady land. But where K'mpec had spent the two years since building a new fortress, strengthening his position, Kravokh had stayed in place.

Now Kravokh's defenses were gone. He stood alone with no one and nothing to defend him.

"Kravokh, son of J'Doq!" K'mpec bellowed the name, his deep voice echoing off the bulkheads of the *Sompek* bridge. At this, the bridge quieted down. "For the second time in as many years, you have let your obsession with Cardassia cloud your judgment—and allow Klingons to die dishonorably. As I stand before these warriors, I assure you—there will not be a third."

On the word *third*, K'mpec unsheathed his *d'k tahg*.

"Do not be a fool, K'mpec." Kravokh took out his own dagger, and looked around the bridge. "We do not have time for such idiocy! I am your supreme commander, and I—"

"*You* are the fool," Kang said. "If somehow you survive K'mpec's assault, you will face a phalanx of warriors who will gladly take their try."

"It is a good day to die, Kravokh," K'mpec said. "Let the final memory of your reign be that you died with honor—in combat."

Kravokh shook his head. "You are *all* fools. You have no idea what is at stake. The fate of the Empire could well hang in the balance, and you do not see it—*cannot* see it."

His voice almost a whisper, K'mpec said, "What I see, Kravokh, are hundreds of Klingon corpses—the victims of your incompetence. The dead cry out for vengeance."

All around the bridge, a chant started. Though he was not sure who started it, soon everyone, even Kang, had joined in: "K'mpec! K'mpec! K'mpec!"

Kravokh whirled around at all of the councillors who had betrayed him. Some of them, K'mpec knew, were the same ones who cheered his victory over Grivak in Council Chambers twelve years ago. Kravokh's eyes fell on one in particular—Ruuv, who had been Kravokh's aide when he was a mere councillor, elevated to the Council when Kravokh ascended to the chancellorship. At the sight of Ruuv cheering on Kravokh's opponent, the chancellor's shoulders sagged. "So be it, K'mpec. If I am to die this day, it will be with my eyes open and a weapon in my hand."

K'mpec smiled. "As it should be."

Then there was no need for words.

Though neither swift nor agile, K'mpec yielded to no one in his ability to wield a *d'k tahg*. In his younger days, he had been feared throughout his home planet of Mempa IV; he achieved champion standing in the Mempa Knife Duels for seven years running before his Defense Force career took away his ability to participate regularly.

Kravokh was most skilled with swords and other, longer weapons. He was good enough with the *d'k tahg* to hold his own, but he was no match for K'mpec. The councillor's own prodigious belly proved more of an impediment than his foe. But K'mpec had challenged him with a *d'k tahg* and—especially given his lack of support among his peers—he was in no position to demand that a different weapon be used.

More fool him, K'mpec thought as he blocked a clumsy thrust of Kravokh's. K'mpec countered with a punch to his enemy's belly, causing Kravokh to bend over forward, then quickly followed with a slash at the chancellor's neck.

Now bleeding profusely from the cut, Kravokh slashed back clumsily, enough to keep K'mpec from moving in for the kill. However, Kravokh chose to hold the wound shut with his right hand, leaving him with only his left to fight. *This,* K'mpec thought, *will end soon.*

"You do not know what you are doing, K'mpec. The Empire will fall to ruin if we do not crush the Cardassians and reclaim Ch'gran!"

"The Empire is already falling to ruin, Kravokh. But the fall stops here—*now*."

K'mpec threw a punch at Kravokh, who instinctively blocked it with his knife hand. The blade penetrated K'mpec's gauntlet and flesh, but the pain was nothing, the wound minor—besides, it left the chest open.

With a powerful thrust, K'mpec's *d'k tahg* penetrated Kravokh's heart.

The erstwhile chancellor fell to the deck of the *Sompek* bridge.

The cheering of K'mpec's name had died down as the fight had progressed—though K'mpec had mostly tuned it out in any case—but now the chanting grew louder and louder, even as K'mpec knelt down besides Kravokh's fallen form. There was no need to pry his eyes open, as they stared straight up at the bridge's ceiling.

Then he leaned back and screamed to the heavens. Most of the bridge crew did likewise.

As K'mpec removed the coat of office from Kravokh's body, Ruuv said, "Long live K'mpec! Long live the Klingon Empire!"

Cheers filled K'mpec's ears.

He allowed himself to enjoy the cheers for several seconds before holding up one hand. "Enough!" That quieted the bridge. "There is much to be done. The Empire has a long road ahead."

In as close to a deferential tone as he was likely to ever hear from the old captain, Kang said, "What are the chancellor's orders?"

"Proceed as before, Captain. Our first priority is Khitomer. The rest—" he looked down at Kravokh's fallen form "—will be dispensed with in due time."

Chapter 36

U.S.S. INTREPID

"No, not like that! You must hold it so it can rest against your forearm!"

Sergey Rozhenko forced a frown onto his face, even though he wanted to smile. Of course, he knew by now how to hold a *bat'leth*—Worf had shown him the proper hold a dozen times over the past few days—but he also knew that the young Klingon enjoyed his role as stern tutor to Rozhenko's bumbling student. And Doctor Tavares said that the time Rozhenko was spending with the boy—virtually all his off-duty time—was aiding in Worf's recovery.

It also aided in Rozhenko's recovery. The more time he spent with the six-year-old Klingon boy, the less the stench of burned flesh lingered in his nostrils.

The *Intrepid* was docked at Starbase 24. As good as the ship's sickbay was, both Worf and the woman they'd beamed up required the superior medical facilities on the starbase. According to Tavares, the boy had suffered brain damage that needed to be repaired. He had come out of surgery just fine, however, and was now recovering in the *Intrepid* sickbay.

Juanita Tavares herself entered as Rozhenko took yet another stab at a proper *bat'leth* grip, and instead almost took a stab at his own abdomen.

Shaking his head and blowing out a breath of frustration, young Worf said, "You are *never* going to be a warrior this way, human."

Smiling, Tavares said, "Good thing he's an engineer, then. How are you feeling, Worf?"

"I am fine." The perfect stoic.

"Good." She turned to Rozhenko. "Chief, can I talk to you for a minute?"

"Of course." He handed the weapon gingerly to the boy, who almost snatched it out of Rozhenko's hands. "Perhaps tomorrow I will get it right."

"I doubt it." The boy's voice was sullen, but Rozhenko could tell that the boy looked forward to continuing the lesson. His face had the same I'm-enjoying-this-but-I-want-you-to-think-I'm-mad look that his son Nikolai got whenever he was feeling especially stubborn.

Rozhenko followed the raven-haired doctor to her office. "I have good news and bad news," she said, sitting at her desk.

Taking the guest chair, Rozhenko smiled. "Experience has taught me that it is best to get the bad news out of the way."

Tavares chuckled. "Maybe, but the bad news stems from the good. All of Worf's brain damage has been healed. It's a good thing we got here when we did—and that Doctor T'Mret was available. However, there's no reason why he can't live a normal, happy life from here on in."

"And the bad news?"

She sighed. "He did suffer some memory loss, and there's no way to get that back. The tissue was repaired, but the damage was done. There will be parts of his life prior to the attack that are lost to him forever."

"If the attack itself is one of those parts, then this was a blessing, Doctor."

Tavares visibly shuddered. "I won't argue with you there. The Klingons who arrived at Khitomer are still sorting everything out, but they double-checked with their Homeworld—

the only people at Worf's family's home there are serving staff. According to them, the entire family was at Khitomer."

Afraid to ask the question, yet knowing he had to, Rozhenko asked, "Have they found any other survivors?"

Tavares shook her head sadly. "Not all the bodies are accounted for, but they could have been vaporized—or captured." She smiled wryly. "From what Captain Deighan told me, if it's the latter, they're dead anyhow. Klingons would rather die than be taken prisoner."

That was an attitude Rozhenko could never understand, but he was not about to get into a philosophical discussion right now—that could wait until dinner. "What about the woman?"

"She's the other reason I wanted to talk to you," Tavares said with a smile. "She finally came out of the coma about half an hour ago. Her name's Kahlest, and she's apparently Worf's *ghojmok*, which seems to be their equivalent of a nursemaid."

So she is the same woman Worf claimed to be protecting back on Khitomer. "Good." Rozhenko was relieved. His act of pretending to be Worf's *bat'leth* student was only going to carry him so far. The boy needed someone who knew how to take care of him, especially if his whole family was dead.

"I told her that you'd been taking an interest in Worf, and she seemed both relieved and scared. Then she asked to talk to you."

"To me?" That surprised Rozhenko. "Why?"

Shrugging, Tavares said, "I honestly don't know. She also asked to be transferred to the starbase medical facility after she talks to you."

"With Worf?"

"She didn't say."

Rozhenko then proceeded to the part of sickbay where the Kahlest woman lay on a biobed. She seemed nice enough, for a Klingon. At least she wasn't bleeding profusely, nor was she missing any limbs—or her head. He liked the idea of having another image, besides Worf, of an intact Klingon to focus his attention on, so it would crowd out all the corpses on Khitomer.

The woman sat upright and spoke in a whispery voice. "You are the human who has been caring for Worf?"

Tilting his head to one side, Rozhenko said, "You could say that. I have been spending time with him when I can. He has been teaching me the *bat'leth*." He smiled. "Worf does not think I am very good at it."

Kahlest did not return the smile. "You must listen to me, human. Worf must be taken away. It is not safe for him."

"What do you mean?"

The nurse looked back and forth, as if expecting there to be spies. Rozhenko had heard stories that Klingons kept their citizenry under constant surveillance, but he had no idea how truthful they were. "Worf's father was sent to Khitomer to find a spy. I do not know if he found him, but if he did, that person's family may take vengeance on Worf, as the last survivor."

Rozhenko's head started swimming. "I do not understand. Vengeance?"

With an impatience that was of far greater moment than Worf's annoyance with Rozhenko's *bat'leth* skills, Kahlest said, "Do you know *nothing*, human? If Worf returns to the Empire, he will be a target."

"Won't you be, as well?"

"No. I am dead. I will remain dead."

Remembering some other stories he heard about Klingons, Rozhenko said, "You do not plan to kill yourself?"

Now, Kahlest looked upon him with pity. "You really do know nothing of us, do you?" She grabbed Rozhenko's arm. "I beg of you, if you want that boy to live to grow into the great warrior I know he can be—do *not* let him return to the Empire. If you do, his life will be as forfeit as that of those people on Khitomer." She let go of his arm, and looked down. "And of me."

The first thing Sergey Rozhenko did when he returned to his quarters was contact Helena on Gault.

When the face of the most beautiful woman in the galaxy appeared on the viewer in the quarters Sergey shared with another noncom (currently on duty in security), his heart sang. Her smile brightened the darkened room—he hadn't bothered to turn the lights on, he knew his way around just fine, thanks.

"*Sergey!*" Then her smile fell. "*What is wrong?*"

He chuckled and shook his head. "I never could keep anything from you."

Then he told her everything. He told her about the *Intrepid* responding to the distress call and Lieutenant Tobias informing him that he'd be on one of the away teams. He told her about the broken, burnt bodies and the two survivors they did find. No details were spared. If he tried to hide something, she'd know. If he tried to downplay how much it affected him, she'd know that, too. She always did. Besides, they took a vow to share their lives—that included the hardships. Helena would never forgive him if he *didn't* divulge it all.

"*That poor boy,*" she said when he told her about Worf. "*He's the same age as Nikolai?*"

Again, he chuckled. "A few years younger, though you would not know it to look at him. He's twice as big as Nikolai. Doctor Tavares says that Klingons develop faster than humans." Then he once again became serious. "There is something else." Slowly, hoping he could convey Kahlest's trepidation—he couldn't really call it fear—he shared what she had told him in sickbay.

Helena frowned. "*I don't know, Sergey.*"

Knowing it was a weak argument, Sergey said, "We did

say that we wanted to have a second child when I came home next month."

Naturally, Helena plowed right through it. "*Yes, a second baby! Who would not come for at least another nine months! Not a Klingon boy that we'd have to take in right away!*"

"We have the space in the house."

"*Wonderful. And how will Nikolai react? Instead of having the better part of a year to prepare him we have, what, a few days? And how will we care for this boy? Do you know what he eats? What kind of clothes he wears? Will he be allergic to the furniture? How does he sleep?*"

"Lenotchka—" He hesitated.

"*What is it?*" she asked gently. Sergey rarely used the diminutive except when they were in person.

"The boy has nothing. No home to go to. Just memories of a—a very bad place. I know because I have that memory now, too." The smell of burnt flesh came back, unbidden, and Sergey's quarters seemed to darken to the same dimness of that engine room he, Tobias, and the damage-control team had beamed into.

A second passed. Two. Then Helena's smile came back, and the room lit up all over again. "*Then we will give him better memories. Bring him home, Sergey, if he will come.*"

"Good." He smiled. "We will not regret this, Helena."

She smirked. "*I already do. I will see you soon.*"

"Not soon enough. I love you."

"*I love you, too.*"

After Helena's beautiful face faded from the viewscreen, Sergey decided to return to sickbay. He wanted to speak to his new son.

Chapter 37

QO'NOS

Lorgh stood in the small room on the upper level of his home that overlooked the HoSghaj River. The room's sole illumination came from a large candle.

He watched the mighty river flow past his estate and toward the ocean into which it emptied.

The mission he had sent Mogh on had not quite been the success Lorgh had hoped. The true identity of the Romulan spy was not known, which meant they did not know who his or her accomplices might have been. Still, he had accounted for that possibility, which was one of the reasons why he had insisted on Kurn remaining behind. Better still, even though Mogh and Kaasin were killed, Worf survived—according to his sources, he had been taken in by the family of one of the humans serving on the *Intrepid*, the Starfleet vessel that first responded to the distress signal on Khitomer.

General Worf's line would remain intact. One son of Mogh remained in the Federation, beyond the reach of any vengeful relations of whoever the spy was.

The other son of Mogh would be a son of Lorgh for the nonce. Lorgh had no sons of his own, so that would provide an adequate excuse for this step. And in the long term, the boy would have other uses. Lorgh intended to make sure that Kurn was a powerful warrior, and a force to be reckoned with in the Empire. He also intended to keep an eye on Worf—see how a Klingon raised in the Federation would turn out.

Both sons of Mogh might turn out to be quite useful to him.

And, even if the short-term consequences were devastating, the long-term prognosis was good. The *Intrepid*'s presence served to drive off the Romulans—and also reveal their responsibility for the attack. K'mpec had been able to ascend to the chancellorship, a move long overdue. The truth—that a Klingon betrayed Khitomer to the Romulans—would remain hidden for now, but there was nothing to be done about that. *A pity*, Lorgh thought. *Proof of that might send us to war with the Romulans.* Instead, the members of the High Council whose Houses owed their strength and position to Romulan assistance would continue to do all they could to keep the two powers from coming into conflict. It would be K'mpec's task to keep those forces at bay—and Lorgh's to try to expose them—over the course of time.

As for Kravokh, he had served his purpose—to get the Empire out of the rut that Kaarg and Ditagh had mired them in—but his Ch'gran obsession proved his undoing. It was almost worth the sacrifice of four thousand lives to speed him on his way to *Sto-Vo-Kor* where he would no longer ruin the Empire with his constant worrying about the past.

Klingons could not forget their past, but it was I.I.'s job to make sure that the Empire had a future. Lorgh was confident that K'mpec was the one to bring them to that future.

If he isn't, then he too will be replaced. The river will flow onward.

He walked over to the candle and unsheathed his *d'k tahg. Mogh, Kaasin, you did your work well. Your sacrifices will not go unheeded. May you join the general in Sto-Vo-*

Kor, *and may your battles continue ever onward. You deserve no less.*

Using the flat of his *d'k tahg,* he extinguished the candle's flame.

Then he went downstairs to speak to his new son.

"You know, if you keep that up, you're going to wear a hole in the floor."

Elias Vaughn had been pacing in the corridor outside the new Klingon chancellor's office for the better part of fifteen minutes. Curzon Dax had never considered Vaughn to be the type to have an excess of nervous energy—well, to be honest, he had never given Vaughn all that much thought at all—but he seemed to be boiling over with it today.

"Since this floor is made of rodinium, I doubt that's an issue, Ambassador."

Dax smiled at Vaughn's disdain. "How do you do that?"

"Do what?"

"The syllables spell out the word 'ambassador,' yet you manage to make it sound like 'jackass' every time."

At that, Vaughn actually smirked. "Call it a gift."

"I'd rather call it an irritant, but suit yourself. In any case, K'mpec will see us when he's good and ready. He *is* the newly appointed head of a massive interstellar empire."

"It feels like we're being stalled. I dislike being stalled."

Dax laughed. "You have no appreciation of the Klingon mindset, Commander. Trust me, if K'mpec can't see us, it's because he's too busy to see us. Klingons don't stall. If he wanted us to sweat, he'd put us in a sauna—or just threaten to garrotte us, or some other such thing."

"Well, you're the expert," Vaughn said, using that same disdainful tone.

The door to K'mpec's office opened, and a surly looking guard stepped through it. "Inside," he said, indicating the interior with his head.

The office, Dax noted as he entered, was spare. The desk was a small piece of metal just large enough to hold a workstation and a few padds. K'mpec's impressive girth made him look like a full-grown adult sitting at a child's play dining room set as he sat behind it, looking over something on the screen of that workstation. Behind him, the wall was decorated, typically, with weapons, as were two other walls, as well as a rather unfortunate painting. Dax prayed that the latter was a holdover from Kravokh's reign that K'mpec simply hadn't gotten around to having destroyed.

"If we were in the Federation," Dax said as they took their places standing before K'mpec, "congratulations would be in order."

K'mpec looked up and smiled. "But we are not in the Federation."

"Indeed. So I will simply wish you success, Chancellor."

"What is it you want, Ambassador?" The smile was now gone, replaced by the face of a busy man who was only having this meeting because of who Dax was.

"We have information that may be of use to you regarding your predecessor—and Ch'gran."

That got K'mpec's attention. "What do *you* know of Ch'gran?"

Vaughn chose this moment to make his presence known. "I'm Lieutenant Commander Elias Vaughn. At Ambassador Dax's request, I did some digging into Kravokh's background. I found out some interesting things about his family—and why he was so obsessed with recovering Ch'gran."

"Recovering Ch'gran is the desire of *all* Klingons," K'mpec said.

"For its historical value, yes. That, however, is *not* what Kravokh was after."

K'mpec frowned. "What, then?"

Dax had been afraid of this. "You aren't aware of what

was in the records of that Ch'gran wreck they found fifty years ago, are you?"

"There *were* no records." K'mpec spoke in a low, menacing tone, as if challenging Dax and Vaughn to prove his words wrong. *Unfortunately, we're about to.*

Vaughn looked at Dax. "I did warn you that he wouldn't know. Those records were sealed by Imperial Intelligence, *not* the High Council."

Sighing, Dax said, "Yes, Vaughn, you were actually right. I suppose the law of averages was bound to catch up with you."

K'mpec was now smoldering. "Of what records do you speak?" he asked, enunciating every word in a manner that Dax found quite intimidating, all things considered.

Vaughn faced the chancellor. "The records on that wreck revealed the reasons why the Ch'gran colony was lost— it was because of a mutiny, led by Ch'gran's second-in-command, a man named Klartak."

"Klartak," Dax added, "was a member of what was then known as the House of Boral, but is more properly known these days as the House of—"

"Kravokh." The word sounded like wheels going over broken glass as it came out of K'mpec's mouth.

"Yes," Vaughn said. "The I.I. agent who decoded the records of the Ch'gran wreck was a descendant of Klartak's, and he is the one who sealed the records. He told no one of this, save his son. It has remained a family secret, one that has been passed down through what is now the House of Kravokh. Dax's proviso that the Cardassians could not touch Ch'gran until the dispensation of Raknal V was determined kept the truth hidden for as long as the competition continued. My personal opinion is that Kravokh's efforts to fortify the Defense Force were primarily with an eye toward taking Raknal by force if necessary, perhaps even invading Cardassia, if Qaolin could not win the planet for them under Dax's terms."

"Ranh!" K'mpec stood angrily. "You mean to tell me that

thousands of Klingons have died so that animal could protect his family's dishonor?"

"Not quite," Dax said with a smile.

That drew K'mpec up short. "I don't understand."

"It's all right, Chancellor," Dax said, "neither did I when Vaughn first explained it to me."

Fixing Vaughn with a penetrating gaze, K'mpec said, "Then explain it to me—*clearly*, if you will, Commander."

Vaughn inclined his head. "Of course. You see, Klartak did not mutiny until he was given the order to turn back."

At that, K'mpec's tiny eyes grew wide with shock, a reaction not dissimilar to Dax's own when Vaughn had explained it to him back on B'Alda'ar.

"Ch'gran had no intention of colonizing space," Vaughn continued. "His plan all along was to return here, destroy the First City from orbit, and install himself as the new emperor. His entire goal in having the fleet constructed wasn't to pave the way to space, it was to give him a weapon by which he could take over Qo'noS. He only traveled with the fleet so far because he needed time to get the other six ship captains on his side."

"Kravokh was not trying to preserve *his* honor," Dax said, "but that of one of the Empire's greatest heroes. He did not wish the legacy of Ch'gran, the man who prompted your people to vault forward into space for the first time after the Hur'q invasion, to be that of a traitor."

K'mpec snorted. "Our people can survive the tarnishing of the occasional legend, Ambassador. We are not human children who require our parents to prettify our stories to make them palatable." He looked away. "And we have had our share of fallen heroes in our time." Then he looked sharply at Vaughn. "How did you obtain this information?"

"I'd rather not say."

Leaning forward, his fists on his desk, K'mpec said, "You will tell me the name of your informant, or I will—"

"Do nothing," Dax said quickly. The last thing he wanted to witness right now was these two men getting into a pissing contest. "We volunteered this information to you as a show of good faith and in the hope that our people's good relations will continue, Chancellor. We are under no obligation to provide you with anything more than we have given you. Humans have a saying about not looking a gift horse in the mouth—I suggest you abide by it in this case."

"If there is a leak in I.I.—"

Vaughn fixed K'mpec with a stern look. "Then it is *your* duty to plug it, sir, not mine."

K'mpec looked back and forth between the two men. Dax was worried that the chancellor would try to take this to the next step, which would be dangerous for all of them—most of all, though, for the Federation–Klingon alliance, which was only just being stitched back together after fifty years of fraying.

Finally, K'mpec sat back down. "Very well. The Klingon Empire is grateful to you for bringing this matter to our attention." He leaned back. "Since both of you were—involved in the beginnings of this absurdity, it is only fitting that you be here for the end of it."

Dax frowned. "What do you mean?"

"What I mean, Ambassador, is that your arrival here has saved me the trouble of contacting you via subspace." He touched a control on his workstation. "You will come with me."

Without another word, K'mpec rose from his chair and left the office. A guard fell into step behind him as he proceeded to the Council Chambers, Vaughn and a bemused Dax right behind both of them. Whispering to Vaughn, Dax asked, "What do you think this is about?"

Vaughn shrugged. "You're the expert."

"Remind me to have you beaten before we leave, Commander."

Soon they were in Council Chambers. Dax recognized

some of the councillors from his last visit, knew others as Defense Force veterans who had been promoted to the Council. K'mpec took his place in the seat under the Klingon Empire's trefoil emblem, a spotlight shining on his heavily lined face, and the other councillors stepped into place in a semicircle on either side of him.

As soon as he took his seat, the room quieted down. Vaughn and Dax stood off to the side, along with other observers.

K'mpec looked around the chamber for several seconds before speaking in a booming voice that belied his near-whisper back in his office. "As of this moment, the Klingon Empire cedes the world of Raknal V to the Cardassian Union."

Dax's own eyes went wide at that one.

"We are willing to discuss ways to obtain the Ch'gran relic through trade, but we will no longer sacrifice warriors in the wasteful manner that they have been cast aside because of the single-minded pursuit of this one insignificant planet. Governor Qaolin will relinquish his post and return to the Homeworld within one week.

"In addition, the ban on Cardassian citizens within the Empire is lifted. It is the wish of this Council that Cardassia do the same for our people—if not, the ban will be reinstated."

Then K'mpec turned to one of the councillors, Ruuv. "What of the Romulan Empire's response to the attack on Khitomer?"

Ruuv stepped forward. "Sir, Praetor Narviat has condemned the actions of the 'traitors' who have attacked Khitomer. He assures us that those responsible will be punished, and offers their lives to us."

"As it should be," said one councillor.

Another said, "We should consider making a formal alliance with them."

"Are you mad?" said a third. "Do you believe these lies?"

Dax put a hand on Vaughn's shoulder, and indicated the exit with his head. They both departed even as the Council's squabbling started. "They'll be at it for hours. I doubt that anything will come of it. Too many important Klingons owe too many important Romulans too much money. I suspect any conflict will be limited to isolated skirmishes."

"Much like what the Klingons and Cardassians have been doing for the past eighteen years?" Vaughn asked pointedly.

Dax shook his head. "Much like that, yes. Well, if you'll excuse me, Commander, I have to inform my superiors in the Diplomatic Corps that the Betreka Nebula incident has finally come to an end."

Chapter 38

CARDASSIA PRIME

Corbin Entek's third trip to the Obsidian Order's public headquarters proceeded in much the same manner as his first two. He approached the sixty-story building in the cul-de-sac—the renovations had just been completed the month before—and was told by the receptionist to report to Room 2552. Entek wondered briefly if this meant he was *not* going to see Tain—with the added floors, 2552 was no longer at the building's epicenter—but apparently Tain liked the office for some reason.

This time a thin, white-haired man sat at the reception desk. He activated his comm unit and said, "He's arrived."

Tain's voice once again sounded over the intercom. *"Send him in."*

Tain's viewer now showed a tactical map of the quadrant. It distressed Entek to see how small Cardassia's territory—marked in yellow on the galactic map—was in relation to such other local powers as the Breen Confederacy, the Tho-ñan Assembly, the Klingon and Romulan Empires, and most especially the United Federation of Planets.

"Greetings, Entek!" As always, Tain sounded like a grandfather saying hello to a child not visited in months. "Please, have a seat."

Entek did so, hoping that the similarities to the previous two trips would remain intact. He had no desire to get on Tain's bad side, not when his career had been going so well. Especially after he was able to handle Khitomer so deftly—though that was with some unknowing help from the Klingons themselves . . .

"You are no doubt aware that the Klingons have ceded Raknal V to us and allowed Cardassians back inside their borders. We have done the same for their people—which," he added with a smile, "is probably the only drawback to the whole thing."

Although he did not find the comment especially humorous, Entek was sensible enough to return the smile.

"Negotiations to restore that silly pile of wreckage to them have commenced. And we owe it all to you. I doubt we'd be at this point if the Romulans hadn't obligingly attacked Khitomer when they did. Your manufactured 'confession' played right into the Romulans' paranoid hands."

Manufactured? "To give credit where it is due, sir," Entek said respectfully, "it was the operative you assigned to leak the confession to the Tal Shiar who fed the paranoia. He did good work in convincing the Romulans of its veracity. I simply provided the documentation."

"True, but the documentation itself was an exquisite piece of work."

Entek smiled. *He doesn't know.* For a moment, he debated not telling Tain—but no, if the head of the Obsidian Order learned that Entek held back such information, it could damage Entek's chances. His career was at too important a turning point right now for him to take that risk, especially since the usefulness of the intelligence had now passed. "For that, you must credit the Klingon we captured. After all, he only spoke the truth."

Tain's mouth actually fell open at that. It took all of Entek's training to keep the look of joy off his face. *I have ac-*

tually surprised Enabran Tain! "You didn't know?" Entek asked innocently.

To his credit, Tain composed himself quickly. "I had simply assumed that the confession was false."

"Not at all. However," he added before Tain could react further, "it was an isolated incident."

Frowning, Tain said, "Explain."

"The Klingon Empire has no intention of developing biogenic weapons. Leaving aside their cultural biases, they have no interest in violating interstellar treaties." He allowed himself a small smile. "But the Klingon Empire wasn't developing those weapons on Khitomer—Chancellor Kravokh was, without the knowledge of the High Council or anyone else aside from the development team. I don't think their Imperial Intelligence even knew of it. Aside from Kravokh, all those associated with the project were either members of the House of Kultan or loyal to it—that House has produced several prominent Klingon scientists."

"Yes, I've seen the reports regarding that House. You suspect Kravokh intended to use that weapon against us?"

Entek nodded. "Oh, the prisoner said as much, though I did not include that in the recording that the Tal Shiar received, nor that the operation wasn't sanctioned by the High Council. Your man provided a forger who did fine editing work that kept the recording seeming authentic. However, all evidence of the research—and all those who knew of it— are quite dead. The only ones who weren't on Khitomer were my prisoner and Kravokh himself."

Tain nodded several times—so much so that Entek wondered if the older man's head would fall off. "That makes what you've done that much more important, my friend. You may well have saved us all from the actions of a madman by setting his assassination in motion."

Deciding not to point out that Kravokh's death was not,

strictly speaking, an assassination, Entek instead simply said, "I merely serve Cardassia."

"And your own desire for promotion, of course." Entek was about to object, but Tain held up a hand. "Now now, it's only to be expected. And besides, the two aren't mutually exclusive goals. In fact, as long as they remain that way, you should do quite well. That's why I've decided to reward your efforts by putting you in charge of Order operations on Bajor."

Now it was Tain's turn to surprise Entek. He had all but given up hope of getting the Bajor assignment after so many years of frustration.

"We have learned that Central Command plans to build a space station in orbit around Bajor. It's still awaiting a final vote, but I'm confident that Legate Kell will get the support he needs for it. While it will do much to streamline the uridium processing, it will also serve as a very nice orbital target for that tiresome resistance movement. I want an Order agent who can get things done in charge over there, before that resistance gets out of hand. Central Command's efforts to curtail them could charitably be called poor."

"I agree," Entek said, "and I'm sure that you will find my efforts to be beneficial to Cardassia."

Tain smiled. "Good." He handed Entek a padd. "This contains a list of your staff. Feel free to make any amendments to the team that you feel are necessary."

Happily, Entek took the padd. *At last, a supervisor, and in the assignment I have longed for.*

For the third time, Corbin Entek left Enabran Tain's office with his life and his career intact. This he considered a sign of skill and success in his chosen field. He felt confident in his ability to continue that success.

It had been many years since Legate Zarin had been invited to Legate Kell's office on Cardassia. The view from the picture window in the north wall was, if anything, more impressive, as this section of the capital city had been built up quite a bit over the past few years. *The spoils of conquest,* he thought. Cardassia was strong, and growing stronger every day.

To Zarin's relief, Kell had apparently gotten over his Lissepian phase. The paintings that now decorated the west wall were primarily Bajoran. In addition to making fine laborers, Bajorans drew very pretty pictures. *Perhaps when I take over this office,* Zarin thought wistfully, *I will keep the artwork.*

Kell's old *urall*-skin couch had long since been replaced by a much more comfortable one made of *keres* hide from Chin'toka VI. Zarin sat on it now, with Kell sitting in the same conformer chair he'd had for over twenty years.

Holding up his glass of *kanar* in toast, Kell said, "To victory over the Klingons."

"To victory."

After gulping down his *kanar* in as boorish a manner as Zarin would have expected from him, Kell set down the glass. "Of course, that victory was a long time coming. Longer than it should have been."

Zarin didn't like the sound of that.

Kell smiled. "Don't look so concerned, Zarin. I know you and Monor did your best. And Raknal V will make a fine addition to the Cardassian Union. Such a pity that all your efforts went to waste."

"We did all that we could within Ambassador Dax's constraints to—"

"That's *not* what I'm referring to, Legate. And you know it." Kell leaned on the table that sat between them and tossed a padd at Zarin. The younger legate frowned as he keyed the display. It showed a transcript of a conversation Zarin had with Monor regarding the sabotage of the communications systems on the Klingon vessel *Chut*. Thanks to the catastrophe on the *Gratok*, the sabotage wound up having a somewhat different effect—to wit, preventing the *Chut* from hearing the panic signal—from what was intended, though the end result of killing the entire complement of the *Chut* was the same.

"What of it?" Zarin asked. "You told Monor and me to do whatever it took to ensure that we secured our claim to Raknal V."

Kell stood up. "Legate Zarin, I am appalled! Do you truly believe that I would authorize actions that would lead to the deaths of a hundred Klingons?"

Staring coldly up at Kell, Zarin said, "Yes, I do believe that you would."

Laughing, Kell sat back down. "Perhaps, but I'm not the one on the transcript—which, by the way, is also in the hands of the Obsidian Order."

Zarin wondered if it was the Order who provided Kell with the transcript or the other way around. The fact that Kell was nonspecific led Zarin to think it was the former. *Kell would never admit to being beholden to the Order for anything.*

"What is it you want, Kell? Obviously, you don't intend to release this publicly."

"Why would I release it publicly?" Kell finished off his *kanar*. "Much better, I think, to release it to the Klingons. I'm sure the descendants of the *Chut* victims would love to know who was responsible for their deaths."

Rolling his eyes, Zarin said, "You haven't answered my question, Kell." These threats were pointless. If Kell wanted Zarin humiliated or dead, the padd would be in the hands of the Detapa Council or the Klingons already.

"You opposed the construction of Terok Nor over Bajor, and convinced several other legates to join that opposition. You will change your position. We need Terok Nor to facilitate the uridium processing."

Zarin was about to point out what a colossal waste of money constructing an orbital station would be—but there was no point. Kell had already heard these arguments when the subject was debated. If Zarin couldn't convince him then, he wouldn't convince him now—especially when Kell had blackmail material.

After several moments, Zarin finally answered. "I cannot guarantee that all the legates who supported my nay vote will switch."

"Oh, don't worry, Zarin, just the fact that you have switched your vote will be more than sufficient to convince enough of them." Kell stood up. "Now get out of my office. And Zarin?"

Zarin stood up. "Yes?"

Kell indicated the picture window. "*Don't* get used to that view. You won't be taking over this office for a long time yet."

We'll see, Zarin thought angrily as he left.

Chapter 39

RAKNAL V

"Governor, the Wo'bortas *has arrived to pick us up."*

Qaolin almost choked on his bloodwine at that. *Once again, fortune sees fit to spit in my drink.* The final indignity in a lifetime of indignities: the very vessel whose command he had to give up to take over this shipwreck of an assignment was the one that would take him away from it.

He looked around at the run-down office that had been his home for eighteen years. The weapons and artwork and furniture had all been packed up and would be transferred to the *Wo'bortas* cargo bay. Knowing the Cardassians, they would probably condemn all the Klingon construction and replace it with their own hideous architecture. *Good. The idea of any of those lifeless cowards making use of Klingon buildings is revolting.*

Taking another gulp of bloodwine, Qaolin laughed. *So this is what it's come to. I had hoped that the deaths on the* Chut *or the collapse of that building would finally end this battle. Even the Cardassians transplanting those damned fish of theirs might have finally led the Great Curzon to declare a victor in this tiresome little war we have been fighting. Instead, it was a simple change in power. A battle that should have been won is instead ended by politics.* He drank more bloodwine, emptying the bottle. *How I hate politics.*

Qaolin had no idea what he was going to do next. After giving it a great deal of consideration, he was seriously tempted to just go home—or perhaps not even that, but take his share of the holdings of his House and purchase some land on a distant world of the Empire. *I can spend my days hunting and my nights drinking. That might not be a bad way to occupy the rest of my life.*

Then he opened the drawer of the empty desk and retrieved the one item he had not packed up.

A vintage bottle of bloodwine from the Ozhpri vintner. *I've been saving this for when I was victorious over Monor and had restored Ch'gran to our people.*

Of course, he had lost to Monor, and Ch'gran's restoration would be at the hands of diplomats and politicians. *Damn Monor, he beat me.* What was worst was that the Cardassian had not shown any signs of weakening. Qaolin had arrived at Raknal V swearing he would not let Monor take Ch'gran from him. A vibrant young man, he was fresh from his first command, with a good life and career ahead of him. He had proven himself to be quick-witted, strong, and one who could thrive in the volatile atmosphere of the Defense Force. Now, he was leaving Raknal V, Monor having succeeded in taking Ch'gran. A drunken wreck with a broken spirit and few prospects, Qaolin was dull-witted, weak, and wouldn't last a minute on a Defense Force ship.

But Monor? He arrived at Raknal V an insufferable clod and he was now taking over Raknal V as the same insufferable clod. It was maddening.

Qaolin stared at the bottle of bloodwine.

Then he smiled.

Prefect Monor stared at the view of his planet from his office. The sun was starting to set behind the solid, Cardassian-constructed buildings that would now serve as the focal point of Cardassia's colony on this world. Monor's World.

"I like the sound of that," he said aloud.

"The sound of what, sir?"

Monor turned to see that Ekron had entered. The years had been kind to Monor's aide. For one thing, age had softened his ridges, so they didn't quite make his face look so craterlike. For another, after a rocky start, he took quite well to living planetside. Monor suspected that change mostly came about when the prefect finally gave in and let him pursue that imbecilic *hevrit* project of his—though even Monor had to admit that the transplanting had been a success, for all the difference it made to the price of *kanar*. Still, it kept Ekron happy, and as long as he was happy, he was efficient, which was what mattered to Monor. He'd have been lost in this post without Ekron's efficiency.

"I was just admiring the view of my planet," he said in answer to Ekron's query. "And it is, you know. Mine. Make a note for me to send a message to Central Command seeing if they can name the planet after me. Least they can do after saddling me with those damned Foreheads for eighteen years. It'll be good to see the last of them, let me tell you. Don't know what it took for one of them to see sense, but I'm glad that K'mpec person at least has a brain. He's probably some kind of mutant—the only Forehead with an actually measurable cranial capacity. Hard to believe, really, that people with such massive heads can have such tiny brains. Make a note of that, Ekron, we should do some kind of study."

"Yes, sir," Ekron said. "Ah, you have a package, sir. It was just delivered from the southern continent."

"What!?" Monor turned around. "Dammit, man, do I have to do *all* the thinking around here? That could be—"

"It's already been thoroughly scanned, sir," Ekron interrupted.

Of course it has, you old fool, Ekron's no idiot. "And what is it?"

"It's a bottle of bloodwine, sir." Ekron handed a box to Monor.

Gingerly, half expecting it to explode, Ekron's scan notwithstanding, Monor opened the box.

Inside was a bottle with some kind of Forehead logo on it, along with that scrawl they insisted was a language. Also inside was an optical chip.

He handed the latter to Ekron. "I'm going to regret this, but put it in the viewer."

"Yes, sir."

Ekron did so, and the viewer on Monor's office wall lit up with the hideous face of Qaolin.

"Greetings, my old enemy. Eighteen years ago, we faced each other in combat worthy of song, and one that intertwined our destinies on this forsaken ball of rock. Today, we part, with victory in your grasp. I must admit, this was not the ending I had in mind for our battle when our ships first engaged over this world, but I cannot deny that you have been a worthy foe. Therefore I give you this parting gift—the finest bottle of the finest bloodwine from our finest vintner. I salute you, Prefect Monor—you have been a worthy foe. Qapla'!"

The message then ended. "At least he wasn't slurring," Monor muttered. Then he handed Ekron the bottle. "Destroy it."

"Sir? It *was* a gift."

Monor's lips curled in distaste. "Please. It's a Forehead abomination. I want all traces of those creatures abolished from my world, starting with this blood vinegar of theirs and finishing with that filthy Ch'gran wreck. That's what started this whole mess, you know. I tell you, Ekron, I wish you'd never found that damned relic. If you hadn't, we'd have just colonized this place eighteen years ago and I could've retired."

Taking the bottle from Monor, Ekron said, "As you say, sir."

"I want that bottle vaporized, Ekron. Hell, I want it *atomized*. I don't even want there to be microscopic traces of that damned Forehead swill on my world, is that understood?"

"Yes, sir. If you'll excuse me, sir."

Ekron took his leave. Monor went back to the window and watched the rest of the sunset on his world.

Chapter 40

BETAZED

Elias Vaughn sipped his single-malt Scotch as he stood on the periphery of the crowd. He saw several familiar faces at the reception, but thankfully no one he knew well enough to actually talk to. Some nodded their heads at him, others ignored him. None came to talk to him, which suited him fine. He was just marking time until the transport arrived in any case. The reception was unusually quiet, as most of those present were telepaths, and so defaulted to talking among themselves psionically.

Finagling the invitation to this reception was the only way Vaughn could justify the trip to Betazed without it getting in the way of the mission he and T'Prynn were about to go on in the Arvada system. But it was something he felt the need to do now, before Arvada III, in case that mission went bad.

Vaughn wasn't even sure what the reception was for—all he knew was that Uhura got him on the guest list.

"Well, well, well, look who's here."

Closing his eyes, Vaughn thought, *Not him. Why did he have to be here?*

Giving in to the inevitable, he turned to see the familiar smug face, irritating smile, shock of white hair, and black spots of Curzon Dax. He was dressed in an ankle-length blue jacket decorated with some kind of sun-and-moon pattern over a white shirt and black pants.

"Ambassador," he said with a minimal inclination of his head. As Dax approached, Vaughn caught a whiff of *allira* punch. Wistfully, Vaughn remembered that Ian Troi was rather fond of that stuff—in fact, it was at the reception on the *Carthage* eighteen years ago that he introduced Vaughn to the beverage. Seeing Dax drink it now seemed wrong to Vaughn.

"Have to admit to being surprised to see you here, Vaughn. You never really struck me as the partying type."

"I have some personal business to take care of on Betazed." That was as much as he was willing to share.

"Fair enough. It seems to be a day for surprises. I thought for sure that Lwaxana Troi would be present—I'm told she *never* misses a party—but she's not around, either." Dax hesiated, then took a sip of his punch. "Listen, I'm glad you're here, actually. I was so caught up in the political nonsense on Qo'noS after we left the Great Hall I never had a chance to thank you."

Vaughn almost choked on his Scotch. "Excuse me?" *Curzon Dax is actually expressing gratitude? To me?*

"Well, for your help, for one thing," Dax said with a smile. *No doubt he's enjoying my discomfiture.* "Your tracking down those records proved to be a very handy bargaining chip. I think it's safe to say that relations with the Empire are stronger than ever."

"That's good."

"Yes." He shook his head. "I have to ask, Commander— how *did* you obtain that information?"

Rather than answer, Vaughn simply stared at the older Trill.

"All right, fine, don't tell me. I suppose it's probably safer this way. In any case, I'm also grateful to you for seeking me out on Risa two years ago. I have to admit, I let the entire Raknal V situation get away from me. I should have been keeping a closer eye on things. Hell, I should never have proposed that solution in the first place."

"Not that I don't agree—" Vaughn started.

Dax grinned. "Considering that you said so from the beginning."

"—but why do you say that?"

"I thought I understood how to make both sides talk to each other, but I couldn't have misjudged the Cardassians more if I tried. Klingons thrive on that sort of competition, but the Cardassians think it's their destiny to overrun the galaxy. I'm not even sure they have a *concept* of competition. They just prefer to run roughshod over everything. As for the Klingons . . ." He smiled. "If I've learned nothing else over the years, it's that the only people who can deal with Klingons are Klingons."

"That's very profound, Ambassador," Vaughn said, almost meaning it.

"Excuse me, Lieutenant Commander Vaughn?"

Vaughn turned at the new voice, which belonged to a young woman with dark black eyes. "Yes?"

"Your transport is ready."

Dax gave a small bow. "I assume this is your personal business. I will leave you to it. Safe journeys, Commander. Perhaps we'll meet again some day."

I sincerely hope not, Vaughn thought. Not quite impolitic enough to say that, but not trustful enough of himself to say anything else, Vaughn simply returned the bow, then followed the Betazoid woman to the transport.

Lwaxana had said she would meet him there. Deanna was not coming along, as the ten-year-old girl did not like to go to that place. Lwaxana probably left her with Mr. Xelo.

Leaving the reception behind, Elias Vaughn got into the transport that would take him to the grave of Ian Troi.

EPILOGUE

GIV'N TO THE STRONG

A WORLD IN THE
CARDASSIAN UNION

The girl could feel the pull of the *hevrit* on the line.

"That's it," Father whispered, a proud smile on his face as they sat in the boat in the middle of the river. The sun was out, reflecting off the crystal clear water. Father held a fishing rod of his own in his hands, but he soon set that aside to make sure that the girl would be able to bring in her catch. Father had been teaching her to fish because his own father had taught him to fish, and his mother had taught him, and her mother had taught her. Families did that sort of thing, he said. It was their second day out on the river in the small wooden boat.

"Bring the fish in," Father then said.

Slowly, gently, she moved the lever on the control that would wind in the fishing line. The mechanism was sensitive, and she had to get the speed just right—not so slow that the *hevrit* would have time to wriggle off the end of the line, but not so fast as to cause the *hevrit* to come loose on account of too much force.

"Take it easy," Father cautioned her.

She eased the lever to a slower speed, then realized that was too slow and made it faster again. Soon she got it just right.

When Grandfather purchased the land on this world, he had invited his entire family to spend a vacation here, and the girl had never enjoyed herself more on a trip in her life. Her sister and brother could play silly war games all they wanted. She preferred spending this time learning to fish with Father.

When the end of the line with the *hevrit* attached burst through the water with a cold splash, she grinned so widely she thought her cheek ridges would fold over her ears. With Father's help, she removed the *hevrit* from the line, where it had been attracted by the sonic vibrations emitted by the device on the end—a wonderful piece of Cardassian ingenuity. The meter-long fish was quite heavy, as big as anything she had ever seen Father, Grandfather, or Great-Grandmother catch—and *she* caught it!

Father placed a hand on the girl's shoulder and grinned. "Your first catch. I think Grandfather will be very proud of you. And Mother will enjoy something new to cook. Good work."

The girl happily replayed those words in her mind over and over again as she and Father steered the boat back toward the shoreline. Mother and her brother and sister were waiting for them, along with Grandfather.

"Father," her sister was whining even before they docked the boat, "he's making me play the Bajoran terrorist again. *I* want to be the gul this time!"

As Father went to settle yet another stupid argument between her siblings, she carried the container with the *hevrit* over to Mother and Grandfather.

"I see you brought dinner," Mother said with a laugh.

"I caught this!" she said enthusiastically. "Father helped a little, but I caught it all by myself!"

"Good for you," Grandfather said. "That's the way it should be done."

Few compared to Mother when it came to cooking. Not only that, but she showed her daughter all the tricks, from how to skin the *hevrit*, the best way to remove the tiny bones from the meat, the proper removal of the head, and so much more.

Night fell, and Mother, Father, Grandfather, and all three children gathered around a fire that was more for illumination than warmth, as it was quite balmy here. As they feasted on the *hevrit*, the girl turned to her grandfather and asked him for a story.

"That seems only fair," Grandfather said. "I think a story's damn fine payment for this meal you've given us."

Grandfather took a moment to adjust the way he was sitting, and he also set his plate aside. Then he leaned forward and started speaking to the three children. The girl was rapt with attention—she loved stories.

"Once there was a people who were very happy. They lived on the greatest planet in the galaxy, and everyone had enough to eat and they were strong. But soon they started to run out of food. And the planet that had given them so much soon ran out of things to give them. The people then became very unhappy. They suffered and starved and they were no longer strong."

Then Grandfather sat up straight, startling the girl. "But soon, they found their way to the stars! And from the stars, they gained salvation, for there they found many more worlds that had food and minerals and so much else. Once again, they were well fed. Once again, they were strong."

Her brother said, "Who are they, Grandfather?"

"*Stu*-pid," her sister said, "he's talking about *us*."

Grinning, Grandfather said, "Yes, I do speak of our people."

The girl was confused. "We were unhappy?"

"Not for very long," Grandfather said in a reassuring tone. "Because we *are* strong. We are, in fact, the strongest people in the galaxy. All that stands against us now are the many inferior species around us—humans, Bajorans, Klingons, Trills, Romulans, Vulcans, Andorians, Ferengi, Lissepians—

but the Cardassian Union will always triumph. It is our destiny to spread our greatness throughout the cosmos."

Grandfather leaned forward again. "Once, we found a world called Raknal V. It was ours for the taking, of course, but Klingon treachery tried to take it away from us. They made a fraudulent claim on the world, and the gullible fools of the Federation took their side. A senile old Trill tried to trick us into accepting a ridiculous competition, to make us fight for what was rightfully ours. In the end, of course, we triumphed. The Klingons gave us the world and the Trill let them. No amount of trickery, no amount of butchery, no amount of posturing could keep us from our destiny—nor will it ever."

"Now then," Mother said, "you should finish your *hevrit*. It's time to get some sleep."

Even as her siblings complained that they weren't tired, the girl wolfed down the rest of her fish, then prepared her bedroll. After a long day of fishing, she was tired. Besides, she was an obedient child. She knew that if she remained obedient, she too would be strong, as a Cardassian should be.

As she lay down to sleep, she turned to her parents. "Mother? Father?"

"Yes?" they said in unison.

"Some day, I will grow up and join the military and be the finest soldier in the Union and I will find more new worlds that will bring glory to Cardassia!"

Mother, Father, and Grandfather all laughed. Father said, "Of that, my darling child, I have no doubt at all. But for now, go to sleep. Tomorrow, we'll go home and tell your grandmother about the first fish you caught."

Content with the day's accomplishments, the girl drifted off to sleep. Her rest was peaceful and undisturbed, because she knew that she slept under the protection of the Cardassian Union . . .

ACKNOWLEDGMENTS

The thanks must commence with editor Marco Palmieri, who conceived *The Lost Era* and has shepherded it into existence. Marco is expert at taking the seed of many of the best stories ("Wouldn't it be cool if . . . ?") and nurturing it into the most beautiful flower—or, in this case, a six-rose nosegay. (Hey, c'mon, people say my prose needs to be more florid . . .) I also must thank Ira Steven Behr and Robert Hewitt Wolfe, who wrote the *Star Trek: Deep Space Nine* episode "The Way of the Warrior," thus providing me with the basis for this novel in a conversation between Bashir and Garak about the eighteen-year Betreka Nebula incident between Cardassia and the Klingons.

My fellow *Lost Era* authors, Michael A. Martin, Andy Mangels, Jeff Mariotte, Margaret Wander Bonanno, and especially the ones on either side of me, David R. George III and Ilsa J. Bick, are all deities among scribes. David and Ilsa had several characters and situations in common with me, and both were a joy to work with. Our cooperative efforts have made our stories more coherent and, I hope, more enjoyable for the reader, which is, after all, the primary goal.

* * *

Also of tremendous use were various *Star Trek* reference tools, particularly *The Star Trek Encyclopedia* by Michael and Denise Okuda, with Debbie Mirek; *Star Trek Chronology* also by the Okudas; *The Klingon Dictionary* by Marc Okrand; and especially *Star Charts* by Geoffrey Mandel.

The *Lost Era* books in general and this book in particular had to weave stories from little dribs and drabs of information that the various TV shows and movies provided at many different stages. In addition to all those onscreen references (far too numerous to list here), I need to acknowledge the contributions of several works of written fiction that provided useful background material for some of the political, social, and physical forces at work in the Federation, the Cardassian Union, the Klingon Empire, and the Romulan Star Empire during this period: the comic book *Enter the Wolves* written by A.C. Crispin and Howard Weinstein; Peter David's young adult book *Worf's First Adventure*; the *Dark Matters* trilogy by Christie Golden; the two-part Martok biographical novel *The Left Hand of Destiny* by J.G. Hertzler and Jeffrey Lang; the Garak biographical novel *A Stitch in Time* by Andrew J. Robinson; Josepha Sherman and Susan Shwartz's *Vulcan's Heart*; and *Lesser Evil* by Robert Simpson.

I make a habit of thanking the actors who play the characters I portray in the text, which is a bit more of a challenge than usual in *The Art of the Impossible*, since so many of the folks herein are either of my own creation, or never appeared onscreen, or did so but briefly. However, I would be remiss if I did not acknowledge the contributions in providing voices, faces, and mannerisms of the following: Michael Ansara (Kang), Frank Owen Smith (Curzon Dax), Majel Barrett (Lwaxana Troi), Theodore Bikel (Sergey Rozhenko), Georgia Brown (Helena Rozhenko), Amick Byram (Ian Troi), John Colicos (Kor), Charles Cooper (K'mpec), Paul Dooley

(Enabran Tain), Michael Dorn (General Worf), John Fleck (Koval), Danny Goldring (Legate Kell), John Hancock (Vance Haden), Richard Herd (L'Kor), Thelma Lee (Kahlest), Mark Lenard (Sarek), Nichelle Nichols (Uhura), Tricia O'Neil (Rachel Garrett), Christine Rose (Gi'ral), Alan Scarfe (Tokath), Gregory Sierra (Corbin Entek), and Ben Slack (K'Tal).

I've always had a great fondness for the Romantic poets of the late eighteenth and early nineteenth centuries, and one of my favorites is William Blake. It is from his *America: A Prophecy* that I took the titles of this book's sections.

The continued support of the online community has been especially heartening, and I must thank all the good folks at the *Star Trek* Books Bulletin Board at PsiPhi.org, the *Trek* Literature Board at TrekBBS.com, Simon & Schuster's discussion board at StarTrekBooks.com, the *Star Trek* Books and *Deep Space Nine Avatar* Yahoo!Groups at groups.yahoo.com, and the Federation Library at StarTrek-Now.com.

The usual gangs of idiots: the Malibu crowd, the Geek Patrol, the Forebearance (in particular GraceAnne Andreassi DeCandido, a.k.a. The Mom), and especially my writers group CITH, who have put up with truckloads of pages dumped on them at once and still managed to go through and make those pages better.

Last, but never least, heaping dollops of thanks to the love of my life, Terri Osborne, as well as our cats, Mittens and Marcus, all three of whom were always there to provide love, affection, and a desire to be scritched. (Okay, maybe I'm sharing too much here . . .)

ABOUT THE AUTHOR

One of **Keith R.A. DeCandido**'s earliest TV memories is being scared to death by the salt vampire from the *Star Trek* episode "The Man Trap." He grew up to overcome these childhood nightmares and make several contributions to the world of *Star Trek* literature, including the novels *Diplomatic Implausibility* and *Demons of Air and Darkness*; the two-book series *The Brave and the Bold*; several short stories; the comic book miniseries *Perchance to Dream* (collected in the trade paperback *Enemy Unseen*); and many eBooks in the monthly *Star Trek: Starfleet Corps of Engineers* series that he codeveloped with John J. Ordover (some collected in the books *Have Tech, Will Travel*; *Miracle Workers*; and *Some Assembly Required*). Coming soon are the first two books in the *Star Trek: I.K.S. Gorkon* series, chronicling the adventures of Captain Klag and his intrepid crew of Klingon warriors, the first time Pocket has published an adventure that exclusively highlights *Star Trek*'s most popular aliens. Keith is the editor of the forthcoming *Tales of the Dominion War* anthology and is presently working on a two-book series that focuses on Ambassador Worf in the days leading up to *Star Trek Nemesis*.

* * *

In addition, Keith has written novels, short stories, and non-fiction books in the universes of *Buffy the Vampire Slayer*, *Farscape*, *Gene Roddenberry's Andromeda*, Marvel Comics, *Xena*, and *Doctor Who*. His first original novel, *Dragon Precinct*, will be published in 2004, and his original short fiction has appeared in *Murder and Magic*, *Urban Nightmares*, and *Did You Say Chicks!?* The editor of the groundbreaking *Imaginings: An Anthology of Long Short Fiction*, Keith is also a professional musician and an avid New York Yankees fan. He lives in the Bronx with his girlfriend and the world's two goofiest cats. Learn way too much about Keith at the easy-to-remember URL of DeCandido.net, join his fan club at KRADfanclub.com, or just send him silly e-mails at keith@decandido.net.

Look for STAR TREK fiction from Pocket Books

Star Trek®

Star Trek®: The Original Series

Star Trek: The Next Generation®

Novelizations

Star Trek: Deep Space Nine®

Books set after the series
Homecoming • Christie Golden
The Farther Shore • Christie Golden

Enterprise®

Novelizations
Broken Bow • Diane Carey
Shockwave • Paul Ruditis

By the Book • Dean Wesley Smith & Kristine Kathryn Rusch
What Price Honor? • Dave Stern
Surak's Soul • J.M. Dillard
Daedalus • David Stern

Star Trek®: New Frontier

New Frontier #1-4 Collector's Edition • Peter David
   #1 • *House of Cards*
   #2 • *Into the Void*
   #3 • *The Two-Front War*
   #4 • *End Game*
#5 • *Martyr* • Peter David
#6 • *Fire on High* • Peter David
The Captain's Table #5 • *Once Burned* • Peter David
Double Helix #5 • *Double or Nothing* • Peter David
#7 • *The Quiet Place* • Peter David
#8 • *Dark Allies* • Peter David
#9-11 • *Excalibur* • Peter David
   #9 • *Requiem*
   #10 • *Renaissance*
   #11 • *Restoration*
Gateways #6: *Cold Wars* • Peter David
Gateways #7: *What Lay Beyond:* "Death After Life" • Peter David
#12 • *Being Human* • Peter David
#13 • *Gods Above* • Peter David
#14 • *Stone and Anvil* • Peter David

Star Trek®: Stargazer

The Valiant • Michael Jan Friedman
Double Helix #6: *The First Virtue* • Michael Jan Friedman and Christie
   Golden
Gauntlet • Michael Jan Friedman
Progenitor • Michael Jan Friedman

Star Trek® : Starfleet Corps of Engineers (eBooks)

Star Trek® : Invasion!

Star Trek® Omnibus Editions

Invasion! Omnibus • various
Day of Honor Omnibus • various
The Captain's Table Omnibus • various
Double Helix Omnibus • various
Star Trek: Odyssey • William Shatner with Judith and Garfield Reeves-Stevens
Millennium Omnibus • Judith and Garfield Reeves-Stevens
Starfleet: Year One • Michael Jan Friedman

Star Trek® Short Story Anthologies

Strange New Worlds, vol. I, II, III, IV, V, and VI • Dean Wesley Smith, ed.
The Lives of Dax • Marco Palmieri, ed.
Enterprise Logs • Carol Greenburg, ed.
The Amazing Stories • various
Prophecy and Change • Marco Palmieri, ed.
No Limits • Peter David, ed.

Other Star Trek® Fiction

Legends of the Ferengi • Ira Steven Behr & Robert Hewitt Wolfe
Adventures in Time and Space • Mary P. Taylor, ed.
Captain Proton: Defender of the Earth • D.W. "Prof" Smith
New Worlds, New Civilizations • Michael Jan Friedman
The Badlands, Books One and *Two* • Susan Wright
The Klingon Hamlet • Wil'yam Shex'pir
Dark Passions, Books One and *Two* • Susan Wright
The Brave and the Bold, Books One and *Two* • Keith R.A. DeCandido